Sign up for our newsletter to hear
about new and upcoming releases.

www.ylva-publishing.com

OTHER BOOKS BY BLYTHE RIPPON

The Love and Law Series

Barring Complications
Benched

Stand Alone

Stowe Away

BLYTHE RIPPON

BENCHED

ACKNOWLEDGMENTS

The fight for LGBTQ rights continues after marriage equality, and a relationship continues after "happily ever after." This novel tackles questions about what comes next, legally and romantically, for Victoria and Genevieve.

I'm exceedingly grateful for all those who have helped me develop this story. Michelle Aguilar's attention to characterization and narrative arc has taught me so much. I really appreciate Astrid's patience and belief in me. My parents and parents-in-law have supported me through my journey as a fiction writer, including reading drafts and helping give me time to write. My kids are stunning and fill me with more joy than I can handle. And my wife inspires me every day to fight to make this world a more just place.

DEDICATION

This book is dedicated to all those who fight for LGBTQ rights, whether in a courtroom, on the telephone, or in the streets. And it's for all those in the LGBTQ community who feel alienated and outcast. You are not alone.

CHAPTER 1

The sound technician clipped a wireless microphone onto Victoria's lapel, then stood back and inspected its placement. He inched it up before moving away to make room for the makeup artist, who applied more powder to Victoria's forehead, scrutinized her face, and walked off.

Surrounded by camera people and sound engineers bustling back and forth, Victoria nevertheless felt alone in the studio. She ignored the slight tremble in her fingers as she sat in the interview chair and wiped her hands on her suit skirt. Add this one to the many surreal moments in her life since her appointment as a justice—all these people were there because of her, but none of them were there *for* her.

When she'd seen the photo on the popular blog I Fought the Law—a picture of her and Genevieve a breath away from kissing—she'd joked about it, impressed with her own blasé response. That, however, was in the privacy of her own kitchen, before the major media outlets picked up the story. Less than two hours later, it flooded the news cycle: Supreme Court Justice Victoria Willoughby, in an undeniably intimate moment with LGBTQ rights advocate Genevieve Fornier, who recently convinced Willoughby and her colleagues to expand marriage rights for the LGBTQ community.

Now that picture seemed to be everywhere. She'd told herself in her kitchen that day that she was prepared for the media firestorm and potential fallout. Her bravado failed her now, as she prepared to discuss it on camera for the first time since the story broke.

At first, she'd been vaguely grateful for the photo's timing. The Court was at the end of its session, and her first impulse had been to hop a plane to England. She was overdue to visit her father, after all.

Genevieve had said that "visit" sounded an awful lot like "run away."

Victoria pointed out that the two didn't even alliterate.

Since then, she'd been inundated with a steady stream of invitations to appear on news programs and pundit-led talk shows. Bill O'Reilly had, unsurprisingly, called for her to resign and, more importantly, answer for her lifestyle on *The O'Reilly Factor*. A few Republicans in the House had echoed his call for her to step down, although they framed their concerns less sensationally. She'd respectfully declined them all, and thus far the political fallout had been nothing but bluster.

The media, of course, was a different issue. The reporters were relentless, and now half a dozen cameras were pointed at her.

"You need to do *They've Got Issues*," Genevieve had insisted when she heard about the invitation. "It's the most respected, non-biased of the Sunday morning news shows."

So now, one month later, she was on the set waiting to be interviewed about, among other things, her private life.

The sound tech returned to her chair. "Justice Willoughby, we're almost ready. We need to test your microphone. Please say something. Anything other than 'testing one-two-three.'"

"Testing four-five-six," Victoria said.

He rolled his eyes and walked away mumbling, "Levels are good."

She studied her hands for a moment, fascinated by the tremors in her fingers, and focused on taking deep, calming breaths. After a moment, the show's host, Vishal Patel, quietly sat down in the plush armchair opposite Victoria. He regarded her with a calm smile, and she studied him. He was strikingly handsome, like most talk show hosts, with jet-black hair that had been expertly coiffed. She hoped the spark in his deep brown eyes indicated excitement at interviewing her, rather than anything more opportunistic.

"Do you need anything, Justice Willoughby? Water, or anything else to drink, or…" He waved his hand in the vague direction of offstage.

She briefly considered making a joke about liquid courage, but the potential headlines that might create stopped her. "I'm fine, thanks."

He was taller than she expected, and his smile more genuine. The filter of television didn't do him any favors.

"I apologize that we weren't able to send out a list of questions in advance of the interview. Journalistic integrity, you understand."

"Of course," Victoria said.

"Just remember: I'm not the enemy."

Victoria contemplated that. She was a confirmed justice with a lifetime appointment; even if he were an enemy, there wasn't much he could do to hurt her. But that thought felt way too rational when set against the torrent of emotions churning in her gut.

"I've never given an interview like this before," she confessed.

"Ignore the camera, and imagine that you and I are having coffee together, getting to know one another."

It was a nice idea in theory, but the irritating tug of the microphone pack on her suit didn't leave much room for imaginary scenarios. She licked her lips and said, "In that case, Earl Grey sounds great."

Patel nodded and waved over an assistant, who took her order. As they waited for the tea, the sound tech returned and fussed with Patel's microphone. After confirming something via his headset, he announced, "On in three," and disappeared again.

The makeup artist returned and fussed with Patel's foundation. He fidgeted slightly and winced when the brush swiped under his nose. As the makeup tech left, Patel sneezed and rolled his eyes. At least she wasn't the only one irritated by all the trappings that accompanied on-screen appearances.

"On in one," boomed a voice through the sound system just as an assistant placed the Earl Grey on a coaster on the table between her and Patel.

Victoria licked her lips and blinked a few times. Her contacts had been bugging her recently, and she hoped they wouldn't dry out during the next half hour. She would have preferred to wear her glasses, but everyone, including her brother Will and her secretary Lynn, told her they would create a glare.

"Thirty seconds," came through the sound system. Patel massaged his jaw and cracked his neck to the right before rubbing his hands together like an evil mastermind. Despite his reassurances to the contrary, all he needed was a hairless cat to complete the appearance of a creepy adversary.

Not the enemy.

For the first time in her life, Victoria wished she were one of those politicians who had handlers and press secretaries and speechwriters. At the very least, she should have reached out to Alistair and asked for help perfecting her talking points. He was charming and whimsical, and given that he'd been on the Court since before sliced bread, probably had insights she hadn't considered.

The show's jingle was startlingly loud as it blared through the sound system. She plastered on a smile and looked right at the camera.

"Today on *They've Got Issues,* my guest is Associate Justice Victoria Willoughby, who will talk about her first two years on the United States Supreme Court, the decisions she's authored, and the now-infamous picture of her with the president of Her Equal Rights, Genevieve Fornier."

A large screen behind the cameras showed the broadcast going out to the public. It cut to the photo in question: She stood inches away from Genevieve, staring at her lips. At least it was a flattering—even sexy—image. The combination of desire and love in Genevieve's eyes took Victoria's breath away.

The camera cut back to Patel and his cheesy grin.

"Justice Willoughby, thanks for being here with us."

"Thank you for having me, Mr. Patel."

"Vishal, please."

She nodded.

"You've been a justice on the Supreme Court for two terms now. What's that been like for you?"

It was predictable, really, for him to lob her a few softball questions before launching a well-aimed fastball. The key for her was not to let her guard down. She took a deep breath and tried to look breezy.

"It's been a whirlwind, Vishal. My confirmation, if you remember, was completed immediately before the October conference of the justices two years ago, so I really hit the ground running."

Vishal leaned forward and asked in an exaggerated stage whisper, "What are those conferences like?"

"Confidential," she said.

He offered a good-natured laugh. "Surely you can give us some more information than that."

"The October conference—like all the conferences throughout our term—is a private gathering. Even the justices' clerks are not invited. It's the first formal event of the new term, and we are exceedingly professional. We discuss the cases that have been appealed to the Court, and we vote whether to hear them. Those conferences continue every Friday that we are in session."

God, even she was bored with her answer. But then, her goal with this interview was to come across as decidedly boring; she'd had her fill of media attention while the Court was considering the first gay marriage case. Life was easier without reporters harassing her in the grocery store and stalking her at the gym.

Perhaps in response to her answer's entertainment level, Patel moved on at a brisk pace. "In your first year on the bench, the Court voted 6-3 to grant federal recognition of gay marriage in *Samuels v United States*. And in your second year, the Court made gay marriage legal in every state. That case was decided on a closer margin, with the chief justice switching sides to vote against marriage rights. What was all this like for you as the first lesbian justice?"

There was something about the word *lesbian* that was always a little jarring to her. Genevieve would argue that it was internalized homophobia, but for Victoria, it was a matter of simple linguistics. *Lesbian* just didn't roll off the tongue—anyone's tongue. Even Patel seemed to hit the word a shade harder than perhaps he intended.

She cleared her throat. "Both cases certainly felt personal to me, although honestly, most human rights cases feel personal. In both of these cases, there was obviously a moral—and more importantly for me as a jurist—a *legal* wrong that my colleagues and I had an opportunity to rectify. And both cases were great victories. Yes, I happen to be gay, but there is a profound truth in Dr. King's words, 'Injustice anywhere is a threat to justice everywhere.' Our decisions in these cases corrected an injustice for a minority group of citizens."

She left out any mention of how personally upsetting it was for her when Kellen switched sides with some half-cocked argument about states' rights.

"It's no secret that because of your vote in the *Samuels* case, you were targeted by a radical, neo-Nazi group called Marriage's Sacred Protector and assaulted in your own house. If you had known what would happen, would you have changed your vote?"

The question surprised her. Rather than digging into the sordid details of her assault or asking her why she didn't recuse herself from the case, Patel had given her a more nuanced question—one that offered her the opportunity to reinforce her image as a jurist with integrity.

Not the enemy.

"Absolutely not, Vishal, and the other justices agree. We aren't doing our jobs if we let fringe political or religious viewpoints dictate our votes. It's rare that cases come with personal ramifications the way this one did, but we consider cases based on the Constitution and our consciences."

"That sounds, I don't know, noble?"

"Executing the office to which I've been confirmed isn't noble. I'm simply doing my job, the way most Americans do every day."

Questions and answers continued in this more or less easy way, touching on her current book project and her interest in cooking, until Vishal paused, and Victoria knew what was coming.

"Madam Justice, a month ago, a blog called I Fought the Law posted a picture of you with Genevieve Fornier. The picture looks intimate. Now, I know a lot of our viewers want to hear juicy details about the nature of your relationship. But this isn't *Access Hollywood*; this is a program dedicated to US politics and government. So what I'm most interested in is this: if you and Ms. Fornier continue to have a close personal relationship, how will that relationship affect her participation in HER's legal cases, should they be argued before the Supreme Court?"

The baseball-sized knot in her stomach ballooned until it filled her whole abdomen and worked its way up her chest and into her throat. The answer to that question was far bigger than any sound bite she could offer Vishal.

"It's a little premature for me to offer you any kind of truthful answer," Victoria fumbled haltingly. She and Genevieve had danced around this difficult conversation for about a year now but hadn't exactly engaged in any meaningful discussion about the effect their romance would have on their professional lives. "I suppose we'll just take things on a case-by-case basis."

Grinning, Patel bumped his knee against hers. "Pun intended, I assume."

She groaned. "Totally inadvertent, I assure you."

"Happens to the best of us," he said. "Justice Willoughby, it was a real pleasure to chat with you. Thank you for taking time out of your busy schedule."

She shook his hand warmly. "I've enjoyed talking with you, Vishal."

The jingle blared again before someone announced through the sound system, "We're off."

As she unclasped the microphone from her lapel, her fingers steady now, Vishal said, "That wasn't so bad, was it?"

In spite of herself, she agreed. "I appreciate your..." She wasn't sure how to finish. *Only minimally invading my privacy?*

"Well, I'm quite a fan, you know."

"Fan?" Victoria asked. Evidently that's what happened when your personal life was the stuff of tabloids: people rooted for you—or against you.

"Well, yes. Of you and Ms. Fornier. A lot of our interview questions came from brainstorming sessions with the network, but that last question was one hundred percent mine. I'm delighted for the two of you, but I'm also a little concerned that the gay rights community will be sacrificing one of its most effective advocates if Ms. Fornier can't argue at the Supreme Court anymore."

The whole event had been surreal. She shook his hand and mumbled some platitude about how lovely it was to meet him.

As Victoria drove home that night, she replayed his final interview question over and over again. The more she considered it, the further she seemed from a satisfactory response.

CHAPTER 2

It had been a long day for Genevieve, filled with administrative red tape and very little substantive legal work. When she'd first considered HER's offer to become the organization's next president, her friends had warned her about this—that she would excel in administration but also dislike it.

At the time, she had shrugged them off, saying, "I'll delegate the boring stuff."

Admittedly, she was also known for being overly optimistic.

She was rubbing her temples at her desk when Frank entered her office with a bottle of Pellegrino and two Advil. He deposited them next to the binder she'd been slogging through and gently slid it from her hands before closing it.

"I'm sorry to interrupt your migraine," he said, "but I thought you might like to know that Nic Ford is stepping down as executive director of NCLR."

It made fuzzy spots float around her eyes to look up so quickly, but she couldn't help it. "Are you kidding?" *Why didn't she tell me herself?*

"They just sent around an e-mail blast," he confirmed.

Genevieve nodded, which made her wince, and she was grateful he closed the door quietly. Migraines brought out the worst in her—it was silly and selfish that her first response was to wonder why Nic hadn't told her personally. Then again, in the past few months, the two of them had had little communication. Genevieve had been wrapped up in the throes of a now very public relationship with a sitting Supreme Court justice. And in addition to overseeing all of HER's operations, the two cases she had spent the last year arguing hadn't helped.

She sighed. Traveling non-stop between Nevada and Louisiana over the last year had made her social life pretty much non-existent.

Even picking up the phone made her dizzy, never mind holding the receiver to her ear. She swallowed the Advil before pushing the button for Frank. "Please call Nic for me," she murmured. He'd probably be surprised she was asking him to place a call for her, but there was currently a jackhammer pounding behind her eyes.

A few seconds later, Frank clicked back to her line. "She's not in the office, but I've got her on her cell. Line two."

She clicked over but never got a chance to say hello.

"I know, I know. I should have called and told you, but seriously, Genevieve, you of all people ought to understand. I met this woman, she's amazing, and she's got this chateau in the south of France. After spending two weeks there, I just realized I need a break. I'm fifty-eight years old, I've been executive director of NCLR for a decade, and I'm tired. I didn't know how tired I was until she showed me."

Genevieve took in a careful breath to say something, fuzzy spots swimming across her vision, but Nic barreled on anyway.

"I'm not retiring—I'm going to take a year off, and then I'll return to appellate work somewhere else—but I'm just so *over* bureaucracy and managing personalities and soothing egos. I want to go back to litigating. It's going to be great. So you can say 'congratulations' and be happy for me, okay?"

Genevieve was pretty sure Nicolette Ford had never spoken so many words so quickly in her life. Headache be damned—she laughed. "Congratulations. I'm happy for you."

"I have no idea who they'll replace me with, and frankly, I'm glad. The board can do their own search, and hopefully, I'll read about who they pick in the papers while I'm wearing a bathrobe on the balcony of my new chateau, drinking wine and eating cheese."

"She must be some woman."

"I've never met anyone like her."

A twinge of jealousy tickled at the back of Genevieve's neck: The minor crush Nic had on her when they worked together on the *Samuels* case had never sounded like this. Was this how she herself sounded when she talked about Tori?

"I certainly hope I get invited to the wedding."

"Will you bring Victoria Willoughby?" Nic asked.

The ensuing pause was awkward and heavy, and Genevieve tried not to sigh.

"Sorry, touchy subject? You'd think a woman who just admitted on national television that she's dating you would be willing to, you know, actually date you."

"So, when do I get to meet this woman?" So much for a smooth change of topic, but with the migraine, it was the best she could do.

Nic graciously rolled with it. "Come to France."

"We've got a full agenda this fall," Genevieve said.

"Good luck with that."

"Good luck in France."

Nic laughed, and Genevieve realized it was a sound she hadn't often heard from her.

"Don't be a stranger, Genevieve."

As they hung up, Genevieve reflected that working together on intense, high-profile, Supreme Court cases was a bit like summer camp: it seemed to create inextricable bonds between people.

Driving in her current state was out of the question, so she left her car at the office and took a cab to Tori's. She was looking forward to the quiet of her girlfriend's house. Maybe she'd be able to entice Tori into giving her a massage.

She rested her head on the back of the cab's seat and closed her eyes. Who would they find to replace Nic? She had been very old guard in a lot of ways. Genevieve wasn't even a full decade younger—did that make Genevieve old guard now too? The thought made her head spin even more.

The cab pulled up to Tori's house, and she managed to pay the driver, despite the numbers swimming on the bills in her hand. She trudged up to the door, fit her key into the lock, and was instantly comforted by the soft smell of lemongrass and the muted palette of Tori's living room.

The absence of classical music coming from the iPod dock indicated that Genevieve was alone in the house. She nudged off her pumps and left them by the door before heading into the kitchen and running a washcloth under cold water. The walk back to the couch took forever, but she gingerly eased down on it and put the compress over her eyes.

When she woke up, still on the couch in the exact same position, Tori was gently massaging her temples, and soft, cascading tinkles of Debussy sounded like raindrops washing away her pain.

"Frank called and told me you were sick. I picked up some soup, and there's a kettle on for tea."

"You're beautiful," Genevieve mumbled.

"You can't even see me with that towel over your eyes."

"Don't need to. I remember. Plus, maybe I was talking about the parts of you I don't need my eyes to see."

She could feel Tori's laughter through the slight shaking of the couch cushion. "You're a nut."

"Oh, that's fair. You're beautiful, and I'm a nut."

Tori kissed her neck softly and murmured, "Nothing in life is fair. Can I get you some soup?"

"Hm. What time is it?"

"After nine."

"Can we just go to bed?"

She could almost see Victoria roll her eyes. "You have to eat a little something. I'll heat up the soup while you gather your strength for the long walk to the kitchen."

Victoria didn't exactly spoon-feed her, but she might as well have. Once Genevieve had consumed enough calories to satisfy her, they headed upstairs, where Tori slipped pajamas on her and tucked her into bed.

As she drifted off to sleep, it occurred to her that she had become awfully dependent on her new—old?—girlfriend.

Genevieve woke up to bright sunlight streaming in from the curtains, the clanking sounds of dishes and utensils, and the smell of toast.

With a long stretch, she luxuriated in her complete lack of headache and the gentle caress of Tori's sheets. It took great strength of character for her to get out of Tori's bed, which was infinitely more comfortable than her own back at the townhouse. She brushed her teeth and hopped down the stairs, humming as she descended, and headed into the kitchen.

"You're in a good mood." Tori kissed her lightly before turning back to the omelet she was making in a ridiculously shiny copper pan. "Migraine gone?"

"Mm-hm." Genevieve started coffee and put on a kettle for Tori's tea. While the omelet finished cooking, she set the table, and they bustled around the kitchen in a quiet routine that felt so normal she wondered why they didn't do this every day.

When they settled at the table with their food and hot beverages, Genevieve sipped her coffee and pondered the view through the sliding glass door into Tori's backyard. "I've been thinking," she said.

"Maybe that explains the migraine?"

"You're not half as funny as you think you are." Genevieve gave her a dirty look.

"That's only because you never understand my jokes," Tori said.

"Did you want to know what I've been thinking about, or would you rather just be a smart-ass?"

"Well, those aren't mutually exclusive. But yes, dear. Please, share."

Genevieve shook her head and smiled. God, nothing could be easy with Tori, could it?

"We've been together for over a year now, and honestly, we've barely seen each other. We get some weekends together here and there, and there was that trip to Europe. But with my travel schedule, I'm out of town more than I'm here, and your work keeps you so busy—"

"I know. But I'm not sure how to make things different."

Two hands wrapped around her coffee mug, Genevieve leaned forward. "Well, I have an idea. I don't want to travel this much anyway. I'm a good spokesperson for HER, but there are a lot of people better than me at raising money, which is half of what I travel for. I've been going over the numbers with my assistant, and I think HER can—and needs to—hire an executive director."

"But isn't that what you do?"

"HER has an odd employment structure—most organizations like us have an executive director instead of a president. HER's never had an ED, though. So, my idea is that I stay on as president and continue to shape the organization in terms of our identity, the cases we take, the way we staff them, that kind of thing."

"So, no more media blitzes?"

"Oh, I'm sure I'll continue to give interviews, and as the public face of the organization, I'll have to do *some* of the galas still. I do really love everything HER stands for, and representing it still gives me a thrill. But an ED could take point on all the glad-handing and the traveling for smaller-scale fundraisers. It would be better for HER in the long term, I think.

"And," she took Tori's hand, "it would mean I'm in DC a lot more. I could see my girlfriend every weekend, instead of once a month."

"And this would free you up to argue more cases?"

"That's what I'm hoping. I miss the excitement of litigation. It's almost impossible to fundraise, run the organization, and take point on cases."

"Wow," Tori said, putting her fork down and coughing a little. "More cases. That sounds…really great for you."

"Good. Because I've already started talking to the board about it, and they have ways to streamline this process. They think we can have someone in place in four to six weeks. So, pretty soon, you're going to be stuck with me."

Tori laced her fingers through Genevieve's. "However this new plan changes things, well, if it means more time with you, then I'm happy." Her smile made Genevieve's stomach flutter.

"Are you sure me being around more will make you happy?" Genevieve traced circles on Tori's palm, a smile curling her lips. "I've heard I have the ability to drive you absolutely crazy. To make you scream in frustration. To make you clench your pillow at night."

Tori drew her finger up Genevieve's arm and across her collarbone. "Only at night? If I recall, none of those things happened last night."

Genevieve stood and pulled Tori to her, and her skin tingled as their mouths met. "Oh, I can make you scream right now."

Her lips hovered a breath away from Tori's neck. As she ran her tongue lightly over Tori's throat, Tori gasped and pulled her hips closer. Genevieve eased a hand between their chests and pushed Tori gently. "Upstairs. Now."

Before they made it through the bedroom door, Tori had turned around and slid her hand into Genevieve's hair, pulling their mouths together again. Genevieve was so focused on the velvety softness of Tori's tongue that she had no idea how they'd made it into the bed, but she loved the way Tori looked on top of her. As Tori's hand possessively ran up and down the length of her body, Genevieve's stomach fluttered.

"You do know this is my bedroom, right? My bedroom, my rules, Genevieve."

The way her name rolled off Tori's tongue made Genevieve shudder.

"God, you're sexy, trembling beneath me." Tori's hand eased between the fabric of Genevieve's shirt and her overheated skin. As she lifted the shirt up and over her head, Genevieve surged upward with it. "Now who's going to be moaning in frustration," Tori whispered, her mouth just out of reach of Genevieve's skin. "If you're a good guest, I might just give you what you want."

To hell with always being the leader of their bedroom activities. By that afternoon, Genevieve decided that she thoroughly enjoyed this role reversal.

It took exactly a month for Genevieve to solidify the hiring of a charming and very experienced executive director named Chuck Green; she immediately tasked him with handling the gala that weekend in Cincinnati. And it was none too soon. She was dying for a break after having traveled to four different cities in three weeks, including a stop in LA for the premiere of a documentary about the *Samuels* case she had won at the Supreme Court. For the first time in months, she called Tori on a Friday afternoon and said, "Hey, can we swim tonight?"

"God, that sounds amazing. I've missed you," Tori said, her voice like warm sunshine spreading through Genevieve.

"For real. Don't know why these past few weeks have felt so hard, but I can't wait to see you."

"It's that thing about the race being hardest right before the finish line, right? I think knowing that your schedule was going to lighten after this last bout of travel probably made it that much harder to wait."

Genevieve exhaled a breath she felt as if she'd she'd been holding for weeks. "See, that's why I love you. You always make me feel better."

"And here I thought you loved me for my cooking skills."

"Oh, don't get me wrong. Those don't hurt."

"Mm," Tori said, and Genevieve could hear the smile in her voice. "I'll see you soon."

It was such a novelty to meet as they used to, outside their personal changing rooms at the most exclusive gym in DC, their names engraved on their respective doors. They smiled at each other and walked hand in hand to the pool. It was certainly hard to feel as though they were making some kind of statement by holding hands when no one saw them. But still, on the off chance that they encountered someone on their way to the pool, well, they were officially out. And Genevieve swelled with pride as she squeezed Tori's hand.

They swam their usual fifty laps, and when Genevieve pulled herself out of the pool, she basked in the view of Tori, flushed and breathless and dripping wet.

"God, you look good." She stepped toward her, wiping her hand across Tori's chest and collecting water droplets. Tori's face grew even redder, and her eyes fluttered.

"You know," Genevieve said, "we've never taken full advantage of those private dressing rooms."

But Tori's features changed from turned on to something that might have been panic before settling on slightly annoyed.

"You and your ideas," she said, and she might have been trying to sound playful, but what Genevieve took from it was exasperation. "I'll see you at home for dinner?"

Home. Genevieve thought about asking "yours or mine?" but she already knew the answer. They never went to her house, no matter how hard she tried to manipulate the situation so that it would make more sense to go downtown instead of the suburbs. Honestly, when she wasn't suffering from a horrendous migraine, Tori's house was one of the least inviting "homes" she'd ever been in—it looked magazine ready at all times and not at all like a place where someone could actually live. Not that she had much ground to stand on, considering her own home had a distinctly neglected feel to it and that there were still boxes here and there. As she stood there in front of Tori's impatient expression, Genevieve vowed to warm the place up, now that she was going to be in town more.

"How about we do my house instead?" she suggested anyway, knowing as she said it that Tori would never go for it.

Tori's towel stilled in the process of drying her hair. "Do you have food there?"

Right, well, the first step in actually moving into the house that had been her permanent address for a year now would probably be stocking the bare fridge.

"I have phone numbers for some great takeout places. And we could always stop at the store on the way home and pick some things up."

"I already have everything for soup and salad back at home." Tori seemed to catch herself. "My home. Let's just go there."

Genevieve nodded. Before she could say anything about the two of them maybe having dinner at her townhouse the following night, Tori turned and walked into the locker room.

Well, that went well. She realized she was going to have to try harder to break Tori's routines. But as she trailed after, admiring Tori's legs, it was hard to feel too frustrated in their domestic life.

One week later, and it was déjà vu—the swimming, Genevieve flirting, and Tori shutting her down when Genevieve suggested they spend the night at her place instead of Tori's. This time her excuse was that she'd spent the day worried that she'd left her garage door open, and could they please hurry home to close it.

It was, of course, closed when they arrived.

Regardless, they ate dinner together, and then Tori chose another way to drive her crazy. Genevieve's sleep that night was filled with sex dreams, and they fooled around again in the morning before Genevieve reluctantly told Tori that she had to go to the office.

"On a Saturday?" Tori asked before shaking her head. "That's fine. I have some writing I'd like to get done anyway."

By the time Genevieve's legs worked enough for her to stand, Tori was partway through her shower and had finished shampooing her hair. Genevieve joined her, brushing her body against Tori's back and sliding her arms around Tori's stomach. She dropped featherlight kisses on her ear, and it brought flutters to her abdomen.

"I had fun this morning," she said. "You know, I don't have to be at the office just yet. We could—"

"Could you hand me the conditioner?"

So this was going to be a purely functional shower. Genevieve closed her eyes and willed the ache between her legs to dissipate.

When she looked at Tori, her girlfriend seemed determined to avoid her eyes. She passed over the conditioner and stepped around Tori to get her hair wet.

They didn't say much as they dried off and dressed. Tori was pulling her hair into a smooth ponytail when Genevieve dared to interrupt the silence. "What's on your mind?"

Tori looked startled and actually tossed her head as if to dispel her thoughts. "Voting rights."

Torn between rolling her eyes and laughing, Genevieve put her hand on Tori's shoulder. "Tori, what percentage of your day is spent thinking about work?"

At least she looked a little guilty. "A lot," she admitted. "Sometimes I try to turn it off and... Well, I think about work a lot."

Genevieve nodded, grateful she didn't have that problem. "I have some meditation techniques for drawing mental boundaries with work. I can help you, if you'd like." Genevieve couldn't imagine thinking about work right then—especially when Tori was naked in the shower and the tasks waiting for her at the office weren't exciting legal questions but dull administrative tasks.

It briefly occurred to her that maybe if she were hotter, or Tori wanted her more, she'd be the one shutting down Tori's work thoughts. But maybe nothing she—or anyone else—could do would successfully stop Tori from spinning out on work sometimes. Neither scenario was especially uplifting.

"Thanks—I'll think about that. I've never tried meditation."

Genevieve took her hand, enjoying the feel of their fingers entwining. "Well. Good luck with voting rights. We need 'em. Fight the good fight, baby. "

She kissed Tori on the cheek, and Tori murmured something back, but she was clearly miles away already.

In her car, halfway down Tori's driveway, it hit her that she'd forgotten, again, to ask Tori about dining at her townhouse that night. Damn. Well, she'd call once she got to the office.

The lobby of her building was empty, save for the security guard, and after flashing her ID in front of the elevator sensor and punching in the top floor where HER's offices were housed, she rode the elevator alone, which never happened during the week. The motion detector lights on her floor clicked on one by one as she walked past the empty cubicles to her office.

She only had one coat sleeve off when her desk phone rang. Before she'd even sat down, Frank was giving her the latest on their staff-restructuring initiative and HR's report on the new benefits package. He was briefing her on the upcoming board meeting when her cell phone rang—Chuck, the new executive director, probably wanting to give her a rundown of the fundraiser in Sonoma the night before. She quickly wrapped up the call with Frank and clicked *accept* on her cell.

Like Frank, Chuck wasted no time with pleasantries.

"Genevieve, glad I caught you. Listen, sorry to say, but the numbers from the fundraiser weren't what they had hoped."

"Well, that happens—and sometimes, we exceed expectations."

"Can't wait for that to happen," Chuck said. "Anyway, so, three wineries had competed for who got the beverage contract for the event, and I guess things had become nasty, and the local woman who organized the event for us gave contracts to all of them."

"Oh yeah, I remember Elaine. She's sweet. Total pushover, though," Genevieve said.

"Right, well, good to know. Next time I'll work more closely with her. But so, the different wineries' staff members kept trying to one-up each other, and poured aggressively. Is that a thing?"

"Great. So, in addition to the event costing a fortune, all the guests got wasted in the first hour and were too drunk to open their pocket books."

"Ah, so. Not the first time this has happened?" Chuck sounded breathless, and Genevieve remembered feeling that way practically every day when she first started at HER.

"No, and I'm sure it won't be the last. Listen, Chuck, you can't solve every problem, and you can't be everywhere at once, as much as you'd probably like to. We're glad to have you on board, and we have every confidence that you're going to be great in this job. You already are."

He took a deep breath. "Thanks for that, Genevieve, but I promise you, as soon as I get the lay of the land, our financials will look very different," he assured her. "This isn't my first rodeo—just my first one here."

By the time she'd hung up with him, had replied to all pressing e-mails, and had taken care of other mundane tasks, it was almost five o'clock and hints of a headache lurked behind her eyes.

She dialed Tori and rubbed her temples while the phone rang.

"Genevieve, hi! I just finished up. Well, I hope I have. I don't know." Tori paused. "No, I *do* know—I'm going to stop here, regardless."

Genevieve smiled and shook her head. "Tori, do you need me for this conversation?"

She laughed lightly, a reminder of how happy her job really made her. "Sorry," she said, the sound of her laptop closing audible in the background. "I'm good. How was your day?"

"Fine, I suppose." She'd only gotten through half of the items on her list for the day and was completely drained. Strange that she used to work fourteen hours in a single day, pouring over briefs or depositions, and felt more invigorated than this. She missed the thrill of litigation.

"You sound tired," Tori said, and the distinct sound of a cork popping out of a bottle came through the phone. "Come over—I'll have some pinot decanted for you."

Shit—beaten to the punch again. "I don't suppose you want to recork that? I was hoping we could do my place tonight. I even went to the grocery store." Okay, that wasn't exactly true, but she could easily stop on her way home.

"Oh, I've had chicken tikka masala in the slow cooker since you left. It smells divine."

Of course it did. Damn Tori for being an amazing cook. She'd never lure her away from that house with offers of food; that much was clear. She'd have to try another tactic some other time. There wasn't a snowball's chance in hell she'd miss Tori's mouthwatering tikka masala.

"On my way, babe," she said.

Despite Tori's slightly uncomfortably laugh whenever Genevieve called her "babe," it somehow brought the first real smile to Genevieve's face all day. Because being shy about terms of endearment was ridiculous, and she was going to convince Tori of that sooner or later.

CHAPTER 3

On the following Monday, Victoria sat in a leather chair in her private chambers and reread her clerks' resumes to assess their strengths and interests. They were an impressive group—that was for sure. But her interviews with them had made it clear that they all lacked the charm of Wallace. Maybe she was sentimentalizing that heady time because it was during the *Samuels* case, or maybe it was simply because he had been one of her first clerks, but Wallace would probably always be her favorite.

She made some notes about which of her clerks would be more suited for tax cases and which would be better equipped for human rights ones.

She set the resumes aside and was contemplating an afternoon cup of tea when Alistair Douglas barged in. "Have you seen this?" he blurted out with a total lack of formality that would have probably annoyed Victoria if it had come from any of her other fellow justices.

He threw a press release down on Victoria's lap and paced to the window.

"Well, hello, Alistair. Good to see you again. How was your summer?" She said it with a smile, hoping to break through his bad mood.

"Irrelevant to today's concerns." He grunted at the paper in her lap. "The Louisiana Attorney General evidently files his press releases before his actual appeals."

It was unusual for her to learn about appeals from the media. She slid on her glasses. The headline read:

SEEKING TO PROTECT CHILDREN, LOUISIANA ATTORNEY
GENERAL APPEALS RULING IN ROWLINGS V. LOUISIANA

"A gay adoption case?" She looked up at Alistair after reading the first few lines.

His back to her, staring out the window, he sighed. "Let's call it a same-sex parentage case—it's not quite adoption." He raised an eyebrow at her. "Victoria, how are you not read up on the details of this case by now?"

"I don't know," she murmured, somehow embarrassed even though the case hadn't even been filed yet with the Court. She wasn't expected to know *every* case that might eventually come their way, was she?

"And people think the gay rights fight ended with marriage equality," she remarked, deflecting.

"Exactly," said Alistair, his hands clasped behind his back. "So this gay couple with two children moved from California to Louisiana. And Louisiana won't recognize the nonbirth mother as a parent."

"God, what is wrong with people?" Victoria said.

"Lord knows. So when the couple applied for a second-parent adoption, Louisiana denied their application, citing a constitutional amendment that denies recognition of two people of the same gender as legal parents of a child. To pour salt on the wound, the women had foreseen this difficulty and had tried to execute a second-parent adoption in California before they moved. The Sacramento judge they appeared before had denied their request because—and this is the real kicker—they were both already the legal parents of the child."

"Well, I have to say that, in her position, I would probably feel compelled to do the same," Victoria said thoughtfully. "A second-parent adoption would be entirely unnecessary."

"That's exactly what the judge wrote in her decision." Alistair's hands had unloosened themselves, and he was gesturing emphatically. "She said that granting them one would be akin to treating them like second-class citizens, rather than treating them the same way the courts treat a straight couple."

She shook her head. "It's like a catch-22. They get a judge who won't grant their request because she's basically too liberal."

"Right. Once they moved, the couple sued the state of Louisiana to declare its ban on same-sex parentage unconstitutional, on equal protection and due process grounds. The district court agreed with them; it ordered Louisiana to recognize existing same-sex parents and struck down its ban on same-sex parents."

"Well, thank God for judges who understand the Constitution."

"Indeed. The state of Louisiana was ordered to issue a new birth certificate form, replacing the blanks currently labeled with the gendered *mother* and *father* with *parent one* and *parent two*." He paused. "Louisiana appealed, of course, but the Fifth Circuit Court of Appeals upheld the district court's ruling, and, well, now Archie Dalton's appealing to the Court, and here we are."

"So, the two previous decisions are strong," Victoria reassured him. "That helps if we hear the case. What do we know about Archie Dalton?"

"Whatever we know now, we'll sure be learning more in the coming months. You know Kellen will want to hear this case. And the rest of them will fall in line," Alistair turned and studied her.

"Okay," she said, "so we'll hear it. From what you're telling me about it, it sounds like we couldn't have asked for a stronger case to work with."

Tori removed her glasses and examined her mentor. His whole body vibrated with agitation.

"Alistair, what am I missing?" she asked softly.

"You don't know, do you?"

"Know what?"

He laughed bitterly.

"It's Genevieve's case."

In the silence that followed, her breath became loud in her ears, and she grew acutely aware of her own heartbeat.

As Alistair sank into an easy chair opposite her, she continued reading the press release. Only this time, her throat felt tight.

> The original complaint was filed by current president of Her Equal Rights, Genevieve Fornier, the legal powerhouse who last year won federal recognition of gay marriage. Fornier, a close personal friend of the plaintiffs, has been quoted as saying that whatever people may think about the religious underpinnings of marriage, no one should ever interfere with two loving parents raising their children.
>
> Fornier has been friends with Crystal Rowlings (nee Sun) since elementary school and officiated the wedding ceremony in which Crystal married Heather Rowlings in Sonoma, California, in July 2008.
>
> The Supreme Court will now decide whether or not to hear arguments in the case. Should they decline, the fifth circuit court decision recognizing Crystal Rowlings as a parent will be upheld, and Louisiana clerks' offices would begin issuing birth certificates with nongendered parental slots.

Alistair wiped his brow and smiled grimly. "I imagine you two will have a fun, lighthearted discussion about this."

"I imagine she and I won't discuss it at all unless the Court decides to hear it." Victoria chewed her lip and tried to ignore the look of sympathy Alistair gave her.

Well, she'd just have to deal with that later, *if* the Court decided to take the case. Maybe they wouldn't. She could always dream.

She cleared her throat. "So, how was your summer, Alistair?"

He rolled his eyes at her. "We're not done here, Victoria."

"What do you want me to do? Bribe Kellen not to hear the case?"

"That man has everything he could ever want. There's nothing you could bribe him with."

She sighed. "There are actual legal questions here. I mean, it might not all be bad. We have the possibility to make same-sex parents' rights the law of the land."

Her attempt at optimism fell flat, and she fiddled with her fingers.

He shifted in his chair. "With a conservative Court? We also have the potential to rip families apart. What if Genevieve insists on arguing the case? Are you going to insist on recusing yourself? Or what if she steps down, and some other lawyer has to learn the case from scratch in a hurry? Either way, it jeopardizes the success of even a case this strong."

Victoria glanced around her private office, taking in the mahogany bookcases, the expensive carpeting, the original Charles Willson Peale painting of George Washington. Her stomach churned. "We perch in these fancy offices and issue directives as though the things that matter to us are who wins which political battles."

Alistair didn't seem to take it personally. "It's easy when you're a justice to feel like you're in some sort of ivory tower, to forget the *people* that your decisions affect. In this case, I can see that happening with five of our colleagues." He sighed. "It would feel particularly callous for members of the Court to deny parental rights for existing families."

The Court hadn't even decided to hear this case yet, and Victoria already found herself wondering if the walls in her office weren't slowly, inexorably moving closer and closer together.

"What are you going to do about this?" he asked.

Her jaw tightened. Why was *this* something she, in particular, needed to do anything about? Weighing her responses, she looked at him—*really* looked at him—for the first time since he had barged into her office. There was a weariness in his eyes she had never seen before, and he looked pale. "Can I get you some tea, Alistair?"

"Chamomile, if you don't mind."

She brewed them both a cup from the machine in the corner, and they drank in silence for a while.

"What would you like me to do about this?" she asked gently.

He shook his head. "That's up to you. But if the Court decides to hear arguments, you're going to have to fight battles on two fronts. Whatever the fallout is with Genevieve, keep your head in the game here."

With such a conservative Court right now, recusing herself clearly wasn't an option, and the list of reasons she didn't want them to hear this case was growing long.

They spent a long while finishing their tea, each lost in thought, before Alistair excused himself. It was Monday, and she and Genevieve rarely saw each other during the workweek; for once

Victoria was grateful. Maybe by the time they faced each other, she'd know what to say.

Later that afternoon, for the first time since joining the Court, she invited herself into Alistair's office the way he routinely did with hers. With the exception of some of the titles in the bookcases, it was remarkably similar to her own.

She closed the door behind her, and from his place behind his desk, Alistair gestured toward two leather chairs by the window that looked identical to the ones they'd sat on earlier.

"With all the excitement earlier, we haven't had a chance to catch up," she said, getting settled.

Alistair rose heavily from his desk chair. "I have chamomile. Can I return the favor?"

She nodded and watched him walk to the sideboard, taken aback by how much more pronounced his limp was than the last time she'd thought to notice. "I wanted to apologize if I was a bit out of sorts," she said.

"Not at all, my dear. Truth be told, I was too." As the tea brewed, he leaned heavily against the window. "I've been thinking a lot about what's next for me."

The look he gave her, equal parts resignation and despondency, told her volumes, and she blinked in surprise. She understood his frustration with Archie Dalton's appeal in a new light.

"Alistair, you can't. You're too young to retire."

He smiled faintly. "Well, I've missed my window anyway, haven't I?"

"Why would you retire now?"

"Learning your wife has stage four ovarian cancer will change your perspective."

She couldn't stifle a gasp. "Oh, Alistair. I'm so sorry."

He held up his hand, and Victoria understood that he had no desire for her pity. "We found out in June and have been making the most of our time together ever since." His gaze drifted out the window, and Victoria's heart ached for both of them. "I've been on the Court since you were in law school, Victoria. It's time."

Still, the tension lines around his mouth indicated that he was conflicted about the decision. Besides, with the Court about to begin a new session, he wouldn't want to leave a vacancy; he'd want to retire in the early summer so that the Senate could confirm his replacement by the start of October term. And there was another issue at play here: if Marcia died and he had retired, he would have no idea how to fill his time.

Not that this was something Victoria would dream of saying out loud. "Can Genevieve and I bring dinner over this week?"

He nodded, brought over their tea, and sat. "As long as it's not soup. I can't handle more soup."

"I make a delicious jambalaya, if you think her stomach can handle it."

His smile didn't reach his eyes. "That works, if it's not too spicy. We went to New Orleans in July. She wanted to tour the mansions in the Garden District."

"I've never been."

"You two should go. I bet Genevieve would enjoy the jazz."

Victoria nodded, although the idea of traveling together as a couple seemed foreign to her. And not really something she even knew how to imagine. "I suppose she would."

"We don't have plans for Thursday," Alistair said.

"We'll be there at seven." She probably should consult with Genevieve before making plans for her, but if Genevieve had another engagement, Victoria could bring over dinner by herself.

Alistair studied his hands and sighed. Before she could inquire about his wife's treatment, he held up his hand and shook his head. Evidently she wasn't the only one struggling to discuss personal matters.

"Well, I look forward to getting to know Genevieve better. Something tells me her energy will be great for Marcia."

She put her hand briefly on his knee and squeezed before changing the subject. They chatted about the summer tennis circuit for a while, but Alistair's heart clearly wasn't in it. As she left his office, she wished she'd been better at cheering him up. Maybe he was right—this was more Genevieve's territory than hers.

CHAPTER 4

Genevieve's leg bounced up and down underneath her desk at HER.

"I'm sorry, Genevieve. I really didn't think you'd mind this much."

"Tori, my schedule is hectic, and I don't even control it—my secretary does. But that's beside the point, really. People ask their partners before committing them to dinner plans. At least, they're supposed to."

"I get it. But it hardly seemed kind to hit the pause button on my conversation with Alistair right after he'd revealed that Marcia has cancer, just so I could call you to compare calendars."

Genevieve squeezed her eyes shut. "Fine. You're driving."

There was a pause, which probably meant Tori was biting back some response about how it made more logistical sense for Genevieve to drive.

"Okay, fine," Tori gave in. "I'm driving."

Genevieve's bouncing grew more erratic, and her knee knocked into her desk. "So, what'd you talk about at work today?"

Tori cleared her throat. "You mean besides my conversation with Alistair?"

"Yes, besides that."

"Nothing I should really discuss with you."

"God, really? You're honestly going to be so ridiculous about this that you won't even admit this is happening?"

"'This'? What's 'this'?"

"Please. Don't play coy with me. That press release was all over the place today, and I'm sure you saw it. Archie Dalton and my case."

"Genevieve," Tori said in a tone that made nails on a chalkboard sound like a symphony. "Let's not—"

She'd heard enough. "No, you're right. Let's not talk about the important things in our lives. What a silly notion I had. I'll see you for dinner with Alistair. Pick me up at six."

Genevieve hung up the phone, instantly regretting how much of an ass she'd just been. But Tori's vise grip on all significant events in their lives sometimes made her want to scream.

She took a drink of the sparkling water Frank had put on her desk sometime during her afternoon barrage of phone calls. Well, at least Tori was finally willing to introduce her to Alistair. Considering how studiously Tori avoided any joint appearances outside of her house—and the very isolated pool at their gym—she was beginning to feel like a dirty little secret. Which was ridiculous, since thanks to that viral photo, everyone now knew what they looked like the moment before they kissed.

Regardless, it was easier to focus on their dinner with Alistair and his wife than the fact that Archie Dalton had appealed her fucking case. What an asshole. What did he hope to accomplish by this? How on earth could he justify this appeal as a good use of his time, when he was ultimately fighting against a loving family like the ones he claimed to support? It was hypocrisy at its worst.

All she could do was hope the Court would decline to hear arguments. She couldn't even think about what she and Tori would do otherwise.

She crossed her legs, and her foot swung left and right rapidly; she was grateful that her door was closed so Frank couldn't tease her. But she was too antsy to sit still.

Her e-mail dinged, and she clicked on it to discover an NCLR announcement of a press conference that afternoon. The e-mail blast didn't explicitly say so, but they had clearly secured a new executive director. Well, good. Genevieve could gather her staff, and they could all watch the announcement together in the conference room. Maybe she could even order food. Mexican sounded delicious.

Her phone rang.

"A woman named Shadi from NCLR is on line three for you," Frank said when she picked up.

She clicked over. "Genevieve Fornier."

"Hi, Ms. Fornier. I'm an administrative assistant at NCLR. I'm sure you're aware that we're announcing our new executive director this afternoon. She would like you to be present at the press conference, standing next to her while she speaks."

Choking back a "really?" Genevieve cleared her throat and asked, "Where and when?"

"Our offices on H Street at three o'clock, please. The conference room is on the eleventh floor."

"I'll be there."

Well, so much for bonding time with her staff. She'd just have to get fajitas for lunch and eat on her own.

The weather was nice, and NCLR's offices weren't far, so Genevieve walked. Since she'd be making an impromptu appearance, she was glad she'd worn a suit to the office, although she usually reserved her maroon one for days when she wasn't going to be on camera.

She was buzzed in and ushered to a conference room with a sleek glass podium and rows of chairs. A few cameramen were testing equipment, and assistants were flitting about. She set her briefcase down on a table in the corner and turned around to find Jamie Chance grinning at her.

"Been a while, Genevieve. Whatever have you been keeping busy with?" He reinforced his suggestive tone with an eyebrow wiggle.

She hit him softly before hugging him. "Nice to see you too."

"Any idea why they wanted us here?"

"Our good looks?"

He surveyed the room for a moment. "Well, we definitely up the hotness factor here."

"How was your summer?" she asked.

He rolled his eyes. "There was a summer? I wouldn't know. There is only work these days. There is no summer. There are no weekends. Hell, for all I know, there is no day and night."

"How you maintain such a grueling travel schedule with a little kid at home, I'll never know."

"Oh, and your workload is a walk in the park? I get e-mails from you at one in the morning. You know, Genevieve, the marriage case was a big exception for me. I don't litigate and administrate. And fundraise. Trying to do them all is just plain wacky."

"It is, but there's this new case about an inmate in Michigan that I just can't walk away from." Genevieve ran her hand through her hair. "You'd think that since gay marriage is legal everywhere now, our jobs would get a little easier."

As if inspired by her gesture, Jamie ran his hand over his own bald head. "Yeah, well, that's certainly what all of our supporters think. Our donations are down forty percent since the SCOTUS decision last year."

"Oh my God." Genevieve struggled to think of something supportive to say.

"'Oh my God' is right. We clearly need to work on our messaging, because we keep trying to tell people that the fight for LGBTQ rights is far from over. Especially for the *T* members of our community. But donors aren't listening."

Casting around for what she hoped would be a happier subject, Genevieve asked, "Well, now that gay marriage is legal, when are you getting hitched? And do I get an invite?"

He shrugged and dropped his eyes. "My partner doesn't believe in marriage."

And Genevieve thought she had it bad, dating a woman who didn't believe in holding hands in public. She gave a soft whistle.

"You're telling me," Jamie said.

Raising a child together seemed to go hand in hand with marriage, Genevieve mused, but she kept that observation to herself. Before she could change the subject, a commotion in the doorway had both of them directing their attention elsewhere.

Amidst a sea of assistants walked one of the most attractive women Genevieve had ever seen. She wore a pinstriped black pantsuit, a low-cut cream-colored shell, and stilettos. It was obvious that she was NCLR's new executive director, and Genevieve was instantly relieved: she looked like she could steer even the most rickety of ships through tumultuous storms.

And it was also high time the organization appointed a person of color as executive director. Some of her lesbian friends had been frustrated that HRC beat NCLR on that front when Jamie became the first African American to head the organization since its inception. The fact that the two most prominent gay rights organizations in the country would now be helmed by black leaders was long overdue and absolutely important.

While these thoughts were parading through her head, the new executive director strode to Jamie and shook his hand warmly. "Good to see you again, Jamie."

He seemed stunned. "And you," he stammered, and Genevieve had never seen him so surprised.

She turned to Genevieve and extended her hand. The moment their palms touched, Genevieve felt a surge of electricity move up her arm, through her neck, and into her mouth. She couldn't remember the last time just shaking hands with someone made her think so forcefully about sex—maybe never.

"Genevieve Fornier. I can't believe we haven't met before. I'm Penelope Sweet."

Her voice was like velvet, and despite her best efforts, Genevieve's eyes dropped to her lips. Penelope's eyes mirrored hers for a fraction of a section before she released Genevieve's hand and took a step back.

"I asked both of you here because our organizations have a history of competing and disagreeing, and I think we can do better. I know that Nicolette Ford had talked about holding check-in meetings with you two every few months. I propose we meet weekly, rotating locations between our three offices over lunch on Fridays. We will be most effective if we collaborate on strategy for existing and future cases, including who's arguing which cases and even which cases to initiate. Gay marriage was only one front of a much larger war, and it's a war that's had too many casualties. It's damn time we win and the other side surrenders."

Evidently, there was a new sheriff in town. Genevieve supposed this must be how Nic and Jamie had felt when she had taken over at HER. Though she gave Penelope points for style; there was something about her delivery that invited them both in and made them feel valued. The scolding she gave Nic and Jamie the first day they had worked together, when the two of them were more inclined to insult each other than collaborate, seemed miles away from this encounter.

She was also acutely aware of her fajita breath.

"So. What do you think?" Penelope asked. "If you're on board, I'd like to announce this new collaboration as part of the press conference."

As far as being steamrolled went, this was actually rather enjoyable. A brief image of Penelope schooling opposing counsel in front of the Supreme Court flitted across her mind, and she smiled.

Appreciation of Penelope's forceful yet welcoming energy aside, Genevieve decided she had a bit of territory to reclaim here. "Welcome to the eye of the hurricane," she told her, hoping to remind her new colleague that she'd been doing this a lot longer. "We're glad to have you."

If Jamie resented that she spoke for him, he hid it well. "We'll have to have some of these meetings via Skype—my schedule has me traveling a lot—but I'm on board."

When Penelope smiled, the atmosphere in the room seemed to relax.

"Lovely. We're agreed, then. Look, let's go smile pretty for the cameras now, and afterward, I'd love to grab a drink with you two and get to know you. Are you free for happy hour today?"

She and Jamie exchanged an incredulous look. Who in DC was free on such short notice? She and Jamie pulled out their phones. "I can move some things around," Jamie said. "Let me call my secretary when the press conference is over."

Genevieve had a strategy session with the team litigating the Michigan case, two briefs for other cases that she wanted to review before they were filed with courts at the end of the business day, and a mentorship coffee date with the newest lawyer on HER's staff. She looked back up at Penelope, who was watching her with an inscrutable look on her face. "I'll make a few calls."

"There's a gastropub between your office and mine," Jamie told Penelope.

There was something jarring about the image of Penelope, who had more Hollywood glamour than a person should be allowed, in a gastropub. But Penelope just smiled.

"Delightful. Shall we say six o'clock?"

The way Penelope strode to the front of the room was unnerving for a host of reasons, and Genevieve wasn't about to stand there and figure them all out. She hurried after her.

The press conference was brief, and she and Jamie left when the formal announcement transitioned into a question-and-answer session. The first thing she did after exiting the doors of the building that housed NCLR was whip out her phone and Google *Penelope Sweet*.

Sweet defied expectations on multiple levels. First, diplomats weren't typically executive director material, and Sweet had spent the previous six years as the United States ambassador to France. That at least explained why she managed to win situations that didn't feel like a competition and convince everyone in the room that they were happier for it. But it left open why a woman who had devoted her life to international law would suddenly want to focus on domestic civil rights issues. Or whether she was at all qualified to do so.

But by the time Genevieve reached the door to her office, she had learned all of Penelope's credentials and history; and she was certainly qualified for a lot of things: Yale Law, then the United Nations Rule of Law task force, working with its Office of the High Commission, for Human Rights and the Office of Legal Affairs. Most of her time had been spent in Africa, assisting fledgling governments draft their constitutions to protect human rights, particularly focusing on gay rights. She left the UN in 2005 to become a law professor at Université Paris 1 Panthéon-Sorbonne. Evidently, France agreed with her, and in 2009 she moved from the classroom to the embassy.

All in all, Penelope Sweet had had an odd career trajectory, and with such an international resumé, she seemed an unlikely choice to succeed a woman who had devoted her life to expanding legal protection for LGBTQ citizens in US law.

Her research generated more questions than answers, and Genevieve was looking forward to drinks for a number of reasons. When she arrived early at the pub Jamie recommended, the maître d' of The Three Branches asked her, "Executive, legislative, or judicial?"

She raised her eyebrows. Obviously annoyed that he was dealing with a newcomer, he rolled his eyes back at her. "Do you want to sit at the bar, at a table, or on the back patio?" he clarified.

The polite thing to do would be to let Penelope, as the one who initiated this gathering, choose where they sat, but curiosity got the better of her. "Which one is judicial?"

"Back patio. Everyone forgets it's there."

Biting back a reply about how everyone wished they could forget the legislative branch, she went for the simpler, "Sounds fine. There are three of us."

The bar and the restaurant were packed; the crowd was mostly young and in suits, suggesting staffers from the Hill. Perhaps it was their naïve optimism that appealed to Jamie; most people who worked in the Beltway acquired a permanently hard-set jaw and a jaded attitude within two years. It was refreshing to see a slew of driven strategists still convinced they might make a difference.

The patio was bricked and, Genevieve noted with amusement, had nine tables. She briefly scanned the tables to see if they were labeled with the names of the nine justices and was disappointed not to see a placard with Tori's name on it—or any of the other justices. Only one table was occupied, and the man and woman seated there appeared to be on a date.

"Anywhere you like," the maître d' said before he walked away. Genevieve chose a table as far away from the couple as possible and grabbed the drinks menu from the rack. It was extensive, featuring three pages for craft beers and about a dozen pages listing every cocktail she'd ever heard of—and even more she hadn't—in chronological order by the date they were created. The wine offerings, listed on the last page, seemed pedestrian by comparison.

Jamie was a beer guy, she knew from their many late nights working together last year. It was a good guess that a woman who had lived in France for years preferred wine. Since this meeting seemed as much about staking out each other's territory as anything else, that left cocktails for her, so she settled on a Front Porch and closed the menu.

Part of her was relieved when Jamie arrived first, and the other part had hoped for a minute or two alone with Penelope—for reasons she wasn't about to examine.

He sat down across from her and immediately leaned in close, as though the CIA might have bugged the table next to them. "What is NCLR thinking?"

Glad her research had equipped her to respond to such a question, Genevieve said, "Maybe they think we can learn something here from human rights work abroad?"

"Obviously, she's got a brilliant legal mind," he conceded. "But it's been forever since she even lived in this country. We have such a patchwork of laws now that I'm sure she's playing catch-up just getting the lay of the land."

"Well, regardless of her knowledge, or lack thereof, she certainly knows how to inspire confidence." Genevieve was about to ask him whether he was really on board with the weekly meetings Penelope had proposed when the woman in question entered the patio.

Her yoga pants and tank top contrasted sharply with the sleek suit she'd worn for the press conference. Her locks were pulled into a ponytail, and her tasteful gold jewelry from the press conference had been removed. Her sneakers reminded Genevieve that it had been way too long since she'd gone for a run. Or done anything physical outside of Tori's bed.

Penelope's thousand-watt smile lit up the patio, and as she sat down, she gestured to her clothes. "I hope you don't mind—I'm going to yoga when we're done."

"Not at all," Jamie said, although from the tone of his voice, Genevieve sensed that he, too, felt keenly aware of his lack of a sustained exercise regime.

The waitress dropped by, and Jamie ordered a stout without looking at the menu. Penelope, likewise, left the menus where they were. "Front Porch," she said.

Unsure whether to feel scooped or an instant connection, Genevieve shrugged and said, "The same."

Penelope grinned at her and bumped Genevieve's knee with hers.

"Okay, so let's just cut to the chase," Jamie said, leaning forward. "You're a bizarre choice for them, and they're a bizarre choice for you. Why are you doing this?"

Penelope took his tactless question in stride. Her eyes seemed open and warm as she looked back and forth between them, and Genevieve was reminded again that diplomatic skills were really undervalued in this country.

"I admit I was also surprised when the board first contacted me. It wasn't a secret in DC that I was ready to move on from my position in France and interested in domestic US politics. Certainly, I wasn't doing a lot of cutting-edge work on human rights as the US ambassador to France, and I missed being in the trenches."

Her voice was warm, like a summer afternoon, and Genevieve thought that she'd never tire of hearing it. Penelope spoke with her hands and conveyed an enticing combination of passion and intelligence.

"There's a lot at stake here, you know. The US likes to think it's a leader for foreign—especially developing—countries to follow. We believe so firmly in our own exceptionalism. But when radical fringe groups from the US target countries like Uganda to advance an agenda that includes capital punishment for gays, well, it's time we focus on fixing our own problems and stop telling other countries what to do."

Jamie studied her as their drinks were deposited in front of them. "That was quite the soliloquy."

She laughed, making Genevieve wonder if the good-natured thing was a well-practiced act or actually sincere. "Well, just because I've been interviewed over a dozen times and rehearsed my answers, it doesn't make them any less true," she said.

He wiped away the froth mustache from his first big drink of stout. "Okay, let's say your motives are pure. What are your priorities?"

The Front Porch was delicious and went down easy, and Genevieve leaned back to watch the tennis match, content to observe and gather information for the time being.

"Trans rights, particularly with respect to health care. And workplace rights for LGBTQ Americans."

Jamie nodded his approval. "Do you think we'll have more success if we advance a state-by-state strategy or if we try for federal protections on these fronts?"

Penelope gazed at him for a long moment before answering, and he squirmed a bit in his chair. "Jamie, I'm not here to dictate strategy," she said. "I'm here to work with you. It's quite possible that the most effective plan for us would be a two-pronged strategy in which one or more of our organizations works state-by-state and the others pursue something federal. I came here to get to know you both better and to brainstorm together about what's next for all of us."

Jamie seemed mollified—a little cowed, even.

For the first time since she had sat down, Penelope turned to Genevieve, who was surprised to feel completely at home under her open scrutiny. One thing was for sure, she was a hell of a lot less abrasive than Nic Ford.

"And I'm not here to grill you," Genevieve said softly. They shared a small smile, and Genevieve hoped Jamie didn't feel she was picking sides.

They shared details of some of the cases their organizations were working on, and when Penelope checked the time on her cell phone, Genevieve looked down at her watch, surprised to find an hour had passed.

"I'm sorry, but I have to run if I want to make that yoga class." Penelope stood up, all legs and glamour, even in workout clothes, and Genevieve didn't want her to go.

Possibly not the best reaction to a colleague's departure, she mused.

"Penelope, it's been a pleasure." Jamie stood up. "I guess we'll see you at noon on Friday. HRC can host our meeting next week."

"Sounds great." She shook Jamie's hand, then dropped cash on the table to cover her drink.

"I look forward to working with you, Penelope," Genevieve said, extending her hand.

"Likewise, Genevieve," she said. They shook hands warmly before she turned to leave.

You've got a girlfriend, Genevieve reminded herself. *Don't watch her walk away.*

Well, she wasn't perfect. But that view certainly was. Damn, this could get dangerous.

Embarrassed, she turned her attention to Jamie, but he was oblivious to Genevieve's wandering eyes. He drank the last of his beer thoughtfully for a while.

Truth be told, she needed a minute alone with her thoughts as well. Penelope was certainly going to shake things up. For one thing, she'd be a dynamite fundraiser. Hell, if she asked, Genevieve probably would have shelled over money herself. It wasn't just her stunning good looks; she simply made you feel like your opinion mattered enough to make a difference. There was something magnetic about her energy, like she was inexorably pulling you closer to her.

"I think it's good," Jamie said at last. "She's a good choice, and I'm glad we're all going to be working together."

Genevieve didn't bother telling him that NCLR didn't really need his approval for their choice of a new leader.

"I am too." She finished her Front Porch and wondered if Penelope often did yoga after a drink. "So I guess I'll see you next time?"

"Guess so," he said. He still seemed a bit uncertain about this new dynamic.

"Well, I'm heading out," she said after he had said nothing for several seconds. "Maybe I'll go for a run."

He gave her a wry look. "Uh-huh. I was thinking the same thing." He paused. "I can't remember the last time I exercised."

"Maybe she'll be good for us in more ways than one."

They paid their bill and left. An hour later, Genevieve gasped for breath, bent over holding her sides. Running after bourbon—definitely a bad idea.

CHAPTER 5

On Thursday night, Victoria picked up Genevieve at six thirty, even though her girlfriend's townhouse was twenty minutes in the opposite direction from Alistair's place in Maryland. Genevieve was sticking to her decision that Victoria's penance for not having consulted her about plans was being the designated driver. She hoped it didn't mean Genevieve planned to get smashed.

Absolutely zero parking spaces were available anywhere near Genevieve's front door, so she double parked, clicked on her hazards, and texted, *I'm outside.*

Three minutes later, Genevieve emerged, locked her front door, and bounded down the steps. Casually elegant, she wore slim-fit jeans, boat shoes, and a blousy blue and white sweater. She might as well have been headed to the Hamptons, and Victoria had an image of the two of them walking down the beach together, the salty ocean air on their cheeks. It made her smile. Maybe someday.

Genevieve got in, dropped a kiss on her cheek, and pulled the door shut. "Hi, honey. How was your day?" She laughed lightly, and the tension in Victoria's shoulders released. Good—Genevieve wasn't going to be passive-aggressively peeved at her all night.

Victoria entered Alistair's address on her navigation system, and they were off. "Today was my last day of freedom. Tomorrow is our first conference, and then it all begins in earnest."

"Ugh. Do you feel the way I always felt on the last day of summer break, before school began?"

"I don't know—how did you feel then?"

"Like my life was ending and everything was terrible."

Victoria offered her hand and Genevieve took it. Their fingers wove together comfortably and the contact sent a wave of warmth up her arm and into her heart. "It's good to know your flair for the dramatic started so young."

"Oh, of course. And by the end of the first week of school, I was so over summer and already crushing on someone new."

"Dear Lord, how did your parents manage you?" Victoria asked.

"Just fine, thank you very much. And since you asked, my crush in fifth grade was Jordan Reilly—boy-Jordan. In sixth grade, it was Jose Martinez. God, he was so cute. And in seventh grade it was girl-Jordan. Eighth grade was Ms. Crawford. She was absolutely dreamy. English teacher, of course."

Only Genevieve Fornier would mark the passage of time with crushes. "Why 'of course?'" Victoria asked.

"Because it's always the English teacher. There's something so romantic about analyzing literature. Probably because so many of the texts are romantic. Who should Hester Prynne choose—Chillingworth or Dimmesdale? And everything about *Gatsby* is romantic, from the alcohol and dancing and aesthetics of the twenties to Gatsby's love for Daisy. Come on, you didn't have a crush on an English teacher at some point?"

Victoria drummed her thumb on the steering wheel, but no one came to mind. "I don't think so. I wasn't someone who had a lot of crushes."

"Right, what was I thinking? You were one of those people who thought school was for learning." Genevieve kissed the back of her hand.

"You must have thought so too—you did end up collecting some prestigious degrees, if I recall."

"School is for many things. Case in point: law school. I got a job out of it and some education and some fun times with this girl I really liked."

Victoria laughed, as images of walking across the Harvard Law School campus twenty years ago with Genevieve flashed across her memory. "Sounds like there's a story there," she teased. "Tell me about her."

"Oh, you know, she was pretty ordinary. Boring, really. Honestly, I don't even remember her."

One finger at a time, Victoria extracted her hand from Genevieve's grasp and then hit her on the shoulder. "Here I thought you spent twenty years hung up on her."

"Yeah, well, everyone remembers history differently."

Victoria cleared her throat. "Listen, Genevieve, I'm really glad you're coming with me tonight."

"Me too. Alistair seems like a good guy. And he's important to you, so he's important to me."

"That means a lot. Thanks."

Victoria was almost sorry when they pulled into his driveway. Time alone with Genevieve was so precious to her, and it was rare that one or both of them wasn't interrupted by something work related.

Genevieve grabbed the pot of jambalaya from the backseat and carried it to the front door. Victoria followed with the salad, and after she joined Genevieve on the front stoop, she knocked lightly on the door. While they waited, she glanced over at Genevieve and nodded at the pot. "Trying to take credit for my work?"

Genevieve shrugged. "Just because I'm carrying it, doesn't mean—"

The door opened, and Alistair's booming voice greeted them. "Victoria! Genevieve! Ooh, Genevieve, did you cook that? It smells delicious!"

"Anything for a friend of Tori's."

Genevieve stepped over the threshold into the house and turned back, as Alistair pulled Victoria into a hug. Victoria glared at her girlfriend over his shoulder.

He led them into the house, calling backward as he walked to the dining room, "What kind of hot sauce did you use? I've found with jambalaya, it all comes down to the hot sauce."

Victoria laughed at the look of panic on Genevieve's face, and Alistair turned around and winked. "It's okay, Genevieve," he said. "I can't cook either."

They walked through the living room and into the open kitchen and dining room. "Does that need to be warmed up?" he asked, pointing to the pot in Genevieve's hands.

"It does. Can I use your stove?" Victoria asked.

He nodded and moved aside for her. "Genevieve, what can I get you to drink? I was thinking margaritas."

"Sounds perfect," she said. "Can I help?"

"No need. Make yourself comfortable."

Victoria fussed with the stove and poked around some drawers, looking for something to stir with, while Genevieve sat on a stool at the island, and Alistair worked on their drinks.

"Where's Marcia?" Victoria asked as she tossed the salad.

"The screened-in porch. She's out there all the time now. I think the birds calm her. She had cytoreductive surgery earlier in the summer, and she just completed her first three-week round of chemo. She's very weak and always tired. But she'll be happy for company."

In addition to the margaritas, Alistair made a cup of tea, and Victoria tried to brace herself for seeing a very different version of Marcia than the one she'd gotten to know over the past couple of years. Alistair patted her on the back, and they carried everything out to the porch.

Marcia Douglas was sitting on a little love seat, her feet propped up on an ottoman, a blanket draped over her legs. Her transformation was startling. Her cheeks were sunken, her skin looked like paper, and she was so much smaller than Victoria remembered. But her headscarf brought out the bright blue of her eyes, which were sharp and, when they fell on Victoria, glowed with happiness.

"Victoria, darling, come see me." She held out her hands, and Victoria took them both in her own. Squeezing them gently, Victoria pushed down her pity for Marcia and Alistair, and gave her a bright smile.

"It's so sweet of you to visit."

Victoria kissed her cheek softly and stood back. "Marcia, this is Genevieve."

"My, my, you're a lovely thing," Marcia said, and Genevieve shook hands with her. "Tall too." She craned her neck. "Sit down so I can really see you."

Alistair pulled over some chairs, Victoria made plates for everyone, and they settled in to eat.

"Marcia," Genevieve leaned close to her and said lowly, "let's compare notes about what it's like to be in a relationship with a Supreme Court justice."

Oh Lord, what was Genevieve doing? Victoria glanced at Alistair, and he grinned and shrugged. "I suppose we should have expected that they'd gang up on us," he told her.

"When she's writing an opinion, does Victoria sometimes walk around the house with a pen in her mouth, talking to herself?" Marcia asked.

"No," Genevieve replied, "but sometimes, over dinner, she says she has a question about one of her cases, and it will just take a second to explain. And then, forty-five minutes later, all she's said are sentences, and I'm still waiting to hear a question."

Marcia patted Genevieve's knee. "Well, at least she talks to you about her cases. He thinks I'm not smart enough to discuss them!"

"Marcia!" Alistair coughed. "That's not true at all! I just don't want to bore you."

"You know, Alistair." Victoria set down her empty margarita glass. "I don't think we need to be here for this conversation."

"Oh, no you don't!" Marcia said. "This will be so much more fun with you two here."

The look Genevieve gave Victoria left little room for negotiation. "More jambalaya, anyone?" seemed the best response.

Marcia and Genevieve ignored her.

"How ridiculous is it when they get picked up in those huge SUVs for the State of the Union?" Marcia asked. Despite her physical alterations, Marcia very much seemed like her usual self.

"Oh, I didn't even know about that! I was out of town last year."

"Honey, you're in for a treat. They get these Secret Service escorts, and they go off to drink with the other justices beforehand in Kellen's basement like some secret society from *The Da Vinci Code* or something. And then, *poof!* Suddenly they're on your TV screen."

Genevieve laughed. "I keep reading all of these articles saying they should start having cameras in the Court, and I'm *so* glad they don't. I hope they never do. I'd hate to see Tori's face on CNN all the time."

"Well, gee, tell me what you really think of my face," Victoria said.

"Oh, please," Genevieve said, "I don't need asinine pundits finding the worst possible screenshot of you and then debating how your hair looked in the courtroom that day. Do you?"

"I agree, Genevieve. If there were cameras, suddenly Alistair and I wouldn't be able to go out to dinner with any kind of anonymity or privacy."

"That's what I keep telling Victoria!" Genevieve said.

"And does she agree?" Marcia asked.

"I think she's conflicted. She sees value in the transparency that cameras would bring—she says they add a layer of democracy."

"You know," Victoria crossed her arms, "*she's* actually sitting right here. You could ask her."

Alistair shook his head. "The sooner you embrace your role as a prop in this conversation, the better."

Victoria followed Alistair's cue and leaned back to listen, as Marcia and Genevieve continued to bond over their roles as partners of justices. Alistair offered to refresh their drinks, and Genevieve paused long enough to nod during one of her tirades about how expensive dry cleaning bills were for justices' robes.

By the time they finished eating, the sun was setting and the temperature dropping. Marcia shivered a little, and Alistair went into protective-husband mode.

"Honey, I think we should call it a night." He stood and rubbed his hip absentmindedly, his attention on his wife.

"Oh." Marcia looked around her in surprise. "It's dark! How did that happen? Well, Genevieve. It's been a long time since I've laughed this much."

Genevieve took her hand. "I'm glad Tori introduced us. Took her long enough." There was an edge to her voice that made Victoria itch at the back of her neck, but neither Alistair nor Marcia seemed to notice.

"I hope you'll come back soon," Marcia said. "And you don't have to make Victoria cook, you know—we can just order food."

"Oh, don't you worry. I'll be back. Maybe I'll even bring Victoria." She helped Marcia stand, and Alistair quickly moved to his wife's side.

"I'm going to help her to bed," he said. "I'll be back in a few minutes to clean up. Please, make yourselves comfortable."

Victoria kissed Marcia's cheek and said good night. After Alistair ushered Marcia inside, Victoria and Genevieve collected the dishes on the porch table in silence, the only sounds the clink of plates and the cicadas outside. Victoria led the way back to the kitchen.

"Thanks for coming, Genevieve. I think you made Marcia's day. You have a gift for this kind of thing."

Genevieve sighed heavily. "I don't have any special gift, Tori—I just enjoy getting to know people."

"What's wrong, Genevieve?" Victoria set her dishes on the kitchen counter and opened the dishwasher to begin loading it, which provided a nice diversion, since she sensed something was about to erupt from Genevieve, who was staring at the floor.

"I had a great time tonight." She looked up and inspected Victoria's eyes. "I think Alistair and Marcia did too. So that begs the question: why did you wait over a year to introduce us?"

She set her stack of dishes on the countertop and paced to the other side of the kitchen. Victoria hesitated, then began loading Genevieve's dishes into the dishwasher. This conversation reminded her of ice-skating when she was young and she had worried about hitting a thin patch.

"I don't understand. You're mad at me for doing something you wanted me to do?" she asked.

"Why do you keep our relationship so secret? I mean, that damn photo is out there, and everyone knows, so what's the big deal?"

Victoria closed the dishwasher and wiped her hands on a towel nearby. Leaning against the countertop, she and Genevieve stared at each other. Victoria tried to think of something she could say that would convey that she was trying to do better but that wouldn't make Genevieve more upset. She opened her mouth but never got a chance to speak.

"Oh, you two didn't have to do the dishes!" Alistair said cheerily as he reentered the kitchen. Victoria instantly replaced whatever concern she was feeling with friendliness and hurried over to hug him.

"Of course we did! We're so happy you invited us."

Over Alistair's shoulder, she watched Genevieve school her features into the picture of congeniality. Alistair turned his attention to her, they hugged, and Genevieve said softly, "Marcia's delightful. And so are you."

He walked them to the door, and they each shared another hug with him before they headed to Victoria's car. They waved as they backed down the driveway.

They hadn't gone one block before Genevieve started again. "We spend all of our time in your house. We never go to my place. We never go out. It takes over a year for you to introduce me to your friends. You're ashamed."

Goosebumps traveled up Victoria's arms, and she shivered despite the blast of heat hitting her from the car vent; this was rocky territory, and it was unlikely either of them could cross it unscathed. "Genevieve, you know I'm a private person."

"That doesn't exactly explain your aversion to spending time on my turf."

"Turf? Really?"

"You know what I mean." Genevieve waved her hand dismissively, the picture of exasperation.

"I'm not sure I do. Are we getting into an actual turf war?" Victoria merged into the exit lane to head toward her house.

Genevieve shook her head. "Please take me home."

A chill went through Victoria's veins, and her stomach knotted. "Really? You really don't want to spend the night with me?"

"I just need a little space," Genevieve mumbled, which made no sense whatsoever to Victoria.

"Space? We see each other a few times a month. Any more space, and we'll hardly count as acquaintances."

"Just take me home."

Clutching the wheel tighter so that her hands wouldn't tremble, Victoria changed lanes and drove past the exit to her neighborhood. "Genevieve, I don't know how to fix something I don't really understand."

"How can you not understand that our entire relationship is on your terms?" Her voice sounded like sandpaper against Victoria's ears. "It takes over a year for you to introduce me to your friends, and you find an excuse not to hang out with mine every time I ask. And when you finally decide I get to meet Alistair and Marcia, you don't even ask if I'm available—you just assume. You say jump, I ask how high. That's how it always is."

Victoria's mind spun, and she couldn't slow it down enough to see one thought clearly. The painted lines on the highway kept disappearing, and soon she was pulling into Genevieve's neighborhood. She still hadn't managed to come up with a response—with every possible thing she came up with to say, she immediately thought of some way Genevieve could twist it into Victoria commandeering control of the situation.

"I never tell you to jump," she finally said after a long silence. "Relationships don't work that way. You're brilliant and creative, and I love you. I don't want to tell you what to do."

"And yet it seems that you're always making *all* the decisions." Genevieve mumbled so softly that Victoria barely heard it. "Where we go, what we do. Now you even get to decide about my career."

"Your career?" she asked, feeling like this conversation was utterly spiraling, as she pulled to a stop in front of Genevieve's townhouse.

"There's whatever the hell you and the other justices decide to do with my case. *You* get to decide, and it's *my* case. Once again, you hold all the cards."

"Oh. So that's what this is about? The conference tomorrow?"

Genevieve shook her head and opened the car door. The interior light made Victoria blink.

"Of course you'd take a complex issue and oversimplify it." Genevieve shook her head. "It's not just that."

"Then what else is it? What am I supposed to do when you spring all this on me?" Victoria grit her teeth at how defensive she sounded.

"Look, I have a big day tomorrow and so do you. I shouldn't have started this conversation now. So let's just talk about this some other time."

A thousand words of protest passed through Victoria's mind, but experience had taught her that pressing Genevieve to talk through things when all she wanted was space wouldn't end well for either of them.

"Okay," she said softly.

Genevieve looked at her with a surprised expression. "Okay?"

The suspicion in Genevieve's voice made Victoria sigh. "I would certainly rather talk more about this, but you don't want to, and I'd like to prove to you that not everything we do is on my terms."

Genevieve closed her eyes, and Victoria couldn't tell if it was in irritation or relief. She leaned over and dropped a quick kiss onto Victoria's cheek before getting out of the car.

"I'll call you tomorrow, okay?" Genevieve said, and she shut the car door.

As Genevieve walked up the steps, put her key in the door, and entered her townhouse, Victoria tried not to focus on the fact that it was the first time since they'd resumed their relationship last year that they hadn't given each other a proper kiss good night.

At seven the next morning, as she dressed and mentally prepared to see her colleagues again, Victoria put on a black suit with a black shell. Might as well dress the part, considering she felt as if she were headed to a funeral.

Besides, she always felt more powerful in black.

As she walked down the carpeted hallway of the US Supreme Court, she passed framed black-and-white photographs of every justice to have served, in chronological order by appointment. The last picture before the conference room door was her own, a stilted portrait taken the day after she was sworn in. The cold, distant woman staring back at her was barely recognizable. Was that how Genevieve saw her right now?

As the people who prized punctuality most, she and Kellen O'Neil were the first two in the room. She took her usual seat, which, given her lack of seniority, was as far away from the chief justice as possible.

"Victoria. You look well."

He looked older, but she wasn't about to say that out loud. "How was your summer?" she asked, feeling like every high school student ever.

"Restful. The wife and I went to Martha's Vineyard." Of course he called her "the wife." Probably both a generational thing and a conservative hack thing. "How did you fare this summer?"

She was saved from answering by the arrival of the other three conservative justices: Eliot McKenzie, Anthony Jaworski, and Matthew Smith inevitably traveled in a pack. As they approached, she could hear them boisterously discussing football, but as soon as they entered the room, they grew silent. The walls themselves seemed to encourage solemnity.

The liberals trickled in one at a time, with Michelle Lin and Jason Blankenstein arriving shortly before Alistair. A good five minutes passed while they waited for the swing vote, Ryan Jamison, to join them, and the justices already present passed the time by reading through the binder of pending cases as if they hadn't seen it before. In a nondescript brown suit, with his wispy hair and weak jaw, Ryan Jamison entered looking like the definition of boring milquetoast. He took the last seat, folded his hands in his lap, and looked expectantly at Kellen.

The chief justice closed his binder and, removing his glasses, sat forward. "Now that we are gathered, permit me to welcome you to the new term. I trust you all used the summer to gather your strength. Naturally, we have a rigorous fall looming ahead. Let us now decide what that fall will look like."

The first case in their binders concerned a mundane tax law. Nevertheless, it sparked a heated debate. If they were going to argue with this much passion about the tax code, Victoria steeled herself for the debates they would have when they reached the voting rights and same-sex parentage cases.

Two hours later, they had declined to hear eleven cases and granted review to three. After only a ten-minute break for coffee, they were right back at it. By lunchtime, they had voted up or down on over fifty appeals.

She dined on a Caesar salad wrap, alone in her office. The first case waiting for a vote after the lunch break was the parentage one. Calling Genevieve was clearly out of the question, so she studied her notes on the case instead. The problem was, it only took four yes votes for the Court to grant review of a case. And the possibility of making same-sex parentage legal nationwide tempted her, even though she knew Genevieve would be furious at her for even entertaining such ideas and despite Alistair's warning that they might lose. The safe bet was for the case not to get onto the docket at all.

When they were again settled in their seats, Kellen turned with an unnecessary amount of enthusiasm to the *Rowlings* case.

"I'll start the discussion here. It is essential that we hear this case—there is a circuit split between the fifth and the ninth, so we must resolve it."

Michelle adjusted her glasses. "All due respect, Kellen, that's not quite accurate: the ninth circuit opinion ruled that second-parent adoption in situations where both parents' names are already on the birth certificate is an undue burden, and therefore discrimination. The petition in the fifth circuit relates to recognition of names on a child's birth certificate. But it's true that the potential outcome is the same: a ruling in favor of the plaintiffs means that same-sex parents nationwide are recognized as just that—parents."

Jaworski jumped in. "Doesn't matter if the outcome is the same. The way we get to an outcome is a fundamental legal question that we can't ignore—and it puts the outcome in question."

Alistair steepled his fingers and leaned toward Kellen, who placed his hands on the table, on either side of his binder. It was such a perfect picture of macho bravado—physical attempts at taking up space—that Victoria almost laughed.

"I see no circuit split, nor do I see any issue with the appellate decision that needs revisiting. Let's let it lie." Alistair turned to her and raised his eyebrows, and she was confronted with the expectation from all eight other justices that she take a side on a case she felt profoundly conflicted about.

During a prolonged blink, the picture of the Rowlings family— two women, two children, all smiles—flitted across her mind. Was she willing to risk tearing them apart?

"I agree with Alistair. This case doesn't require our attention."

She could almost see tangible disappointment seep from O'Neill's eyes, float across the table like smoke, and engulf her; she coughed.

"Well, if there are no other comments, I call for a vote," O'Neill said.

All four conservatives voted to hear the case. Since his vote wasn't needed, Jamison abstained, giving no indication of his views.

Victoria's only consolation was the Voting Rights Act case— the conservative justices declined to hear the appeal, but the four liberals voted to grant review, giving them an opportunity to reinstate voting protections for minorities. The conference adjourned, and the justices drifted away to their offices or cars.

She had work to do.

CHAPTER 6

Genevieve tried not to think about Victoria and what the other justices were deciding at that very moment, as she sat in one of HRC's conference rooms for her weekly meeting with Penelope and Jamie. After the third interruption by one of Jamie's staff, Genevieve politely suggested that maybe instead of rotating offices, they should hold their weekly meeting at The Three Branches. The other two enthusiastically agreed.

"Okay, well, let's see what we can get done before someone else tries to ask me something that absolutely can't wait," Jamie said.

Genevieve sighed and handed them each a printout of a news article from Arizona. "I assume you two have seen this? It seems that that awful, racist sheriff in New Mexico—Rourke—found out that one of his employees is thinking about transitioning. In addition to firing young Jonathan Riley, Rourke or one of his lackeys knocked out one of the twenty-two-year-old's teeth and dislocated his shoulder."

"We've been following it closely at HRC," Jamie said. "We want to give Riley a chance to recover in peace, but once he's released from the hospital, we intend to reach out and ask about filing a lawsuit."

Penelope poked at her salad thoughtfully. "What does Riley do for the sheriff's office?"

"He's a guard at the jail," Jamie answered. "Good at his job too, from everything I've heard."

Genevieve cleared her throat. This potential case exemplified the many reasons their respective organizations should be meeting regularly. "Before you contact Riley, Jamie, we should discuss the case's implications and whether or not HRC is the best organization to spearhead any legal action."

"Agreed," Penelope said. "Given that the HRC already has four high-profile trans cases in the pipeline right now, and that you just lost one, perhaps it would best for NCLR to take point on this one."

"Now, wait a minute," Jamie said, his expression suddenly stormy. "This collaboration of ours isn't about stealing business from each other."

"Listen, Spot, no need to piss on your territory," Genevieve cut in. "Penelope has a point; this case will be a media darling, and you know it. Rourke is a lightning rod with national name recognition. And he's not even apologetic about what happened to Riley. If the case goes to trial, Rourke's antics on the stand will be historic, to say the least. HRC doesn't need to hog the spotlight."

"That's rich, coming from you, Genevieve," Jamie said. "What's this I hear about you representing a trans inmate in Michigan who's seeking coverage for sex reassignment surgery? I don't remember you offering to share the glory."

"She contacted us, Jamie. What you're talking about here— contacting the victim and, knowing you, strong-arming him into a highly public, likely invasive trial—is entirely different."

"Okay, let's just take a moment here," Penelope said. Her rich, soothing voice was made for ending disagreements and forging alliances. It was also a bedroom voice, and Genevieve closed her eyes briefly, willing away inappropriate thoughts.

"Jamie," Penelope continued, "what if NCLR partnered with HRC on this New Mexico case, and HER continued to work solo on the Michigan one, which likely won't have as high a profile?"

"So, what? We're putting our efforts toward equalizing the number of media points between our organizations now?" Jamie's hands gripped the edge of the table until his knuckles turned white.

"You know," Genevieve said, "it's exactly this kind of infighting that made me hesitant to take over at HER. Our organizations focus too heavily on publicity, competing with each other for airtime instead of collaborating on legal strategy."

"I agree," said Jamie, who looked anything but agreeable.

Penelope nodded. "As do I."

"That's great in principle, but what's happening here is a perfect example of each of us looking out for our own organization, rather than looking to the big picture," Genevieve said.

Jamie glared at her. "Weren't you the one who raised concerns when I said HRC was taking this case?"

They were getting nowhere. Were they as frustrating to Penelope as the heads of state she'd worked with as a diplomat?

"If I recall correctly, Jamie," Penelope said, her hands folded on the table in front of her, "Genevieve didn't raise concerns, per se. I took her comment to involve situating this case in the larger context of the legal landscape of LGBTQ rights, which is our ultimate goal with this collaboration."

By the time the meeting ended, they had established legal strategies for a dozen cases, in addition to organizing responsibilities for a dozen more. Under Penelope's deft hand, all parties concluded the meeting by saying their organizations had been treated fairly and the agreed-upon agenda reflected their collective strengths.

As she walked back to HER's office, Genevieve thought back to their conversation about the New Mexico case: Jamie had wanted it to himself; Genevieve offered a challenge, hoping for a piece of the action; and Penelope played the diplomat by somehow cutting Genevieve out and dividing the case with Jamie.

Essentially, she'd lost that entire negotiation. Yet somehow, she didn't really mind. Maybe she was learning to practice what she was trying to preach, focusing on the bigger picture.

Or maybe that was just the effect Penelope had on people.

Genevieve pulled into Tori's driveway, turned off the car, and sat, staring at the door. It had been a long day, made even harder by the anxiety of knowing that Tori and her colleagues were discussing her case. And by the churning in her stomach every time she debated how to behave around Tori.

The front door opened, and Tori leaned against the jamb, crossing her arms. "You just going to sit there in your car all night?" she called out loudly.

Genevieve removed her sunglasses and squinted in the late afternoon sun. No sense putting off the inevitable.

She walked up to Tori and pulled her into a hug. Tori's body against hers, so familiar and steady, slowed her frantic heartbeat. She gave Tori a sweet, affectionate kiss to smooth over some of the rough edges between them.

"Hungry?" Tori asked, taking her hand and shutting the door behind them.

"Always."

They settled into their familiar kitchen routine, and Genevieve struggled to read Tori, who excelled at masking her emotions. Tori couldn't reveal anything that went on in the conference, and the Court wouldn't release the docket for another week. Instead of asking a question she would never get an answer to, Genevieve poured them glasses of wine and got to work on a faro salad while Tori started the grill.

What would they talk about over dinner, since they couldn't very well talk about their day at the office? Well, Tori couldn't. Genevieve just didn't want to. Monologing wasn't really her style— why reveal her professional successes and challenges when nothing would be reciprocated?

At least she wasn't dating someone in the CIA.

The last time they had salmon, they were on vacation in France, a much simpler time that seemed to mock her now. They had talked about art, architecture, landscaping—the kinds of carefree topics that contrasted sharply with the focused and tense environment of DC. Well, she'd listened to NPR on her drive over and had picked up a few stories she could share if conversation stalled.

Tori's kitchen would make Martha Stewart jealous, and Genevieve always felt out of place in it. Copper pots and pans hung from a rack above the range, providing yet another reason Genevieve would never even *try* to cook for her girlfriend. A few months back, she had seriously contemplated bringing over a couple of her own nonstick, Teflon pots and trying out a Thai curry dish. At least that way, if she burned it beyond recognition, she'd be able to clean the cookware, rather than throwing it away. She didn't even want to know how much those bright, hanging pots cost.

There was one domestic, dinner-related bit of flair Genevieve did better than Tori, and once the table was set, she located a pair of scissors and a woven basket and headed into the backyard. The breeze was chilly, and she turned up the collar on her jacket. The low orange streaks of the sunset made the trees in Tori's backyard glow, hinting at the colors their leaves would turn in a few short weeks. In fact, a few of the leaves on the farthest maple tree were already a yellow-orange, so Genevieve snipped a handful of small branches and dropped them into the basket. Next to the maple stood a crabapple tree, its fruit already fading from brilliant red to a darker shade with hints of purple. After cutting a few thin branches, she glanced at the herb garden on her right and contemplated the rosemary. Too Christmas-y. On the opposite side of the yard, where Tori's flower garden ran the length of the fence, she spotted some crimson chrysanthemums that would complement the crabapple branches.

She brought her loot back to the dining room table, rummaged around Tori's cabinets until she located a large footed bowl, and began tinkering. By the time Tori came back inside with the grilled salmon, the chrysanthemums formed a bed of color just above the lip of the bowl from which the maple branches sprung up, and the crabapple branches snaked around the base of the bowl, extending to the two sides of the table without plates.

She was standing back to admire her work when Tori came up behind her and wrapped an arm around her stomach.

"That's gorgeous," Tori breathed into her ear.

"Well, I know how you like flowers in the house. When was the last time you bought flowers from Rosie, anyway?"

"Never. That woman is a genius with flowers, and she doesn't let me buy." Tori kissed her cheek, her lips lingering long enough for Genevieve to close her eyes and sigh. "Thank you."

"I'm glad you like it. I wasn't sure if the flowers in your backyard were fair game."

"Well, I don't usually cut them, but I think that's mostly laziness. Or hesitation to take a risk—I wouldn't know what to do with them or which ones look good together. You're welcome to experiment with anything that grows out there. Except the basil plant—that thing is finicky."

"Sounds like a good arrangement."

She felt Tori chuckle against her back. "Pun intended, I hope."

"Always."

After giving her another kiss, Tori stepped away. "I'll dress the salad. Will you bring the salmon to the table?"

Genevieve did her one better, pouring more wine too. When they were settled at the table, she asked, "How was your day, darling?" and winked.

Tori laughed, but it sounded forced, and her eyes darkened a shade. "Good. It was nice to see everyone again. My new crop of clerks seems promising and decidedly overeager."

"How's Kellen?"

"He wore that stupid bow tie I hate. Honestly, I think he must do it just to annoy me. It's all droopy and cockeyed, and I spend far too much time distracted from the conversation just thinking about how badly I want to retie the damn thing."

"Must not have had any interesting, contentious conversations, then," Genevieve said between bites of salad.

"Genevieve." The hint of warning in Tori's voice compelled Genevieve to take a healthy drink of wine.

"I get it. You can't talk about anything that happened today. I'm just trying to make conversation."

"No, you're fishing." Tori's volume was soft, but there was steel in her voice.

"Can you blame me?"

Tori sighed and leaned back in her chair. "I thought we had established boundaries last session."

"Last session you weren't considering one of my cases."

"Right now, we're not considering anything. We're considering what to consider, and since that's all I'm legally permitted to communicate, let's talk about your day instead. What's on your plate right now?"

To buy time while considering whether she wanted to press the issue or change subjects, Genevieve tried the salmon. It melted in her mouth, the way all of Tori's food did, and she moaned a little. "Jesus, Tori, if you ever want to change careers, you could cook for the president."

"You know, I offered once. At the White House holiday party last year, he was raving about the crab cakes, and I told him mine were far superior and offered to prove it."

Genevieve shook her head. Of course Tori could take a simple joke about the president and turn it into a real-life scenario. "Is he going to take you up on it?"

"Actually, we got sidetracked when a waiter brought over a tray of stuffed mushrooms and we started debating the best cheese to use for the filling. He never gave me an answer. About dinner, I mean. He thinks blue cheese is better than feta for stuffed mushrooms."

"For the record, you've never made me your crab cakes. Or stuffed mushrooms. So now I know where I stand."

"I haven't? Well, now we know what's for dinner tomorrow night. Come hungry."

"Do you want to invite the president to join us?"

The fact that Tori thought about it for a minute drove Genevieve to laughter.

"I'd rather it were just us," she said. "Besides, I'll just bring you to the White House holiday party this year, and you can meet him there."

Genevieve almost choked on her wine. "Really?"

Tori gave her a look she couldn't quite decipher. "Yes, really."

"But that would be so…" Genevieve's sentence hung in the air, filled with the things she'd never accuse Tori of, at least out loud.

"Yes, it would be 'so.' I'm not saying an event that public would be easy for me. Still, I'd like to take you as my date to the holiday party," she insisted.

Genevieve raised her wine glass. "Well, then: to dinner at the White House. "

They clinked glasses. Would Tori really follow through with this offer, or would she find some excuse to back out? Being ripped out of the closet hadn't exactly diminished the vise grip Tori kept on her privacy, and Genevieve could count on one finger the number of joint public appearances they had made in the few months since I Fought the Law had posted that picture of them almost kissing. Well, she'd just have to wait and see. In the meantime, if Tori couldn't talk about her day, well, Genevieve supposed she could fill the void.

"HER just filed a new suit in Michigan on behalf of a transgender woman in prison who's seeking access to sex reassignment surgery."

Tori put down her fork and stared at Genevieve. "You'll never win."

"Oh, I think we will. When she first petitioned the state for surgery, they balked, and she turned to the media there. *Detroit Free Press* ran the story a few months ago, and we got involved. We put some pressure on Michigan prison officials until they hired an expert to assess her. They brought in a psychiatrist from Johns Hopkins who determined that her gender dysphoria was so acute that denying her reassignment surgery would cause severe and undue pain, and that surgery would significantly alleviate her anxiety, depression, and likelihood of suicide attempts."

"The prison's own expert said this?"

"He didn't just say it—he signed a declaration."

Tori nodded and, for the first time since she'd come home from work, genuinely smiled. "Sounds like you've got a good case on your hands, Counselor. What's her name?"

"Amelia Garcia."

"Can I ask what she's in for?"

"Jesus, Tori, haven't you watched *Orange is the New Black*? You're not supposed to ask that!"

Tori rolled her eyes. "I suppose it's not really relevant."

"Well, it shouldn't be. We're going to make this case about medical and psychological issues, but I'm sure that the prison's lawyers will try to make it about character." Genevieve finished her wine and fetched the bottle from the kitchen to refill their glasses.

"That can cut in your favor, of course—you just need to spin any negative character traits so they appear to be the result of discrimination, or lack of access to proper care and procedures, or her dysphoria, which reassignment surgery would address."

"Telling me how to argue my case, Madam Justice?"

Tori blushed, which was about the cutest response she could give.

"I appreciate the input," Genevieve said, "and I'll take it under advisement. But, as you well know, I can't discuss strategy with you."

She grinned to take a little of the sting out of her dig—she could, of course, discuss strategy with anyone she wanted. That was the difference between her job as an advocate and Tori's job as a judge. She'd never stopped to wonder how Tori would take it if their situations were reversed and Genevieve was the one withholding information. Badly, she surmised.

"Anyway, I'm flying out there next week to meet with the client and take a couple of depositions of fellow inmates. I leave Wednesday morning, and I'll be home in time to swim on Friday."

"I can work with that," Tori said.

"*Work* being the operative word there. If I had to guess, I'd say you'll work the whole time I'm away."

"Probably. I like to feel on top of research before we start hearing arguments. And my editor got back to me with comments on my book manuscript," Tori said.

"Is this the book about international law? I hadn't realized you'd finished it."

"Well, as much as any book is ever finished. But yes, I finished the chapter on capital punishment when you were in California for those fundraisers, at the end of summer."

"See? It's a good thing my job requires travel—otherwise, you'd never get any work done."

"Well, I have to do something to keep from missing you."

Genevieve reached across the table and took her hand. "That's sweet. You can be very sweet, Victoria Willoughby."

"Shh. Don't tell anyone."

"I wouldn't dream of it."

After dinner, they retired to the living room, where Genevieve won a hard-fought Scrabble game. Tori rallied in their second match, drawing all the high-value letters, while Genevieve was stuck with six vowels for most of the game, no matter how many she managed to dump out each turn with words like *louie* and *aioli*. She suggested a tiebreaker, but Tori demurred, saying she'd had a long day.

They were brushing their teeth when Genevieve asked, "When will you all release the docket?"

Tori glared at her. "You know I can't answer that."

"I don't see why not," Genevieve said through a mouthful of foam. "You wouldn't be telling me what the docket will reveal, only when I can expect to see it."

Tori's electronic toothbrush buzzed, and she swiveled it in her mouth. Her answer came out muffled. "We release it when Kellen decides it's ready, and press releases are sent simultaneously to all the major news outlets. I'm sorry, Genevieve, but you'll have to find out when everyone else does."

Genevieve spat and wiped her mouth. "And here I thought being your girlfriend would come with perks."

Heading into the bedroom, she pulled open the dresser drawer where she stored pajamas. She hadn't often worn them here, but somehow she felt compelled to arm herself in a layer of flannel. The pants felt cozy and warm, and she was buttoning the shirt when Tori slid behind her and stilled her hands.

"It does come with perks. Very personal, very physical ones. Perks reserved for you and you alone. Would you like to see them?"

Genevieve sighed. "Not particularly. Let's just sleep, Tori."

Disappointment permeated the bedroom, as they pulled the covers over themselves and lay without touching.

"I don't feel particularly drawn to sleep with someone who won't even talk to me about basic things," Genevieve said.

"Not won't—can't. And we talked about tons of basic things. Look, our jobs are only going to come between us if we let them."

"That's easy for you to say."

Tori rolled over and snuggled against Genevieve's side. "No, it's not. You're being uncharitable."

She might be right, but Genevieve wasn't about to say as much. Instead, she wrapped her arms around Tori, kissed her head, and whispered, "Good night, Tori. I love you."

Tori said it back, and Genevieve drifted off to sleep, wondering how long those three words could hold back the storm threatening them.

CHAPTER 7

A prison guard with a *Michigan Department of Corrections* badge led Genevieve into an interview room, a dark, soulless cube with fluorescent lighting. A metal table and two chairs stood in the center of the room, the only furniture. Both the metal door through which Genevieve had entered and the one on the opposite wall had panels for guards to peek into the room, but otherwise they were entirely smooth; neither door had a handle on the inside.

She wasn't allowed to bring a bag through the security checkpoints. After placing her notebook, a binder filled with legal briefs, and the prison-issued pencil on the table, she sat down, folded her hands, and waited for her client.

She hadn't met Amelia yet—so far, they'd communicated through phone calls and one handwritten letter from Amelia, detailing the ways in which she had deteriorated mentally and physically since becoming a ward of the state a year and a half ago. Although transgender inmates in Michigan were supposed to receive their hormone medications while incarcerated, Amelia's had disappeared as soon as she reached out to the media about her sex reassignment surgery.

A guard led Amelia in from the other door, nodded at Genevieve, and left.

Genevieve rose and extended her hand over the table. "It's good to finally meet you, Ms. Garcia."

Amelia's fingers were freezing, but her handshake was firm. "Ms. Fornier."

"Please, Genevieve is fine."

"Okay. Amelia for me, then."

The chairs ground against the concrete floor as they sat. "You look good—healthier," Genevieve said, studying her client. Although Amelia looked older than fifty, Genevieve knew her to be forty-one. Her black hair was pulled back into a ponytail, which drew attention to her guarded eyes. But her dark skin looked clearer than in the picture she'd sent a few weeks ago—or maybe it was just that the florescent lighting failed to show any blemishes. She was taller in real life than she looked in the pictures.

"I think you scared them. The guards and stuff. They're giving me my hormone treatments again, thank God."

"Good, I'm glad to hear it. Do you happen to remember the day that the hormones disappeared and the day they reappeared?" She wrote down the dates Amelia gave her. "And who dispenses medicine to inmates?"

"A nurse named Milo, but I don't think he's responsible. He can't give me what he doesn't have. This kind of thing came from the prison administration."

"I'll have my people look into it. If we can pinpoint a few individuals responsible, that's easier for a judge to rule against than the entire administration."

"Judge? So you think we'll have a trial?"

"Hard to say. We'll see how things go with depositions and our preliminary motions. Frankly, we might do very well before a judge with an Eighth Amendment argument about cruel and unusual punishment. If the state takes custody of you, it's the state's responsibility to care for you."

Amelia's laugh was cynical, matching the chill in the concrete room. "Care. Please. I restocked shelves at a medical facility. When I was on the outside, I mean. I can tell you all about basic medical supplies and how the corrections department doesn't give them to us."

The look of suspicion she gave Genevieve reinforced how different their life experiences had been, how little Genevieve knew about her client's circumstances, and how much power she had to impact Amelia's life. How much damage could she do if she reported to a guard that Amelia had criticized the facility?

Well, Genevieve would have to win her trust the best way she knew how—by putting together a strong case and being honest. "The problem is if the case goes to trial, it means that we weren't able to settle the case during preliminary stages, so it will just take longer before you get the medical procedures you need. For that reason, my goal is to wrap this up as quickly as possible. But I'd be remiss as your lawyer if I didn't make clear to you that this could take a while. Years, even, if there are appeals."

A couple of decades of experience giving clients tough truths didn't make Amelia's disappointment any easier to swallow. Her eyes fell, and her shoulders drooped; Genevieve's news depleted any boost she may have been riding from receiving hormone treatments again.

"I can't promise you many things, Amelia, but I can promise you this: I'll never lie to you. I'll never sugarcoat bad news, and I'll call you immediately with good news. I'm transparent with my clients about everything, including legal strategy. I believe that we have a good case here, but I won't try to guess what our chances are or in any other way give you false hope."

Amelia wrapped her arms around herself and nodded. "I appreciate that. It's good, being real like this."

"I expect the same from you, Amelia. I want to know if anyone threatens you. If you feel endangered, you tell me. Don't be a hero."

"That's not something you need to worry about. I've never been especially brave."

Deep lines between Amelia's eyes and across her forehead spoke of a life of frequent stress dating back years, long before the eighteen months she'd spent in the prison. Genevieve briefly wondered about her client's life on the outside, what it had been like before she had ended up here. Did she have family? Had they been supportive of her transition? Did she have someone to care about, someone who cared about her?

Genevieve flipped through her notebook to focus her thoughts. "After we talk, I'll take depositions of some of your fellow inmates." She slid a packet of stapled papers across the table. "Here are the questions I intend to ask them. Please look these over and let me know if there's anything you're uncomfortable with me asking."

The silence in the room as Amelia read was oppressive. Metal and concrete provided no sound insulation, and every turn of the page sounded like a tornado. Was the whole prison like this? For a moment, Genevieve imagined the sound of hundreds of forks clinking against plates in a cavernous dining area, before she realized that inmates wouldn't be given metal or ceramic.

She released a breath she didn't know she'd been holding when Amelia returned the questions and nodded. "This is all fine. Did you come up with these?"

Genevieve cleared her throat. "It was something of a group effort. I'm lead attorney on this case, but we have a legal team working together on every aspect of it. In fact, it's likely that someone else will take the next round of depositions."

The alarm on Amelia's face made Genevieve pause. "I'll continue to be your primary point of contact, and if there's even a chance that you're going to meet another attorney, I'll be sure to let you know ahead of time. You're in good hands, Amelia."

"I'm in the hands of the state." She picked at her fingers and affected a bored look, but her leg started bouncing up and down, and the table vibrated with her movement.

"Fair enough," Genevieve said. "I mean, you've got a bunch of lawyers in your corner. And my staff is very good."

"Got anyone on staff who's trans?"

"We do. A woman named Cherice, and she's staffed on your case, actually. Does that make you feel better?"

"Yeah, a little. I mean, none of this makes me feel better, really. But yeah. I'm sure you all are great. And I'm glad you got me my hormones back."

Genevieve nodded. "I'm going to take the depositions now, but I'll try to see you again before the day's over to give you an update."

Amelia's shoulders fell for the briefest of moments, before she squared them and sat up straighter. "Guess I don't get to sit in, then."

"Oh. Um, most clients don't want to. The questioning can be pretty tedious."

"Probably most of your clients aren't in prison, then."

Truth be told, Genevieve wasn't overly fond of taking depositions in front of clients. Depositions were tricky beasts. The person being deposed was under oath, and everything he or she said was on the record, as were the questions Genevieve asked. It was all about wording, and good attorneys were able to tease out perfect sound bites without looking like they'd coached their own witnesses or harassed the opposing side's. Clients' reactions to the deposed person giving testimony were distracting—they were always grunting in frustration or nodding in agreement.

But there was no doubt that Amelia would spend a better day in a deposition than harassed in a prison yard. And since today's sessions were with other inmates and were happening on-site, she could probably make it happen. "Let me talk to the guards and see what I can do."

"Guards don't know shit. You're gonna have to talk to the warden."

"Is he here, on-site?"

"Not usually. But I'm sure he's got a phone."

"Will they let you wait here until we get this sorted out?"

Amelia scrutinized her for a moment before giving Genevieve an overly casual shrug, but it seemed like something had changed between them. "Maybe. Depends on whether they had their coffee or not. Or whether they got laid last night or not. Or whether they got something against Latinas, or women, or me." She raked her eyes down Genevieve's body and back up. "You could ask, though. Pretty white girl like you, you could probably charm the keys right out the guards' hands."

"I'll see what I can do." The chair scraped harshly against the ground when Genevieve stood up, and her heel clicks echoed around the room as she made her way to the door. She knocked twice on the panel, and a guard appeared.

"I'll be taking three depositions today. Do you know what room has been set aside for this?"

He glared at her as if she'd asked him to explain quantum physics or why women don't like it when men order food for them at restaurants. "Be right back," he said and disappeared before Genevieve could ask him her other questions.

Sighing, she leaned against the door to wait. "You know this guard?"

"Oh, honey, I know 'em all. This one's fine. Bit of a Neanderthal when it comes to brains, but harmless."

"You'll point out any guards who've given you a hard time?"

"I do that, I get beat up." Her eyes looked tough, as if the admission were nothing to her, but her body shrank almost imperceptibly.

"Well, obviously, don't do it so they hear you. But I'd like to be able to recognize them."

Amelia thought about that and then grinned, and her whole face changed. The tension in her forehead and cheeks dissipated, and Genevieve had a brief vision of how different Amelia would be—inside and out—if she won this case. "Tell you what. I'll hum something by Lady Gaga if one of those pricks shows up."

"I can work with that," Genevieve grinned.

"I saw her in concert once. That first year after her *Fame Monster* album dropped. Bitch has pipes. Did you know she's classically trained?"

"Doesn't surprise me. I'd love to see her live."

Amelia's face shifted to wistful—not as luminous as it had been, but still a far cry from the desperate air she'd carried into the room with her. "I took piano lessons when I was young. Made it all the way to Chopin. Our neighbor had a piano. But then my dad's company did layoffs, and we moved, and that was that."

"Ma'am? I got that info for you," the guard said from the other side of the door. "You'll be right here. So you can make yourself at home."

She'd hoped for a cheerier room, but at least she had a better chance of keeping Amelia if they weren't relocating.

"Great. Here's my list of witnesses, in the order I want them. Amelia will be staying with me until we're through. I'm ready for the first deposition whenever you can get her here."

The guard nodded and left again.

Genevieve and Amelia's eyes met. "Maybe it's as easy as that," Genevieve said.

"Probably not, because this is prison, and my life, and nothing is ever as easy as that. But we can always hope."

"You have a lawyer on your side now. We can do better than just hope."

The depositions went well enough, and Genevieve enjoyed laying the foundations of their case. The witnesses all agreed that Amelia suffered from anxiety and depression, and her cellmate described in detail a failed suicide attempt. Amelia stared stone-faced at the wall during that part, and Genevieve curbed her impulse to reach out and touch her shoulder, unsure if it would be welcome.

The witnesses also testified to the guards' mistreatment of Amelia, and the prison's general intolerance for all things queer. Between the second and third deposition, the guards changed over, and Genevieve could feel Amelia's tension as she worried that she'd be sent back to her cell. Genevieve flashed the new guard a thousand-watt smile and told him she and Amelia would be finished up in a couple of hours. He dropped the bottle of water he'd been carrying, stammered, and almost ran into the wall as he left.

"See what I mean about pretty girls like you?" Amelia's voice dripped with cynicism, but her eyes were laughing.

Privilege was an insidious and awful tool of oppression, and Genevieve had dedicated her life to eradicating it, legally if not socially. But she wasn't above using hers if it would keep someone whose life was already hard enough out of a prison cell for a day.

CHAPTER 8

Victoria looked up from the kitchen counter where she had been reading the news on her tablet, as Genevieve stormed in through the front door and stalked into the kitchen.

"I see you released the fall docket this afternoon."

Victoria tried to read past Genevieve's measured tone. Before she could fully assess the distant look in her eyes, Genevieve turned and opened the cabinet that held the liquor.

"I'm having scotch. Can I get you something?"

It was annoying to be offered her own alcohol. Yet another thing she would need to adjust to if she and Genevieve were going to share a living space in any more permanent arrangement. "There's a bottle of chardonnay in the fridge."

Genevieve pulled open a few drawers looking for a corkscrew, and Victoria wondered how long it would take her to just ask for its location. She had always loved Genevieve's stubbornness when it was directed elsewhere.

After she successfully located the corkscrew on her own and poured a glass for Victoria, Genevieve settled into a seat at the kitchen island and nursed her scotch.

Victoria held back a sigh. "If there's something you want to say, now's as good a time as any."

Genevieve's eyes went dark. "I can't believe you took the appeal on the *Rowlings* case."

"I suppose it's not necessary to remind you that I don't work alone."

"The fifth circuit decision is perfect. Why would you mess with that? There's no real legal question that you all need to decide."

"I agree with you, you know. But some of my colleagues see things differently."

Genevieve abandoned her chair, taking her drink with her. She stared out the glass door into the backyard.

Fighting the urge to go to her, Victoria sipped her wine and waited for the explosion she could see lurking beneath Genevieve's stormy features.

"Well, I've argued in front of the Court before with you there. It'll be just like déjà vu."

"Genevieve—"

"Don't even say it."

"We weren't in a relationship then. Can't you see the difference? Now that everyone knows about us, you can't argue in front of the Court."

"I can't believe you." Genevieve started pacing across the kitchen. "There's nothing—nothing—that prevents me from arguing in front of you. There's no real conflict here. There's only you and your ridiculous—"

"I'm not sure there's no real conflict here, Genevieve."

"Please," Genevieve said, running her hand through her hair. "It's not like there's a clear law governing recusal or impeachment of justices—you are the law. I argue the case, you hear it….no problem."

"Genevieve, it's not that simple. If you argue the case, I'd have to recuse myself."

"You don't have personal bias or prejudice concerning a party, or personal knowledge of disputed evidentiary facts concerning the proceeding."

Victoria raised an eyebrow. "You're seriously going to quote—"

"You haven't served as a lawyer in the matter; you haven't provided counsel nor are you a witness in the case; you haven't publicly expressed an opinion concerning the merits of the case; you don't have a financial stake in the case. Your spouse—or in this case girlfriend—isn't a party to the proceedings."

"Pretty sure there's a clause about knowing your *girlfriend* has an interest that could be substantially affected by the outcome of the proceeding."

Genevieve stopped pacing and put her hands on the kitchen island. "That interest isn't fiduciary, nor is it personal."

"And you memorized that section of the ethics code when, exactly?"

"This morning."

"You anticipated this argument and wanted to enter it armed with evidence."

"I had hoped you wouldn't be so predictable."

Victoria opened and closed her mouth, unable to think of a single thing to say in response. Genevieve refilled her glass and stormed out of the kitchen. Victoria gave her a minute to stew before following her into the living room, stopping just inside the entrance. Genevieve stood in the far corner with her back to Victoria.

With the whole room between them, Victoria spoke to her girlfriend's back. "Genevieve, if you argue the case, I'll recuse myself. I can't tell you what outcome that would produce in terms of votes—I honestly don't know. You'd only need four votes—if the

Court's tied, it'll go back to the appellate decision, and you'll win. It's really the same situation whether or not I'm there—you still have to sway one conservative."

Genevieve turned to her, hands outstretched, looking desperate. "Which I'd have a better chance of doing if you were on the inside, writing the kind of decision one of them would be willing to sign on to. Can't we work together on this?"

"Don't you see that's the exact reason that… We can't collude like that. Absolutely not. I won't."

"Always so uncompromising," Genevieve said, clearly not intending it as a compliment.

"Look, either way, the trial record you created at the district level still maintains. The testimony you elicited and the cross-examination you conducted combine to create compelling evidence. Honestly, oral arguments at the Supreme Court will be just a formality."

Genevieve spun around. "Bullshit. Nothing about this case is any different than any other case."

"I don't—meaning what?"

"Meaning it always matters who argues cases in front of your bench. And who sits on it and decides."

"Genevieve—"

"Goddamnit, if one of us is going to have to recuse themselves, then why shouldn't it be you?" She almost spat the words.

"Excuse me?"

"It's my case. The transcripts and decisions you all will read to prep for it will have my name all over it. A name you cry out in bed these days. Haven't I already influenced you?"

"I… Look, like you said, the guidelines about recusal are… murky at best."

"Then I honestly don't see why either of us has to walk away from this."

Victoria dared to enter the room, feeling like she was approaching a trapped animal who might lash out at any given moment. Genevieve's feet stayed firmly planted, and Victoria perched on the couch, hoping to convey an invitation. "Genevieve, the media—"

"Fuck the media. They have absolutely no legal power here. No more so than they do for any case that comes before the Court. They can't make me step away or you recuse yourself. All they can do is recycle the same two pundits—on opposite sides, inevitably—arguing self-righteously that they know more about the Constitution than you or I do."

Victoria swallowed. Genevieve had a point. The media could bluster about but couldn't really do anything. No one could, exactly—she had a lifetime appointment and, well, Genevieve was right. She sort of was the law.

"Fine, forget the media. This kind of situation is utterly unprecedented. What if the situation were reversed? What if, I don't know, the attorney general arguing against you was married to Matthew Smith? You don't think you'd be outraged at that?"

"Matthew Smith would never marry a woman with that much authority."

Victoria rolled her eyes. "Genevieve, come on."

"Fine, yes, I'd raise hell about it." Genevieve threw up her hands.

"So let's not put that shadow over this case. Let's not give idiots any reason to doubt the outcome. Call it integrity, call it me being a closet case, call it overcautiousness. Call it whatever you want. If you argue, I'm stepping down."

Genevieve's eyes narrowed, and a staring contest ensued. Genevieve lost and mumbled, "I need another drink," before stalking back to the kitchen.

This time, Victoria left her alone. She'd said what she needed to. Genevieve could decide how the case proceeded—she could give her that, since it might be the last decision Genevieve would make on the case.

Genevieve returned and sat on the couch as far away from Victoria as possible. She stared into her glass.

"Crystal and I grew up together. Sleepovers at her house. Climbing trees together. Soccer practice. When we were sophomores, we both had crushes on the prom queen. When we were juniors, I had… problems with a teacher. He was a woman-hating asshole, and for some reason I was the one he went after. Gave me Fs on all my history papers for no reason. Mocked me mercilessly in front of the other students. It got so bad I was crying in the bathroom before class every day. Crystal stood up to him. Called him out whenever he was cruel to me in class and wrote it all down. Got the school board involved. She taught me how to stand up for myself and how important it is to stand up for other people."

Finally, she turned bruised eyes to Victoria. "I can't believe you're putting me in this position."

"Look, I want you to know that I don't—"

"Just stop. I will step down, because I do think the case needs your vote and needs your…integrity behind the scenes, as the other justices figure out what decision to sign on to."

Victoria dared to scoot closer to her. "I'm sorry that our jobs… our relationship… I'm sorry about this professional conflict. I'm sorry that you won't be able to argue a case that you've put so much work into. That involves your friends."

"Yeah. Well." She drained her third scotch of the evening. "I'm flying Crystal and Heather out here as soon as possible. I need to explain in person why I won't be arguing their case and help them decide who will. They'll stay at my townhouse. With me."

The implication was clear: Genevieve wouldn't be staying with Victoria.

"Of course." Despite her best efforts, she knew her voice sounded flat. "Would you like some privacy to call them and make arrangements?"

"Yeah, I would."

Victoria stood and started to head upstairs.

"Don't bother. That's not the kind of privacy I need right now."

When Genevieve headed toward the front hall closet for her coat, Victoria felt as though she had been slapped. Risking an actual slap, she walked to the front door and stood in front of it. "You're not driving right now. You're drunk and angry."

"Well, you live in the middle of nowhere, so I certainly can't walk or take a train."

It felt like an old-fashioned standoff, only she surmised they would look pretty ridiculous to an outsider, Victoria in a skirt suit and bare feet with her hands on her hips and Genevieve clutching her coat in one hand and her keys in the other, squeezing so hard her fingers were white.

"Please. Just stay tonight. You can sleep wherever you want. I'll go upstairs and close the door."

She held out her hand and, defeated, Genevieve dropped her keys into it before snatching up her cell phone from the coffee table and storming back into the kitchen. She seemed to have forgotten the coat in her other hand and, the belt of the trench dragged on the floor.

Obviously it would be a mistake to suggest that drunk and pissed might not be the best state in which to call her friends-slash-clients, but that didn't mean Victoria didn't seriously consider it.

When she heard the unmistakable clink of the scotch bottle against Genevieve's tumbler, Victoria plodded upstairs, turning off lights as she made her way to the bedroom.

Unsure whether she'd have company, she climbed into her side of the bed and stared at the empty other half.

CHAPTER 9

When she awoke at 9:00 a.m., Genevieve's head felt like a freight train had run through it, and Tori's side of the bed was cold. Still a bit groggy, she wandered downstairs and spied a note on the table. *Ran to the store. Back by 9:30.*

Swallowing her pride last night had been difficult. Whether Tori had actually been asleep when Genevieve finally eased into the bed was anyone's guess, but it was probably for the best that she hadn't tried to find out, since she had been in no state for a repeat performance of that evening's sparring. She had watched the minutes tick by until somewhere around 3:00 a.m., when she finally fell asleep.

How was it possible that the things that attracted her to Victoria in the first place were the same things driving her nuts now? It was endlessly sexy to her the way Victoria was impeccably dressed for any occasion. She had been so drawn to the immaculate, if perhaps a bit remote, decor of her house and her unparalleled work ethic. But seriously, who puts on makeup to go to the farmers' market? Far be it for Genevieve to complain about the delicious home-cooked food she was now privy to, but a greasy pizza delivered right to their door never killed anyone. And Genevieve wasn't an excessive TV watcher, but she did enjoy watching some Shondaland shows or, really, anything that wasn't *Meet the Press*.

Although she was getting better at remembering to hang up her coat, rather than just dumping it on the back of the couch, for the life of her, she couldn't ever seem to load the dishwasher correctly. Never mind that there really wasn't such a thing.

It was the first Saturday in, well, she couldn't remember how long, when she wouldn't be going into the office.

And, hell, if Tori kept taking cases away from her, maybe she'd never have to go into the office on a Saturday again. Maybe she could retire.

Grateful for thirty minutes to actually be herself, she swapped devices in the docking station and cued up an old Garbage album. She knew she should get dressed before Victoria returned, most likely wearing pressed slacks and a blazer. But dammit, it was Saturday morning, and yoga pants were so comfortable.

She was scrolling through her tablet, reading the news on Tori's couch, when vibrations from the floor indicated the garage door was opening. She thought briefly about hopping in the shower, which might at least seem mildly productive to her hyperefficient girlfriend and would also give them an excuse not to talk right away. Instead, she turned off the music, steeled herself, and headed into the kitchen to help unload the groceries.

She wondered, not for the first time, how different, how much better, this dynamic would be if they spent more of their time in her townhouse than in Tori's place.

"Did you get bananas?" Genevieve unpacked the first of six matching cloth bags lining the countertop.

"I'm sorry, I didn't. Were they on the list?"

"Let's say that they're permanently on the list."

"I'll get some next time." Tori hesitated, then kissed her cheek as she made a trip from the kitchen island to the fridge, hands filled with produce.

"I was thinking. What if we went out tonight for dinner?"

Tori visibly stiffened, but when she stood up and turned to face Genevieve, her eyes were impassive. "I just returned from a rather impressive shopping trip, as you can see. I picked up all the ingredients to make a stir fry."

Genevieve willed herself not to feel guilty asking for what she wanted. Because she certainly hadn't asked for Tori to go to the store and get dinner ingredients, and she had just given up a hugely important case because her girlfriend wasn't going to. So, for better or worse, Genevieve felt she was owed something right now.

"Tori. I'd like to go out to dinner tonight. Together."

Something she thought might be panic flitted across Tori's features, but she smiled serenely. "Of course. Make us a reservation wherever you'd like to go."

She turned back to the refrigerator, and just like that, there it was again: Tori's unfailing politeness was the perfect combination of overwhelmingly sexy and irritating, all at once. Well, Genevieve had gotten something she wanted; she should feel a sense of victory, or at least validation.

Yet the air between them felt too thin, like she had summited some great peak only to discover the view was obscured by fog. Tori was still messing around in the fridge, and Genevieve honestly didn't know if it was an OCD thing or simply a handy way to avoid eye contact, because after knowing her for over twenty years, she still didn't *really* know Victoria Willoughby.

"I'm going to take a shower," she said. If her voice sounded hollower than she'd intended, it was because she couldn't help feeling she was retreating.

Through the whirr of the shower water, Genevieve could hear Tori messing around in the bedroom. Making the bed, most likely. Genevieve considered that she should have done it while Tori was at the grocery store; making the bed was one of the few chores she did regularly and without complaint. So it stood to reason that being annoyed at Tori for doing it was completely irrational.

Everything about their relationship right now felt irrational to her.

CHAPTER 10

Victoria was not overly fond of sushi, but given how tenuous their hold was on any kind of civility right now, she just smiled and nodded when Genevieve informed her that they were headed to a fancy place called The Dragon and Eel.

Genevieve also left no room for debate about who was driving, and Victoria took her place in the passenger seat of Genevieve's BMW. The restaurant was downtown, and when they got close, Victoria pointed out a parking garage; but Genevieve shook her head and insisted on weaving up and down nearby streets until she found an open spot. Victoria folded her hands in her lap and didn't say anything.

Clearly, despite the mostly civil conversation they'd had this morning, Genevieve was not done with her anger from last night.

The Dragon and Eel had a distinctly yuppie vibe, with brightly colored paintings of fish on the walls and a large community table in the middle of the room. The clientele was younger than the two of them, although Genevieve blended well in her jeans and boots. Par for the course, really—Genevieve looked good in any environment. Maybe Victoria's pencil skirt and blazer weren't the best choice. Too late now—they were led to a small, two-person table on the side of the room, and Victoria took solace in the fact that it was unlikely that anyone in the restaurant would recognize them.

They ordered rolls and sake, and when the waiter left with their menus, there was nothing between them to hide behind. Victoria fidgeted with her napkin and wondered if it was her responsibility to break the ice. Genevieve probably thought so, considering she felt like the wronged party here. But really, anyone in their right mind would look at their situation and say that the obvious choice would be for Victoria to stay on the bench for the same-sex parentage case and for Genevieve to step away. Maybe she could ask something benign about Genevieve's trip to Michigan.

"Look, I get it. I do," Genevieve said, continuing a conversation they hadn't ever really started. "I understand your point that we have a conflict of interest. But that doesn't mean I'm happy about how this whole thing is working out."

"I don't expect you would be. I'm sure I'd be pissed too. Genevieve, I want you to know that I didn't do this to you. I didn't vote to hear the case this fall, and I would never intentionally take a case away from you or in any other way sabotage your career."

Victoria wanted desperately to take her hand, and if they had been at home, she probably would have. But there were too many people around, and besides, Genevieve didn't seem particularly receptive to physical affection at the moment.

"Rationally understanding that this isn't your fault doesn't make it any easier. I still have to sit this one out, and you get a front row seat to a fight that should have been mine."

She sighed. "What can I do to make it up to you?" Maybe if she could convey how much she wanted Genevieve to be happy, how she cared as much about Genevieve's career as her own, this tension between them would dissipate. Because if she had to be awfully, pathetically alone for another night when they were in the same bed, she would probably cry. Which wasn't something she did very often.

But her offer only seemed to make Genevieve angrier. "That's not how this works, and you know it, Victoria."

This situation was more serious than she'd realized. Obviously, Genevieve was annoyed when she'd asked to go home after Alistair's. And she was clearly pissed last night when she stormed around Victoria's house getting drunk. But perhaps Victoria had underestimated the extent to which Genevieve was unhappy with their relationship.

She swallowed hard.

"Your career will always be more important than mine." The quiet resignation in Genevieve's voice felt worse than her anger the night before.

"I don't want that to be the case," Victoria said. "And actually, there are ways that you can look at this and see that your career trumps mine. You get publicity and recognition—more people know your name and face than know mine."

"I seriously doubt that. And besides, media fanfare hardly compares to having your name in history books."

"Are we really doing this?" Victoria's shoulders slumped a little. "You never wanted to be a justice, Genevieve. Please don't punish me now for achieving my dream."

"Your dream always seems to come at my expense," Genevieve said, making no attempt to mask the bitterness in her voice.

The comment hit Victoria right in the gut, and she took a few deep breaths, trying to decide how to proceed. "Genevieve, there needs to be a statute of limitations on what happened with us in law school. If you can't forgive me for leaving you back then, I'm not sure we have much of a future here."

Genevieve put a piece of sushi in her mouth and turned green, either because of too much wasabi or the frank way in which she had just questioned their future. But really, if Genevieve was going to dance around their problems like a monkey, well, screw that.

Victoria had no patience for passive-aggressiveness. Let Genevieve hear out loud what she was clearly thinking about and dissect the feelings those words inspired.

The server arrived to ask if they needed anything, saving them from rehashing old grievances like a child picking at a scab. They ate their rolls in silence, and just when Genevieve seemed about to say something, a man and a woman holding hands approached their table.

"Hey, you're Justice Victoria Willoughby, right?" the woman asked.

The man slipped behind her and put his hands on her shoulders. Victoria resisted making a face; it was one of her least favorite postures for straight couples. Men who did that always looked simultaneously possessive and parental.

This guy was wearing a tweed jacket with elbow patches that screamed "professor" in the most tired way possible. Victoria glanced down at his shoes—yep, loafers with no socks. Ridiculous. He was older—much older—than his date, who was probably twenty, very sexy, and painfully idealistic. His student, perhaps? Gross.

"I just wanted to say that I think you're really cool," the woman said. "I'm thinking of going to law school after I graduate Georgetown."

The mask Victoria wore when talking to strangers slid on, and Genevieve inexplicably glared at her. "Good for you. Law school is challenging but very rewarding. And there are a lot of career options that a law degree would open for you," Victoria said, repeating phrases she'd used a thousand times.

Genevieve drained her sake and eyed the door to the bathrooms. Victoria kicked her in the shin, hoping to dissuade Genevieve from abandoning her with two interlopers.

After a pronounced eye roll, Genevieve refilled her sake glass and was about to drink when the couple turned their attention to her.

"And you're Genevieve Fornier, right?" the man said.

Genevieve nodded, her eyes narrowed. Despite her vast experience with interviews and glad-handing, she showed no interest in being civil to these strangers.

"I've been following this gay adoption case of yours—my cousin and his partner live in Louisiana, and they've always wanted kids." He glanced between Victoria and Genevieve, his hands still gripping his date's shoulders. "Does this mean that you can't argue the case anymore?" he asked Genevieve.

Victoria blinked at him. Was he for real? She was tempted to ask him how he'd like it if she and Genevieve had moseyed over to his table and asked him if dating his student meant that he couldn't teach anymore.

"Quite the quandary," he continued, unfazed. "It's really fascinating, your relationship." He glanced at Victoria. "I teach an upper division course on law and the media at Georgetown. I was thinking of ending the semester by talking about you two."

Victoria might have had a flawless poker face, but she couldn't maintain it in that moment. She glanced at Genevieve and saw pure fire in her eyes. The storm brewing behind them actually scared her. Damn these two for interfering. She shifted in her seat so that her knee rested against Genevieve's, which seemed to calm her slightly.

Genevieve took a deep breath and turned a completely fake smile to their unwanted visitors. "Good luck with that. Let us know how it goes. Now, if you don't mind, we were just about to eat. I hope you two enjoy your date." She turned and, in a voice she usually reserved for television interviews, said pleasantly, "You *have* to try some of my dragon rolls, Tori—they're amazing."

As Victoria nodded slowly and fumbled around the table for her chopsticks, Professor No-Boundaries and his student left.

Victoria drained her sake. "Jesus," she snarled. "I wanted to strangle that jerk."

Genevieve stared at her like she'd never seen her before.

"What?" Victoria's pitch rose. "What'd I do?"

"Tori, do you realize that you showed more emotion just now than you did all last night during our argument? Honestly, it's like I don't even know you. You have this impenetrable public persona, and it's like steel, and no one ever breaks through, not even me sometimes. And then some stupid idiot totally unnerves you, and you, like, almost lose it. After all this time, I have no idea what makes you tick."

"That's ridiculous. You know me better than anyone."

"That probably says more sad things about you than good things about our relationship. You hold everyone at a distance, and I'm not sure I've ever actually been inside."

Closing her eyes and taking a deep breath, Victoria tried to find a way to convince Genevieve that she really wasn't such an enigma, that Genevieve had broken through her walls that first time they'd met at Harvard Law, and she'd never successfully been able to keep Genevieve out. When she opened her eyes again, Genevieve was shaking her head.

"Look," Genevieve said, her voice warmer than it had been in days, "I can see that your public persona, your walls—they cost you something. Whether you know it or not." She ran her hand through her hair. "I'm sorry I dragged us out here. You were right— we would have had a better time at home."

Victoria gave a shaky laugh. "But then we would have never known that undergraduates are going to spend an entire class discussing our relationship. And that they might even get graded on how well they debate our love life. Hell, we could be the topic for a term paper: *Fornier, Willoughby, and the Romanticization of the US Legal System.* Maybe there'll even be a book."

"God, I could have died happy never thinking about any of this."

Their eyes met, and some of the frost between them melted. Victoria swallowed, reached out, and took Genevieve's hand.

"Genevieve, I don't know what the hell we're doing. You know I'm not used to making accommodations for someone in my personal life. I understand—apart from the legal complications of our relationship, I'm just difficult to be with."

"What an understatement," Genevieve said, but there was enough affection in her voice to take the sting out.

"Hey, I'm trying here. Can you meet me halfway?"

Genevieve squeezed her hand. "You're right. I do appreciate that. And I know this isn't your fault. I committed to this relationship just as much as you did, even knowing that something like this might happen."

The tension that had tightened Genevieve's entire body relaxed, and only then was Victoria aware of how taut Genevieve had been for the past week. Exhaling and leaning back in her chair, she smiled tentatively. "So, we're okay?"

"We're okay."

They left the restaurant holding hands, another first for Victoria. She tried to relax into Genevieve's touch and not to glance this way and that to see who was watching them, but it wasn't easy. Genevieve's hand felt stiff, and Victoria wondered if they had actually solved anything between them at all.

CHAPTER 11

Saturday morning, Will called Victoria and announced that he and Diane had hired a babysitter for that evening and were going out to dinner. He invited her and Genevieve on a double date, which seemed the perfect opportunity to make progress on her ongoing project to prove to Genevieve that she wasn't afraid to be seen in public with her.

On a stool at her kitchen island, Victoria dialed Genevieve's cell phone, because she was at the office. On a Saturday. And people thought Victoria was a workaholic.

"Tori, hi, just a moment."

Victoria could hear her talking about depositions in Michigan to someone, presumably on her office phone. "Thanks, Frank—once you've got flight options, please send them to me. Bye for now." She cleared her throat. "Thanks, babe—sorry about that."

"Flying to Michigan again?" Tori asked.

"Next week. Final depositions on Thursday."

Victoria nodded, even though Genevieve couldn't see her. It was great that Genevieve had been more available since hiring an executive director, but there were certain parts of her job that simply required travel, and Victoria would probably always be missing her.

"Well, since you're actually in town tonight, Will and Diane invited us to dinner. Go on a double date with me?"

"Oh, I'd love to, Tori, but I promised Bethany we could go to a *Labyrinth* sing-along. It's playing at a theater downtown, and evidently they give you bags of bubbles, balloons, and whoopee cushions. She's been looking forward to this all week."

Victoria glanced at the recipe for herb-encrusted halibut that she was going to make them for dinner before Will called, and almost asked her when she had been planning to tell her about Bethany. "I didn't realize you had plans," she said.

"Sorry, Tor—didn't know I needed to run my social schedule by you." The edge in her voice belied her breezy tone.

"You don't—that's not what I mean. I just... It would be nice if we could find a way to coordinate schedules."

"What, like synching calendars or something?"

"Sure, why not? When you were traveling so much for work, our default was time apart. Now that you're here more, it seems like we should spend more time together—isn't that what you want?"

"Yes, of course."

Victoria waited for her to say something more but was met with silence. "Look, I don't want you to feel tied down or anything," she said, though that wasn't exactly true.

There was another pause, and then Genevieve said hurriedly, "Tori, I'm sorry—I just got an e-mail that my client in Michigan is sick, and there's some question about whether she will be classified as male or female for a hospital trip. I have to go."

"Genevieve, are you checking e-mail while we're on the—"

Click.

Well. She would be going to dinner without Genevieve, and that was that.

At eight that evening, she drove over to Legislative Lobster, an upscale seafood restaurant. Will and Diane were seated at a conspicuous circular table in the center of the room, and with this crowd, Victoria didn't have much hope that the presence of a Supreme

Court justice would go unnoticed. As she joined her brother and sister-in-law at their table, she tried not to feel like a third wheel.

After they got caught up on mundane life events and ordered drinks, Diane turned to Victoria and grabbed her hands. "Darling, it's been weeks! We've been worried that Genevieve kidnapped you and whisked you away to some tropical destination."

"I've been working," Victoria said. *Let's not talk about my love life, please.*

"What's on the docket this fall? Anything I need to really care about?" Will asked.

Victoria had long ago given up on convincing Will that all cases—even the unsexy ones about taxes—were worth caring about.

"We're hearing an important case on voting rights this fall, and it's going to be contentious, particularly considering the Court issued a controversial ruling on this topic just three years ago."

"Voting rights? I guess I should know this stuff, huh?"

"Only if you think enfranchisement is a fundamental part of the American democratic system."

"My darling sister, are you picking up Genevieve's flair for the dramatic?" Will asked.

Victoria started at the sound of Genevieve's name, but Will and Diane didn't seem to notice. Their food arrived, and they began a complicated process of passing plates around and sharing. Her heart had been set on halibut since she'd picked out a recipe for dinner, and Victoria decided she couldn't have made it any better at home. Will's salmon was delicious, but Diane's bouillabaisse was to die for.

Diane leaned back in her chair and patted her tummy when she was done. "Yep. I definitely feel guilty for this dinner. I ate way too much."

"When was the last time you two went out for dinner without the kids?" Victoria asked.

"Was it…last month? Honey, you couldn't have even combed your hair?" Diane returned a lock of hair sticking up on the back of his head to its proper place.

He batted her hand away. "What month is it now? October? I think we went out in August."

"Oh yeah. That new Asian fusion place where you got the sushi burrito. It was awful."

"Let me get this straight." Victoria cocked her head. "The last time you two went out for dinner was two months ago, and you didn't like the food? I think you can hold off on the guilt right now."

Will pushed his plate away and sighed. "That salmon was so good. Almost as good as my wife makes, and we don't even have to clean up after it." He leaned over and kissed Diane's cheek.

"And by 'clean up,' he means 'pull chunks of it out of Rebecca's hair,'" Diane said.

"Don't forget fishing it out of the rug under the table," Will added.

"*Fishing it?*" Victoria poked him in the ribs. "Like, fish? Like salmon? Get it?"

"Oh God," Will groaned. "That one wasn't even intentional."

"You two. How did your parents put up with you?" Diane asked.

"I've got to say, Tori, it's really nice to spend an evening talking about something other than Power Rangers. I feel very adult all of a sudden," Will said.

"Then why are you dressed like a teenager?" Victoria asked. "Diane and I are wearing dresses and jewelry, and you're in what amounts to a T-shirt and jeans."

He rubbed the back of his neck. "Um, let's talk about that voting rights thing again."

Victoria laughed. "And I was just going to ask if we could talk about Ninja Turtles."

Will waved his hand in the general direction of the server. "Check, please!"

"Oh, Tori, by the way, when's Genevieve's birthday?" Diane pulled out her phone. "I was updating my calendar the other day, and I don't have hers."

"July 6. She turns fifty this year."

"Oh shit, that's huge!" Will said. "You need to start planning now!"

"It's only October," Victoria said. "A lot could happen between now and then."

Why did I just say that? She could kick herself.

"What, like, you two break up? Jesus, Tor, have a little faith." Will stared at her, and Victoria fidgeted. His eyes narrowed. "Unless you're planning on walking away again."

"Me? No. I won't make that mistake again."

"Well, then, how are things with Genevieve?" Diane asked, bringing the conversation in the exact direction Victoria didn't want it to go.

"Good. Our jobs are, well, messy right now. But we're working through it."

"Are you being a jerk again?" Will asked. "Because you were a jerk in law school, so I'd suggest being nice this time."

Diane rolled her eyes. "I think we've all moved past that one, Will."

"I'm not sure, actually," Victoria said softly. "Genevieve brought it up again last night."

"Ouch," Will said.

"You know," Diane cut in, "I've seen the way Genevieve looks at you. I sincerely doubt she'll make that mistake either. So let's assume you two are still together for her birthday. What do you think she wants for her fiftieth? A stripper?"

It was an awful time to have just taken a drink. Victoria coughed and tried not to spray vodka all over the table. Her eyes watering, she sputtered, "No strippers. I honestly haven't thought much about it, but I'll come up with something."

The waiter, having taken Will's earlier gesture seriously, arrived with the bill, which Victoria claimed before her dinner companions could. When Will started to protest, she cut him off. "You had to pay a babysitter so you could come out tonight. I've got this."

As they hugged good-bye on the sidewalk outside the restaurant, Diane whispered in her ear, "Let me know if you want to talk about Genevieve. I can't imagine navigating a relationship with all the scrutiny you two are under."

"Thanks, Diane. We'll be fine, I'm sure. Just some bumps in the road."

After she climbed into her car, Victoria checked her phone and discovered a notification:

Genevieve Fornier would like to merge calendars.

She tapped *accept*, and her calendar app populated with fundraising events, hearings, depositions, and conference calls. The only event listed for that day was a phone interview with *The Advocate*; the calendar didn't say anything about going to a movie with Bethany. Had she forgotten to put it on the calendar, or had she just made it up as some ridiculous power play so Victoria would stop scheduling things for her?

She hated that she even entertained such doubts.

CHAPTER 12

A week later, Genevieve surveyed her living room one last time before she headed to the airport, and sighed.

Trying to convince herself that her anger was directed at Archie Dalton for appealing the case wasn't working. The idea that someone else would argue a case she had worked up from scratch, almost single-handedly, made her skin crawl.

Well, it wasn't her personal frustration that mattered right now. Heather and Crystal were on their way, and they would look to her for strength and optimism, which she vowed to give them, regardless of whatever emotions were swirling around inside her.

When she had called them to say that the Supreme Court would be hearing their case, she had been vague about why they needed to meet in person to discuss what came next. Her friends were devoted parents who didn't spend a lot of time following gossip in the legal field. And she hadn't exactly kept them posted on her romantic situation.

In her defense, every time she called to talk, Crystal interrupted her twice a sentence to call out things to her children like "put the dirty diaper back in the pail" and "stop biting your brother."

The phone call last week hadn't been much different. In between "get back in bed" and "you just had a glass of water—you don't need another one," she had said to Genevieve, "Well, the kids have never seen DC before. I'll look into flights."

So Genevieve had done what she could to childproof the house for Jackie and Jasper, one of whom was probably two. Or four. She mentally added, *come up with a graceful way to ask the kids' ages* to her to-do list.

When all of her breakable items were either elevated to higher shelves or stashed in the closet, and a new game of Connect Four was on the coffee table for the older child, she grabbed her car keys and headed to the airport. Heather had promised that three adults and two kids could fit in Genevieve's BMW and had hinted that there was something pretty hot about the way Crystal, who was in no way butch, installed the gear her kids needed to ride in a car.

Everything from the moment they first hugged outside the airport to the moment both kids were asleep in her home office on an air mattress felt like chaos. Before Heather had closed the office door and Crystal had taken off her earrings, Genevieve was pouring wine.

The three of them got settled in the living room, and Genevieve studied her friends while they nursed their drinks. Crystal's hair was in a messy ponytail, and she looked like a single glass of wine might knock her out at any moment. Heather had dark shadows under her eyes.

When they had recovered enough of their energy to talk, Crystal offered her a weak smile. "Well, on the plus side, we made it here in once piece."

"Congratulations," Genevieve offered.

"Genevieve, you look great," Heather said.

Crystal turned to her and smirked. "Really? I was about to say she looks awful."

"You're one to talk. Is that yogurt on your sweater?" Genevieve asked.

"Mashed-up Cheerios, I think," Crystal said.

"Do you want to treat it and put it in the washer?"

Crystal just laughed. "If I worried about washing my clothes every time the kids covered them with food, I'd probably give up clothing altogether."

"I have no problem with this," Heather announced, and Crystal swatted her shoulder.

Their glasses were nearing empty, so Genevieve headed into the kitchen to fetch the bottle. It was surreal, she thought as she poured refills: Crystal was in many ways the same girl she had played dodge ball with in gym class, but their lives felt so different now. Genevieve hadn't ever stopped to think about whether she wanted kids, and Crystal had started talking about names long before Heather had become pregnant.

When she had settled back into her corner of the couch, Heather turned to her. "Well, we're headed to the Supreme Court. Who would have thought?"

"Do you think we'll win?"

The hope in Crystal's eyes sent a wave of guilt through Genevieve. She suppressed a sigh as she stood and paced around the room. "Do you want the good news or the bad?"

At the same time that Heather said, "There's bad news?" Crystal said promptly, "Good news, please."

"I'm seeing someone, and it's kind of serious."

Crystal squealed a bit and hopped over to pull her into a tight hug. "About time!"

Over Crystal's shoulder, she could see Heather raise her wine glass in salute. "What's she like?"

"She's great," Genevieve admitted, producing more squeals and hugs from Crystal. "Brilliant, funny, beautiful. And total pain in the ass too."

Heather laughed at her wry tone. "Good. Sounds like you've found someone who can keep up with you."

"Some days, I'm not sure I can keep up with her."

Crystal held her hand, solemnly. "If she feels the same way about you, that's the foundation for a good partnership."

It was unsettling, receiving advice about relationships from someone who actually understood how to make them last.

"What's her name?" Heather asked.

"Victoria Willoughby."

Recognition dawned slowly on each of their faces.

Heather spoke first. "*Justice* Victoria Willoughby?"

"Damn, girl. You're dating a Supreme Court justice?" Crystal clapped her on the back.

"And now we get to the bad news," Genevieve said. "I can no longer argue your case at the Supreme Court."

After a beat, their faces fell. Crystal sat next to her wife, who wrapped an arm around her shoulder. "Does this mean—" Crystal's voice wavered.

Heather seemed more in control of her emotions. Understandable, Genevieve thought, considering her parental rights regarding the children would always be secure. "Do we lose now?"

"No, not at all," Genevieve rushed to reassure them. "Honestly, it probably means very little for the outcome of the case. We just need to find you new counsel. In many ways, it's just a technicality—the case record we've developed still stands, and the justices will read all of it."

"You can't just, like, pretend you're not dating her?" Heather asked.

Crystal rested her hand on Heather's thigh. "That seems highly unethical and like something Genevieve would never do."

Genevieve shook her head. "Even if I wanted to, there's a photo. And some television interviews in which Victoria doesn't deny it."

She polished off the wine and briefly considered breaking out the scotch. If she wasn't careful, this whole situation could easily lead to a drinking problem. "I flew you here because I want to talk with you about who could argue the case, and, if we decide on someone, introduce you so you can get started. December fifth seems far away now, but I promise it will sneak up on all of you. I want to make sure you're in good hands."

Crystal rubbed her eyes. "I'm sure there's some joke to be made about how good you are with your hands, Genevieve, but I'm too tired to make it."

"Let's talk through your options," Genevieve said, as she walked to the one of the bookcases and extracted a binder she'd spent the week putting together.

It was remarkably hard to replace herself, both emotionally and logistically. She sat on the couch next to Crystal, who spread the binder across her lap and Heather's.

"I wouldn't recommend a private-sector attorney—they're too expensive, for one. Plus, they're always pulled in multiple directions and don't necessarily have a background in human rights litigation.

"My first thought was Jamie Chance," she said, flipping to the first page of the binder. "But honestly, he's got a full plate right now, and he's better at fundraising and strategizing cases than actually arguing them."

She flipped through the binder, publicity photos of men and women in suits staring back at them, and evaluated the candidates. There, in the middle, was Penelope Sweet, gorgeous as ever, with eyes that seemed to cut through all of Genevieve's BS.

She was going to try to present the options neutrally, but after spending the week researching profiles, who was she kidding? Penelope was the strongest candidate out there.

When she reached the end of the binder, Genevieve asked, "Do you want time to discuss without me?"

Heather laughed. "That's ridiculous. We don't need to confer alone. Please, stay and help us decide."

"Yeah, I want to know who you'd pick, if it were up to you," Crystal said. "I know you have opinions."

"Exactly—I don't know the first thing about these people or why to pick one over the other. Actually, if the last thing you can do on this case is help us find a new lawyer, please just tell us who to choose."

Genevieve took a deep breath and angled herself to see her friends better. "There's no one on this list better suited to represent you than Penelope Sweet."

"Is that the one from NCLR?" Crystal flipped through the binder until she landed on the right page. "Don't you, like, compete with them or something?"

"It's complicated," Genevieve admitted. "Yes, there's a history of competition between our organizations—mine, NCLR, and HRC. But Penelope and I are both pretty new to these organizations, and we're trying to collaborate now. I think NCLR would provide great support for you two, and Penelope would put forward excellent oral arguments. And also, because she and I are friendly, I can continue to help develop arguments behind the scenes—I won't have to walk away from the case completely."

Heather studied the photo. "Her eyes look smart."

Swatting at her, Crystal laughed. "You're ridiculous—that doesn't even make sense. If you think she's hot, just say it."

"She's hot, for sure," Heather said. "But I meant it; she's sharp and, I don't know, curious? I can tell from the photo that I like her."

Oddly relieved, Genevieve leaned back in her seat and studied the two of them for a moment. Their shoulders were touching, and as they pored over the fact sheet, they adjusted their eyeglasses with identical gestures. It was sweet, and Genevieve felt keenly how much she'd missed her childhood friend. Yet another reason she wished she was going to be their lawyer this fall—it would give them a chance to spend time together.

"I'll set up a meeting with Penelope, then?" Genevieve asked.

Crystal's expression fell, and she slumped against her wife's side. Wrapping a protective arm around her, Heather said, "I guess so. This feels so weird, though. Like we're firing you or something."

Not that she would ever say it out loud, but Genevieve wholeheartedly agreed. "Let's not focus on that right now. I'll figure out Penelope's availability, and we'll go from there." She stood and wiped her hands on her pants. "You two have had a long day and some big news. Let's get some sleep, and then tomorrow we can do something a lot more fun than this. Drive around looking at monuments—that's something little kids enjoy, right?"

Heather and Crystal looked at each other and laughed. "People without kids say the darnedest things, don't they?" Crystal said.

Genevieve rolled her eyes. "Fine. I think there's a zoo somewhere. Does that work?"

"Now you're talking," Heather said, as she carried the empty wine glasses into the kitchen.

Crystal took Genevieve's hands. "You've already done so much to help us. I promise I'll be appropriately curious about your new relationship tomorrow."

They hugged again, and Genevieve said softly, "I wish things were different."

She felt rather than heard Crystal's small laugh.

"I wish we didn't have to sue the government in the first place."

CHAPTER 13

The next Friday, when Penelope breezed through the door of The Three Branches for their meeting, she was speaking before she'd even sat down.

"I want to strategize with you two about the same-sex parentage case, but this is uncharted territory for me. Genevieve, can you discuss the case or is that some breach of ethics?"

"I think so—that we can discuss it, I mean. If I don't tell Tori what we talk about, and she doesn't tell me what she thinks about the case… I don't know. The whole thing is messed up, and there aren't clear rules set down on paper for this situation."

Jamie nodded. "Exactly. I think you are all upstanding, ethical people. Follow your instincts and don't do anything you think is questionable, and I'm sure you'll be fine."

They all ordered burgers, and then Penelope jumped right in.

"Okay, so, the other side wrote in their briefs that marriage rights aren't coterminous with parental rights and that children can only have a mother and a father."

"Here's my thing," Jamie cut in. "What's the state proposing as an alternative in this situation? There are two kids—real, breathing kids—who need to live someplace."

"No one's suggesting taking the kids out of the home," Genevieve said. "As long as their birth mother is alive and lives with them, everything's fine. So, in a sense, if Crystal and Heather were fine living with the risk, they could do nothing here and hope for the best. But if something were to happen to Heather, well, even if she had left a notarized document saying that Crystal is to be their guardian, that document would have no legal force. The surviving parent would be 'a complete stranger in the eyes of the law.'"

"So, in that hypothetical situation, the state would take the kids away from their other mother," Penelope said.

"Yes, because that's the Christian thing to do," Jamie rolled his eyes. "What hypocrisy."

"My plan," Penelope said, "is to make a historical argument about the nature of family. How we consider—and have always considered—family to be those individuals who live together, share their food and fortunes, and rely on and support each other."

"But you're going to run into some problems with that argument," Jamie told her. "That argument is pretty much the opposite of what we used to advocate for gay marriage—we've always said that people evolve and that looking at history and tradition for answers is limiting."

"Right, so how do I argue that this is a family unit in all ways save one—the law—and that the state needs to get on board?"

"I think you talk about the well-being of the children," Genevieve said. "The Court seemed particularly moved by those arguments in last year's gay marriage case. It wants children to be raised by loving parents, and removing a child from a parent will be detrimental to both the child and society."

"O'Neil's going to be a problem here," Jamie said. "He's going to say that Louisiana can determine for itself whether or not it wants to recognize another state's birth certificates."

"That's just absurd," Penelope said. "There's zero history of a given state refusing to recognize another state's birth certificates."

"Well, I think that's your best defense if the other side raises states' rights issues," Genevieve said.

"Noted," Penelope scribbled in a notebook. "I also wondered what your thoughts were on the reach of this case. I assume that the justices wanted to hear arguments because they want to issue a broad ruling that would apply to more couples than just my clients. So how much time should I spend in briefs and arguments about my clients' biographies and histories?"

"Not much," Genevieve said. "In other circumstances, I'd say go for sentimentality and talk about how much those kids love their moms. But the justices aren't going to be swayed by emotions. Keep it about the well-being of children and society."

Penelope nodded, closed her notebook, and removed her glasses. "Listen, Genevieve, I wanted to say thanks for asking me to take this case on. It's great for NCLR, and I'm honored to be arguing a case that means so much to you."

Underneath the table, her knee bumped against Genevieve's. She left it there for a moment, then moved away and stole a quick glance at her. When their eyes met, Genevieve could have sworn actual sparks erupted between them.

A millisecond later, it was over. Penelope turned to Jamie and cleared her throat. "But after this one, I won't be taking lead on arguing cases myself. It's too much, dividing my attention between administrating and litigating. I don't know how you two do it."

"Well," Jamie said, "to be clear, I don't really. The gay marriage case Genevieve and I argued together—with Nic, of course—was an exception. I wasn't about to let that case go to the Supreme Court without me. But since then, I've dramatically scaled back my involvement in actual cases. I agree—it's too hard to do both."

Their eyes turned to Genevieve, an unspoken question hanging in the air.

"I'm a litigator. I've always been one. I'm not going to walk away from that just because I'm an administrator now." She shrugged. "I'm making it work, doing both. Isn't that the dream—having it all?"

They looked at her a bit skeptically, but the conversation moved on to other topics. Penelope's knee brushed against hers one more time, and she felt a thrill ripple through her. Having it all, indeed.

CHAPTER 14

Now that Penelope was officially their attorney and she'd had a couple of weeks to review their case, Heather and Crystal were back in DC for a series of meetings with her. Their neighbor was watching Jackie and Jasper, and according to Crystal, traveling without the kids was so amazing she was just going to check them with her bags next time.

It was an unseasonably warm day in November, so Genevieve took them to the National Mall for a city walk. After filling them in on her new life in DC, including dating Tori, she asked, "How's living in Louisiana?"

"Oh, it's fine. Baton Rouge isn't as conservative as the rest of the state. But it's not Oakland, either," Crystal said.

"I think most people who see us don't even register that we're a couple—that both of us are parents to our children," Heather added.

"There are some homophobic taunts here and there," Crystal said. "We try to just ignore it."

"It's harder for Crystal," Heather said, taking her hand. "It's not just homophobia she has to face. At least once a week, someone treats Crystal like she's an alien because, you know, they've only ever seen Asian people on TV."

"What kills me about the people who jeer at us because Heather's white and I'm not is that they're implicitly acknowledging that we are in fact a couple. So sometimes when I hear it, I think, *at least they don't hate us for being gay.* But then they turn around and call us dykes."

Genevieve touched Crystal's shoulder. "Are you sure this new job is worth it? Living there? There are tons of jobs here in DC."

"I know," Crystal said, patting her hand. "It's tempting. I think about leaving at least once a day. But honestly, green energy companies are a dime a dozen on the coasts. The fact that I'm working for one in Louisiana—well, it feels important."

"That's not the only good work we're trying to do either," Heather cut in. "Back when congresspeople were proposing constitutional amendments to ban gay marriage, we talked about what it would mean to live our politics. It's not an easy choice, and I'm not sure how much headway we're actually making, but we are trying to convince people that lesbians aren't evil incarnate and that breathing the same air as us isn't going to liquefy their lungs or anything."

"At least now, fewer people in our neighborhood can honestly say they've never met a gay person."

"Wow," said Genevieve. "I mean…wow. I would never do that. I've never lived anywhere other than superliberal places where, for the most part, people don't hate other people for being different. I'm not that brave."

"Oh, please," Crystal said, nudging Genevieve's shoulder. "You run one of the foremost civil rights organizations in the country. I don't think you need to worry about not making an impact."

"We're careful not to hold hands in public," Heather said. "And we've talked to the kids about it a lot. They're cautious about who they talk to about their family, and so far, no one's bullied them. We were going to pre-emptively talk to the principal, but evidently, he's pretty awful. Blames it on his religion, but he doesn't believe women *or* gay people deserve equality."

"Sounds like exactly the person you want in charge of a school," Genevieve said.

"The guidance counselor is more open-minded, and we've talked to her a few times. She's keeping an eye on the kids, and we trust she'll let us know if anyone tries to start something with them."

Given how warm it was, the paths were lined with pedestrians, runners, strollers, and even someone on Rollerblades. Ahead of them walked two women talking animatedly; at that moment, one kissed the other on the mouth, and Genevieve could faintly hear her say, "You're ridiculous."

She glanced at her friends, who were looking wistfully at the couple. "Well, if you're committed to Louisiana, I applaud you. And I offer you refuge any time you need it, for however long you need it, with or without the kids."

"You know, you're not half as awkward around kids as you pretend to be," Crystal said.

Genevieve's eyes got big, and Heather cut in. "Jasper even has a little crush on you."

"He's, like, four, isn't he?" Genevieve asked, hoping her cheeks didn't look as red as they felt.

"Eight," Crystal said. "And I'm pretty sure I told you that twice last time we were here."

Heather laughed. "Don't worry, Genevieve. Every time we bring them to see you, they'll be older and less scary for you."

"Ha-ha," Genevieve said, but the thought did give her some comfort. "So, what do you think of Penelope?"

Crystal and Heather fell over themselves gushing about how brilliant, warm, and gorgeous Penelope was. Genevieve let them talk over each other, trying to sing her praises using increasingly sweeping superlatives. Finally, when Heather said, "I've never seen clothes fit a person better," Genevieve put a hand on her arm.

"I'm going to stop you there before you drool on yourself." They rounded a corner and the Lincoln Memorial Reflecting Pool stretched out in front of them. "I'm really glad you like looking at her. And even more glad that you feel confident in her legal skills."

Heather and Crystal both hesitated. "She's not you, of course—" Heather said at the same time that Crystal blurted out, "We'd obviously rather have you arguing the case."

Genevieve chuckled and shook her head. "It's okay, you two. It's fine that you're happy with her. And I get it. She's...really something."

"Oh?" Crystal raised her eyebrows. "Says the woman in a relationship with a Supreme Court justice."

"Oh?" Genevieve countered. "And you two forgot for a minute that you're married to each other while you were fawning over her?"

"Fair point. Let's all agree that she's 'really something' and leave it at that," Heather said.

The conversation moved on, but for the next two days, every time Penelope's name came up, Crystal looked at her a little too knowingly, and Genevieve tried not to squirm.

❧

The settlement conference for Amelia's case was scheduled for December 5, the same day as oral arguments in Heather and Crystal's case at the Supreme Court. Genevieve was relieved that she'd have something else to do that day to take her mind off of how frustrated and helpless she felt about being sidelined.

The team she assembled from HER worked tirelessly to sift through evidence and prepare arguments. Although it wasn't as sexy as a trial, especially in terms of getting the media interested, Genevieve would take a positive and, more importantly, a *binding* outcome—which she'd get at a settlement conference. Her team understood that, for Amelia, a settlement was an opportunity to reach a resolution quickly. Trial, should it be necessary, was set for June, which would mean six more months of waiting, plus potential appeals.

Genevieve and her team were set to fly to Michigan on December 4, and they worked until eleven the night before, preparing documents and finalizing strategy. When Genevieve woke up the morning of the fourth, her head was pounding.

She peeled the covers off and stumbled into her bathroom, where she rummaged around in the medicine cabinet until she found something for migraines. She managed to toss a pill into her mouth and swallow a bit of water with it before her stomach churned and a wave of dizziness washed over her. She clutched the sink, hoping to wait it out, but nausea surged through her, and she fell to her knees.

Two hours and a lot of throwing up later, she'd made it back to bed with a glass of water, a box of Kleenex, and a cold compress for her head. Blindly, she poked at her phone until she woke up Siri, whom she instructed to call Frank.

"Hi, Genevieve," he said, breathlessly, "I know your driver's late. I'm on it—I'll drive you to the airport myself."

"Frank," she mumbled, "please slow down. Talk softer."

He paused, then said, "Oh God, you sound awful. Is it a migraine again?"

"Whatever it is, I'm throwing up, and I can't see straight."

"Okay, give me five minutes. I'm going to shift some things around, reassign your plane ticket to send someone else from the team, and then I'll head over with some antinausea medicine I got last year when I went on that cruise. And soup."

"Please don't talk about food," Genevieve groaned. She tried to say good-bye, but her eyes were so heavy, and she closed them instead.

When Genevieve woke up, she was drenched in sweat, but her vision was clearer than it had been all day. She rolled over and noticed a note on her nightstand.

> *Genevieve, there's soup and ginger ale in your fridge. I don't know if you'll remember this, but you did take the antinausea medicine I brought, along with some migraine medicine. I hope they helped you sleep this off, and you wake up feeling better! Call me whenever, and don't worry about Amelia—she's in good hands.*

Amelia? What did she have to do with—oh shit. She closed her eyes again. When she opened them, she glanced at her alarm clock. 2:30 p.m. Her flight, along with her legal team, had left hours ago.

She sat up, relieved that her head felt its normal size and the floor wasn't swaying in front of her. It was early enough—she could probably catch another flight to Michigan. The settlement conference began at eight the next morning, and surely there were evening flights that would get her to the hotel in time to grab a few hours' sleep beforehand. Her mouth felt like a disaster zone, and her eyes still ached a little. Her trip to the bathroom was a lot less nerve-wracking this time, and throwing cold water on her cheeks and brushing her teeth made her feel more human. And if toothpaste could make this much of a difference, imagine how amazing a shower would feel.

Bathing and dressing, however, sapped all her energy, and she crawled back into bed and passed out.

It was dark when she woke up again, and her alarm clock read 6:45 p.m. She rolled onto her back and stared at the ceiling. There was no way she was going to Michigan. So now, in addition to disappointing Heather and Crystal, she was disappointing Amelia.

She trudged downstairs for some soup and ginger ale and checked in with Frank, who assured her that the excellent team of lawyers she'd sent to Michigan was well prepared.

After hanging up with Frank, she fiddled with her phone for a minute, then dialed Tori.

"Hi, Genevieve," Tori greeted her cheerfully. "How's Michigan? How are you feeling about tomorrow?"

"Miserable," Genevieve said.

"Oh no. What's wrong, babe?" Tori asked and Genevieve laughed.

"Babe?"

"Yeah, I'm trying it out. How'd it hit you?"

"Best thing I've heard all day." Genevieve took her glass to her living room and curled up on the couch, grateful that the change in elevation didn't cause her to see stars. The remains of a headache haunted her forehead and eyes, and she felt weak as a kitten, but generally the pain was gone.

"So what's going on?" Tori asked, and Genevieve could hear the sound of a chair scraping against bricks, suggesting that Tori was sitting on her back patio.

"Well, for starters, I'm not in Michigan." After filling Tori in on her day, Genevieve closed her eyes—talking that much was exhausting.

"God, Vee, I'm so sorry. Can I bring you something? Soup? Sprite?"

"I'm covered, but thanks. What are you up to tonight?"

After an awkwardly long pause, Victoria said with a sigh, "Prepping for tomorrow's oral arguments."

"Oh." Of course that's what she was doing. And if Genevieve hadn't spent the day in oblivion she would have remembered. Whether it was the turn their conversation had taken or whatever bug was infesting her body, she suddenly needed to sleep again. "Sorry, babe—I gotta rest. Like, now."

She hung up before Victoria responded and made it to her bed, where she collapsed and the world spun. Her insides churned a few times, accentuating just how sore her stomach muscles were from throwing up earlier.

When she opened her eyes again, there was a soft glow coming from the chair in the corner of her room—a book light clipped to a binder illuminating Tori's face.

"Your briefs from the district-level trial are beautiful. You're a brilliant writer, Genevieve."

She wasn't expecting that, and her heart swelled a little. "Thanks. That means a lot."

Tori took off her glasses and closed the binder on her lap. "I'm not sure if saying this will make you feel better or worse, but I really do wish it were you arguing tomorrow."

"Yeah. Me too."

They were quiet for a moment, but the silence felt more comfortable than it had in a long time. Genevieve sat up in bed and adjusted the blankets around her. "Do you know what questions you're going to ask from the bench?"

"There are things I'd like more information on, but no, I don't plan questions in advance. Good questions are direct responses to what the attorneys say in arguments, so I'll just have to wait and see."

"Well, good luck tomorrow."

"Will you listen?" Victoria asked.

"I had planned on being in a settlement conference, so I hadn't thought about listening live. Maybe."

"How are you feeling?"

"Like I've been hit by a truck."

"Can I make you some tea?" Tori asked.

"That sounds nice. I'll go down with you."

The stairs didn't make her seasick for the first time that day, and she sat at her kitchen table while Tori put on the kettle and located Saltines. They nibbled crackers and drank tea, Victoria's leg resting against Genevieve's underneath the table.

"Would you like to come over for dinner tomorrow, since you're in town?"

"Honestly, I'm not sure how I'll feel tomorrow."

"Physically or emotionally?"

"Both," Genevieve admitted.

"That's fair. But if you're up for seeing me and still not feeling that well, I'll happily bring over food. Just let me know."

Genevieve nodded. "Going to be a weird day tomorrow."

"I know," Tori said, taking her hand. "I love you, Genevieve."

Genevieve studied their interlaced fingers that fit so well together before looking up into Tori's open eyes, filled with tenderness. "I love you too."

"Do you want me to stay, or would you rather be alone?"

"It really means a lot to me that you came over, Tori. I think I'd like to wake up alone tomorrow, though. I'm not sure I have it in me to watch you get dressed to hear tomorrow's arguments."

Tori nodded. "Want me to tuck you in, then?"

"That sounds divine."

She crawled back into bed, and Tori bustled about getting her more water, crackers, and her copy of *A Separate Peace*—"in case you wake up in the middle of the night and can't get back to sleep."

"Thanks, Tori." They kissed, a sweet kiss that reminded Genevieve how much she really did love Tori.

When Genevieve woke up the next morning, she felt like a million bucks compared to the day before. Her head was clear and, despite barely eating the day before, her energy was high. She checked in with the legal team in Michigan before they headed into the settlement conference. Once the conference started, there wasn't anything she could do to help them, but they seemed to have everything in hand. She ate a little and went out for a run.

By the time she'd showered and dressed, it was almost ten. She made herself a cup of coffee, took her laptop to her living room, and pulled up the live audio stream of the Supreme Court arguments. With her feet on her coffee table and caffeine in her hand, she listened as the clerk called the court to order and introduced the case.

The attorney general of Louisiana gave his arguments first. He got out two sentences before Alistair Douglas interrupted him: "Do you honestly think that what's best for the two children in question, should something befall one of their parents, would be the foster care system?"

"Foster care provides children all over this country with safe homes and loving families," Archie answered.

"That's quite the rosy view of the system," Alistair responded.

"Studies have proven that what's best for children is to grow up with a mother and a father. Louisiana takes those studies seriously, and the state has a right to—"

"I'm glad you brought up states' rights," Michelle Lin cut in. "Doesn't every state have a right for the birth certificates it issues to be recognized by every other state?"

"Michelle raises a good question," Jason Blankenstein said. "But I'd like to go back to your assertion that studies have proven children do best with a mother and a father. Drawing your attention to the Johns Hopkins study, it seems as if there are a number of misrepresentations you've made in your handling of that study."

The liberal justices continued to pepper Archie with questions, and twenty minutes passed before it occurred to Genevieve that she hadn't heard Tori say anything. It was common practice for justices to ask questions from the bench—especially of the side they were more skeptical of—and Tori was one of the most vocal justices during arguments.

Arguments continued until Archie's time elapsed and the floor was given over to Penelope, with still not a word from Tori. Well, sometimes justices opted for the reverse strategy—they asked leading questions of the attorney whose side they favored. Maybe Tori planned on giving softballs to Penelope.

"Your Honors, I'm here on behalf of Heather and Crystal Rowlings. But I'm also here on behalf of families all across this country—not hypothetical families, but real ones. Children and their parents. Families who eat breakfast together and scramble to get out the door on the way to school with backpacks and lunches and homework. Who talk about their days at the dinner table. These families have a civil right to legal recognition. Because they exist, whether some people want them to or not."

"That's a lovely picture you've painted for us, Ms. Sweet," Kellen O'Neill said. "But this is a case about states' rights."

"I respectfully disagree, Mr. Chief Justice. This case is entirely about family."

Penelope spoke passionately and insightfully, fielding questions with grace and deftly redirecting the conversation back to the welfare of the children at every turn. Genevieve was impressed with the way she tightrope walked the conversation—always focusing on family without veering into anything emotional or sentimental.

Smith, Jaworski, and McKenzie asked questions ranging from legally nuanced to personally offensive. And still, Tori remained silent, along with Jamison, whom she mocked endlessly for never saying anything from the bench.

Genevieve had newfound respect for those calling for video cameras in the Court—she wanted desperately to see Tori's face while the debate surged around her. Hell, was she even there? Maybe she'd skipped work today. Because nothing about Tori was making any sense right now.

Penelope was wrapping up her oral arguments, when Genevieve heard a throat clear and Penelope stopped speaking. Maybe Tori had saved everything up for now?

"Ms. Sweet, is your desired outcome here that gay couples be allowed to conduct second-parent adoptions or that Louisiana recognize California's birth certificates?"

There was a small pause—no one had expected Jamison to ask a question. Ever. Genevieve only recognized his voice by process of elimination.

"Thank you, Justice Jamison. Our desired outcome is that all states must recognize the two people listed on a birth certificate as legal parents, regardless of gender, and that all states issue birth certificates for new babies with blanks labeled *parent one* and *parent two*, as opposed to *mother* and *father*."

Penelope concluded, and Genevieve exhaled for what felt like the first time since arguments began. She unclenched her grip on her coffee cup and flexed her stiff fingers.

She had to hand it to Penelope—she'd put forth excellent arguments and answered questions well. Archie had a weak case, and the questions the liberal justices asked of him seemed to poke holes in all his arguments. Well, all the liberals except Tori.

Genevieve stood to stretch her legs and was trying to make sense of her emotions when her cell rang.

She spent the afternoon on the phone with her legal team in Michigan. The settlement conference hadn't gone well, and they were looking at trial in June.

By six o'clock, they had a legal strategy for trial and had scheduled with the jail a series of prep sessions for Amelia and some of their other witnesses. Genevieve rubbed her ear as she hung up the phone, and her stomach growled.

Well, Tori always had food, and, frankly, Genevieve had a couple of questions for her. She grabbed her coat, purse, and keys and pointed her BMW toward Tori's house. It took half the drive for her car to warm up, and she was grateful for her gloves.

After parking in Tori's driveway, crunching up the snow-covered walk to the front door, and knocking, she waited.

Tori opened the door a couple of minutes later, looking surprised. "Genevieve. Hi. I wasn't expecting you."

"Is now a bad time?"

Tori stood aside and gestured toward the living room. "Not at all—come in."

Genevieve kicked off her boots and tossed her coat on the back of the couch, then followed Tori into the kitchen.

"I was going to have a salad. Does that interest you?"

"Sure," Genevieve said, and she leaned against the kitchen island. "Why didn't you say anything today? I looked it up online—this is the first time since you've joined the Court that you didn't say anything during arguments."

Tori glanced at her, then buried herself in the fridge as she gathered salad ingredients. "Alistair and I discussed it, and the optics wouldn't have looked good."

She dumped lettuce, strawberries, and parmesan cheese on the counter and pulled a big wooden bowl out of a cabinet.

"Optics? Are you kidding me?"

Tori knit her brow. "No. We thought it wouldn't be a good idea for me to get too close to this case."

"It's the Supreme Freaking Court. Why the hell would you care about optics? That's for congressmen who have to get money for elections. You're not supposed to be political. Or care what the media says."

Sighing, Tori located some pistachio nuts and started assembling the salad. "We would be foolish not to care what the media says. We just don't let it dictate our decisions."

"Well, you decided not to say a damn thing today. You might as well not have even been there. In which case, I might as well have been there. Arguing my case."

"Genevieve, don't—"

Genevieve looked down and was surprised to see she was pacing across the kitchen. She returned to the island and clutched the countertop. "Seriously, you stayed on this case to make a difference. But you just sat there."

"I still get to vote. And I will talk in our conferences."

"Yes, I know. You writing your name on a piece of paper is way more important than anything I could have spent a half hour saying during oral arguments."

"Genevieve—"

"You know what? Don't. You're still calling all the shots. I'm... I'm not playing this game anymore."

She stalked toward the door and vaguely heard Tori calling to her.

"What does that mean? Genevieve, come back! Genevieve, please, let's—"

Genevieve closed the front door, cutting off anything else Tori tried to say.

Genevieve had stormed out of the house without her cell phone and coat. She sat in the car, wondering if she should go back for them, but that would ruin her dramatic exit. The appropriate thing to do, she supposed, would be to drive to Bethany's. But somehow that wasn't the energy she wanted right now. She drove to a ritzy corner market and picked up a six-pack of craft beer before leaving Tori's neighborhood and heading toward Mount Pleasant, DC's hottest neighborhood. The phrase "playing with fire" flashed through her mind; she shrugged it off and drove faster.

Penelope answered the door wearing a Yale hoodie and silk boxers with little bulldogs. In lieu of staring at her legs, Genevieve mused that she couldn't imagine Tori wearing anything with the word *Harvard* on it.

When she saw who was standing on her stoop, Penelope raised her eyebrows. "Come to talk about how arguments went today?"

"I brought beer." Genevieve held up her recent purchase. "Are you busy?"

Penelope stood aside and motioned for Genevieve to enter. "I've waited this long to watch the pilot of *How to Get Away with Murder*. What's another night?"

Genevieve helped herself to a spot on the couch and put the beer on the coffee table. "Do you have a bottle opener?"

Standing just inside the door, arms crossed, Penelope studied her for a moment before shrugging and heading into the kitchen. While she fetched an opener, Genevieve extracted a bottle and started peeling off the label. She'd shredded it into small pieces when Penelope returned.

"You want to talk about it? Whatever's bothering you?" Penelope asked, handing her the opener and sitting down on the other half of couch. She turned so her back was against the armrest and pulled her legs up underneath her. This time, Genevieve made no attempt to hide her staring.

It had been a long time since she'd seduced another woman, and if that was really going to be her endgame here, she was going about it all wrong. She took a drink of her beer and smiled appreciatively at Penelope's legs before slowly raising her gaze to eyes so dark they seemed to envelop her.

"Genevieve," Penelope said with a hint of warning in her voice.

"Would you like a drink?" She grabbed a new bottle and held it out.

Penelope hesitated, then opened hers and offered a toast. "To unexpected visits."

"I'll drink to that," Genevieve said.

They sat in silence, just drinking, before Genevieve said, "You've never seen *How to Get Away with Murder*?"

"I have a love-hate relationship with Shondaland shows. She handles race well, but her female protagonists make awful, weak choices about the men in their lives." She squinted at the television for a moment, even though it wasn't on, before continuing. "I'm also hesitant to watch legal dramas because they get so much wrong about how the law actually works. And then I get mad. And watching TV isn't supposed to make me mad—it's supposed to be relaxing."

"Fair points, all. I haven't seen it either. Tori has a television, but it's in a built-in cabinet in the living room, and the doors are always closed. She used to have one in the bedroom, but she got rid of it after she was attacked. She associated watching it with staying up late, too anxious about stalkers and such."

"Understandable," Penelope said, and Genevieve was reminded once again that she was the consummate diplomat.

"I suppose. Anyway, if you end up watching *How to Get Away with Murder*, let me know what you think."

"You didn't come over to talk about television."

The bottle in her hand was mostly empty, and she finished it off. "You did great today. I couldn't have done any better. Really—well done."

Penelope smiled at her. "Thanks. That means a lot to me." She took a drink and then grinned. "I almost laughed when Jamison asked that question. The look on Kellen's face was priceless—it was as if he'd seen a ghost."

"I wish I could have seen it."

Giving her a long, open look, Penelope nodded. "I wish you could have too."

"I mean it—I couldn't have done any better today. My friends were in excellent hands."

"I'm still sorry it came to this."

Genevieve nodded. "Relationships are tricky."

Penelope resituated on the couch, propping her head up with her arm. "I don't think I've ever told you why I left France, did I?"

Genevieve shook her head and opened a second beer. It was good—dark and crisp, with none of the heaviness of mass-produced brews. The label came off in one satisfying piece, and she slowly ripped it into pieces as she listened.

"I loved everything about teaching in the Sorbonne—the students weren't driven by money, like in the US. They wanted to understand the law in all its applications. I was teaching subjects I cared deeply about—the history of law, international human rights law, a course comparing constitutions of First World countries. My colleagues were great—open and supportive, beautiful and sophisticated; and I actually had opportunity to get to know them, which was a stark change from my transient life traveling for the UN."

It wasn't hard for Genevieve to see where this was going. "You met someone."

"Raina. She was like waking up after a hard rain to find that the skies had cleared, the grass was greener, and the flowers were brighter. She had an eight-year-old daughter, Alaine, and I fell for her too. For a short time I thought we could be a family. Raina and I were so happy together, and at night we'd lie in bed and talk about how Alaine was going to grow up to be a legal scholar just like us.

"We spent a summer together, the three of us. And when the fall started, Raina met a man that she thought could be a good father to Alaine, and that was that. I thought I could continue to teach, that we could be colleagues together, but it was too hard to see her when she'd thrown everything away for such an arbitrary reason. France was starting to feel like home, and I'd heard rumors that the US ambassador was stepping down, so I reached out to the State Department."

Somewhere during this story, Genevieve had put her bottle down and shifted so she was leaning toward Penelope. "I'm so sorry, Penelope," she said, and it felt wholly inadequate. "She was a fool if she thought her daughter would be better off with a man she's not in love with than with you."

The smile Penelope gave her was laced with sadness. "I said as much at the time, but she was unconvinced."

"That explains why you moved to the State Department but not why you moved back to the States."

"I like a challenge, and being the US ambassador to France wasn't cutting it."

"But advocating for gay rights within the US would?"

"I'm sure I don't have to tell you that the conservative streak in this country runs deep and wide."

"So 'easy' doesn't interest you." Genevieve said. Yet another thing she admired about Penelope.

"Another reason Raina's decision to choose a man over me was disappointing—she took the easy way out."

Genevieve shrugged. "Some people might say she chose the harder option. Depends on whether you're evaluating her place in society or her emotional state. I can't imagine leaving you would be easy on someone's heart."

"You're missing the point, Genevieve. People like us, we don't do easy. Easy is fundamentally not in our constitution. This is why you're drawn to Justice Victoria Willoughby, whose nickname, if I recall correctly, is Just-Ice. And why staying in a relationship with her will always be challenging. If it weren't, you'd have walked a long time ago."

The aftertaste of beer in her mouth turned sour. "I didn't come here to talk about Tori."

The look Penelope gave her made her feel as transparent as glass. "Then why did you come here?"

Penelope's lips were full and slightly parted and nothing like Tori's thin lips that were often set in a grim line. They were perfect for kissing, and maybe other things too, and all Genevieve wanted to do was lose herself in them.

"Genevieve." Penelope's voice was soft. Gentle. Like being surrounded by cashmere. "I'm no one's other woman."

She thought briefly about denying Penelope's interpretation of the moment, but really, what would be the point? She put her beer down and looked away. "I know."

"Then you've got a choice to make. I find you very attractive. And," Penelope said wryly, "my track record clearly indicates I have no problem dating colleagues. You and I have a lot in common, and I'm…" Her gaze brushed over Genevieve's lips, which tingled in response. "…interested. But you and Victoria—are you ready to give up on that relationship because of professional difficulties? Isn't that how Victoria broke your heart in the first place? I've read the articles about your history."

"Why do diplomats have to make so much sense all the time?" Genevieve asked, running her hands through her hair.

"What do you want, Genevieve?" Penelope asked, her voice husky. Those bedroom eyes roaming Genevieve's body were going to be her undoing.

"God, when you look at me like that, how can you expect a responsible answer?"

"You don't expect me to fight fair, do you? I'm not the one here who doesn't know what she wants."

"And if I say I'll break up with Victoria tomorrow, but tonight…"

"I'd say I don't believe you. I'm not asking for a lifetime commitment, but I won't touch you while you're with someone else. If you want to call her tonight and end it, you and I can see where this thing between us goes. Otherwise, you should take your sad eyes, your beer, and your ridiculously hot body and go home."

"Home. I don't even know where that is anymore."

"Then it sounds like your problems are bigger than Victoria."

Genevieve leaned back against the couch and closed her eyes. "When I first moved here, I was so focused on the trial and seeing Victoria again after twenty years that I never really settled in to DC. Other than locating a grocery store and a coffee shop, I barely found my way around the city. I prepared for oral arguments in the trial, and once they were over, I launched into a crushing interview schedule that had me flying all over the country. And then the decision came down, and Victoria and I were together again, and what little time I wasn't spending on work, or traveling for work, I spent with her. It was like last time, when we were together in law school—everything in my life became fuzzy and out of focus, and the only thing I could see was her. She blinds me to everything else. Honestly, if it weren't for this same-sex parentage case pulling me out of the haze, I might have continued like that without even noticing."

"Then thank God for the case. You know all this is very unhealthy."

"I suppose." Genevieve opened her eyes and gazed at Penelope, hoping the desperation she felt couldn't be heard in her voice. "Isn't this the shit they write movies and songs about? Where you love someone so much that nothing else in the world matters?"

"Those movies are crap."

"The songs are okay, though?"

Penelope shrugged. "Depends on the bass line."

"Well, how was your relationship with Raina? Did you maintain healthy friendships outside of it, and were you able to continue focusing on your work with as much rigor as you had before you two fell into bed together?"

"It's hard to compare a three-month relationship to however long you and Victoria have been in love with each other."

"So you're as guilty of obsession as I am."

The slow, seductive smile on Penelope's face indicated that being on the receiving end of her obsession would be nothing short of a sublime experience. "Oh, I know how to fixate."

They stared at each other for a long moment, and all Genevieve could hear was the thud of her heartbeat in her ears and the soft breath that made Penelope's chest rise and fall. The thing was, if she wanted great sex, she could go home to her girlfriend. The real debate here, she was beginning to realize, was whether she wanted to commit to Tori or whether she wanted to embark on a brand new relationship with someone she was just getting to know. A relationship without twenty-plus years of baggage.

But wouldn't she be bringing that same baggage from her past with Tori with her into any new relationship? Wasn't that the definition of baggage?

"You look tired, Genevieve. Why don't you borrow some pajamas and sleep on the couch? We can talk more in the morning. A bright new day always brings clarity. Or, so I've heard."

The two beers had gone to her head. She nodded, and while Penelope went to find clothes and sheets, Genevieve cleaned up the beer and the tattered bottle labels she'd shredded onto the coffee table and couch. Penelope returned with a pillow, some blankets, a Yale bulldog T-shirt, and a spare toothbrush still in its packaging.

Later that night, she stared at the ceiling and wondered if Tori was sleeping. She briefly considered calling but had no idea what she would say or what she wanted to hear.

Besides, she'd left her cell at Tori's, which gave her the perfect excuse for doing nothing.

She threw her arm over her forehead and managed to fall into a fitful sleep.

CHAPTER 15

The third time she called Genevieve's cell phone, she was on her way down the stairs after changing out of her work clothes, and Genevieve's ringtone sounded in the kitchen. Right next to her bowl of uneaten salad that Victoria didn't have the heart to clear away.

Well, that explains why Genevieve has been screening her calls.

Or maybe it didn't—maybe Genevieve wouldn't have answered even if she hadn't forgotten her cell at home.

Home. Was this even a home to Genevieve? Victoria sighed and grabbed Genevieve's cell, lighting it up. She'd missed three calls from Victoria and one from Jamie Chance.

On the plus side, having Genevieve's cell gave Victoria an excuse to track down her pissed-off girlfriend. At which point, maybe they could talk more rationally about Genevieve storming out.

Victoria located her purse and keys and was selecting her black trench coat from the front hall closet when she spied Genevieve's coat draped over her couch. Genevieve must have been freezing when she left. Victoria draped the coat carefully over her arm. The garage was chilly, and as she slid into the driver's seat, Tori was tempted to put Genevieve's coat over her lap. Instead, she gingerly hung it over the back of the passenger seat, making sure it wasn't wrinkled.

The drive to Genevieve's had never taken so long. A thousand thoughts flittered through her mind, each one more dire. What if Genevieve couldn't get past this same-sex parentage case and refused to be with a Supreme Court justice because she wanted to argue before the Court again? Maybe now that she'd spent actual time with Victoria, Genevieve had decided that the memory was better than the reality. Or she was fed up with Victoria's slight OCD tendencies and didn't want to date someone so tightly wound.

Whatever the reason, it was clear Genevieve was running, and since *Victoria* was supposed to be the runner, she had no idea how to handle this role reversal. She was either supposed to chase Genevieve or give her space, and given her track record, it was highly likely that Victoria was choosing wrong.

But this was who she was—tenacious and uncompromising—and if Genevieve didn't like it, maybe they *shouldn't* be together.

Damn. The right answer was probably that she should stop overanalyzing and just wait to see what happened when she and Genevieve were finally face-to-face.

It was always hell finding parking near Genevieve's townhouse, and on the third time around the block, Victoria had to remind herself that showing up on her girlfriend's doorstep irritated wouldn't help anything. When she finally found a parking spot, it was five blocks away and tested every parallel parking skill she had.

She arrived at Genevieve's door out of breath from the chill in the air and the brisk pace of her walk. Closing her eyes, she inhaled slowly and tried to calm her nerves. It wasn't like she and Genevieve had never fought before. They'd get past this. Or they wouldn't, and she'd get over Genevieve.

Right. Just like she did during those twenty years she'd spent imagining running into her randomly and rekindling their connection.

She knocked and waited. And waited some more. And knocked some more. When no answer came, she took a couple of steps backward and peered at the upstairs windows. All dark. Not at home then, or else she really didn't want to be found.

Maybe she was at Bethany's. Feeling desperate and yet unable to stop herself, Victoria punched Bethany's address into her GPS when she got back to her car and started following the instructions of the automated voice.

When she got to the door, she wondered at the wisdom of this. She was nervous enough about fighting with Genevieve—she certainly didn't want to do it in front of Genevieve's old roommate. But it would be even worse if Genevieve just threw her out and didn't want to talk to her at all, she supposed. At least she had the phone as an excuse: *It's okay if you don't want to talk yet, but I thought you should have your phone.* That seemed like an acceptable opening line—certainly not one that would produce highly embarrassing responses.

Bethany's voice boomed behind the door, and there was no way she could pretend not to be home when Victoria rang the bell. *Here goes*, she thought, and pushed the button.

The door was thrown open with the vigor Bethany brought to all she did. She made no attempt to hide the surprise on her face when she saw who had rung her doorbell.

"Victoria! My, my. To what do I owe the pleasure?" She crossed her arms and leaned against the doorframe.

It hadn't occurred to Victoria that Genevieve wouldn't accompany Bethany to the door.

"Uh. Hi, Bethany. I have Genevieve's phone." She held it out, feeling like a compete dolt.

Bethany raised her eyebrows. "It appears you do. I have a bra of hers from law school. Are you here to propose a trade?"

"Can I talk to her, please?"

"Evidently not, if she doesn't have her phone."

"Please don't be obtuse. If she doesn't want to talk to me, could you please at least give this to her?"

Bethany stared at her blankly for a moment. "Oh! You think she's here!"

"She's not?"

"Haven't seen her. In weeks. No thanks to you, I'm sure." Suddenly Bethany's posture looked less casual and more menacing.

"Oh. I had no idea."

"Clearly." Bethany sighed and gestured inside. "I was just yelling at my television. You might as well come in and join me."

Victoria followed, wary. "What are we watching?"

"The Dallas Cowboys. And they're losing. I swear our offensive coordinator has no idea what a screen pass is."

As she entered the living room, Victoria wasn't about to mention that she had no idea either. A plush, burnt-orange couch dominated the room, and a huge blanket with a longhorn on it was draped over the back. Between the couch legs and the hardwood floor of Bethany's townhouse was what Victoria imagined could only be a genuine cowhide, which also extended underneath the low wooden coffee table. A large flat-screen television, mounted on the wall opposite the couch, was showing the football game. On either side of the TV, horseshoes hung on the wall.

"Drink? I'm on my second margarita," Bethany said, heading into the kitchen.

"Sure, thanks. A margarita sounds great."

Alone in the living room, Victoria sat down next to the couch on a large chair upholstered with short, coarse brown and white fur that matched the rug. Even perched on the edge of the seat, Victoria felt the bristles poke through her trousers.

Bethany was, without question, Genevieve's friend and not hers. They'd never spent time together without Genevieve. While her host bustled around the kitchen preparing their margaritas, Victoria racked her brain for safe topics of conversation.

The drink deposited in front of her was pink, not light-green, and when Victoria gave her a puzzled look, Bethany said, "Strawberry. Hope that's okay." She sprawled on the couch and gazed at Victoria. "Well. I assume since you thought she was here that you and G-Spot had an argument."

The margarita was strong, and Victoria mentally decided she'd have to stop at one if she wanted to drive. "Things have been a bit…rocky of late. And today was a rough day for her. I mean, I can't say I blame her—she must be feeling really awful. And I'm sorry for the role I played in that. But honestly, storming out is no way to handle a disagreement, and—"

"Mm. God, where did you learn how to tackle, kindergarten? Fucking defense. I swear, Victoria, you could tackle better than our secondary."

"I've obviously come at a bad time. I should let you get back to your game. Thanks for the margarita," Victoria said, slightly irritated that her host was more interested in television than conversation.

Bethany muted the TV and gestured at her with the remote. "Look, that's entirely up to you. You've made no secret in the twenty years we've all known each other that you care about me and my opinion not at all. If something's changed, by all means let me know. Otherwise, you're welcome to watch the game, as long as you don't root for the Giants."

Bethany's eyes were blazing, and for the first time, it occurred to Victoria that she was probably an excellent litigator. Having her casual dismissal of Bethany thrown back in her face stung. "I care what you think," she said, and she knew she sounded defensive.

"Bull. Not only do you have no respect for me, you have no respect for my friendship with Genevieve. It's just like back in law school—you've claimed her, and you keep her on the tightest leash imaginable, and no one else ever gets a piece of her."

"Don't be ridiculous. Genevieve is an adult, fully capable of making her own choices."

"Victoria, how many times in the past few months have you asked Genevieve how she wants to spend the evening, instead of having already made dinner and just assuming the two of you will spend the night playing Scrabble at your place? Jesus, Tori, you're not eighty."

Victoria shifted uncomfortably in her chair. What kind of masochist would upholster a chair like this? And what kind of idiot would put it in her living room?

Bethany sat up and turned the television off. "You haven't created any room in the relationship for her. Do you have any idea what she's given up for you? Seriously, close your eyes for a second. I mean it—close your damn eyes. And imagine what it would be like if the rules governing recusal were different, and because your girlfriend filed the original complaint in this case, you automatically had to recuse yourself."

"But that's ridiculous—that would never happ—"

"This is a thought experiment, Victoria. Get on board. Imagine that as soon as Dalton appealed the case, you were off it. How would it feel to listen to arguments from your living room via a live audio stream, not from your comfy chair behind the bench? Imagine hearing Genevieve arguing the case in a way that's disappointing to you, and there's nothing you can do about it. Imagine knowing that the other justices were debating the case behind closed doors, while you have no say in the matter."

Victoria's stomach churned and her neck itched.

"What would you have to say to Genevieve in that scenario?"

"God, I don't know," Victoria said, opening her eyes. "Everything. Nothing. I have no idea."

"And what she's giving up because of you—it doesn't stop with this same-sex parentage case. When was the last time the two of you spent the night at her place instead of yours?"

"I offered last night!"

Bethany raised her eyebrows, and Victoria knew she sounded defensive. "I can never find parking there."

"Bullshit. Take a cab. Or, I don't know, invest ten minutes of your time looking for parking so that you can be in her space, with her furniture and food and shower products."

"Has she said something to you?" Victoria asked, equal parts angry and embarrassed. How could Genevieve discuss their private life with someone else?

"See, this is the problem. Genevieve tries to talk to me, even while she feels guilty about it because she knows you'd have a problem with it, and she gets all twisted up, and I have to read between the lines and, really, it's not working. She needs someone to talk to about all the changes in her life—someone who isn't part of those changes."

"Like a therapist?"

"Lord knows I'd need a therapist if I were in a relationship with you. How can you be so smart and so dense at the same time? Like a friend, Victoria. If you're not sure what that is, look it up in the damn dictionary."

"Don't be insulting, Bethany."

"Please. It's one of the reasons Genevieve loves me. Which you would know if you ever paid attention."

"Let me get this straight." Victoria recrossed her legs. "Jesus, Bethany, what's with this awful chair? Are you intentionally trying to make guests uncomfortable?"

She laughed. "No one ever sits there. I promise I won't bite if you move to the couch."

The fabric was soft, the cushions enveloped her, and Victoria was instantly a thousand times more comfortable. "Am I supposed to apologize for the fact that you're her friend and not mine?"

"Doesn't it get exhausting having such a black-and-white world view? People can be friends with their girlfriend's friends. They should be, in fact."

"But wouldn't Genevieve get jealous?"

"Unless we have some kind of sexual tension that I've never picked up on before, I suspect not. But I'm her best friend. You're her girlfriend. She shouldn't have to choose between us."

"But you don't like me. Why would I want to spend more time with someone who doesn't like me? For that matter, why would I want Genevieve to spend time with you if all you're going to do is tell her I'm awful?"

"God, there are a dozen places I could go with that. First off, who the hell knows if I like you? I don't even know you. Maybe we'd be thick as thieves. But second, you have to trust her. Do you really think I could convince her to leave you if she didn't want to?"

"Does she want to? Are you trying to convince her to leave me?"

"Seriously? That's what you take from what I just said? You're a frigging judge—can't you recognize a hypothetical argument when you hear one?"

"Not when it comes to Genevieve."

"Why?"

Victoria retrieved her margarita from the table. The liquid in the glass looked like the color she imagined her cheeks were turning. She couldn't say it louder than a whisper, and she couldn't believe she was saying it out loud. "Because I spend every day afraid that she's going to leave."

Bethany took what Victoria could only assume was her first real breath of the evening. "That's an awful way to go through life. Has she given you any indication that she wants to?"

Victoria shook her head. "We've been arguing a lot, and I keep thinking she's going to just give up, but no."

"Victoria, darling, stop operating in your relationship like she's going to leave you at any moment. For one thing, you sound desperate, which is the least attractive quality I can think of. But more importantly, if you don't believe in this relationship, she'll stop believing in it too. It's unfair to ask her to have faith for the both of you."

"I'd never thought about it that way."

"It doesn't seem like you've thought of many things from her perspective."

"No, I have! I spend hours trying to imagine why the hell she's still here, what the hell she sees in me. There's no way she's forgiven me for walking away all those years ago. She says she has, but she can't have."

"Let's face it, Victoria. You're a control freak, to the point where you're even trying to control when and why your girlfriend's going to leave you. And, if you ask me, you haven't forgiven yourself. But don't put that on her. You two were kids. Kids do stupid shit."

"But I was so cruel. And she has brought it up again lately, that I ran away back then."

Bethany tucked one leg underneath her and rested her arm along the back of the couch. "Victoria Jane Willoughby, I can tell you in all honesty that Genevieve Fornier has forgiven you for being a shortsighted fool when you were twenty-four years old. If she's got problems with your relationship, it's not because of that, believe me. She's long past moved on from that bit of history. So now it's on you: are you going to be a shortsighted fool at forty-whatever-the-hell-you-are, or are you going to move on too?"

"I'm not very good at moving on."

"No kidding. Find a way."

"Bethany, if Genevieve isn't here or at home or at my place, where is she?"

Bethany dropped her hands and reached for her drink. "Beats me. Probably having a stiff drink somewhere."

Victoria finished her margarita and stood. "Yes, that's what I'm nervous about."

"The alcohol, or the other women at the bar?"

"Take your pick. I should go. Shall I put this in the dishwasher?" she asked, indicating the empty glass in her hand.

"Nah, leave it there. I'll take care of it later." Bethany rose and led her toward the door. "You know, this is the most you and I have ever said to each other. You're crazy, but not half as crazy as I pretend you are."

"Thanks, I think. You're a good listener. And questioner."

They reached the door, and Bethany paused in front of it, turning to face her. "So. Friends, then?" She held out her hand.

"You're a nut. But yes, friends." Victoria shook her hand as though sealing a business deal, and Bethany pulled her into a hug, engulfing her face in hair and Aqua Net.

"I'm sure you two will make up soon. And then maybe this time you can give me the sexy details instead of Genevieve."

Victoria pulled away in alarm. "She talks about sex with you?"

Laughing, Bethany opened the door. "Good-bye, Victoria. Drive safely."

She drove home, deep in thought, and before she knew it she was in her kitchen again, Genevieve's phone in her hand. She didn't remember much from the drive home, just the way her thoughts churned and churned. For perhaps the first time, she saw the appeal, and was grateful that Genevieve had a good friend in her life. It made her momentarily jealous before she remembered her brother and his wife—she had friends too, if only she'd open up to them.

Well, activity for another day. It was late, and she was going to bed, trusting that Genevieve would return in the morning and they would talk. And vowing to find new ways to let Genevieve take the lead in their relationship.

The next morning, she awoke to sunshine streaming through her window. Dreams in which she and Genevieve were in Paris, holding hands and kissing their way down the Champs-Élysées, filled her with warmth and contentment. For weeks, she'd been dreaming about work; it was ironic that the night Genevieve stormed out on her, she finally had happy dreams about her. Maybe Bethany's sage words from the night before had given her some comfort.

Putting on her glasses and heading into the kitchen for some coffee, she vowed to call Bethany and thank her. That seemed like what friends would do.

The coffee was brewing and she was rifling through the fridge, searching for yogurt, when Genevieve's phone, still resting on the kitchen island, beeped. She glanced at the screen, and her heart stopped.

PENELOPE SWEET: *I'm glad you stayed last night.*
You can keep the shirt—it looks better on you.

Her first instinct was to throw the phone across the room. Before she did something rash, she gently placed it on the counter, grabbed her coffee, and headed into the living room.

On her pristine, white couch, with her legs elegantly crossed, she sipped coffee because Genevieve preferred it to tea and, contrary to popular belief, she had made alterations to her life to accommodate her girlfriend's habits. Concessions that, it now seemed, were a waste of time.

Honestly, she couldn't even be surprised. This was exactly what she had been trying to say to Bethany the night before—Genevieve was gorgeous and had spent her adult life in and out of casual relationships. The idea that she would suddenly settle down with an uptight closet case was absurd. Getting involved with Genevieve… Well, Victoria was basically asking for this.

Unbidden, thoughts of Bethany came to her, and she was pretty sure she knew what Bethany would say to her right now: *Yes, Victoria, you basically asked for this when you didn't trust her. You worried so much about the other shoe dropping that you didn't leave her a lot of options.*

Well, she had lived without Genevieve for most of her life; surely she would be fine without her again.

It occurred to her that she had gone through about fifteen levels of assumptions and defense mechanisms, all before having finished a single cup of coffee. There *might* be a reasonable explanation.

But Chief Justice Kellen O'Neil wouldn't care one iota that Victoria's personal life might be falling apart. The justices' conference started in two hours, she still needed to shower, and there was a pile of briefs on her desk that she needed to glance at first.

On mornings when Genevieve was there, once she'd had her coffee, she left the cup on Victoria's table in the living room or the kitchen island or, really, anywhere other than the sink or dishwasher. Bethany, too, seemed not to care about errant drinking receptacles loitering about the house.

Fuck it, she thought. And when she left the mug on the coffee table, she didn't even use a coaster. *I can be relaxed.*

Turned out she couldn't leave the house without putting the mug in the dishwasher. Some personality traits were just too hard to change overnight. Or maybe ever.

She arrived in her private chambers with thirty minutes to prepare for the conference. The same-sex parentage case was the last one they'd hear until January, and they would be reviewing the arguments of all the cases so far this term.

Kellen's suit was wrinkled, Alistair had huge bags under his eyes, and even Michelle Lin looked drained. The judicial calendar wasn't unlike the academic one, and Victoria was reminded briefly of a bunch of undergraduates worn out at the end of the semester, trudging through a grueling finals period.

"We begin with the voting rights case," Kellen said. "Alistair, your thoughts."

"I still maintain that the Court made a grave error in 2013 when we overturned large portions of the Voting Rights Act. The arguments in this case put forth compelling reasons to reinstate the spirit of the original act, while avoiding some of the constitutional gray areas."

"I agree with Alistair," Jason said. "The Fourteenth Amendment issues here require us to intervene in state laws that put undue demands on would-be voters, especially minority voters. The number of polling places in minority-concentrated districts that have been closed since the 2013 decision came down is staggering."

"I see no evidence of actual harm here," Jaworski chimed in. "The plaintiffs have no cause to have filed, much less appealed, this case."

Michelle rolled her eyes. "Really, Anthony, you want to consider this on procedural grounds? This is a civil rights issue, and you know it. Hiding behind procedure is at best kicking the can down the road, and at worst a weak attempt to avoid grappling with the very real, very serious racism in this country."

"Racism? Really?" Matthew Smith, who was about the whitest man imaginable, was actually turning pink. "How dare you imply someone is a racist if they feel that the Constitution simply does not support the contradictory and even irresponsible demands that the Voting Rights Act put on select states? You're an artist, so let me put this in terms you can understand: style is substance. Procedure is content. We are required by our oaths to interpret the Constitution in all of its technicalities."

Victoria could practically hear Michelle's blood boil. "Our oaths? You're bringing up our oaths right now? Supporting and defending the Constitution requires us to use common sense, not use phrases like 'constitutional textualism' as reasons to avoid doing our jobs."

"Michelle," Kellen cut in, a hint of warning in his voice, "it's Ryan's turn to speak."

Ryan Jamison took his sweet time, and when he did finally open his mouth, nothing of substance came out. "I'm leaning toward restoring the VRA, but I'd like to read the opinion drafts once they're written before I choose which one to sign my name to."

It was Kellen's least favorite answer from him. Hell, it was everyone in the room's least favorite answer. Kellen sighed heavily. "Eliot?"

"As written, the original Voting Rights Act had constitutional problems and was an inconsistent piece of legislation. We have an opportunity here to rectify some of those problems, to, with surgical precision, issue a decision that offers the protections minority voters need while not discriminating against southern states."

The silence in the room was so thick it was almost palpable. Not one single justice would have predicted Eliot McKenzie would side with the liberals on this case, or speak eloquently about why.

When Kellen said, "Very well," no one in the room believed he meant it. "Victoria?"

The unenviable position of speaking last meant that she seldom had original arguments to contribute. Instead, she found herself saying words she had never expected to utter: "I agree with Eliot."

Kellen nodded gruffly. "Well, I don't. Matthew and Anthony, I assign myself the task of writing our position. Alistair, who's writing for your side?"

Alistair glanced at Victoria. They'd done more than discuss Victoria writing this opinion—she'd shown him drafts already. She nodded at him anyway, knowing what was coming.

"Eliot, I'd like to give this assignment to you," Alistair said.

It was the strategic choice. There was always a chance that a justice who voted in an unexpected way in conference would change his mind at the last minute. But if he wrote the decision, he was sure to agree with it. In other words, if the liberals wanted to keep Eliot, their best chance was to let him speak for them.

"I'd prefer not to, if that's all right, Alistair. I have my hands full with the estate tax decision, and frankly, I think this case is more suited to Victoria."

Just when she thought Eliot was done surprising them.

Consideration of their other cases proceeded much more predictably, and by lunch break, Victoria was yawning.

She ate a kale salad at her desk, reviewing the afternoon's cases. On her way back into the conference, she stopped by her secretary's desk.

"We're officially handling the majority decision on the voting rights case. Please let the clerks know that I'd like to meet about this as soon as the conference ends—we're going to need to coordinate a lot with Eliot's clerks."

"I'll e-mail them straight away," Lynn said.

Victoria turned to walk away.

"Oh, Justice Willoughby. I thought you should know that Genevieve Fornier called for you. I asked if she wanted to be transferred to your voicemail, but she declined."

She studied Lynn's face, but found no judgment or artifice there. "Thank you for letting me know," she said, cringing inwardly at the stiffness in her voice.

The afternoon dragged on, with benign disagreements here and there. The same-sex parentage case came up last, when all the justices were weary and ready for the weekend. No surprises as they moved around the table, and everyone's expectant eyes turned to Jamison when it was his turn.

"This case couldn't be more clear-cut," he said. "The Court should issue a sweeping decision that parental rights have nothing to do with gender, and we should require states to change birth certificates so that they ask for the two parents' names, not a mother and father."

If a pin dropped on that plush carpet, it would sound like a canon, it was so silent in the room. Jamison had never spoken so clearly and strongly on a case before.

It took O'Neill a moment to recover his voice. "Okay, then. Eliot?"

"I agree with Ryan," Eliot said, and he and Jamison shared a smile.

Victoria glanced at Kellen, who looked like he was ready to ask, "What the hell is happening?" Instead, he blinked and turned to her.

"Ditto," she said.

With a heavy sigh, Kellen asked, "Alistair, who's writing for your side?"

Alistair cleared his throat, clearly unsure how to answer. He glanced at Victoria, and she nodded at Jamison.

"Ryan," he said, "will you do the honors?"

"I'd be happy to," Ryan said.

"Right, then," Kellen said, gathering his papers quickly and standing. "Happy holidays, everyone. See you in January."

He was typically the first to arrive and the last to leave, so O'Neill's rapid departure left the rest of them staring at each other for a moment before they, too, collected their things and headed toward the door.

"Thanks, Victoria, for letting me write this," Jamison said softly as he held the door for her. "I know you would have loved to write this decision."

"Not at all, Ryan," she said. There was no way she was ever going to write it—she and Alistair had already agreed.

"Merry Christmas, Victoria," He held out his hand.

She shook it and smiled at him. "Merry Christmas, Ryan."

So the parentage case would be 6-3. Genevieve and Penelope would win their case.

Just thinking about their names together in the same sentence made her skin crawl.

She wasn't sure if this healthy margin of victory would make things better or worse between her and Genevieve, if there still was such a thing as the two of them. The case hadn't needed her vote—or her powers of persuasion—after all. She could have recused herself, Genevieve could have argued, and the result would have been, for all practical purposes, the same.

Holding her happiness at the decisive victory for gay rights against her anxiety about what would come next with Genevieve felt disorientating, to say the least.

CHAPTER 16

Sitting in her car staring at Tori's house was becoming a bad habit. Genevieve shivered against the winter chill seeping into the car, put on a brave face, and marched to the door.

Tori opened it shortly after she knocked and leaned against the doorjamb, a copy of Kellen's god-awful new book on US tax law tucked under her arm.

"Hi," Tori said.

"Um, hi." Genevieve drew it out, but Tori made no move to let her pass. "Uh, can I come inside?"

"I suppose. We have a lot to talk about." She reached into her pocket and pulled out Genevieve's phone. "Like, for example, why you spent the night at Penelope Sweet's house last night."

She casually tossed the phone to Genevieve, whose brain scrambled. She barely managed to grab the phone before it fell into the snow.

By the time she'd scrolled through the messages and found the one from Penelope, Tori had long since retreated inside. Chilled to the bone for multiple reasons, Genevieve trudged after her, kicking off her shoes just inside the door and frantically thinking of what to say.

Tori was huddled in the corner of the couch, a cup of tea resting on her legs. Genevieve sat down as close as she dared, given that she had no idea which direction this conversation would go.

"Tori, it's not what you think. Nothing happened between us. I slept on her couch, and she loaned me some clothes. That's all."

Tori turned and scrutinized her, and Genevieve suddenly felt naked. She tried to hold Tori's gaze but failed, and she was sure Tori saw the heat in her cheeks.

"I see," Tori said as if she'd just decided something, and Genevieve's heart thudded in her ears.

"What—what do you see? I just said nothing happened."

"Well, regardless, you went over there for a reason."

"You pissed me off, and I wanted to be with someone who...I felt like was on my side." It sounded unconvincing, even to her.

"Mm. I don't think you're telling the truth—to me or yourself."

"I—what's that supposed to mean?" Genevieve's face turned red for an entirely different reason. "Don't assume you know—"

"It's hard not to make assumptions when you disappear, sleep over at another woman's house, and then can't even look me in the eye when explaining why." Tori looked away, her eyes bright with tears.

Which somehow made Genevieve more angry than sympathetic. "Look, it's no secret that things between us haven't been great—"

"Here it comes. Just say it. I know you've been wanting to."

"You *know*? How the hell... God, if you've got it all figured out, I don't even need to be here for this relationship, do I? You can just imagine whatever version of me you want, make it your reality, and that's that."

Tori turned back to her, shoulders slumped. "You think I want you to cheat on me? To decide this relationship isn't worth it? I'm not worth it?"

"Look, you're the one who doubted this relationship from the start. Never introducing me to your friends, refusing to be seen with me in public—you never fully committed to me."

Tori stood slowly, as if it hurt her, walked to the fireplace she never used, and stared into its darkness. "Maybe we should take a break. Some time apart. To sort out what we want."

Taking a break—that was a ridiculous thing that couples did when they were too weak to call a spade a spade and just break up.

Well, maybe she wasn't that special after all, because she wasn't ready to call it quits yet, just like every other sap out there currently *taking a break* from their relationship.

"Sure. Yeah. A break."

She walked to the door, and Tori didn't stop her. The cold hit Genevieve's face like a wall, and the click of the door behind her echoed against the snow and the trees and the dark purple sky.

Genevieve stared at the steering wheel. She wanted to rage. Or cry. But nothing came.

Looking up, she saw that the window to Tori's bedroom had the curtains drawn, but a faint glow indicated that the lights were on. Maybe she was curled up in bed, on top of the comforter, shivering. Too angry and lost to climb under the sheets. Wondering how Genevieve could do this to her. Confirming all her suspicions that she'd never be enough.

Genevieve reversed out of the driveway, and the next thing she knew, she was home.

Her townhouse was dark and cold. She turned up the heat and clicked on all the lights in the living room and kitchen. The fridge held only condiments and an unopened bottle of chardonnay, in case Tori ever came by. A thin layer of dust topped a bottle of merlot, the only item in her tiny wine rack. The liquid made a satisfying sound as it gurgled into a glass, and it swelled around her insides. She wouldn't be able to drink her problems with Tori away, but drinking a lot this one night sounded perfect.

She found a truly awful movie on Lifetime, laughed at its oversentimentality, and eventually fell asleep on the couch.

Too-bright sunshine woke her up, and before standing she knew she'd be late to work, even though it was Saturday. Since taking over at HER, weekends had come to mean something a lot less fun for her. The team working Amelia's case would be spending the day in the conference room strategizing.

Her first glass of wine from the night before, barely touched, rested on her coffee table next to her phone, which she picked up and unlocked, wondering if Tori had sent her anything.

And then she remembered.

She couldn't say what exactly she was trying to achieve, but she texted her girlfriend:

> *Tori, nothing happened with Penelope. Like I said yesterday, I borrowed her shirt and crashed on her couch. I'm sorry for any doubt her text gave you.*

It was eight thirty, well past the time Tori normally rose from bed. She was probably already at the farmers' market, or else on her way there. Genevieve typed another message.

> *Regarding this "break," let's talk again in a couple of days.*

She stared at the screen for a long time, debating how to end it. Finally, because it was true and probably always would be, she wrote *I love you* and tapped *send*.

Well, she had work to do, and she wasn't about to wait around for a reply. The shower helped wash away a night spent on the couch.

At the intersection of U and 16th streets, her phone buzzed. She knew she shouldn't, but the light was red, and she picked up the phone to read Tori's reply.

> *A couple of days—sure. Let me know when you're ready, and we'll see if I am too.*

For crying out loud. Passive-aggressive much? Genevieve certainly hadn't intended to set up some kind of power play, but evidently she'd lost. Now it was on her to reach out next, with no guarantee of a meaningful response.

Karma probably thought she deserved it, what with almost seducing another woman and all.

Alone in the elevator on her way up to HER's offices, Genevieve punched the button with unnecessary force and sincerely hoped for their sakes that every single one of her staff had brought their A game today.

CHAPTER 17

Drink in hand, Victoria slowly walked the length of Alistair's library. As she read book titles, she noted with amusement the perfect alphabetical order to every bookcase.

The soft clink of plates and forks being loaded into the dishwasher down the hall faded when she noticed a first edition copy of Poe's *The Tell-Tale Heart*. The pages were brittle, framed by darker shades of tan on the edges. Turning them gently, she fell into Poe's darkness, where hidden fears that should be deeply buried were instead starkly exposed.

She was returning the book when Alistair's slightly uneven footsteps on the hardwood floor grew louder behind her.

"Well, what do you think of my little library?" He swept his hand toward the floor-to-ceiling bookcases, the wainscoting between each one sparkling with light from the delicate chandelier that hung from the ceiling. In the middle of the room, two benches with leather seats on top and books beneath called to her, and she sat.

"I installed these two pocket doors myself," Alistair said.

"It's amazing. Who did the woodwork?"

"I hired a contractor half my age, who seems immune to the effects of such backbreaking work."

"Well, he did a beautiful job."

Alistair sat down on the bench opposite her and swiveled his cocktail in its glass. "That's what you have to say? Nice woodwork?

What about the years and years I've spent curating such an impressive literary collection?"

"Alistair, this place is just like you—overwhelmingly sophisticated and impressive. And utterly impossible to do justice to."

"Oh, pshaw." He shrugged, but his eyes danced with happiness.

"You have a lot of Poe. Are you particularly interested in the gothic?"

"More the tragic. You'll notice Poe is situated in the same section as the ancient Greek tragedies. And Shakespeare."

"And *Wuthering Heights*? How are you defining tragedy?"

"The same way everyone else does. *Hamartia*."

Victoria rolled her eyes. "In English, if it wouldn't be too much trouble."

"A fatal flaw. A trait that should be someone's strength, but turns out to be his—or her—biggest weakness. A world where one's undoing comes from within. *Hamartia*."

"Thanks for the literature lecture. So, what's your fatal flaw?"

"I prefer to think of my life as a comedy populated with low characters whose biggest struggles in life involve miscommunication leading to pratfalls. Where there are lots of doors that constantly get opened and closed."

"So, *Molière*?"

"Precisely." He clinked his glass against hers and took a drink. "What about you, Victoria? What's your fatal flaw?"

"As if there were only one."

"Ah, but you see, Victoria, only *one* will actually be your downfall." His delivery was so deadpan that she almost snorted.

"I'm sure you meant to say that I'm not a deeply flawed human being and that I should stop being so hard on myself."

"You say potato…"

"Gee, thanks. I know where to turn if I ever need a pep talk."

"Well, really, Victoria, do you honestly believe your life is a classic tragedy? I've always viewed you as more of a Western. Or maybe steampunk."

"I can't believe you even know what steampunk is."

"Well, I confess that came from my daughter. She kept raving about this steampunk novel she was reading, so I looked it up after she left. Evidently it involves Victorian England and science fiction. And steam engines. I think I connected it to you because, well…" He waved his hand vaguely at her.

"Any chance you could finish that sentence?"

"Oh, the Victoria/Victorian thing. But then again, what's in a name?"

"Following conversations with you is like following directions when Genevieve's navigating."

"We were comparing your life to literary genres."

"Can I be a Jane Austen novel? I realize she's not an entire genre, exactly."

"Of course she is. And that's the point, Victoria—you can be anyone you want to be." He paused and scrutinized her for a moment. "Besides, I'm detecting distinct threads of pride *and* prejudice weaving in and out of your life."

Victoria made some kind of indistinct noise and turned her attention to her glass. "What do you call this again?"

"You mean the gin fizz or your transparent change of subject?"

"Genevieve and I might be breaking up."

The glass in Alistair's hand slipped, and he barely caught it. Maybe she'd hit him with too much truth at once. Gin had sloshed onto the back of his hand, which he wiped on his pants before clearing his throat. "And you think this why?"

"She spent the night at Penelo— another woman's place. And she left the next morning wearing this woman's clothes."

"That all seems circumstantial. Do you have any evidence? Have you accused her?"

"What is this, criminal court?" Victoria took a deep breath and tried unsuccessfully to prevent her shoulders from slumping. "She pled not guilty."

"Well, I for one have some reasonable doubt and am not prepared to convict her."

Victoria put her drink down on the bench and walked around the library, gazing at books without really seeing them. "My head's spinning enough already. I can't talk about this in terms of some third-party court case. It's personal."

"Of course. So, what are you going to do?" His tone softened, and she stopped her pacing to look at him, her arms hanging helplessly at her side.

"I don't know. When I confronted her about it, I acted like I wanted to end it, but I was bluffing."

"I guess you have to ask yourself how badly you want a relationship with her—what you're willing to give up, for one, and what you're willing to put up with from her."

"That all sounds so logical. I can't answer a single one of those things." She stared at her drink, but it offered no answers.

"Relationships are always work. This is the work you have to do now, it seems. If you two end up continuing, you'll have other work to do, I'm sure." He placed a hand on her shoulder. "It's work that never stops. I suppose that's what makes it so rewarding."

"I keep waiting for that part."

"Oh, you two have been together for a little while now. It can't all have been bad."

"The first ten months or so, we were still pretty closeted. Or, I was, I guess. I took her out to one dinner to woo her back after leaving her twenty years ago, and then once we were together, I kept finding excuses for us to eat at home rather than in public, or else reasons to be too busy to eat together at all. Between my fear of going out in public with my…girlfriend, and Genevieve's busy travel schedule, we saw each other every other weekend, maybe. It's made for a pretty prolonged honeymoon period, but reality has hit now."

"You two did lay pretty low last year. I think by the time we went into our winter recess I'd figured it out, but that's only because I know you. The other justices had no clue until that photo was suddenly everywhere."

"Since we've been outed, I don't really have an excuse for staying home with her, and I think she's starting to feel stifled by me. She's been delegating more travel responsibilities to her staff, so that there are more opportunities for us to spend time together, but we're not taking them. I think we're both trying to figure out what all this means."

She trailed her fingers across some books and pictured Genevieve's smile. "Remember when we decided the gay marriage case? Not two years ago—last year's, when it became legal everywhere? She stormed over to the Court and cornered me as I was leaving the building from the justices' entrance around back. She kissed me, right in front of all the people who had gathered outside, who had cameras and cell phones. Turns out no one cared—they were all too busy celebrating to notice us. I think I took it as a sign, and when we were in France the next week, I tried to be more open. Hence the picture of us kissing on the bridge."

"Almost kissing."

Victoria raised her eyebrows. "And that detail matters why?"

"Just makes for a better photo."

Placing his glass next to hers, he walked over and put his hands on her shoulders. "I don't have any advice for you, Victoria. All I can say is that there aren't clear or right answers when it comes to love. There are choices you make—and choices you decide not to make. And I'll tell you one thing—you regret the choices you don't make."

His eyes held kindness, tinged with worry. And his whole face wore the strain of a long day caring for an ailing partner and a hot mess of a friend.

Victoria sighed. "I don't even know what that means."

"It means don't run away if she's what you want."

After gathering their glasses and returning them to the kitchen, Alistair walked her to the door, and they shared a long hug.

Later that night, after a little more scotch, Victoria climbed under the covers. Alistair was right—she wasn't a runner. She would fight for what she wanted.

Tomorrow, she would call Genevieve. Smooth things over. Figure out what to do next.

She slept soundly for the first time in weeks.

CHAPTER 18

It had been three days since she and Tori had agreed to take a break. Three days in which Genevieve snapped at her staff and gave a few off-her-game interviews. She toyed with the phone in her hand, wondering whether or not she was ready to call Tori.

Then, on her way home from the gym, her phone rang, and Tori's name lit up the screen. If she screened, then the ball would be in her court to call back again, and, well, fuck it.

"Hi."

"Hi, Genevieve."

The ensuing pause felt so thick with doubt that it couldn't be coming just from her. Considering it was Tori who called, Genevieve didn't think it was her responsibility to speak next. But as the pause lengthened, she caved first—which felt like the story of their entire relationship. "Do you want to get together and talk?"

Tori cleared her throat. "Yes. I bought a bottle of that Chilean pinot noir you love so much, and I was going to make you tacos."

It was sweet, how food was love in Tori's world. Tori, who hated tacos but knew they were Genevieve's favorite.

Genevieve swallowed. "That's really—thanks, Tori. But I'd rather go out. There's a new wine bar in my neighborhood that I really like. I'll text you the directions. Thirty minutes?"

She could almost see the way Tori's face fell. "Yes, of course. Let's make it forty-five, just to be safe."

Genevieve charitably chose to believe that Tori just couldn't get ready that quickly, rather than viewing the timing as yet another power play. As she stood in the doorway to her closet, she wondered what one wore on a date that might very well end in a breakup.

She chose a pair of jeans and a relatively boring sweater, which she spiced up with a necklace. With her purse and keys in hand, she walked the three blocks to Ambrosia in her favorite pea coat and boots and sat down at the small table in the corner. She ordered a flight of reds to drink while she waited.

The first and third wines danced across her tongue, but the second reminded her of chewing leather. The fourth swelled pleasantly in her mouth until her taste buds felt like they were soaring, and she ordered a full glass of it. It arrived at the same time Tori did.

Her first impulse was to stand and kiss Tori, but instead she waved at the waiter.

If Tori was put off by her less than warm welcome, she hid it well. "This place is cute. How long has it been open?"

The waiter came by with a menu, but Tori simply said, "I'll have a glass of whatever cabernet you recommend." He nodded and left them alone, staring at each other with tense shoulders. Tori's foot was tapping.

"Uh, I think it's been open for three weeks or so. The word hasn't gotten around just yet, so it's still pretty quiet. I'll be sad when it's packed every night, but I'm sure it's headed in that direction."

Tori nodded and they sat in uncomfortable silence until the server arrived with her wine. "So, there's really nothing between you and Penelope?"

"Penelope's not the issue here. Not really. We have other problems."

Tori slid the glass away and sat with her hands in her lap. "Tell me. Help me understand."

Genevieve took a healthy drink of absolutely delicious wine and tried to figure out how to explain it. "I feel like it's the Tori show, and I just make cameos here and there."

"Well," Tori adjusted her glasses. "Don't hold back or anything."

"I'm just being honest. This doesn't feel like an equal partnership, and I don't want to settle for anything less."

"I wouldn't want you to. Believe it or not, Genevieve, your happiness is very important to me." Her voice cracked on *happiness*, and Genevieve willed her heavy eyes not to leak.

"Likewise. And I can tell you're not happy either. I think… Maybe we were in love with the idea of us."

If Tori was fighting a similar battle with her eyes, she was losing; they glistened in the dimly lit bar. "Don't. Don't you dare belittle this. I'm in love with you. I might not have figured out how to show you just how much, but that doesn't mean I don't feel it."

It was Genevieve's turn to look away, and she studied the placemats made of old wine corks. "We used to be really happy. We used to have fun together."

"That's a lot of past-tense language. Is that where we are now? The past?"

Genevieve thought about months of feeling sidelined in her own relationship. About how she and Tori still hadn't seemed to find a comfortable rhythm after over a year of dating. Her night with Penelope had been both validating and thrilling.

She hadn't expected to say it, but at that moment, it seemed the only thing she could say: "Yeah. That's where we are." She picked at her napkin while she waited for Tori's reaction.

Finally, Tori put shaking hands around her wine glass. "So that's it, then? We're through?"

"We're through," Genevieve said, feeling awful and sort of liberated at the same time.

"You're making a mistake. You're every bit as in love with me as I am with you."

"Maybe. But I'm also tired." Genevieve rubbed her face with both hands.

"The great Genevieve Fornier. Warrior of gay people everywhere. Too tired to fight for the woman she loves."

"Why should it be a fight?" Genevieve pushed her shoulders back against her chair.

Tori leaned across the table toward her. "I can't believe you. I've loved you forever. I know we're not easy. But I also know there's no one out there for me besides you. And I know you'll regret this."

"Maybe. Maybe I'd regret staying even more."

"Fine. I won't grovel." She squared her shoulders, reached into her purse and extracted some cash, which she deposited on the table. "I love you, Genevieve Fornier. And I hope you wake up soon."

She moved to walk past Genevieve toward the door, then stopped and rested her trembling hand on Genevieve's shoulder. "I'll be in touch about when you can come by and collect your things."

She placed a kiss on Genevieve's cheek, pressure so soft that Genevieve might have imagined it. Then Tori was gone.

Alone with the consequences of her decision, Genevieve finished her wine and Tori's. Bethany would gladly comfort her if she called, but she wasn't ready for that. She wasn't ready to talk or justify herself. Although she'd expected to feel relief, and feared feeling regret, she mostly felt anger. Why couldn't Tori have given just a little bit more? Why couldn't she have been more reasonable, more willing to meet her halfway? Instead, Tori lived with fear and internalized homophobia, with deeply ingrained habits that she showed zero inclination to change, and with an intransigence that sucked the air out of the room. And screw her for making those qualities seem appealing from the outside, when the reality was anything but.

As she walked home alone, Genevieve paid particular attention to her empty hands, which had only once held Tori's when they walked down the street together. She was leaving the bar with exactly what she'd gone in with.

And she was going to learn to be just fine with nothing.

The evening of the State of the Union, Genevieve watched from the chair in Tori's room while she did her hair and makeup. She chose a charcoal skirt suit, and Genevieve bit back a comment about the weather being below freezing and pants being more practical. She toyed with the drawstring of her sweatpants and enjoyed feeling comfortable while Tori tucked in her blouse.

She tried not to watch as Tori sat on the bed and worked black stockings up her legs. After situating earrings in her delicate, perfect ears, Tori slid on a pair of black stiletto pumps and was good to go.

They stared at each other, a sea of unsaid things ebbing and flowing between them. Finally, Tori gave Genevieve an entirely fake smile and asked, "Am I camera ready?"

"You look the same way you do every time you to go work. The height of class."

"There aren't usually cameras when I go to work."

"Well, just remember to keep a neutral face the entire time, because you know the moment you itch your nose or something, the cameras will turn right toward you."

"Yes. That's our job—sit there and don't clap at anything. Because we're nonpartisan. How silly."

"Well, get Jamison drunk at this preparty of yours, and see if he breaks character during the speech."

"I'll see what I can do."

It was probably the most civil conversation they'd had in a long time. Maybe it was a sign. Maybe they were better off as friends—and could actually be friends, at some point.

Who was she kidding—Victoria Willoughby didn't really have friends. She had close relationships with family, maybe, but she didn't do casual in any sense. And there was too much history between them for them to be…close without falling into old habits.

Tucking her hair behind her ear, Genevieve stood and stepped away from the chair. "Is the alarm code still the same?"

"No, I've changed it again. Here, I'll write it down for you." A quick trip to her nightstand, and she returned with a notecard bearing five numbers. Her fingers shook slightly during the handoff. "Help yourself to anything in the fridge."

"Thanks, I'll be fine. And I'll be…out of your hair by the time you get back."

If Genevieve had punched her in the gut, Tori couldn't look more winded. Ever the paragon of composure, she shook it off immediately.

"That's fine," she said, but her voice wavered slightly.

Genevieve nodded, unsure of the protocol in this particular situation. Should they hug it out? Kiss good-bye, even? They seemed to have mastered the fine art of standing there awkwardly.

She was on the verge of taking a step toward Tori when the doorbell rang. "That'll be my car."

"I'm glad. I'll walk you downstairs."

At the front hall closet, Victoria pulled out two hangers, one with her coat, and one bearing her Supreme Court robe, with the scarf tied neatly around the top. "Might as well put this on now, since it's so cold out."

Helping Tori into her robe and coat felt gallant in a way that made Genevieve uncomfortable, but less uncomfortable than standing there doing nothing. When Tori opened the door, a Court police officer was on the other side, and beyond him a black SUV idled. Another officer waited by the rear passenger door.

"How many agents do you get? This is like the aftermath of—"

"Don't even say it," Tori cut in. "This is standard—I've had this many officers accompany me to the State of the Union every year. Security to get into the chamber is... Well, this and inauguration are the biggest security events of the year for them, or so I've been told. After our little preparty at Kellen's house, all the justices will be driven to the chambers in individual cars with three officers on each of us."

"So. Break a leg? Or do I say something else?"

"Break a leg works."

Genevieve stole a glance at the officer standing mere feet from them, grateful for an excuse not to prolong their good-bye. "Okay, well."

"Well, I'm off. I'll see you..."

"Yeah. Bye. Have fun tonight."

They stood there staring at each other, clearly both wanting to say more, before Tori gave a perfunctory nod to Genevieve, turned toward the car and the officer, and closed the door.

Watching through the window, Genevieve waited until the dark SUV had pulled away, before she pulled on her sneakers and trudged out to her car to grab a few flattened boxes.

Once she'd dragged the boxes into the living room, she opened the cabinet doors to reveal Tori's seldom-used television and clicked it to CNN, which was basically doing a red-carpet show for the State of the Union. It was all so ridiculous, but also kind of thrilling.

One by one, she taped the boxes into shape. Okay, she had stuff in the bedroom, the bathroom, and the office. And then it was probably just little things she'd left here and there, much to Tori's annoyance, surely.

God, why was everything about Tori so hard?

She found her purse where she'd dumped it on the first step of Tori's stairs, located her phone, and called Bethany.

"Sweetpea! Why aren't you glued to your TV like the rest of Washington? Well, all of us B-listers who aren't invited to the big dance, anyway."

"I'm using this time while Tori's…occupied to get my crap out of her house."

"Well, you can't do that alone. I'll be right over."

Genevieve relayed the address before hanging up and settling back into the couch.

CHAPTER 19

Schmoozing at Kellen's felt like being in the smoking room of an old boys' club. The male justices were all drinking scotch and laughing together, while she and Michelle stood on the side of the room, nursing wine. In his finished basement, Kellen had what he called a "drinking room," a cozy, windowless space that smelled vaguely like a tap room. Three dark walls held paintings of vineyards, and through the fourth, glass wall, a temperature-controlled wine cellar contained hundreds of dusty, unopened bottles. Kellen had selected a Château Kirwan, which Victoria had actually heard of, since she and Genevieve had toured the Bordeaux region the previous summer.

"Why didn't we do this last year?" Victoria asked Michelle, swirling the wine around in her glass.

"Something about Kellen giving up alcohol while they changed his blood-pressure medicine. God. Every now and then, don't you just stop and think about the age differences between all of us?"

"I know. Did *everyone* their age watch *Bonanza*?"

"Seems like it," Michelle said. "You and I should establish common ground so we can make TV references none of them understand."

Victoria was debating whether or not to confess that she preferred reading when her name boomed out behind her.

"Get over here, Willoughby," Alistair called. "Jamison has a question for you."

"Wow, how many have they had?" Michelle whispered.

"Scotch goes to Alistair's head."

They joined the circle, Victoria next to Alistair, just as Kellen drifted away to the far corner of the room and made a phone call. Victoria tried not to take his disappearance personally.

"Scotch, Victoria?" Alistair clapped her on the back.

"I'm fine with wine, thanks. What kind of shenanigans are you gentlemen getting up to?"

"Oh, the usual," Alistair answered. "Go on, Ryan. You wanted to ask Victoria something, right?"

If possible, Jamison looked embarrassed. But since he'd so rarely shown emotion, she might be misinterpreting it.

He rubbed the back of his neck. "Um, I was wondering… well… I have a niece, see. In high school. And she's gay. She saw Genevieve on television once, and she's been dying to meet her. Wants to work for a civil rights organization when she gets older. Of course, she's fifteen, so she'll end up changing her mind a dozen times or so, and who knows? But would it be okay if I gave her Genevieve's phone number? Or if I gave you my niece's to pass on to Genevieve?"

Nothing like having your breakup thrown right in your face. Of course his niece would want to meet Genevieve, not her. What was a Supreme Court justice next to a charismatic, gorgeous attorney who had reporters eating out of the palm of her hand?

Tori squared her shoulders. "Sure, Ryan. Of course I'll give you Genevieve's number. I can't speak for her, but I suspect she'll be very flattered and happy to talk with your niece."

Jamison took his cell out of his pocket, unlocked it, and handed it to Victoria. As she programmed in her ex-girlfriend's number, she wondered how long she'd have it memorized.

Probably forever. With a quiet sigh, she returned the phone.

"Okay, I want to know who's read Senator Hick's latest book. Is that guy gunning for a spot on the bench or what?" Matthew Smith said.

"He'll never get it," Eliot McKenzie said. "I doubt there'll be an opening on the bench for the rest of Obama's term, and there's no way a conservative will nominate him."

Victoria exchanged a silent look with Alistair but said nothing.

"He's too liberal for Obama to nominate, even if there was a vacancy," said Anthony Jaworski. "Barack knows that the Senate would never confirm someone that liberal."

"Ah, but there's where you're wrong," McKenzie said. "The Senate won't stonewall one of their own. They're a proud group. I think that's why he thinks he can get away with such a brazen public play for the bench."

"So, is this what you all do in your spare time? Debate potential justices?" Victoria asked.

"We also aren't above gossiping about appellate judges," Smith said. "Evidently Carroway, on the third circuit, fell asleep on the bench last week."

"You're kidding," said Jaworski. "That's extremely unprofessional. Is he going to be admonished in some way?"

McKenzie laughed. "Admonished by who? Us? I've got better things to do."

"See, this is exactly why what we do is so important," Victoria said. "Because it matters what happens once, in a live courtroom, where people come together in the search for the most just outcome," Victoria said.

"Well, Victoria Willoughby, I would have thought we'd scared that idealism away by now." Smith grinned at her.

"Where's the fun in that?" she said, offering up her glass, which he toasted.

"Speaking of fun, I wanted to talk to you all about Kellen's birthday," Alistair said. "He turns eighty next month, and I'd like to surprise him with some kind of outing."

"Should we really be surprising an eighty-year-old?" Jaworski said. "What if we can't resuscitate him?"

"I'll put the paramedics on standby," Alistair responded, dryly. "You do know I'm a year older than he is, right?"

Jaworski squinted at him. "You don't look a day over seventy-eight. Anyway, Kellen's been talking about an exhibit at the Natural History Museum on the evolution of nautical… I don't know. On boats. He seems really excited about it. We could all go together, and then take him out to dinner."

"A museum? Shouldn't we do something a little less…playing to type?" McKenzie asked.

"I like boats. I'm in," said Smith. "Besides, we're boring legal scholars. Might as well embrace that our idea of a good time is a museum."

"Well, it doesn't really matter if it's our idea of a good time—what matters is if Kellen will be happy," Victoria said. "If he'll enjoy it, then I'm in. And I know a great French bistro in Georgetown that we could go to afterward. It's small enough that we could probably buy out the few other tables and have the place to ourselves."

"That will make the Court police very happy," Alistair said. "I'll handle the museum—I happen to be friends with the executive director, and I suspect he can get us in after hours so we won't have to fight the crowds and security will be easier. We can do a late dinner, in that case—maybe at nine. Victoria, you'll take care of the restaurant?"

Victoria nodded. "When are we doing this?"

"I spoke with Kellen's wife when I first arrived. Let's do the day before his birthday and let her spend the actual day with him alone."

"Sounds like a plan," Victoria said.

"Victoria, you're empty, and so am I," Smith said. "Shall we?" He indicated the bar, where a wine decanter and various liquor bottles awaited them.

As soon as they'd refilled their glasses, Kellen hung up and called for everyone's attention.

"They'd like us in our seats in twenty minutes, so we should wrap up and head to our cars. I know you've all done this before, but it's my duty to remind you that we do not take sides in partisan issues, and it is therefore inappropriate for us to clap or smile at policy agendas that we find to our liking."

"Blank face? I think I can handle that," Jamison said, and they all laughed. *Where did this sudden personality come from?*

"Thank you all for coming over this evening." Kellen raised his glass. "To a great group of colleagues, and a great group of friends!"

A chorus of "hear, hear" filled the room, and Victoria and Smith clinked glasses again. "Bottoms up?" He drained his scotch.

"I don't think I can chug wine," Victoria said, but she took a very healthy gulp.

Smith took her glass and put it on the bar next to his before offering her his arm. "May I escort you to your car?"

Her chest felt warm, and her throat tingled a little from the wine. Something about sliding her arm through her colleague's made her think of Genevieve in her house, packing. She shook her head, feeling a little hazy. "We should get a drink some time, Matthew."

When he smiled down at her, she was reminded that he was, hands down, the most handsome man on the bench. Tall, blond hair, blue eyes—he looked like a Disney prince at fifty. As they exited Kellen's drinking room, they must have looked like quite a striking couple, at least in a very classical sense. If only things were that easy.

After Smith helped her get settled into an SUV and closed the door, quiet and loneliness replaced the warm frivolity of Kellen's drinking room. The driver turned on a playful jazz station, but the bright music hardly permeated the darkness of the black leather seats.

To take her mind off depressing thoughts, she pulled up the number for the French bistro in Georgetown and reserved the restaurant for Kellen's birthday gathering. The fee for reserving the entire restaurant was cheaper than she'd expected it to be. She also sent an e-mail to Pollard with the details. He'd want to prepare security measures since all nine justices would be together for the evening.

As the cars pulled up in front of the building where the House of Representatives was hosting the president, she hit *send* on her e-mail to Pollard. Looking out the window, she was momentarily stunned by how much worse the weather had gotten during the drive. Driving snow was pelting the ground, and visibility was so bad she couldn't see the building.

After pulling on her hood and buttoning her coat, she slung her bag over her shoulder and held her breath, bracing for the sting of cold air that was about to hit her face. An officer opened the door for her, and she gasped at the piercing snow that bit her cheeks. But by the time she was fully upright, a second officer had an umbrella opened for her, and her trip to the door was mercifully brief.

The din of the chamber replaced the whistling of the snow, and before she knew it, Matthew Smith was beside her. "That scotch made me pretty sleepy. Elbow me if I start to nod off, okay?"

She smiled at him. "If you promise to return the favor."

"Deal."

As the justices waited outside the door, watching staffers bustle to and fro in the hallway, the president's cabinet entered behind them. Victoria waved at the secretary of labor, who had gone to law school with her, right before the sergeant at arms announced the chief justice and associate justices of the United States Supreme Court.

The nine of them filed into their seats in order of seniority. Wait, no. There were only eight. Victoria counted again, but Alistair was absent. Once they were standing in front of their seats and the sergeant at arms was announcing the cabinet, turning the attention of the cameras elsewhere, Victoria squeezed past her colleagues until she was next to Kellen.

"Where's Alistair?" she asked softly.

He leaned close to her and whispered in her ear, "He got a call and had to go. His wife."

Victoria pulled away, and they shared a sorrowful look. She was pretty sure the two of them were the only justices Alistair had told.

Kellen leaned in again. "I phoned the White House, and the chief of staff's office has made arrangements to fill his seat. It's all theater tonight, you know."

She nodded and patted his arm before returning to her seat.

After ten minutes of schmoozing with some of the cabinet who were seated behind her, the sergeant at arms announced the president, and the entire chamber stood and applauded. She took advantage of the one moment she could show real emotion and clapped enthusiastically for the man who had nominated her to the bench.

CHAPTER 20

On the television, Dana Bash and Anderson Cooper were discussing Obama's legacy, and making predictions about his policy agenda for the year.

Twenty minutes later, when Bethany knocked on the door, Genevieve was in the same position, riveted by the pundits who so often infuriated her. Sometimes she found herself frustrated by the sensationalism and oversimplification of their coverage. Sometimes she just had to get on their train and enjoy the ride.

She opened the door to find a ginormous puffy coat, layers upon layers of scarves, and bright-red mittens. From somewhere under all those layers, Bethany's voice sang, "Let me in, will you? It's worse than the North Pole out here!"

Standing aside so Bethany could waddle in, Genevieve closed the door and watched as a pile of winter insulation grew and grew on Tori's floor. "How did you even fit in your car?"

After peeling off the last layer, Bethany stood there in a turtleneck sweater and jeans, her hands on her hips. "I'm quite petite, you know."

"Yes, but that coat must have feathers from two hundred geese."

"Well, at least it's not fur," Bethany huffed before walking into the living room to survey her surroundings. "So. This is where the great Victoria Willoughby hangs her hat. Neat as a pin and no personality. No surprises there."

"Oh, come on. She's not that bad," Genevieve said, plopping down on the couch.

The look Bethany gave her could have curdled new milk. "All right, G-Spot. Let's get clear on something: am I here to make you feel better about your choice by insulting your ex-girlfriend, or am I supposed to help you wallow in your self-pity by reminding you of everything you're giving up?"

"There has to be another option."

"We could play State of the Union drinking games!" Bethany pulled a flask out of her back pocket. "I thought the evening called for whiskey."

"Oh Lord. Do you carry booze with you everywhere you go?"

"Only into the lion's den. Ooh, is Anderson Cooper covering this?" Bethany clapped her hands and bounced on the couch cushion next to Genevieve like a little puppy.

Torn between rolling her eyes and laughing, Genevieve asked, "When did you start having a thing for gay guys?"

"I have a thing for hot guys. Hot, smart, silver-fox guys."

"So, we're watching the preshow instead of packing?"

Bethany put her foot in a box and moved it closer to the couch before dropping a few throw pillows into it. "Packed?"

"Those aren't mine."

"Well, they're nice. Nicer than yours. Maybe she won't notice?"

"Tori, not notice something amiss in her house? God, that's the whole reason I'm getting out of here in the first place."

"Fine." She returned the pillows to the couch. "I'm good at multitasking. Shall we start upstairs?" Pointing the remote at the television, she cranked the volume until surely, the politicians in the House chamber could hear their own voices echoing back to them from Tori's TV eight miles away. A look of supreme satisfaction on her face, Bethany grabbed two boxes and headed upstairs.

Well, what was she expecting when she called Bethany? She grabbed the other one and followed.

When she entered Tori's bedroom, she ran smack into a Bethany statue in the doorway.

"How is this anyone's bedroom? I mean, who lives like this?" Bethany dropped the boxes but continued to gape at the formal bedroom.

The antique bed frame matched the long, low dresser, the two lingerie stands, and a nightstand. A chair upholstered with a floral print and a round table formed a sitting area in one corner, and a dressing table and chair occupied the other.

"Seriously, does she actually use that dressing table?"

Placing her box on the smartly made bed, Genevieve strode to the closet to begin the unsavory task of vacating Tori's life. "It's actually really handy. The lighting there is good, and she's got this nice system of organization for all her products."

Three suits, half a dozen blouses and dress pants, and four or five dresses. It wasn't much to show for an eighteen-month relationship, thanks to her travel schedule and her discomfort with the idea of really moving in.

When Genevieve emerged from the closet, hangers dangling from her hands, Bethany was sitting at the dressing table dabbing perfume on her neck.

"Fancy lady, that Victoria." Investigating various lipsticks, she selected one, applied it, and smacked her lips. "Well, how do I look?"

"More understated than usual. I think you need something bolder for your coloring."

"Nonsense. You're only saying that because that's how you always see me. I could do understated."

"Doubt you'd want to, though."

Bethany turned and gasped. "Genevieve! You aren't planning on putting your suits in a box, are you? Didn't you bring a garment bag?"

Genevieve shrugged. "It would have made more sense to bring empty suitcases than empty boxes, but, alas, this is what I'm stuck with."

"Well, lucky for you I always carry a spare garment bag. Be back in a jiffy!"

By the time Bethany had returned, Genevieve had filled a box with products, makeup, a flat iron and hairdryer, and the various parts of her electric toothbrush. High heels and boots left very little room in a second box.

"What took you so long?"

"Anderson Cooper was recapping some of the highlights from Obama's previous State of the Unions."

"Yeah, I heard all the way up here. He walks into the chamber in ten minutes?"

"If the little countdown on CNN is to be believed."

"We can finish in here by then, and do the downstairs while we watch. And listen at a reasonable volume."

"I'm on the suits."

Genevieve returned to the closet for a stack of sweaters, which went into the final box. One final trip to the closet confirmed she had extracted all of her clothes. She spun around, taking in the sight of Tori's suits, her dresses, her blouses and pants, organized by type and color, before running her hands down the sleeve of the velvet blazer Tori had been wearing when the Pont Saint-Bénézet bridge photo had been taken, when she'd felt carefree enough to kiss in public.

"No time for reminiscing, darling! I don't want to miss all the handshaking before the speech."

With the boxes closed, taped, and stacked by the front door, and the garment bag hanging in the front hall closet, they settled back into the living room couch. The boring coverage of who was in the room continued, and the clock by the crawler at the bottom of the screen put Obama's entrance at four minutes.

"So, Hot Spot, who's next?" Bethany asked.

"Next?"

"Yeah, who have you got your sights set on? Who's going to be your rebound girl? Who's going to make you remember what it's like to be fun?"

"Jesus, Bethie, we're sitting in Tori's living room. I can't talk about this here. It's creepy."

"Well, you have to talk about it somewhere. You've been mopey forever. Time to buck up, buttercup. I know how you operate— there's got to be someone who's caught your eye already."

"I—well—there is kind of someone." Just saying those words out loud felt like a betrayal, never mind that she was saying them while sitting on Tori's couch.

Bethany clapped Genevieve on the shoulder. "Of course there is. Who is she, what's she like, and when do I get to meet her?"

"Hold on, Bethie. It's not like I'm moving in with her tomorrow."

"Why not—isn't that what you lesbians do?"

Genevieve rolled her eyes. "It's Penelope Sweet, the new—"

"The new executive director of NCLR, I know. Wow, Genevieve. You don't mess around."

The irony of that statement was almost too much, and Genevieve laughed. "I like her… She's got fire. She's—"

Bethany's squeal cut her off just in time to watch Obama's grand entrance. The chamber erupted in applause, and the president shook hands with politicians, dignitaries, and unfamiliar people who were probably wealthy donors, as he made his way to the chamber.

"Hey, as a prominent gay rights leader, how come you weren't invited?" she asked.

"It's not a very big room, and I'm not that important."

The camera switched to a zoomed-out view of the whole chamber, and her eyes were immediately drawn to the pocket of black justices' robes in a sea of more colorful suits and shirts. Tori's huge, enthusiastic smile for the president seemed to light up the chamber—at least as far as Genevieve was concerned.

Get it out now, sweetheart, before you have to sit there stoically and pretend you don't care.

They watched the standing ovation at the end of the speech, and when CNN cut to their pundits, commencing hours of commentary, they gathered boxes and loaded Genevieve's car.

After the last trip, Bethany clicked off the television. Genevieve turned off the lights, and in the darkness, she set the alarm and closed the door on a house that had given her happiness and even more frustration.

CHAPTER 21

Genevieve boarded the plane for Michigan loaded with binders and her laptop. Grateful for HER's policy that its executives always fly business class, she used the extra space to spread open her binder, typing notes as she read. Arguments for summary judgment in Amelia's case were tomorrow. If she wasn't on top of her game, the other side could get her case dismissed before arguments on the actual substance of the matter even began.

She reclined her seat and began by reading the other side's briefs to the court. After she read through the first draft of her arguments, she moved paragraphs around, deleted one entire argument thread, and added another. Satisfied—at least for now—she turned to another binder and began reviewing similar cases and decisions. Identifying each argument against her, she typed a bullet-pointed list and interspersed how she would respond if the judge or opposing side raised that point.

After she deplaned, she sent her notes to Jamie and Penelope with a request to e-mail feedback on her proposed responses. Because she was doing so much travel on this trip, HER had hired her a driver, who took her to a hotel. By the time she'd checked in and settled into her room, both Jamie and Penelope had replied. Jamie wanted her to respond slightly differently to the slippery slope issue, and Penelope tweaked her wording about gender dysphoria.

She read cases about inmates and health care until well past midnight and slept fitfully, her dreams flitting between being imprisoned herself and her client having a total breakdown while she waited for a resolution in her case. It was a relief when her alarm finally gave her permission to wake up. She trudged to the shower and stood under the spray longer than she should have.

Maybe Penelope and Jamie had a point. Maybe she was taking on too much, trying to manage HER *and* litigate cases herself. Even with the addition of an executive director, she was still doing the job of multiple people, and it was taking a toll.

Jamie managed the organization's caseload and oversaw litigation strategies but seldom stood up in court to deliver arguments and field questions. Penelope had hired a litigation manager as soon as she took the helm of NCLR. Apart from taking on Genevieve's case, she confined her responsibilities to overseeing personnel and fundraising. As a non-profit, NCLR's books were somewhat public, and Genevieve had looked up their numbers a few weeks ago; with Penelope's charisma, the organization had never had so much money coming in, and it had significantly expanded its number of active cases.

HER, meanwhile, seemed stuck in a rut. Maybe Genevieve was being overly self-critical, but the impact of her leadership seemed lackluster to her—on the organization's budget, its caseload, and its national profile.

At some point she might need to choose between an administrative position and a litigation one. Would she rather be in charge of a lot of people and responsible for boring things like expense reports, or would she rather stride around a courtroom delivering impassioned arguments? Put in those terms, it felt like the difference between being the talent and the talent agent.

Well, that was a question for another day. She felt good in her suit, and whatever she decided about her career, she definitely looked the part of an attorney. She slid on her trench coat, picked up her briefcase, and headed to court.

Typically she met her client beforehand, and they entered the courtroom together. It was a ritual she missed when she walked in alone and sat at one of the attorneys' tables waiting for a prison guard to escort in Amelia. Theirs was the first hearing that day, and the room was virtually empty. As their arguments proceeded, attorneys and clients for other matters would trickle in.

When Amelia entered from a side door, her eyes darted to and fro nervously until she spotted Genevieve. Her shoulders dropped a little of their tension, but as she sat down next to Genevieve her leg immediately began bouncing up and down, rattling her shackles. Genevieve reached out and gently stilled her knee, hyperaware of the prison guard seated directly behind them.

"Relax. Take a deep breath. Try not to let anyone else see that you're nervous."

"Easy for you to say. Last time I was here, they threw me in the slammer. This place gives me the creeps. And they're gonna ask me really personal questions. Questions that I don't want to talk about in public."

"Not today, Amelia. Today is just procedural. In fact, most clients don't even come to summary judgment hearings, but I thought you'd like a chance to leave the yard for a bit."

Amelia nodded as her leg started bouncing again, and Genevieve gave up trying to set her at ease.

Opposing counsel entered and sat down at the other table, nodding in Genevieve's direction. Judge Reagan Hart came in, and they all stood, waited, and then sat down again, reminding Genevieve, as always, of going to church when she was a child.

The judge banged her gavel. "Up next, case number 56324, *Garcia v. Michigan*, hearing on summary judgment. Ms. Fornier, please."

"Your Honor," Genevieve said, standing. "The defense has moved to have this case dismissed because they say it has no legal merit. We submit that there is a history of animus against transgender residents of the state, and the other side is more concerned with its budget and image than with giving my client her rights under the law. When the state incarcerates one if its residents, it takes responsibility for that person's health. And it is vital that we understand health broadly to include physical and mental health. My client is suffering from depression and anxiety, and the state has a responsibility to look after her well-being, which, in this case, includes taking steps to alleviate her stress. This stress is directly caused by my client's gender, and the mismatch between its physical manifestation and its inherent nature."

"Objection, Your Honor, counsel is testifying, and assuming facts not in evidence," opposing counsel said.

"Sustained. Watch yourself, Ms. Fornier," Judge Hart said.

"Your Honor, this is exactly my point. There are points of contention here—facts that haven't yet been put into evidence, such as my client's relationship to her gender. We need to hear testimony from my client and from expert witnesses from the medical and psychological community before this case is decided. We therefore move that the court reject the defense's summary judgment motion."

"Thank you, Ms. Fornier. Mr. Orr, let's hear from you."

Genevieve sat as opposing counsel stood, but she remained on the edge of her seat in case he said something objectionable.

"Your Honor, this case has turned into a media stunt, and it has no legal merit. There is no precedent for the state of Michigan footing the bill for expensive, elective medical procedures such as the one this felon—"

Genevieve sprang up. "Objection, Your Honor. Inflammatory."

"Sustained," the judge said, and Genevieve sat down. "Mr. Orr, do I need to remind you that we haven't actually gone to trial yet and that there are no jurors here? There's no need to try to prejudice me against the plaintiff."

"Understood, Your Honor. As I was saying, this—plaintiff—may want an elective surgery, but that does not mean the state has to pay for it."

"Objection, Your Honor." Genevieve stood again. "The question of whether this surgery is elective or not is very much undecided and is the reason we need to hear arguments in this case."

"Indeed, Ms. Fornier. Mr. Orr, I take your point about a lack of precedent in the state of Michigan, but there are precedents in other states that I think are quite relevant here. I therefore find in favor of the plaintiff, motion for summary judgment denied. Oral arguments in this case will be heard in June as planned. Unless there are any more motions before the court?"

"None, Your Honor," Genevieve and opposing counsel said at the same time.

"Well then. I look forward to hearing your arguments." Hart banged her gavel, and the clerk called forth another case.

The guard moved to escort Amelia out the way she had come in, and Genevieve followed them. Once in the hallway outside the courtroom, the three of them stopped.

"Two minutes. And no touching," said the guard. He stepped away to give them a modicum of privacy.

"That went really well," Genevieve said, and Amelia's nervous energy quieted for the first time that day. "The judge seems fair—I like her, even."

"So, what's next? Do I take the stand and stuff? Because I never watched *Law and Order* or anything like that."

"Well, you might testify. We'll have to see—if it comes to that, we'll go through witness prep for you. But first, we find expert witnesses who will support our claim that this surgery is vital to your health and well-being, and that the state would be delinquent in their responsibilities if they denied it to you."

"You gonna get doctors to say all that?"

"Pretty much. I've got a few names in mind, and I'm meeting with two of them later today. The third is traveling, so he and I will talk over Skype. I'm leaving tonight, but my staff has made arrangements with the prison for you and me to meet at the end of the day."

Amelia nodded. "It's real nice, what you're doing for me."

"It's not nice, it's just. This is the very reason organizations like mine exist—the reason we hold fundraisers and galas. We build up funds so that we can represent people seeking justice."

"Well, I can still think it's nice, you know."

"Yes," Genevieve said, smiling. "I suppose you can." The guard stepped closer to them and pointed at his watch. "I'll see you in a few hours, Amelia."

The driver who took Genevieve to Henry Ford Hospital let her know that he was heading to lunch but that she could text him when she was done and he'd return within ten minutes. She spoke with a receptionist and was directed to a conference room to meet the first potential expert witness, who turned out to be an unqualified disaster. She lost her train of thought in the middle of every sentence, didn't use dysphoria appropriately in sentences, and couldn't maintain eye contact. After the doctor shook her hand—which felt like squeezing a wet fish—and left the room, Genevieve double-checked the profile her staff had given her. Yep, this woman had gone to University of Chicago as an undergrad and had gotten her MD from Northwestern. Just went to show that fancy schools didn't teach you everything.

The meeting had also gone way over time, and if she took a cab back to her hotel, she'd be late for her Skype meeting with the next potential expert. She poked her head out the door and got the receptionist's attention. "Would it be all right if I stayed in this room for the next hour? I need to take a call."

The receptionist checked the schedule, then nodded. "Room's open until three. Do you need our Wi-Fi info?"

"That'd be great, thanks," Genevieve said.

Twenty minutes later, she had responded to half of the new e-mails in her inbox and signed on to Skype.

This candidate had an MD/PhD and spoke like a textbook. He said all the right things and made great eye contact, but Genevieve had to fight to suppress a yawn, and her thoughts kept straying to her flight home and how nice it would be to read a novel. After clicking *end* and closing her laptop, she went straight to the coffee bar on the first floor of the hospital and texted her driver while she waited in line.

The third possible expert worked in a private practice in Grosse Point Park, where wealthy residents could actually afford his services.

He was a plastic surgeon, primarily, and Genevieve didn't like the optics of that. Considering the other side would try to frame this procedure as an elective, frivolous expenditure, a highly qualified hospital surgeon would be better. But her other options were pretty subpar, so she tried to keep an open mind as she entered the posh waiting room.

"Genevieve Fornier, to see Dr. Carson," she said to the receptionist, trying to decide if she'd had work done. She was gorgeous, and if Dr. Carson had gone at her face with collagen, or Botox, or a scalpel, he was very subtle about it.

"Nice to see you, Ms. Fornier. Dr. Carson is just finishing up with a patient. Can I offer you sparkling water, tea, or wine while you wait?"

She raised her eyebrows, trying to decide whether it was unethical for a plastic surgeon to offer wine to clients.

"Don't worry, the wine's not for patients. We keep it on hand for when the four doctors who work together here have their end-of-the-week meetings. I just figured, since you're not a patient and it's nearing the end of the day…"

"Thanks. I'm good with water."

The chairs in the waiting room were plush and comfy, and the reading material was a far cry from the outdated *US Weekly* magazines in normal waiting rooms. This month's *National Geographic*, *The Atlantic*, and *The Economist* were on the table nearest to her seat.

She didn't have to wait long; within five minutes, a handsome white man with very coiffed hair and a thousand-watt smile approached her, his large hand extending to engulf hers.

"Ms. Fornier. So lovely to meet you. Please, right this way."

He took her past the exam rooms and into his office, closing the door behind her. "I hope Cynthia offered you tea or wine?"

"She did, thanks."

"Excellent, excellent. Well then, let's get to it. I've been an expert witness before, so I understand the gig. Your office sent me some materials last night, and I looked them over. There's no doubt in my mind that your client requires this surgery. I'd be happy to testify to such."

"And if you're asked why sex reassignment surgery isn't an elective procedure?"

"Then I'll point to pages and pages of research indicating that gender dysphoria is a very real and very dangerous medical condition, and the treatment for such is sex reassignment surgery. I can cite multiple peer-reviewed studies, some written by me personally, that indicate the effects of having—and, more importantly, not having—this procedure."

"And if you're asked about whether this surgery isn't simply cosmetic, like most of the work you do?"

"I'd have to take issue with that question. Cosmetic surgery is a complete misnomer. We do skin grafts for burn victims. Those procedures might give the patient a more aesthetically pleasing appearance, sure—but that new skin will be significantly less susceptible to infection. We repair cleft palates.

"But also, there are important reasons to have cosmetic surgery that our society undervalues or overlooks because, on first glance, they seem frivolous. Nevertheless, these procedures can have a profound effect on the well-being of the patient. I've done skin repair for a teenager who had scarring acne. He was bullied mercilessly in school for it and was so miserable that he swallowed an entire bottle of pills. If his mother hadn't found him in time, he might not have been alive to undergo surgery with me. That 'cosmetic' surgery saved this boy's life.

"Self-esteem issues can be an immediate threat to someone's well-being, and until we can change our culture's fixation on a single, unattainable standard of attractiveness, these kinds of procedures save lives."

It was an impressive and impassioned speech, but she wasn't sure the judge would buy it. He wasn't a psychologist, after all. But he was making a good case for being a medical professional whose work should be taken seriously as part of the tapestry of physical and mental health, not some sort of glorified body artist. "How does any of this relate to gender dysphoria?" she asked.

"This procedure aligns a person's physical attributes with his or her innate gender identity. When these things are out of alignment, a person's psychological state plummets. Put it this way: if someone's atlas vertebra was out of alignment, the result could be gastrointestinal disorders, heart arrhythmia, sensitivity disorders, chronic fatigue, sleep disorders, and malfunctioning of sense organs. When gender and sex are out of alignment, the results include sleep disorders, depression, chronic fatigue, and anxiety. And hundreds upon hundreds of studies link these disorders with a risk of suicide. But even apart from suicide, these disorders are cause for concern in and of themselves. They are indicators of poor health and require medical attention."

Genevieve hadn't expected that much substance behind his shiny veneer. She nodded at him, and he looked pleased. "Does this mean I've got the job?"

"Well, it's not quite as simple as all that. I'll need to talk to our legal team, and we'll have to discuss your rates, which are quite high."

"Sorry, but my rates aren't negotiable."

"Understandable." She stood and extended her hand over his desk. As he shook it, she said, "I'll be in touch, Dr. Carson. Thanks for your time."

"Thank you, Ms. Fornier. I look forward to hearing from you."

Back in the car, she directed the driver to the prison before calling Frank. "Please circulate Dr. Carlson's name to the team—he's the best candidate we have for an expert. Have him completely vetted. I want everything he's ever written to be read with a fine-tooth comb—this includes any papers he wrote in med school, if we can get our hands on them. Tell everyone that we're meeting about this at the end of the day on Friday, and I want to hear any objections at that time—otherwise, we're hiring him."

At the prison, she had to wait in the concrete room for a while before a guard brought Amelia in—evidently there was a problem with the inmate count. She was restless, as usual, but there was an optimism Genevieve had never noticed before in Amelia's eyes.

"Well? Find any good ones?"

"God, Amelia, you should have met the first two. Total train wrecks. I wish you had seen them."

"Don't worry—I hear plenty of crazy shit in here. Don't need to leave these walls to meet crackpots."

"Ah, I'm sure that's true. Well, anyway, the last doctor I met with—I think he'll work for us. My team's looking into his background more. We want to make sure he's squeaky clean so the other side can't disqualify him for something he said to his neighbor when he was in third grade or something."

"Good. What's next, then?"

"Well, I'll be back in two weeks to depose some of the prison administrators. And I'll have my people coordinate things so that you can be present for those, if you want to be."

"Dunno about that. Probably best that I don't go, right? I don't want any retaliation."

"Retaliation would be illegal, of course, but you know better than I do what happens here when no one's looking. Think about what you want, and give my office a call next time you have access to the phone."

The guard came and escorted Amelia to the door, and before she exited the room, she turned and gave Genevieve a smile and a thumbs-up sign.

There was a lot of work left to do on this case, but right now the important thing was that Amelia had hope and knew someone was fighting for her.

After tipping her driver generously, Genevieve endured airport security and preboarding procedures before settling into her seat and closing her eyes. God, what a long day. She downloaded her e-mails before the plane took off and wrote responses to the time-sensitive ones, settling them up to send after she'd landed.

With an hour left before landing, she pulled up her Kindle app and opened Margaret Atwood's latest, happy with what she'd accomplished that day and equally happy to find a way to escape it all.

CHAPTER 22

"I know my gym's not as fancy as yours, but it gets the job done," Diane said, leading Victoria down the stairs toward two side-by-side basketball courts, which were empty except for the nets strung across them. Diane grabbed a couple of racquets and a shuttlecock and handed one to Victoria. "I was surprised you called. Don't you usually play badminton with Sonya and Tara?"

"Yeah, in their backyard. Too much snow now." Victoria headed to the far side of the court while Diane gave her a knowing look. "What?"

"Have you seen them since…"

"No," Victoria said quickly. "Do you want to serve first?"

Diane looked at the shuttlecock in her hand and tried bouncing it on her racquet a few times. It fell to the ground on the third bounce. "I haven't played badminton since gym class. Why don't you serve first?"

Victoria's serve wasn't particularly impressive, but Diane returned it into the net anyway.

"How long are you going to avoid your friends?" Diane asked, as Tori served again. Diane managed a passable return, before Victoria hit it out of her reach.

"I'm not avoiding anyone. I just figure… Bethany's her best friend, and Tara's Bethany's sister, and Sonya's Tara's wife… They're all more her friends than mine."

After a sharper serve from Victoria, they rallied back and forth a couple of times before Victoria's shot hit the net.

"Ooh, my serve!" Diane scooped up the shuttlecock and headed to the service line. "So, you haven't heard from any of them since the breakup?"

"I didn't say that." Victoria bested her with a drop shot and set up to serve. "Sonya and Tara are having a dinner party next week. Evidently, they've invited a lot of lesbians. And Bethany." Her serve went straight to Diane, who returned it to the opposite corner where Victoria couldn't reach it.

"Are you going?" Diane's serve was a bit of a floater, and they had a lengthy rally before she hit a shot wide and Victoria collected the shuttlecock to serve again.

"I haven't decided."

"I've heard of fag hags and lesbros… What do you call a straight woman who hangs out with a bunch of lesbians?"

That got Victoria laughing so hard that her serve didn't even make it to the net. "I guess you call her 'Bethany,'" she said, tossing the shuttlecock to Diane to serve.

"Maybe we can get that added to the Urban Dictionary. She'd be so proud."

She served an ace, which was probably because Victoria was wondering if she could legitimately find a way to contact the Urban Dictionary and get Bethany's name in there. "So seriously, Tor, how are you holding up, with this breakup and all?"

"Hell if I know," Victoria said as she won another point.

"God, how are you so good at this? How often do you play with them?"

"Twice, ever. I'm very inconsistent." Victoria served again.

"I have a couple of single colleagues I can introduce you to. They're not as famous as Genevieve, but maybe that's a good thing."

After their longest rally yet, Victoria won the point and reclaimed the serve. "I'm definitely not ready for that yet. Honestly, if I couldn't make something work with Genevieve, I doubt my chances with anyone else."

"Oh, don't be so hard on yourself. I adore Genevieve, but she's got a lot of pride. And she thinks she's low maintenance, and I just want to tell her, 'Au contraire mon frère.'"

"Pretty sure she'd tell you your French needs work."

"Pretty sure I'd laugh and tell her I don't really care."

Victoria served, lost, and grabbed a drink of water. "I wish I could tell her I don't really care," she said, a little wistfully. "Instead, I just keep making the same mistakes over and over again. I… It was a mistake to make Genevieve step away from her case when it got appealed to the Supreme Court."

Diane's serve sailed past Victoria, who stood there flatfooted. She trudged after the shuttlecock and tossed it back to Diane.

"It was? Why?" Diane knit her eye brows. "Can you even *imagine* the media frenzy you'd face if you heard her argue a case? You'd spend more time defending your choice than actually working on the case."

"That's true. But I would have been defending more than the case… I think, in Genevieve's eyes, I would have been defending our relationship."

Victoria pretty much stood there and watched while Diane won a point.

"Okay, how so?" Diane asked, then lobbed another serve at her.

"I think…in her mind it was another example of me valuing my career over her, which is what I did in law school. And I… I don't put her first. She's right about that. We have—had—this relationship where we spent time together if it was convenient, but we didn't…make room for each other. We didn't do sweeping romantic gestures. We never once got each other flowers."

"You two, man. I don't know about you two." Diane won another point, and Victoria pretty much gave up on recovering her earlier winning streak.

"You and me both. Regardless, I don't think I'm ready to be in the same room as her. I don't think I'll go to the party. It would just feel so strange—and so awful—to be near her and not be with her. I don't know how to do that. I guess…I still don't believe it."

She lost the next two points. Or maybe three. She stopped keeping track.

"Victoria, you are a fighter, and you've always been one. Either you want Genevieve back, in which case you should go to this dinner party and make her remember how amazing you are, or you want to get over her, in which case you should go to this party and, you know, confront your pain so you can move on. Hiding from her—and, you know, yourself—won't help you."

Victoria gave her an uneasy look.

"So, which one is it?" Diane asked her. "Fight to get her back, or fight to get over her?"

Victoria picked up the shuttlecock, which had fallen at her feet.

"Because, honestly, Tori, you've lost the badminton fight."

Victoria smiled. "True. Very true. Okay, um…" She fiddled with the shuttlecock. "How about I go to the party, and between now and then I decide which one I want to fight for?"

"Good. I approve. Should we maybe do something besides try to play badminton?"

Victoria nodded, and they returned their equipment.

"What else is going on besides Genevieve?" Diane asked as they started up the stairs.

"I'm advising this high school mock-trial team, and their competitions are coming up. It's… It's been really great to have something other than work and Genevieve to think about. Actually, I was wondering if you'd be interested in being a scorer."

"You don't need a lawyer for that?"

"No, not at all. The person who plays the judge is usually a lawyer, but most of the scorers are laypeople. This year's case is about a high school student accused of stealing expensive artwork from her boyfriend's parents' house."

"Ooh, sounds juicy. Count me in—thanks for asking."

As they neared the doors, Diane put her arm around Victoria's shoulders. "Listen, whatever ends up happening with your love life, you can't blame yourself for this. Genevieve's the one who walked away." She stopped walking and looked thoughtful.

"What?" Victoria asked. "Just say it, whatever it is."

"Do you think, on some level, she's just trying to get even with you for leaving her all those years ago? Like, now you've both broken each other's hearts, so you're on a level playing field?"

As the automatic doors opened, a freezing blast of air hit Victoria's face. "It's occurred to me. But it felt very uncharitable to even think."

"Maybe it's not a conscious thing," Diane said, pulling on a pair of gloves.

Victoria stomped her feet to stay warm against the frigid winter air. "Thanks for playing today."

Diane pulled her into a tight hug. "Keep me posted, okay? Love you, Tori," she said, kissing her on the cheek.

When she got home, she sent an e-mail to the mock-trial organizers giving them Diane's name as a potential scorer, only to be told that they already had enough volunteers. The reply also included the date of the competition: the same date as Sonya and Tara's party.

Diane was going to give her a hard time for not going, but it was a legit excuse to avoid, well, everything. And maybe, since Diane wasn't going to be a scorer, she wouldn't even need to tell her about the scheduling conflict.

When the night of the mock-trial competition came, Tori's team put forward their best performance yet, and narrowly lost to their opponent, a school with a lot more funding and a coaching staff of eight. By comparison, her team had three coaches, plus the handful of advising sessions Victoria did for them. But on the plus side, some of the kids on her team won individual awards, and they all hugged her after the competition and said they'd learned a lot. She drove home happy, feeling confident that she'd had a better night than she would have had at the dinner party.

Chapter 23

The following Friday, Genevieve headed to The Three Branches to catch up with Penelope and Jamie. She had studiously avoided being alone with Penelope since the night she slept on her couch, but of course, when she walked through the doors of the restaurant, the only other patron in the entire place was Penelope, sitting in the legislative section. They gazed at each other across the restaurant, electricity sparking between them, every ounce of the sexual tension they had failed to relieve the last time they saw each other flooding back. As heat from Penelope's smoldering look washed over her, Genevieve's phone buzzed and she glanced down.

> *Got pulled into a meeting—probably won't be able to make it. Sorry! –Jamie.*

She squared her shoulders and strode over to the table, selecting a chair right next to Penelope and draping her coat over the back of it. Their knees bumped as Genevieve pulled her chair in, and despite the warmth that spread across her cheeks, she left her leg resting against Penelope's.

"Jamie's not coming." Her eyes dropped to Penelope's lips.

Surprise flitted across Penelope's features, before transforming into something that looked a little more suggestive. "Hmm. Whatever shall we do in his absence?"

"I can think of a few things." Genevieve's nerve endings came alive with anticipation. God, she'd missed flirting.

"You've been avoiding me," Penelope said, and the look she gave Genevieve sent warm tingles down her spine.

"I've had a lot going on. Issues in my personal life. Tori and I broke up."

"Are you okay?"

Genevieve looked at Penelope's lips, which were slightly parted, and leaned closer. "Hmm, I will be."

"Are you ladies ready to order?"

Genevieve leaned back and glared at their waiter, but his gaze was fixed steadily on Penelope. Not that she could blame him; in a navy skirt suit, wearing deep-red lipstick and a blouse so low-cut it was flirting with the edge of professionalism, Penelope was utterly captivating.

"I'm ready—Genevieve, do you need a minute?"

She knew exactly what she wanted to devour, and it wasn't on the menu.

Willing her heartbeat to slow back down, she shook her head. "Go ahead—I'll be ready by the time you're done."

"I'll have the kale salad, but can I have lemon vinaigrette instead of pomegranate? And no onions, please."

Both Penelope and the waiter turned to look at her, and she remembered she was supposed to use that time to figure out her order, not watch the way Penelope's mouth moved when she spoke.

"What's your soup today?" she asked to buy time.

"Carrot curry," the waiter said.

"Great—I'll have that. And a house salad."

They both ordered coffee, and Penelope handed over their menus.

"Where were we?" Genevieve asked, leaning close again.

Penelope traced her finger down Genevieve's jaw before outlining her lips. "Hm. I think we were going to get to know each other better."

Genevieve turned her head and wrapped her lips gently around Penelope's finger, watching with satisfaction as Penelope's eyes fluttered, then closed. When she bit down slightly, Penelope's eyes flew open, her surprise quickly replaced with a devious smile. Her hand moved to Genevieve's thigh and began inching upward. Genevieve squirmed, wishing she had chosen a skirt that morning. Penelope squeezed the fabric of her pants, and Genevieve's self-control teetered on the edge. Fuck it. She slid her hand behind Penelope's neck and pulled their mouths closer. Their lips had barely grazed each other when someone cleared his throat, and Genevieve looked up again, this time ready to tell the waiter exactly what she thought of his timing.

"Sorry to interrupt," Jamie said, rocking on his feet a little and studiously avoiding eye contact with either of them.

Genevieve took a deep breath, pushing away her desire. "Sorry, Jamie. Please, have a seat."

She stole a look at Penelope, who looked as flustered as she did. When their eyes met, Genevieve wanted to skip the rest of lunch and invite Penelope back to her place. She allowed herself to sink into that fantasy for a brief moment, while Jamie took off his coat and got settled. As Jamie flagged down the waiter, Genevieve resolved not to look at Penelope until she had her imagination under control.

"Well, I'd ask what I missed, but…" Jamie laughed. "I'd really rather not know."

"What was this meeting you got pulled into?" Genevieve asked, hoping he'd launch into some lengthy story that would give her time to calm down.

"The president of our board of directors just won a special election for the Colorado state legislature, and he's stepping down from the board. We needed to strategize how to replace him, and whether we need to appoint an interim president until we're able to hold elections."

"Oh, that's too bad," Penelope said politely.

"Well, it's great for the cause in Colorado politics, but yeah, it's too bad for us," Jamie said.

They took turns looking at each other, and Genevieve couldn't think of a single thing to say. The silence was growing oppressive when the waiter actually demonstrated a good sense of timing for once and approached Jamie.

While Jamie ordered, Genevieve risked looking at Penelope. Big mistake. Penelope looked ready to devour her whole, and there was no way in hell Genevieve was going back to the office after this lunch.

"Genevieve, how was your trip to Michigan?"

Damn, she'd forgotten that her team for Amelia's case was meeting that afternoon to discuss the expert witness—a meeting she herself had scheduled and that she couldn't in good conscience postpone.

"Uh, good. It was good. Actually, can I ask your opinion about this potential expert witness?"

She explained her concerns about having Dr. Carson testify, and for most of their lunch they debated the pros and cons of using a cosmetic surgeon

"Jamie, what's new at HRC?" Penelope asked.

"Well, I wanted to run something by you two, actually. It's been a few years since anyone in Congress has introduced a ban on workplace discrimination for LGBTQ employees. I think it might be time to try again, and if we work together, maybe we'll stand a better chance of getting something passed."

"That's what I love about you, Jamie," Genevieve said. "You're optimistic to the point of foolishness. There's no way in hell this Congress passes a non-discrimination bill this year. Maybe after the next election, if Democrats can regain control of the House. But the Senate isn't budging."

"It's a damn shame that these are our concerns, really," said Penelope. "Democracy can be such a fucked-up political system."

"Meaning?" Jamie asked.

"Well, meaning that the majority almost always wins. And sometimes the majority is a bunch of bigots."

"Actually, that's not quite right in this situation," Jamie said. "The majority of Americans favor a non-discrimination bill. That's why this whole thing is a head-scratcher—if congresspeople were really representing their constituents, they'd support this. But their funding sources are opposed. That's where the real problem is."

"Campaign finance reform, where are you when we need you?" Genevieve said.

They debated which congresspeople were vulnerable when it came to the next election cycle, and brainstormed some tactics for swaying legislators to their side before agreeing that they were somewhat out of their depth. They took out their phones and each e-mailed their organization's legislative director, briefly explaining the situation and telling them to meet with each other in the next week or two.

After they paid the bill, Genevieve said good-bye and headed to the restroom before the cold walk back to her office. She'd just washed her hands when the door opened and Penelope entered and stood just inside. At the sight of Penelope's chest rising and falling heavily, Genevieve's heart rate doubled. She crossed slowly to Penelope, pushing her against the door and bringing their lips together. Jesus, it felt so good to crave someone and be able to act on it. Their lips and teeth and tongues demanded more and more of each other, and Penelope's hands on her lower back drew their bodies even closer.

When they finally pulled apart, breathless, Penelope looked at her with hooded eyes.

"My place," she said. "Tonight."

Genevieve nodded. "I'll bring dinner."

"Screw food—I don't care about food."

"You'll need your energy."

Penelope gave her a shaky laugh. She gently pushed Genevieve away and ran her thumb around her lips, wiping off lipstick. "I'll see you then," she said.

Genevieve let her leave first, and when she was alone again in the bathroom, she clutched the edge of the sink and studied herself in the mirror. She didn't look like the hot mess she felt, thank God.

Her whole body thrummed with anticipation, but her mind took an unexpected detour, and she thought of Tori. She reminded herself that they weren't in a relationship anymore—she didn't owe Tori anything.

But Tori would be devastated if she found out. And wouldn't Genevieve be too, if the tables were turned and Tori suddenly had…well, had someone?

Dammit. In the dim lighting of a stupid restaurant bathroom, Genevieve finally admitted it to herself: she might be pissed at Tori, and they might not have figured out how to be in a relationship together, but she still loved her beyond measure. And she was really hoping Tori would get her head out of her ass and try to win her back.

Which was probably horribly unfair of her.

It was such an uncomfortable, unsettling thought that Genevieve stormed out of the bathroom. She walked to work without putting on her gloves or hat, enjoying the way the cold burned her skin.

What the hell was she doing?

The afternoon meeting went well, or at least that's what Frank said as they left the conference room and headed toward Genevieve's office. She wouldn't really know since she'd barely heard a word anyone had said.

She narrowly avoided causing two accidents on her drive home, and when she dumped her coat and purse on her couch she paused a moment, then dumped herself there too. She growled in frustration, a pillow pulled over her face.

No doubt she wanted Penelope. But that didn't make it a good idea. Penelope had made it clear to her that she was interested in sex and maybe something more. Sleeping with Penelope now, in light of her recent realization about Tori, would be more than unfair to Penelope.

Or would it? Did she really need to be completely over her ex in order to try to move on? Wasn't finding someone new the best way to move on?

God, why was this so complicated? She could call Bethany, but she was pretty sure that conversation would go something like, "Penelope wants to sleep with you and you're single? What the hell's the holdup?"

She needed to get out of her own head. She turned on the TV and headed into the kitchen for wine. She filled a huge glass—she could take a cab to Penelope's if she decided to go. Leaning against the kitchen counter, she savored the taste of an expensive pinot noir and closed her eyes. She heard Tori's voice in her head, and she stood there, enjoying the warm caress of Tori's rich alto.

"And that's why I've worked with the mock-trial program ever since law school."

She opened her eyes quickly and hurried into her living room, where Tori was on CNN, extolling the value of high school mock-trial programs. Dressed in a teal skirt suit, black blouse, and black pumps, she looked like a million bucks. Genevieve fixated on her long, delicate fingers and the way they moved as she gestured. They were bare, save for the ring on her right middle finger, the ring her father had given her mother on their wedding day, which she in turn left to Tori in her will. It was the first time Genevieve had really noticed how bare Tori's left ring finger was, and she wondered what kind of ring Tori would like to wear there—a thought which compelled her to sit down.

How stupid was she being? In her most honest moments, she could admit that her anger about Heather and Crystal's case was entirely irrational—even though she couldn't figure out how to let go of it. God, viewing their relationship as a competition and keeping score of wins and losses felt terrible—she was losing on multiple fronts.

Looking back at the screen, she saw through Tori's brilliant smile and upbeat inflection. Her eyes held that haunted look that meant she wasn't sleeping. Shoulders slightly slouched, she reminded Genevieve of the way she looked after working well into the night, hunched over her laptop and numerous research binders. When she'd finally come to bed, Genevieve would lay her on her stomach, straddle her, and massage the tension away.

Her cell phone buzzed, and she read a text from Penelope:

> *Let me know when you're on your way. Can't wait to see you. All of you.*

Genevieve paced, feeling like so much rested on what she did in the next hour. Sighing, she dialed Penelope's number.

"Mm, I hope you're calling to ask what I'm wearing. Because my answer will be very, very brief."

Genevieve's stomach clenched. Of course Penelope wasn't going to make this easy for her.

"I'm sorry, Penelope, but I don't think this is a good idea."

Penelope sighed heavily. "Look, Genevieve, I like you. I'm attracted to you. But I don't want to play these games, and if you can't decide what you want, then I think we shouldn't pursue this any further."

Genevieve's whole body slumped, and she wanted to protest. "I like you too, Penelope, but I'm still… Well, I'm not emotionally available, I guess."

"I look forward to the day when I can meet Victoria Willoughby, so maybe I can understand the hold she has over you," Penelope said with a hint of bitterness.

"I really am sorry, Penelope."

"I know." She hesitated. "I'll see you on Friday for our next lunch meeting."

Genevieve opened her mouth to respond, but Penelope hung up. Before she could feel the disappointment, she heard Tori's voice again.

"Well, I'm sure many of these kids will go on to be lawyers, but many of them won't. Mock Trial provides an opportunity to work on public speaking, critical thinking, collaboration, research, and writing. Students on mock-trial teams hone skills that they will use no matter what career they choose."

"Justice Willoughby, thanks for taking the time to talk with us today," the reporter said.

"It was my pleasure—thank you for having me," Tori said with that smile that... Fuck. She loved Tori's smile. Genevieve ran a shaky hand through her hair, and the camera cut to more "breaking news."

Genevieve located her remote control and hit rewind; rewatching Tori's interview probably wasn't healthy, but neither were most of her decisions these days.

The following Friday, The Three Branches was crowded for lunch—evidently some lobbying firm was celebrating something. It took Genevieve a minute to locate the table where Jamie was seated, alone.

"Well, well. If it isn't Genevieve Fornier, kisser of colleagues. Am I next?" he asked.

"Very funny, wise guy," she said, taking off her coat and sitting down. "Besides, she's not my colleague—not really. We don't work for the same organization."

"I suppose you're technically right. So you've traded in Victoria for Penelope, huh? I think you came out ahead in that deal."

Leave it to Jamie to say something flippant about a situation keeping her up at night. She rubbed her eyes, then put her hands firmly on the table. "Okay, since you're asking. Tori and I aren't together. Penelope and I aren't together. And what you saw last week, well, that won't be happening again."

Jamie's eyebrows knitted together. "Wait, why? You two have so much chemistry it makes *me* want to sleep with you. You'd be perfect together."

"I suppose I don't have to ask which of the two women I just mentioned you're talking about."

"Duh, Penelope," he said, rolling his eyes.

"It's not the right timing," Genevieve said, hoping he'd drop it.

The look on his face said he saw right through her, but he moved on. "Our legislative directors are meeting on Monday to discuss federal non-discrimination. Do you think we should be there too?"

"Nah, let's let them get the ball rolling, and they can bring us up to speed in a couple of weeks."

The waiter came to take their order, and Genevieve looked at the empty seat at their table. "Let's wait a few more minutes," she said. "We're expecting someone else."

The waiter left and Jamie whispered, "Yeah, unless she's too brokenhearted to be in the same room as you. That's what you get for messing around with collaborators."

"Sorry I'm late, everyone," Penelope said, breathless. "What did I miss?"

Jamie threw Genevieve an inscrutable look. "Nothing of importance, dear. And we waited for you to order."

"Oh, you didn't have to do that. Listen, I was hoping we could brainstorm some talking points for the media blitz we're doing about the parentage case."

So this was how Penelope was going to play it—all business. That seemed the mature thing to do, after all.

As they noshed on burgers and fries and considered other strategies for Penelope's arguments, Genevieve found it easier and easier to make eye contact with her. Twinges of regret began to prickle in the back of Genevieve's mind: Penelope's sharp wit and discerning intellect drew her in, just like Tori's always had. But more than that, Penelope radiated a warmth and ease that was unique to her.

Still, Penelope seemed to have flipped some kind of switch in her attitude toward Genevieve; the electricity between them had fizzed out. Positive that sexual tension that profound couldn't just disappear, Genevieve knew it lurked just under the surface. But if their path forward led to friendship and not romance, she vowed to do her part to keep it buried too.

Their lunch meeting over, they all walked out together before moving in different directions toward their respective offices. Genevieve glanced over her shoulder as people on their way to important places hurried to and fro between her and Penelope. With a bittersweet smile, Penelope turned and walked away.

Chapter 24

The following Friday morning, Genevieve sat in her office at HER and opened her calendar. Miraculously, the afternoon was free of any meetings. She'd tasked one of her team members to fly to Michigan that morning to meet with Dr. Carson, whom they'd decided to hire, and check in on Amelia. The only thing on her schedule for the whole day was her lunch meeting with Jamie and Penelope.

She wasn't really up for seeing Penelope, or enduring Jamie's odd blend of irreverence and earnestness, or any of it. Hoping they felt the same way, she composed an e-mail.

> Hi Jamie and Penelope,
>
> All my cases are well in hand, our legislative directors have been strategizing a plan for the non-discrimination bill, and it's been a long week. I'm not sure we need to meet today. Let me know what you think.
>
> GF

The cup of coffee she'd made herself at home that morning didn't get the job done, so she dragged her feet to the break room. By the time she returned to her desk, both Jamie and Penelope had written back agreeing to cancel that day's lunch; she deleted it from her calendar.

Part one of her plan having fallen into place, she grabbed her cell and hit speed dial number two.

"G-Spot! Isn't it a beautiful day? I just love Fridays," Bethany gushed.

"You're in a good mood."

"What's not to be in a good mood about? It doesn't feel like a blizzard outside, I'm wearing a new pair of cowboy boots for casual Friday, and…I have a date this weekend!"

"Well, hot damn, Bethie! I'm happy for you," Genevieve said.

"You know what, sweet cheeks? I'm happy for me, too!"

"With all this happiness, I think you and I need to celebrate. Play hooky with me today."

"Hmm, let me check my schedule. I have a meeting at two, but I'll cancel it. One sec."

Sounds of her long nails typing away clicked through the phone. "Done! Okay, what are we doing?"

"I hadn't gotten that far," Genevieve admitted. Channeling her inner Ferris Bueller, she leaned back in her desk chair and swiveled, hoping for some inspiration.

"Spa day? Or, we could go sit in the balcony of the House of Representatives and throw food at people we don't like."

"Spa day sounds less likely to get us arrested."

"I know just the place, and I'm scheduling us for mani/pedis, facials, and a couples' massage."

"Bethie, what makes it a *couples'* massage?"

"Oh, nothing that scandalous. We're just in the same room, is all."

Genevieve raised her eyebrows. "So, we'll be pretty much naked together?"

"Nothing I haven't seen before, babycakes."

Seen before? When? Oh, their trip to Cancun.

"Bethany, you could hear the shower water running, and you knew the curtain was clear."

"Well, I had to pee!"

She bit her lip to keep from laughing at that ridiculous logic. "There was another bathroom, *sweet cheeks*," she said, in her best Bethany voice.

"Oh well, I guess I forgot about that. Anyway, what's the big deal?"

What, indeed. "Absolutely nothing. This all sounds perfect. I'll make us an early lunch reservation so we can eat first."

"Peachy! Text me the details."

Genevieve poked around online until she found a hot lunch spot called Diplomacy. It reminded her of Penelope. Well, good—going there with Bethany would be exactly what she needed to get over whatever she still felt whenever she thought about Penelope. Disappointment? Lust? Guilt?

After gathering her coat and bag, along with some paperwork she'd need to look at over the weekend, she closed her office door and walked to Frank's desk.

She pointed to his headset. "Are you on the phone?"

He shook his head. "I just leave this on because it's easier."

"Makes sense. Hey, I'm going to take the day off. I'm powering down my phone, and I won't be on e-mail either. If there's an emergency—"

"Genevieve, we're not exactly trauma surgeons. There won't be any kind of emergency worth interrupting whatever it is you have planned with Bethany."

She raised her eyebrows.

"Oh!" He looked embarrassed. "I was just guessing. Since you cancelled lunch with Penelope."

He didn't add Jamie's name—instead he gave her a knowing look that clearly said he knew way more about her personal life than she'd ever imagined. Well, it was hard to fault him—he probably knew more about her comings and goings than anyone else.

"Go, Genevieve. Have some fun. You deserve it."

She smiled at him, and while she rode the elevator to the ground floor, she located a number for HER's courier service and requested they deliver a bottle of very nice wine to Frank by mid-afternoon, making sure they charged her personal credit card number.

With ninety minutes before their lunch reservation, she hailed a cab to DC's shopping district. It wouldn't be fair for Bethany to be the only one in new boots. Besides, shoe shopping served her better than therapy.

After browsing to gather her options, she tried on a handful and selected a pair of gray knee-highs that worked well with the skinny jeans and red blouse she wore that day. Her purchase complete, she wandered around other stores for a while, before emerging into the late morning sun, which was almost warm. She slid sunglasses on and walked to the end of the block to hail a cab. As she stood on the corner, a woman probably ten years younger than her walked past, turned around and took her sunglasses off, and blatantly checked her out. It was so obvious that Genevieve almost laughed, and when the woman walked away, she knew she had a stupid, self-satisfied grin on her face. Maybe it was the boots or maybe it was something else. Maybe, despite everything, she still had it.

When she joined Bethany at the lunch table, she got kisses on both cheeks and a martini already waiting for her. Bethany ordered their food, then launched into a lengthy discussion about the new ownership of the Dallas Cowboys. Genevieve took the opportunity to look around the restaurant, which was chic and not very crowded. Evidently, most people in DC had better things to do than eat lunch at eleven. Well, too bad for them. She sipped her martini and basked in not being at work.

"…overlooks the importance of special teams, and has a penchant for cutting the most expensive players. He's just awful."

"Hmm," Genevieve said, enjoying the faint buzz in her ears, brought on no doubt by the vodka. When Bethany paused in her diatribe to drink, Genevieve jumped in.

"Darling, I'm very sorry about this new development in the safe-as-kittens, not at all hypermasculine, one hundred percent head-trauma-free world of the NFL. But I'd really rather talk about your date."

Well, who knew Genevieve actually had the ability to silence Bethany—even if for a moment. Instead of launching into a monologue about the merits of the man she'd be spending tomorrow evening with, Bethany pensively swirled her martini around, and looked out the window.

Finally, when Genevieve was about to apologize for asking, Bethany shrugged and turned her attention back to the room. "I wouldn't ever have predicted him. For me, I mean. He's British, for one."

Genevieve had to bite back a snort, because all Bethany had ever talked about wanting was a native Texan who could rope a steer as well as write a legal brief. She cleared her throat and took another drink, but why she ever tried to fool Bethany was beyond her.

"Laugh all you want, G-Spot. I'd laugh too. But he's… I don't know. I just like him."

She'd never seen Bethany so...reserved. "What's his name? Where did you two meet?"

"Edward—that's his name. The Bar Association threw an event for law firm partners who had done a lot of pro bono work in the past year. It was kind of an awards thing."

"Oh, Bethie, why didn't you tell me! I would have come to support you!" Bethany's ability to prattle on about insignificant things, while completely failing to mention important ones, never failed to amuse Genevieve.

"You're sweet, but really, it wasn't a big deal." She wiped her mouth with her napkin, despite not having eaten a bite of the salad in front of them, and Genevieve wondered how preoccupied she was in that moment, thinking about this mystery man's lips. "Anyway, he won a couple of housing-related cases for low-income clients who couldn't afford to pay for proper representation. He's lived in DC for fifteen years, and in addition to being a partner at Skadden, he also consults on housing-related legislation. And he's a Big Brother—not, like, he's related to someone else. Or, like, I mean siblings. It's...he's..."

Bethany shook her head and finished her martini.

Genevieve sat back in her chair, stunned. "Whoa. He's rendered you speechless, and he isn't even here. Give me his number—I need to get pointers."

"Ha-ha. You're hilarious, Genevieve."

"Okay, so, let's recap. He's civic-minded and mentors youth through a Big Brother program? He's got dough because he's a fancy-pants law firm partner just like you. So you don't have to tread lightly around someone who might feel threatened by your professional and financial success. And he has you entirely flustered and probably doesn't know it. I mean, have you even kissed him yet?"

If she thought this lunch had been full of surprises, the biggest was happening now—an honest-to-God blush crept up Bethany's neck and flooded her cheeks. Unsure how to interpret that, Genevieve just stared.

"Um, no. Not at all. We talked during the cocktail hour before and sat next to each other during the speeches and stuff."

"Let me get this straight. Talking and sitting next to this guy makes you as red as a tomato?"

Bethany's hands flew to her face, and her eyes bulged. "Oh no." Impossibly, her blush grew even redder. "Um, our legs sort of. We were touching. Just, like, our knees."

Genevieve abandoned all efforts at masking her response. She guffawed so loudly that the bartender threw her a dirty look. Tears in her eyes, in between snorting laughs, she managed to wheeze out, "Jesus, Bethie, are you a Victorian novel?"

Bethany wadded up her napkin and threw it at Genevieve, who batted it away with effort, considering her arm—hell, her whole body—was weak with laughter. But at least the spell was broken, and Bethany's coloring returned to normal. "Yes, okay, he makes me hot and bothered that easily."

Retrieving the rogue napkin from the floor, Genevieve dabbed at the tears in her eyes. "We are going to need to seriously strategize how you'll handle it when you two finally kiss. Do you need me to be on hand with smelling salts? Shall I program the local apothecary's number into your cell phone?"

Bethany tried to give her a stern look, but her eyes were sparkling. "You know what, Genevieve Fornier? I have had to watch you do some pretty ridiculous stuff for Victoria Willoughby—*twice*—and not say a damn thing either time. The least you can do is cut me some slack here."

"That's fair," Genevieve said, sobering instantly at the sound of Victoria's name. Bethany gave her a quick glance indicating she noticed, but Genevieve moved on. "Well, what's he look like?"

"Not very tall. Not ripped. Just, you know, normal. Except he's got this great wavy hair that I can't wait to run my fingers through. And this dimple that is outrageously distracting when he talks. And his lips are... I don't know. Perfect? Whatever, he's... I like him."

She seemed to have noticed for the first time that there was food on the table, and she picked up a fork. The blush had returned, full force, and Genevieve contemplated exploiting it for more laughs. Bethany gave the tiniest shudder, though, and Genevieve took pity on her. She was clearly not ready to laugh about this.

"You know what, Bethie? I never would have guessed."

Once she changed the subject to work, the remainder of lunch passed without Bethany passing out or disintegrating or experiencing any of the other responses that discussion of her new beau seemed to be producing. Genevieve even managed to forget for a few minutes the exact shade of red on Bethany's cheeks when the subject of Edward came up. While they were waiting for the bill, however, Genevieve shifted in her chair so she could gently rest her knee against Bethany's, and gazed at her as if smitten.

"Oh, Bethany. I'm so glad the Bar Association brought us together. I can't wait to kiss the inside of your wrist in a chaste yet passionate way that communicates my feelings for you without damaging your virtue. Then, if your father gives his blessing, I shall propose to you, and, after a church wedding, we shall do that thing we've heard people whisper about but never directly discuss."

Bethany refused to talk to her, and when their bill arrived, she crossed her arms and glared. It was worth it.

Genevieve stuck her credit card into the envelope, and when the waitress returned, handed it to her. Their fingers brushed, which couldn't have been an accident, and Genevieve glanced at her. She was hot in a hipster artist kind of way and not at all hesitant to give Genevieve a slow smile that made the temperature in the room escalate. She backed away from the table, dragging her eyes up and down Genevieve's body before turning and disappearing behind the bar. Bethany smirked at her. Because it was too much to ask for a lunch where the teasing went only one direction.

When the waitress returned with Genevieve's card and the receipt, she brushed her hand lightly over Genevieve's shoulders this time. "I hope you enjoyed yourself. Dining out can be so much fun," she said with enough suggestiveness in her voice that even Ryan Jamison wouldn't be able to miss her meaning.

Bethany did a poor job of stifling a snort, and as soon as the waitress departed, she snatched up the receipt. Grinning like the cat that caught the canary, she turned the slip of paper over and pointed to the phone number written on the back. "How does that saying go?" Bethany asked. "You keep getting older, but they stay the same age?"

Genevieve yanked the receipt out of her hand and stared at the number. It felt like cheating somehow—why, after all this time, could she not escape the notion that she and Tori were together? With great effort, she managed to remember thoroughly and soundly dumping Victoria Willoughby.

Tori had been right, of course, when she said Genevieve was every bit as in love with her as she was with Genevieve. When she wasn't thinking clearly, she seemed to just assume that they were together. Her natural state of being seemed to be with Tori. An image of Tori with tears in her eyes at that damn wine bar flashed across her mind and she blinked.

"Come on, Genevieve, it's got to feel good to know you still got it. Those abs, those boobs—dynamite combo." Bethany said, winking obnoxiously at her.

Genevieve laughed and slipped the receipt into her wallet, more as a show for Bethie than anything else. "Well, now that we've had martinis, have you come up with a plan for your new beau? Are you sleeping with him on date one, or waiting until after marriage?"

Bethany fluffed her hair, making it even larger than usual. "There must be something in between. I figure I'll just play it by ear. In the meantime, facials and massages."

Genevieve stood and turned toward the door when Bethany gasped.

"Those!" she said, pointing at her boots as though Genevieve hadn't been wearing them when she walked in. "Ohmygod, those are yummy. They're so delicious I could lick them. I want them. In black. I'm buying them immediately. And you can wear yours on Mondays, Thursdays, and every other Saturday. I get the rest."

"I've got a better idea. You wear the new cowboy boots you just bought, whenever you want. And we'll both be happy."

Bethany glanced at her own feet, and her face lit up in delight, as if she were seeing them for the first time in her life. "Oh yeah, these old things! Okay, I accept your deal. But you drive a hard bargain, Genevieve."

"You and logic aren't friends, you know that?" Genevieve shook her head and shrugged into her coat.

"To the spa!" Bethany said, linking arms with her and dragging her to the door.

When they left the spa, legs replaced with Jell-O after hours of pampering, Bethany murmured, "Drinks?" and Genevieve said, "The wine bar in my neighborhood. That way we can both park at my place and walk."

"I may as well just stay over, don't you think?" Bethany gave her a guileless smile and pointed at a bag in her backseat. "I'm all packed, anyway."

Genevieve raised her eyebrows. "You just assumed I'd be that easy to sleep with?" she asked.

"I've lived with you. I don't have to assume."

Genevieve unlocked her car, tossed her purse in, and turned to give Bethany her sweetest, most innocent expression. "You know, I've been wondering about Edward. And those perfectly kissable lips of his. Would you draw me a picture of them, so I don't have to rely on my *very active* imagination?"

Bethany tried to give her a murderous expression, but her eyes glassed over, and her neck and cheeks turned pink. Before Bethany fainted or threw keys at her head, Genevieve got into her car and drove away, wondering how long it would take Bethany to catch up.

Word had spread about the wine bar, and they had to squeeze past crowds of Capitol Hill wonks who'd left the office a little early for Friday happy hour. She and Bethany landed the last open table in the place and were soon comparing notes on their wine flights. By the time they'd ordered another round, two women had stopped by their table to hit on Genevieve.

When a third woman threw Genevieve a look so smoldering it seemed to scorch her clothes from across the room, Bethany slapped the table.

"What the hell, Genevieve. Did you take some kind of 'fuck me' pill this morning?"

"It's the boots," Genevieve said.

"It's not the boots. Why are you just oozing sex right now?" She crossed her arms and stared. "Spill."

Genevieve looked around the table, taking stock of anyone who might overhear. For all the looks she received, no one paying them any attention was within earshot. She leaned forward. "I almost slept with someone. But I didn't. And now I'm... What did you say? Oozing sex?"

Bethany put on an expression that conveyed mild interest. Genevieve had never seen her in court before, but she imagined this was her professional expression. She folded her hands primly on the table. "Does this involve the incomparable Penelope Sweet? Do tell, Genevieve," she said.

So she told. The whole story. Bethany's eyes grew wider and wider until she finally held up her hand, as if in surrender.

"Genevieve Fornier, I'm only going to say this once. You're not getting any younger. Quit messing around—with your own heart and everyone else's. Because, girl, when you are sexually frustrated, it's like a homing beacon for every lesbian in three states."

As she said this, the door opened, letting in a blast of cold air that made its way to their table in the corner. A woman who could have been a dead ringer for Eva Longoria shook the dusting of snow off of her coat collar, looked around, and raised an eyebrow at Genevieve. Before Genevieve could react, Bethany leaned forward, blocking the woman's view of Genevieve, and vigorously shook her head. The woman spared Bethany a dirty look, located her friends, and turned her back to them.

"That wasn't necessary."

Bethany turned to look at her, fire in her eyes. "For Christ's sake, are you emitting some kind of sonar only lesbians can hear?

Turn it off!" She sat back down, shaking her head. "Honestly, sort your shit out, lady."

"I'm trying!" Genevieve protested, and even she knew it sounded weak.

"Try harder. Look, far be it for me to encourage *anyone* to pursue Victoria Willoughby. That woman has a stick up her ass the size of the Washington monument." Her expression turned thoughtful. "But she loves the pants off of you. And you have been over the moon for her since the damn day you met her. This seems like a no-brainer."

"Well. Yes." Genevieve cleared her throat. "I'm not sure love is always enough." She ran her fingers through her hair as old frustrations threatened to abscond with her good mood. "She drives me crazy—and I don't mean in bed. Well, I mean, yes, in bed. But everywhere else too. And, I'm no one's…lapdog. Or whatever. Everything has to be on her terms. It's exhausting. And I don't feel like an equal partner."

"I think you're misinterpreting her agenda, Genevieve. If she likes things on her territory, it's not because she's selfish—she's scared. The woman is the biggest closet case this side of Queen Latifah. So, you know, hold her hand and help her through it, or wash your hands of her neuroses forever. That's what I say." She leaned back in her chair, clearly proud of herself.

Genevieve had one sip left of her second wine flight, and she twirled that glass around, watching the legs of the wine ease back to the bottom.

Bethany snorted. "Oh, boo-hoo. My name's Genevieve, and I've got women all over me. I have to decide between playing house with a beautiful, powerful Supreme Court justice and a gorgeous, brilliant human rights executive. My life is so hard. I might as well wear a bag over my face, because that's the only way women will stop dropping their pants for me."

Genevieve stared at her. "Sorry to destroy your little fantasy, Bethany, but with a body like this, it won't matter if I cover my face. They'll still come...uh, running."

Bethany glared at her. "Well. I'm on the verge of having a very cute boyfriend."

"And I can't wait to meet him." Genevieve hesitated. "I guess I never thought of it that way. Thought of Tori as afraid. I mean, I always knew she was scared, but I focused more on the way her fear affected me, not her. I...I haven't had as much compassion for that fear as I should have."

"No, you haven't. She's made mistakes, you've made mistakes. So, what now?"

"Mm. What now, indeed. Shall we stumble back to my place, watch something we've seen a thousand times, and order Thai food?"

"I see what you did there. With the glaring change of subject. But I'll let you off the hook this time, on the assumption that you will think long and hard about this, and actually make a decision, nimrod. In the meantime, *Devil Wears Prada* and pad see ew, here we come!"

On the walk home, with snow flurries tickling their faces, Bethany sang KT Tunstall's "Suddenly I See" and danced in the street. Genevieve reflected that while her love life might be a mess, she was hitting homers at work. And she had a very funny, very thoughtful, very tipsy best friend that she could turn to for anything.

CHAPTER 25

Alone at her kitchen table, Genevieve turned the invitation over and over in her hands before taking a sip of her morning coffee. The invitation was simpler than last year's design and more to the point. Last year's event was well attended, and she'd heard fun stories; she hadn't been able to go, of course, because she had been traveling for something or other.

She read the invitation for a fifth time.

> *The District of Columbia Bar Association invites you to our annual Women in the Law gala. This year's keynote address will be delivered by Justice Victoria Willoughby. Cocktail hour begins at 6:00 p.m. Please RSVP by March 15.*

Well. The universe couldn't be clearer if it had delivered Tori to her doorstep. The question was, could she put aside her anger?

The thing was, if she RSVPed, her name would be on the guest list, Tori would likely see it, and…well, it was supposed to be a special night for Tori, not one hijacked by Genevieve.

She checked her watch. Almost nine—she should leave for the office soon. She called Frank while she gathered her coat and bag and headed to the door.

"Genevieve, hi. What's up?"

She swore she could see his smile through the phone. God, morning people.

"Frank, can you RSVP to the Bar Association gala? Just tell them someone from HER will be there, and we don't know who yet. I'll let you know when I figure it out."

"Okay," he said with enough hesitation in his voice to make Genevieve wish she hadn't called. Of course Frank would know why she wouldn't commit to going. Well, in addition to his pity, at least she could count on his discretion. "Anything else I can do?" he asked.

"I'll be there in a bit. Can you e-mail back MSNBC and tell them I'll only do the interview if it's in DC? I'm not trekking up to New York."

"I'm sure they'll be fine with that—they've been salivating over the chance to interview you. They'll take whatever you give them."

"Then make sure they know that it's Maddow or no one," Genevieve said, climbing into her car. She started it, and her phone switched over to Bluetooth.

"Roger that. And don't forget that you have that forum on the Hill next week. I think our legislative folks have put together a packet for you."

"What's this?" Genevieve said, double-checking her appearance in the rearview mirror. She looked pale. Maybe more lipstick would help.

"The forum on violence against the trans community."

Genevieve rifled around in her purse until she found the perfect color, then reapplied her lipstick. "Who all is going to be there?"

"Hang on, let me check." He clicked away on his keyboard while she backed out of the driveway and began her traffic-filled drive to work. At least she could be productive while in transit.

"A few senators, a dozen or so congresspeople, some state officials, and some members of the trans community. Jamie and Penelope too. Looks like about thirty people, total. And the forum will be televised on C-Span, so, you know, expect a wide viewing audience."

Genevieve rolled her eyes. "Well, I'm sure some idiot will pick up on a few sound bites, strip them of their context, and repackage them for public consumption."

"Sounds delicious. Anyway, I'll leave the prep materials on your desk. Oh, also, Chuck wants to meet with you about the fundraiser in Atlanta and some staffing issues."

Their conversation continued in much the same vein until she walked into the office. She hung up the phone only when she was standing in front of Frank's desk, and they finished their conversation face to face. She went from meeting to conference call to brainstorming session, and by the time she finally caught her breath, alone in her office, it was six thirty. She'd forgotten about lunch.

Her head was a bit fuzzy and her stomach grumbled. "Frank?"

No answer. She stuck her head out of her office and discovered that the floor was dark except for the light in her office. Well, it was Friday, after all.

She returned to her desk and opened her calendar to see what was on tap for Monday, which would determine what binders and materials she brought home with her. Because there was no way she was coming into the office this weekend. According to the meteorologists, the weather was going to break, and if there was work to be done, she'd do it in her backyard.

Fifteen new calendar notifications from Frank. She clicked through them one by one, confirming as she went, until she got to the last one.

Evidently food wasn't the only thing she'd forgotten about during her hectic day.

Bar Association Gala, March 29, 6:00 p.m.

He hadn't assigned the task to anyone. She closed it without confirming or rejecting the notification. All she had the energy for at that point was the drive home and the effort it took to collapse onto her couch and pull on a blanket as the beginnings of a headache started behind her eyes.

Her weekend had pretty much been spent on the couch, battling a migraine and working from her laptop and phone whenever she could focus enough to respond to e-mails. Her head felt better when she woke up on Monday, and she was nibbling on toast when her cell phone rang with a call from the Michigan Department of Corrections.

"Hello," she said and waited through the recording asking her if she was willing to accept the call. She pressed the number one on her phone and said, "Hi, Amelia."

"Uh, hi, Genevieve. Listen, I've been thinking about this a lot, and I don't wanna do the case anymore. So I wanted to call and let you know."

The spots that had been floating in Genevieve's vision for the past two days returned, and she bit back a groan. "What? Why?"

"I just. I'm worried we won't win. Or, you know. Like, it's a risk to take, and if we win, great, but if we don't... I'd rather not risk it."

"Amelia, what aren't you telling me?"

"Nothing. Everything's good. And I really appreciate all the work you've done for me. It means a lot."

Genevieve could hear raised voices in the background but couldn't make out any words.

"Gotta go now. Bye, Genevieve."

She stared at the phone for a full minute trying to process what had just happened before asking Siri to call Frank.

"I need a flight to Michigan tomorrow. Tell the prison I'm coming to talk to my client. And I need more migraine medicine today, at home. As soon as possible."

If he replied while she stumbled back to her couch, she didn't hear it.

When she woke up later, medicine and crackers were on a plate next to a bottle of ginger ale on her coffee table, and a note from Frank read *feel better soon*. Tori had taken care of her a few times when she'd felt this awful. Frank had pretty much done the same thing—who needed girlfriends, right?

Her inbox had an itinerary for a flight that left at 6:00 a.m. the next day, plus seventy-eight other messages. She made it through half of them before falling asleep again. The headache was a mere shadow when she woke up that evening, and she settled into the workday she should have started at eight that morning. She worked through the night, the morning, the flight, and the car ride to the facility housing Amelia.

It was a dreary winter day, and the harsh sounds of the prison as she was escorted from the guard booth through the yard and to the concrete and metal meeting room felt like the pounding that had been in her head for the past three days. How did inmates not have constant headaches? It was the longest she'd ever had to wait for Amelia, and when her client finally arrived, she gasped.

She had a black eye and scratches on her cheeks and chin, and she limped to the chair where she gingerly sat down, leaning to one side as if pressure on her back or behind was too much to bear.

"Who did this to you?" Genevieve asked, and Amelia refused to look at her.

"It's not what you think. Just a disagreement in the lunchroom."

"You're going to tell me this is unrelated to you suddenly telling me to drop your case?"

"Oh, that. Is that why you're here? I didn't mean for you to get on a plane."

"Amelia, if someone is intimidating you, I need to know."

"No, you don't. What could you even do about it? Sue? We're already doing that, it's taking forever, and it doesn't really change how things are in here. The law doesn't matter in here. Not really."

Genevieve sat back, the wind knocked out of her. "Amelia, I—" But she didn't know what to say.

Shifting in her seat, Amelia grimaced. "Look, Genevieve, I like you and all. And we've had some nice talks. But—"

"Amelia, I've done civil rights work my entire career. What you need to know about intimidation is that it doesn't go away if you give in to it. Someone tells you to give up this case, you do it thinking they'll leave you alone, and then they just give you more demands."

"But I can't lose my hormones again!" Amelia practically shouted, then clamped her mouth shut and looked away.

"I see," Genevieve said. Based on the stories she'd heard—from Amelia and others—it would be just like the warden to threaten her hormones if she didn't drop the case.

It wasn't immediately clear to Genevieve what she could do to ensure that once she left the prison gates, Amelia would still be cared for as the law required. For an institution that acted as the enforcement arm of the law, prisons were pretty lawless.

"Listen to me, Amelia." She reached across the table to take her hand—the prison guard be damned; he was picking at his fingernails anyway. "This is your fight. It's entirely up to you whether we proceed or not. But I believe in your case. I believe in you. I'll keep fighting for you as long as you let me."

Amelia squeezed her hands, and tears filled her eyes, but her back was stiff. "I'm scared, Genevieve. I'm fucking scared. But I… I'm not a person who gives up."

"I know. Okay, look, I'm going to investigate what kinds of oversight we can have into your care—now and after your case is decided, whatever the outcome. We're going to start a whole new team for your case that's focused entirely on oversight. And I'm going to get a court-appointed sketch artist to come draw you tomorrow, before these bruises fade."

"Oh, this?" Amelia pointed at her black eye. "Honey, I meant it—this is just a cafeteria brawl."

"Are you serious?"

"I'm telling you, it sucks in here. People are nasty, no matter which uniform they wear."

Genevieve shook her head. "This has nothing to do with the administration threatening to take away your hormones?"

"No. But it has everything to do with closed-minded asshats who are threatened by someone different." She bit her lip and paused. "Okay, fine, we can keep suing. You're right. I'm not going to let those fuckers win. And I… I trust you, Genevieve."

They smiled at each other across the table.

"Then let's get back to work," she said.

CHAPTER 26

The night of the gala, Genevieve stood in her closet, naked, hair dripping wet from a quick shower, telling herself it didn't matter what she wore. Tori would never even know she was there.

When she'd finally made the decision to represent HER at this event, she gave herself permission to arrive late, stand in the back of the room, and slip out before anyone noticed her. And that would be that.

So there was nothing behind her decision to wear the blue dress that clung to every curve, the one she felt powerful and sexy in, the one Bethany told her never to wear again unless she had a bodyguard to fend off other women. And the black-and-white pumps that Tori told her once to leave on, before stripping off all of Genevieve's other clothes, was a completely coincidental choice. Absolutely.

Well. All right. But, there was no way in hell she'd wear the pendant necklace Tori gave her, even though it did go perfectly with the dress, dropping right between her breasts. Tori had licked her lips the first time she'd worn it. But it didn't matter—even Genevieve had her limits when it came to self-denial.

She rifled through her jewelry box and came up empty. How was it possible she didn't own a damn necklace that would work?

Okay, fine, she'd wear the pendant necklace. Maybe she'd just leave her coat and scarf on, and no one would notice.

No one would notice, because the choice to wear the necklace meant nothing, just like her going to this gala meant nothing.

Absolutely.

As soon as she walked into the ballroom of the hotel, she stopped dead in her tracks. Tori and Jamie were chatting not five feet from the entrance. He said something and put his hand on her arm, and she laughed.

Genevieve spun around and strode back the way she came.

If she smoked, she'd have the perfect excuse for loitering outside in the cold. Instead, she took out her phone and…nothing. The whole Internet at her fingertips, and she couldn't think of a damn thing to do with it.

Sighing, she texted Bethany:

> *How are things with Edward? Drinks tomorrow to discuss?*

She waited a few minutes for a response, stalking back and forth in front of the hotel. Occasionally she got too close, and the automatic sensors opened the doors, making her feel even more ridiculous.

Bethany clearly wasn't going to text back right now. She checked her watch—six forty. Twenty minutes until the keynote. Maybe Tori had moved away from the door. Oh, wait—of course; she had the solution in her hand.

She punched up Jamie's number and dialed, hoping he hadn't silenced his phone just yet.

His voice was muffled, and the din from the ballroom almost drowned him out, but to her relief he answered.

"Hey, I wondered if you were going to the thing. The Bar Association thing," she asked, trying to sound casual.

"Yeah, I'm here. Not sure how I scored an invite because, hello, I'm a guy. But there are a few of us here. And, uh, your ex-girlfriend. But I guess you knew that."

Genevieve flinched, grateful she wasn't having this conversation face-to-face. "Oh, that's right. She's speaking. Have you seen her?"

"Um, yeah, she's…well, right now she's chatting with that woman who runs lobbying for Planned Parenthood."

"The hot one? Or the old one?" Genevieve asked in her most disinterested voice.

"The old one. Anyway. What's up?"

Shit. She forgot to come up with a reason to call him.

"I, uh, was wondering. If you wanted…to go running together some time."

What? *Say no, say no, say no.* Jamie was super slow and would totally cramp her style.

"Really? Sure, I guess. I've never had a running buddy before."

"Great!" she said, even though it was anything but. "I've been in the market for one. Ooh, someone's clicking in—gotta go!"

Perfect. Smooth, Genevieve.

At least now she knew that Tori had moved away from the door. But if Jamie saw her there, she'd have some explaining to do. She checked the time on her phone again—6:55. The lights would probably dim in another three minutes—just enough time to visit the ladies' room and confirm that she looked okay. She peeked through the doors and found the lobby empty. Evidently, everyone had already moved into the ballroom.

The lighting in the restroom was too bright, but she looked good. At least she had that, because she was an emotional wreck.

Her palms were starting to sweat, and her cheeks were too pink. Whatever—she yanked open the door, strode to the ballroom, and ducked inside. The lights were low, and she walked along the back wall until she found the perfect spot in the middle to lean against. Considering everyone else was seated at circular tables, drinking wine and eating salad, she had a great view of the stage at the far side of the room.

Someone from the DC Bar Association stood onstage and rattled off a handful of Tori's accomplishments—which didn't even begin to touch the breadth of her impact on the law in this country. Everyone applauded, and then there she was.

Genevieve had been so startled by Tori's presence when she first arrived that she'd failed to notice the dress. It was a red and white wrap dress that showed off her perfect legs and the collarbone that always drove Genevieve nuts. The dress was new, and a painful ache struck her chest at the knowledge that Tori had things in her life now that Genevieve didn't know about. But then she noticed the earrings she'd given Tori for Christmas the previous year. Her heartbeat suddenly sounded like timpani in her head, and she had to strain to catch Tori's voice, which might have been a bad idea, because the way her rich tones caressed Genevieve's ears made her weak in the knees. It dawned on her then that she'd made a terrible mistake in coming.

"…honor to be here tonight, among such distinguished and brilliant women, and a few of you men too."

Scattered laughter brought a smile to Tori's face, which only made Genevieve's condition more tenuous.

How was it possible that after all these years, Victoria Willoughby still had this effect on her?

"I'm here tonight to talk about what it means to be a woman working in the law. I thought a lot about what I wanted to say tonight. Should I focus on the trailblazers, without whose tireless efforts we wouldn't be here? Maybe instead I should talk about agenda items for the future. Or I could list the roadblocks that we continue to face at every turn. But none of those topics seemed to suit this event. What I really want to talk about today is coalition building."

A murmur went through the crowd, although Genevieve couldn't tell if it was surprise or approval.

"As I look out there at all of you, I see women of all colors, who express their gender with varying degrees of femininity and masculinity. I see people who were born as women, whether or not their sex has always matched their gender. We are a diverse group in all ways save education—which also means that at this point in our lives, we are also not very diverse in terms of class.

"As women, we face tremendous obstacles in this country. The nature of those obstacles varies depending on whether you're a woman of color or not, whether you are cis or trans.

"So I find it strange that I would stand up here and talk to you about being a woman in the law. We might have a lot in common, but my experiences aren't yours. I don't want you to just hear from me. Nor do I want you to just hear from, and talk to, the women you came here with—the ones you've known since law school, the ones whose offices you stop by on a daily basis. I want you all to talk to someone you don't know. Learn her story. Share yours. Brainstorm ideas for how you can be allies to each other." She held her hand over her eyes and squinted. "Can we get the lights back on?"

Of course Tori would come up with an innovative, dynamic take on what was typically a tired speech. Murmurs in the room were unmistakably excited now.

Oh shit—she couldn't just stand there—the lights. Yep. Lights. Great.

She moved quickly to the door, pulled it open a crack, and glanced over her shoulder. Thankfully, Tori was talking again, giving instructions for bringing strangers together and making suggestions for what they could talk about.

Genevieve eased out the door and leaned back against it once it closed. Tori's voice was muffled now, and she couldn't decipher the words.

Oddly, she knew in that moment exactly what she'd say to Tori, if the two of them had a chance to talk. And she wanted nothing more than to go back in, participate in Tori's coalition building, find Tori when the event had ended, and say she wanted her back.

But she knew that her presence there would send Tori spinning. She rubbed her face with her hands, squared her shoulders, and walked to her car.

Genevieve's phone was ringing. Phone. Wake up, Genevieve. The phone. She dragged her eyes open and squinted at the clock. Seven fifteen. Not outrageously early, but still, who called before noon on the weekend?

"Hello?" she mumbled, then tried to cough the sleep away from her throat.

"Why were you there last night?" Tori demanded.

"Um…hi. Good morning, Tori." Great. This certainly wasn't what she hoped for when she imagined talking to Tori again. "How did it go last night?"

"You tell me, Genevieve. You were there. And then you disappeared." Tori practically choked on Genevieve's name. Was it from anger or something else?

Genevieve sat up and leaned her shoulders against the headboard, accidently hitting her head against it much harder than she wanted to. "I don't suppose you'd be willing to postpone this discussion until after I've had some coffee?"

The pause on the other end went on so long that Genevieve had to remind herself not to doze off again.

"I've had three cups of coffee already. I never went to sleep." Her voice cracked with the admission, and Genevieve's heart cracked right along with it.

"I'm sorry," Genevieve said, and she wasn't sure how much more she should say. She never had much of a filter this early in the morning, and she couldn't decide if that would be a blessing or a curse in this instance. "I didn't mean to… Wait, why couldn't you sleep?"

Tori exhaled heavily. "Look, Genevieve, I know that the legal community is small, and we're bound to run into each other. I wasn't sure how I'd feel, seeing you again. But now I know—it's too hard to be near you and not be with you. I'd rather not see you for a while. So, if possible, please don't…be places where you know I'm going to be." The request seemed torn from her throat.

Genevieve rubbed her eyes. On the way home the night before, she'd practiced a little speech to give to Tori, but Tori didn't seem to be in the mood to hear it. And besides, she didn't really want to have *that* conversation over the phone.

"I thought your idea was really brilliant. I've been to hundreds of events like that, and this is the first time I've seen someone give up the microphone for a more interactive, community-building experience."

"Coalition building," Tori corrected, mumbling.

"How do you think it went?"

"We didn't have as much time at the end as I had wanted, for people to report back to the group what they'd discussed and learned. But we still had some great stories. And some of the women have formed new listservs and, I guess, also monthly potlucks."

"Look at you, Tori. Making actual change in the world," Genevieve said, unable to keep the pride from her voice.

"Don't do that," Tori said, softly.

"Hmm? What? Don't do what?"

"Don't act like we still mean something to each other, or you care, or—"

Genevieve sat up in bed and tossed the covers off. "Tori, I will always care. We will always mean something to each other."

"So have you changed your mind?" Tori said, and her voice cracked.

Genevieve paused. If she was going to tell her she still loved her and, yes, she wanted Tori back, now was the time. But as soon as the prospect became real, Genevieve forgot her speech. Yes, she loved Tori, but they were doing more fighting than anything else before Genevieve ended things, and it wasn't at all clear to her things had changed—that they wouldn't fall back into the same patterns and both end up unhappy again. She thought of the way Tori's voice had sounded that last night in the wine bar. She never wanted to make her sound like that again.

"I'll take that as a no. I'm going to hang up now, Genevieve. Good-bye."

"Tori, let me explain—" Genevieve said, but the line went dead.

Genevieve dropped her phone onto her pillow, leaned her head against the headboard, and closed her eyes.

She could go over there. Try to explain in person. But they would either fight, or end up in bed together having not worked anything out, or both.

After rubbing the sleep out of her eyes, she picked up her cell phone and dialed Jamie. His "hello" sounded as groggy as she imagined hers had a few minutes earlier. "Morning, Jamie. So, about that run …"

CHAPTER 27

When she'd given her interview to *They've Got Issues* six months ago, before this year's SCOTUS session began, Victoria hadn't expected to be back so soon. And she certainly hadn't anticipated how different things would be. She should probably be relieved that her personal circumstances were no longer going to be a topic of conversation.

As she watched the technical staff bustling about the studio, she took a sip of her tea and returned it to a saucer on the table between her chair and Vishal's empty one, next to a copy of her book, *International Law and its Implications on the US Judiciary*. Not exactly a catchy title, but then again, as a celebrity in her field, she didn't really need one to sell books. And the title was apt. Her editor had suggested some other ones, but they didn't really suit the subject matter, and in the end Victoria's original title had stuck.

The book hit the shelves last week, and she'd grudgingly agreed when her publisher set her up with three different interviews to promote it. In addition to *They've Got Issues*, she'd be talking to Terry Gross of NPR next week and stopping by *Good Morning America* the week after that. Victoria had given her publisher a lot of pushback on the last one—she knew the Court police wouldn't be overly fond of her hanging out in Times Square. After multiple phone calls between Pollard and her editor, they'd decided on some sort of schedule of events and security detail. Eventually they would even share it with her, and maybe she'd feel like less of a puppet.

She took another sip of tea, endured some fussing from the makeup crew, and reviewed talking points in her head. This interview promised to be much easier than her last one since she wasn't the subject; her book was.

A voice came through the sound system, asking for a sound check, and when someone asked her to test her microphone, she said, "In a globalized world, it is essential that the US judiciary weigh international law when reaching domestic decisions. On issues ranging from the death penalty to—"

"Thank you, Justice Willoughby," the unseen technician said through the sound system. "Someone get Vishal out here to check his mic, please. He's late."

Some commotion to her right caught Victoria's attention, and she turned to see Vishal coming from offstage, his jacket in his hand, dripping. "—find me another, or else I can change suits entirely," he said.

Vishal took his seat next to her, and an assistant swapped out the coffee-stained jacket for a new one.

"Victoria!" he said, holding out his hand to her.

When they shook hands, it felt like greeting an old friend, and she marveled yet again at his ability to put people at ease.

"Lovely to see you again, Vishal," she said.

"Thanks for giving me some fascinating reading material," he said. "Has Kellen read this? I'd love to see the different shades of red his face must have turned when he got to the part about—"

"One minute, everyone!" someone called out, and the energy in the room immediately transitioned from frantic to quiet. Vishal winked at her, sat back in his chair a bit, and smoothed his jacket. Victoria took one final sip of tea before: "We're live in five, four, three…"

The show's theme song blared, and they were off. Victoria relished the opportunity to talk with someone knowledgeable not only about US and international laws, but also the inner workings of the Court and its politics. She had to bite her tongue more than once, cautioning herself not to speak out of turn about the things the justices shared behind closed doors. They went through the book chapter by chapter, and Vishal concluded by asking her what she was going to write next.

"An e-mail to my editor telling her I'm taking a year off!" Victoria said, and Vishal laughed.

She was about to thank him for having her, when he resituated in his chair and the tone in the room seemed to change. Her right hand was resting on the arm of her chair, and she squeezed it, bracing herself.

"The last time we talked, Justice Willoughby, I asked you if you thought your relationship with Genevieve Fornier would change your respective professional careers. Mere months later, Ms. Fornier stepped down from a case that seemed very personal to her, apparently so that you could vote on it. Have you two worked out how you're going to negotiate your careers going forward so as to avoid this kind of conflict? And, I have to ask, how did that particular case affect your relationship?"

Victoria closed her eyes for the briefest of moments. "Well, Vishal, it ended it."

His eyes widened. "I wasn't aware of that," he said not unkindly.

Evidently, the discretion Victoria always displayed when it came to her personal life was working, and the media was way behind the times.

"Yes, well, I don't know if you've noticed, but I'm kind of a private person," Victoria said.

Vishal laughed. "So, then, can we expect Genevieve to argue in front of the Court again?" he asked, his eyebrows knitted.

Victoria felt the color drain from her face, but she managed not to wince. "I don't know, Vishal. I think this is uncharted territory."

"Last time you were here, I expressed concern that your romance might have an adverse effect on civil rights cases in this country. I apologize if that was a bit thoughtless on my part. My condolences that the reverse came to pass."

"Yes, well, as much as I'd like to blame the rules of professional conduct for lawyers, I think this one's on me."

If possible, Vishal's eyes grew even wider. It was perhaps the most personal statement Victoria had ever publicly made, but somehow saying it out loud didn't fill her with regret or make her palms sweat. "We all make mistakes," she said and shrugged, but she knew her voice sounded sad. "So," she cleared her throat, "I can't really say if she'll be arguing in front of the Court again. But I can tell you that my book is available in bookstores everywhere, and also through online retailers."

Vishal laughed good-naturedly at her transparent change of subject and turned to the camera. "And even if you're not a legal scholar, it's a great read. Excellent stories and events from history that I'd never known about before. And Victoria's writing style is accessible and refreshingly funny." He turned back to her. "Justice Willoughby, wonderful to have you back on the show. You're welcome any time."

"Thank you for having me, Vishal." They shook hands, the theme song blared again, and someone offstage announced, "We're off!"

Later that evening, Victoria sat at the table on her back patio drinking a glass of wine. The June sun was flirting with the horizon, and a slight breeze tickled the leaves in the trees. Her tomato and basil plants were starting to grow, and the daffodils were already on the back end of their blooms.

She'd moved here when she'd first started out as a judge on the DC Court of Appeals. In the past decade, she'd come to love this house—the quiet of it, the space. The backyard with her garden and the hummingbird feeder, and the hammock she'd never once used. The kitchen, which couldn't have had a more functional layout or better appliances.

But the house was big. Three bedrooms, three baths. A huge dining room table where five chairs sat empty every night unless her brother and his family came over for dinner, which almost never happened. It was way more space than one person needed. She had always thought it was perfect, but maybe it hadn't served her very well after all.

She needed a change. She heard Genevieve's voice in her head and revised her statement: she needed *to* change. After a trip inside to refill her wine glass and grab her laptop, she returned to her patio table and started searching for real estate in the DC area.

Maybe she should live in a hipper neighborhood. Some place where new restaurants were regularly opening and college kids drank beer. She did a quick search for properties in Foggy Bottom, where, according to this particular website, the median age was twenty-eight and only 2 percent of families had children. The listings overflowed with apartments and condos but no houses that interested her. A search for Cleveland Park brought up a lot of places that looked ideal for Genevieve and not at all appealing to Victoria.

She sighed and searched for Georgetown. There were a dozen places that she found attractive, especially a $6.8 million house on the Potomac. Okay, perhaps that one was a teensy bit out of her price range. She was about to close the browser when she glanced at the final property on her screen.

It was a white townhouse with a red brick driveway leading to a two-car garage. The shutters were black, and the front door was red. The pictures of the kitchen had her practically drooling, and the sunroom facing the backyard looked perfect for reading the morning paper. There was even a back patio that would suit the table she was sitting at right now.

It was walking distance to everything but the Metro, which she couldn't take anyway. Imagine the look Pollard would give her if she suggested it.

Pictures could be misleading, of course, but from everything she'd seen so far, she'd love it. And it would probably be a lot healthier for her to be less isolated.

She wasn't ready to up and move—not by a long shot—but doing a little research might be fun. She fired off a quick message to the agent listed on the posting to schedule a viewing.

The wine was delicious, and the sky was almost orange as she leaned back in her chair, feeling proud of herself.

She was about to head back inside when her phone rang with a number she didn't recognize. A quick glance at her laptop confirmed it was the agent's phone number, and she accepted the call. After going back and forth on dates and times, they landed on the end of the week for a viewing—Friday at 7:00 p.m.

As she hung up the call, the significance of that day and time wasn't lost on Victoria, and she wondered if Genevieve still swam then. She suspected they'd both been studiously avoiding any appearances at their mutual fitness center at their former rendezvous time.

As she headed back inside to clean the kitchen and settle down with a book, she wondered what else they'd both given up because of their split.

CHAPTER 28

Wrapping up the Court's session had never felt this stressful or frustrating. There was an unusual amount of last-minute jockeying as justices suddenly refused to sign opinions they'd previously given verbal agreement that they'd join. Clerks were scrambling to write concurring opinions, and the outcome in some cases was as yet undetermined.

On Tuesday night, Victoria typed away at her laptop in her home office, trying to tweak the wording on her voting rights decision in order to keep Jamison on board after he waffled. She revised the same section for the eighth time that evening, then pushed back her chair and rubbed her face. After sighing and squaring her shoulders, she looked at the document open on her computer... and her shoulders slumped. She just didn't have it in her to rework this opinion one more time. Closing her laptop gave her much more satisfaction than any of the work she'd done that night, and she turned off the lights in the office.

She was heading upstairs when her cell phone beeped. Glancing at the screen while she climbed, she saw a text from Genevieve, and her feet forgot how to navigate steps. Communicating in any way with Genevieve left her tied in knots, and it would be best for her mental health if she avoided it altogether. But she never did have much strength of will in this area.

After stumbling into her room and perching on her bed, Victoria opened the text message:

I'm choosing to be flattered and amused by these.

There was a link to a website. Victoria adjusted her glasses and tapped the URL, which opened a Wordpress website for an undergraduate course at Georgetown called Media and Law. Naturally, Professor Dating My Student and Interrupting Your Dinner Date would make his course website public—the man had serious boundary issues.

She scrolled down his class syllabus to the link for week thirteen, "Romance in the Legal Community: The Curious Case of Victoria Willoughby and Genevieve Fornier," and almost gagged. Steeling herself, she tapped the link.

> Your assignment for this week is to propose
> a media representation of the relationship
> between Willoughby and Fornier. This
> representation can take the form of a TV
> pilot, a music video, a graphic novel—you
> get the picture. Think creatively, but
> as with all your assignments, you'll be
> assessed on how well you incorporate our
> course material and themes. The proposal
> should be 2-3 pages.

Below the assignment prompt were the files students had submitted.

Oh, for crying out loud. This should be interesting. Victoria clicked on the first student's submission, which was a proposal called *SCOTUS Love, the Musical*. Victoria was to be played by an alto and Genevieve by a soprano. Rolling her eyes, she texted Genevieve:

What's your vocal range?

The student called for the musical to end with a rousing group number where all nine justices sang on the steps of the Court. The student obviously had an idealized view of the harmony between justices, both metaphorically and musically.

Her phone beeped with Genevieve's reply:

> *Oh, I can definitely hit the high notes in "A good lawyer knows the law, a great lawyer knows the judge."*

Victoria smiled as she wrote back:

> *Really? Because I always imagined you as an alto.*

As soon as she saw Genevieve's reply, Victoria laughed before she could help herself.

> *I'm flexible.*

Victoria clicked on the next student's submission, a Lifetime movie entitled *Lawyer's Appeal*, and snorted. The opening shot was of a redheaded woman sitting in a bay window, looking mournfully out at the trees beyond while rain dripped down the panes, accompanied by Yanni.

Genevieve texted again.

> *Did you get to the second one? Because when I picture you, it's always with rain and Yanni.*

Victoria's first impulse was to ask, *You picture me?* But she went with:

> *Oh, give me a bay window and some rain, and I can brood with the best of them.*

Victoria glanced sadly out her window, the perfect embodiment of what that student envisioned her to be.

> *God, Tori, I hope this student failed the assignment—*
> *that wedding at the end is too sentimental to stomach.*

> *What's too much—the beach, or fact that we're on*
> *horses?*

> *Both—and that we braided each other's hair first.*

Victoria let out a bark of laughter—she'd missed that part. She skimmed the proposal again and yep, there it was: before they walked—no, wait, *rode their horses* down the aisle, they sat underneath a waterfall and braided each other's hair.

> *I'm confused—are we on the horses for the hair*
> *braiding, or do we mount them after?*

> *She doesn't say. Looks like a plot hole.*

Victoria glanced back at the student's name: Quinn O'Brien. Pretty gender neutral.

> *How do you know it's a "she?"*

> *More importantly, how does the third student know*
> *about the secret removable panel in your chambers*
> *where I sneak in?*

Victoria navigated to the next submission, a graphic novel called *Law Suits* that—if the capes, masks, and flying were any indication—was a comedy.

> *What would your superhero name be?*

Genevieve texted back immediately.

Amicus Breeze.

That was fast—been thinking about this for a while?

A mock-trial student I worked with in Chicago gave me that name a long time ago.

The image of a younger Genevieve mentoring high school students filled Victoria's heart.

That's very sweet.

Your turn—what's your superhero name?

Sighing, Victoria stared at the ceiling for a full minute and came up empty.

Um, Wonder Judge?

The reply text came quickly.

Oh, we can do better than that. How about Justice Jax?

Jax?

Why not? Sounds cool. Sounds like someone people won't mess with.

Victoria shrugged.

I'll take it.

She tapped through some of the other proposals students had submitted about her relationship with Genevieve. They were uniformly supportive—not a single student was homophobic or found ethical issues with a justice and lawyer seeing each other. Some representations were more saccharine than others, but Victoria and Genevieve were without fail the heroes of each play, novel, or action movie. The students seemed to idolize them as individuals and as a couple—or else, that's what made the best story.

Victoria looked back at her texting conversation with Genevieve, but she hadn't received a new message in five minutes. She stared at the last one Genevieve had sent: *Sounds like someone people won't mess with*. How deeply should she read into that?

It was late, she was tired, and tomorrow promised to be an equally frustrating day at work. As she got ready for bed, she clicked through a few news sites, starting with CNN. Nothing particularly newsworthy seemed to have happened that day. She crawled into bed and checked her phone one last time—no new texts from Genevieve. After rereading their text conversation and wondering what it all meant, she wrote, *Good night, Genevieve*, turned off her volume, and put the phone on her nightstand without waiting to see if Genevieve would write back.

C～⤶♋

The following afternoon, Alistair's pacing across her office in the Court was driving her bananas, and she had to bite her tongue from telling him to sit down or get out. She turned the page on the decision she was reading, and he grunted.

"Victoria, I asked you to skim it, not to copyedit the damn thing."

She removed her glasses and reminded herself to be patient with him—he'd spent years being patient with her. "Alistair, I think it's very good. I would be proud to sign my name on this."

He stopped pacing and stared at her. "But?"

She shrugged. "But I think you need to soften the language about animus if you are serious about courting Kellen. His record on LGBTQ rights is pretty spotty, and he might take anything you say about animus personally. Telling states to issue birth certificates with gender-neutral parentage would be a big deal for him."

After giving her a good glare, he dropped into one of the chairs on the other side of her desk. "Damn Jamison for dumping this on my lap."

"Alistair, you know you're secretly thrilled. Although I'm still laughing at the idea that Jamison 'had too much on his plate.'"

He sighed. "How can I soften the language? The only possible motivation for separating children from their gay parents *is* animus. It's bigotry masquerading as some kind of concern for the children, when in reality, their lives would be destroyed if suddenly they had to go live with strangers."

"Listen, Alistair, I agree with you. I feel strongly about this too. But Kellen will never sign an opinion that calls this animus. He believes it's a legitimate concern arising from religious convictions, even if he might also believe that the law should not bow to that concern."

Alistair looked at his tea. "I'm going to need something stronger than this."

Smiling, Victoria pointed to a cabinet beneath her tea maker. "Whiskey?"

After giving her an eye roll, Alistair stood. "I meant caffeinated tea, not spiked." He pulled out his phone and scrolled through something. "Tomorrow we release the decision on the Clean Air Act and the two health care cases. Those three are done—nothing more to do there. The gay parentage decision is scheduled for release on Monday…"

He looked up at her, brows knitted. "I'm so close to getting Kellen to join us. I really want this 7-2 victory—it would be such a decisive win for LGBTQ rights."

"Do you want me to try to talk to him?" Victoria offered with as much enthusiasm as if she were suggesting she could birth a calf.

"I'm not sure that would be good for his health—or yours. I'm off to revise this *again*. Expect to read another draft in two hours." He mimed a hat tip and left her office.

Her head was spinning, and it was long past lunchtime. She pulled out the leftover pasta she'd brought from home, knowing she wouldn't have time to step away from her desk once she walked through the door. While she ate, she clicked through the news, bored with the events of the world and her own habits of procrastination.

For lack of anything better to do, and with mixed feelings, she navigated to I Fought the Law. Sure enough, the second post down was about her. The infamous picture of her and Genevieve almost kissing had been cut into two, the outline of a broken heart superimposed over the pieces, and the blog post read: *Splitzies for our favorite legal couple?*

The post began with a summary of Victoria's interview on *They've Got Issues* and concluded with speculation about what she might have meant when she said "this one's on me." The writer suggested that Victoria had put her career over their relationship, which she supposed wasn't far from the truth.

Without really overanalyzing why, she opened her iMessage, copied and pasted the link to the blog post, and texted it to Genevieve, along with the message,

This site should start paying us for material.

She had finished her pasta, and still no reply, so she turned her focus back to work.

Alistair breezed back into her office around four, an hour later than he'd promised when he'd left. "I got caught up in a conversation with Michelle about architecture. Sorry!"

"Architecture? Who has time for casual conversation this week? It's crunch time, Alistair," Victoria said.

He smirked at her. "Well, I liked your idea about the whiskey—just a splash, mind you. And I think you'll find that this draft reads much better." He dropped a binder-clipped stack of paper on her desk. "I printed a redlined version, so you can easily see my edits."

She held out a similarly thick stack of paper, this one not binder-clipped. "Here's the final of Michelle's opinion on the Clean Air Act. It's good."

He sat, and they read in silence for forty-five minutes. When she finally pushed back from her desk and took her glasses off, he did the same.

"Michelle's is good," he said. "I can't for the life of me imagine why it won't be unanimous, but evidently, some justices don't believe in science."

"I don't think it's science so much as they don't believe businesses should bear the financial burden for solving global warming," Victoria said.

He cocked his head at her. "That's charitable, Victoria."

"I think it's reasonable," she said with a shrug, "but it's also shortsighted. Industry has created the problem. Industry needs to work to fix it."

Pointing to the papers in her hand, Alistair raised his eyebrows. "Well?" he asked. "Is it better?"

"Yes, I think you can show this to Kellen. And who knows? He might even sign it."

His shoulders lowered. "Whew. God, I won't miss wooing that man with my writing."

"I call foul. You'll miss it intensely."

He gave her a crooked smile. "I suppose I will."

"This is it, then? The last decision you'll write?" Victoria waved the papers in her hand.

"Yes, ma'am. And I'm immensely proud of it."

She passed it back to him. "You going to walk it down to Kellen's office?"

He nodded, wistfully. "Guess so. Thanks for your feedback, Victoria." He headed toward the door, and his hand was on the knob when she called out to him.

"Alistair, Kellen's a pain in the ass, but it's okay that you're going to miss him."

"Yes, I know." His voice tightened almost imperceptibly. "I'll miss all of you, you pains in my ass."

As he closed the door behind him, Victoria tried not to think about how much *she* would miss *him* and how quiet her office would be without him inviting himself in multiple times a day.

After gathering up binders and her laptop, Victoria headed home, where she would spend the night doing what she'd done all day: researching and writing.

Alistair's wife was in remission, and Victoria still wasn't convinced that retirement would make him happy, but during crunch-time weeks—especially the last few weeks of June when all outstanding cases had to be decided—she could certainly understand the appeal of work-free evenings.

Four hours and a salad later, Victoria was done working for the night. Not to say that she didn't still have loads more work she could be doing, but she was just done. She closed the French doors to her home office, padded to the living room, and flopped down on the couch.

Maybe a little television would help quiet her brain. She clicked the remote and stopped when she got to a Pavarotti concert on PBS. He was performing her favorite song from *Tosca*, but she clicked around again until she found a rerun of *Cheers*, which seemed just mindless enough to help her zone out.

Sam was pouring beer, and Woody was being oblivious as usual when her phone beeped. She'd managed to forget all about texting Genevieve earlier.

Should we charge them by the word, or flat fee?

Victoria felt that familiar rush of adrenaline as her fingers typed.

I was thinking per post.

Ah, well, we need a plan to make more headlines then—otherwise, this income source is going to dry up.

Victoria tapped her finger to her lips a few times, pondering.

One sec—I've got an idea.

She collected her laptop from her office, navigated to the blog post on I Fought the Law about their breakup, did some speedy typing in the comments section, identified herself as Justice Jax, and hit *submit*.

*Handled. Check out the most recent comment on that
blog post.*

A few minutes passed while Victoria scrolled through all the
article's comments, most of which expressed sadness at the breakup.
Well, it was nice to know that the legal community was behind
their relationship, even if Genevieve wasn't.

Genevieve still hadn't responded when Victoria reached her
own comment at the bottom:

Shame about the breakup—especially since an entire class of
undergraduate students has written comic books and television
pilots about them!

And there was a link to the course website.
Her phone buzzed with Genevieve's reply.

I can't believe you just did that.

Victoria's heart skipped a beat, and she bit her lip hard. Crap,
she clearly hadn't thought this through.

*I'm so sorry—I should have asked. Do you want me
to delete it?*

*Hell no! I think everyone in the legal community
should read those assignments. And some Hollywood
producers, too.*

*LOL! I'll reach out to Lifetime about that melodramatic
one.*

Genevieve seemed to hesitate—her response came a few seconds
later than the rhythm they'd established. Then:

Are you serious? I can't tell with you right now… I'm still in shock that you shared that website with the entire legal community.

Well, that was fair. She was kind of in shock too. But she shrugged and typed back:

I'm trying this new thing where I don't hide all the time.

When Genevieve didn't write back immediately, Victoria tried to return her attention to the television. Why wasn't Genevieve saying anything? Maybe she was mad Victoria had posted that link after all?

Spinning out about Genevieve definitely wasn't going to help her get to sleep. She moved to turn off the television when her phone rang.

Gazing at the screen that read *Genevieve calling*, Victoria contemplated not answering. Talking right now would only confuse her and weaken her resolve to move on. But Genevieve would know… And it was impossible, really, not to take whatever kernels were being offered to her, as awful as that felt. She tapped *accept*.

"Hey."

"Hey. Listen, Tori, I watched your interview. You know that this—our breakup—wasn't 'on you,' don't you? You're right when you said that we all make mistakes. You made yours in law school. I made mine this past December."

The books lining the walls of her living room swam a little, and her voice caught as she tried to respond. If they'd been texting, she would have written back *what are you saying?* But she wasn't about to say that out loud in the more intimate medium of a phone call.

"You sound tired," was the best she could come up with.

"I'm not surprised. I flew home late last night, woke up in DC for a breakfast fundraiser, gave an interview in New York, and finalized case prep in Michigan this afternoon. I'm in a shitty hotel room with itchy sheets."

"That sounds awful."

"Well, it's a hell of a lot better than the cell my client's in."

"How's she holding up? Amelia, right?"

"She's okay. I've got to say, my staff managing the media for this case has done an amazing job, and the prison administration has suddenly become remarkably accommodating to her mental health and hormone needs. She's been given access to a therapist once a week, which has made a huge difference in her overall well-being. I have to wonder, though, if they're taking these more minor steps in the hopes of winning the case and avoiding more robust support for her. Also, seeing the way that the prison staff is bending over backward for this one inmate because she's the plaintiff in a high-profile lawsuit throws into sharp relief how hard it is for other inmates to access these basic services."

"You can't save everyone, Genevieve," Victoria said. "Focus on the ones you can save—each case you win changes real lives."

"I'm not sure that's the best attitude to have if you want to change the world," Genevieve said, her voice lowering. Victoria pictured her lying on her back in a crappy hotel-room bed. "Aren't I supposed to dream bigger?"

"Dream big, and find satisfaction in small victories."

"Well, look at you. That's a very optimistic attitude. I wouldn't have expected—"

"I'm trying to change some things, Genevieve. I think I know the things about me that you found…unworkable. I'm trying to be more open. More generous, less exacting."

"Look, Victoria, I want to talk to you about this, but I'd rather do it in person than when I'm in Michigan."

"Great," Victoria mumbled, "I just love waiting."

Genevieve laughed, a sound that warmed Victoria's heart.

"Sorry, did I say that out loud?"

"Little bit," Genevieve said. "Anyway, arguments are tomorrow, and I'll probably take Friday to catch up on work. Or sleep. So... dinner Saturday night?"

"I'd love to," Victoria said.

"Want me to come to your place?"

Genevieve probably didn't mean the question as a test, but Victoria was determined to pass it anyway. "No, let's go out. Or I can come over, if you'd like. You pick."

"Oh! Sure, come over here. I'd like that."

"Me too," Victoria said.

"Great. I'll text you on Saturday, then."

"Get some sleep, Genevieve. And, good luck tomorrow." She hesitated, then added, "I'll be thinking about you."

The smile in Genevieve's voice sounded guarded but genuine. "I'll be thinking of you too. Good night, Tori."

After turning off the TV and closing the blinds, Victoria headed upstairs, feeling lighter than she had in days. The next day at work would begin with the justices seated at the bench in the Court and releasing decisions, which would be a fun break in her routine of researching, writing, and editing opinions. When she crawled into bed and closed her eyes, she heard Genevieve's rich voice in her head saying over and over again, *I'll be thinking of you too. Good night, Tori.*

She slept better than she had in months.

CHAPTER 29

With everything else on her plate as president of HER, Amelia's case was the only one Genevieve was taking point on. She felt a familiar thrill buzz through her as she walked into the courtroom for arguments, accompanied by her team of HER lawyers. Amelia was already seated at their table, and she'd been allowed to wear civilian clothes. She looked beautiful in a light-blue dress and blazer, although upon close inspection Genevieve could see that her eyes were puffy and her hands were shaking.

She sat down and rested a hand on her client's shoulder. "The last time we were in court together, when the other side tried to get your case thrown out, we won. We've got a good track record so far."

Amelia nodded. "I practiced all the things we talked about. I know what to say and what not to say. I worked really hard on not saying 'um' between sentences."

"You're well prepared. And that's all you need to be," Genevieve said.

The judge entered, the room was called to order, and they were off.

As the plaintiff's attorney, Genevieve gave opening arguments first. She stood and buttoned her jacket.

"Your Honor, my client, Amelia Garcia, has been in the custody of Michigan's Department of Corrections for two years now.

During that time, her mental and physical state has deteriorated, and she has attempted suicide twice.

"You see, Your Honor, my client suffers from gender dysphoria. Multiple experts have attested to this, including the defense's own psychologist. The *Diagnostic and Statistical Manual of Mental Disorders* defines gender dysphoria as the condition one experiences when biological sex and the gender that person identifies with are in conflict. Amelia Garcia is female. But her biological sex contradicts this identity, and this contradiction is causing her immeasurable harm. I will call three witnesses who will demonstrate that my client requires sex reassignment surgery, and because the state is holding her, it is the state's responsibility to make this surgery financially and logistically available."

Judge Reagan Hart nodded and scribbled something on the papers in front of her. "Mr. Orr?" she said, turning to opposing counsel.

Orr nodded at Genevieve as they passed each other, and he began his opening statement. "The state stipulates that the plaintiff here is transgender, and that we have been providing her with hormone therapy to help her."

"Objection, Your Honor," Genevieve stood. "The state has intermittently provided my client with hormones, and only once we filed this lawsuit has my client had consistent access to those necessary medications."

"Your Honor," Orr said, "the medication access has been uninterrupted for the last seven months. The fact that there was a lawsuit pending is irrelevant."

"Well, I think it's obvious why the state suddenly decided to fulfill its responsibilities to Ms. Garcia when it made hormones available," Hart said. "But Mr. Orr is correct, Ms. Fornier. There's no real objection here."

Genevieve sat down, and Amelia whispered, "Is that bad?"

"Nah. The judge knows that the state has been somewhat delinquent here and that our filing this lawsuit has changed things. That's good."

"The state contends that sex reassignment surgery is an elective procedure, and an expensive one at that. Taxpayer dollars should not go to medically unnecessary procedures such as this. With the hormone drugs we commit to providing Ms. Garcia, there is no reason to undergo such a costly and cosmetic surgery."

Genevieve's team of HER lawyers deftly examined and cross-examined witnesses all morning, with little help from Genevieve. Dr. Carson's testimony turned out to be worth every penny, and she actually wondered if Orr's heart was in it, given that his witnesses weren't very strong and his cross-examination of hers seemed lethargic. Amelia took the stand right after lunch.

They had debated whether or not she would. Cross-examination was always difficult, and there was no mechanism requiring Amelia to speak on her own behalf. But she was determined to do everything she could to win her case, even if that meant enduring insulting questions intended to trick or trap her.

Genevieve's first few questions for her client were straightforward and biographical, and Amelia answered confidently; any anxiety she might be feeling she hid away so well that even Genevieve couldn't detect it.

"At what point in your life did you realize your sex and gender didn't match?" Genevieve asked her.

Amelia shifted in her seat slightly but gave no other indication of tension.

"I was four," She kept her answers simple and straightforward, just as they'd practiced.

"And how did you realize this?"

"I was playing with my neighbor—she was a girl, Gabriella. I asked her to pretend I was a girl. I told her to call me Amelia. We played together all day, and I realized."

"What did you realize?"

"That I was a girl. Whatever other people thought I was, I knew was a girl."

"And how did the people in your life react to this realization?"

"Well, I didn't tell anyone else for a long time. Gabriella was my best friend, and whenever we played together, she called me Amelia. No one else knew until high school."

"How did it feel, living two different lives?"

"Painful. I developed an eating disorder when I was twelve. When I was thirteen, I started cutting myself."

"And did anyone intervene to help you?"

"Yes, a guidance counselor at school. At first I wouldn't say anything to her, but she insisted I start seeing her every day. Finally, I told her. Everything. That I was really a girl. That I threw up after I ate. I showed her the scars on my arms."

"And what did she do?"

"Well, she started calling me Amelia when we would meet, when no one else was listening. She got me appointments with a therapist—I didn't understand this at the time, but I think she paid for them out of her own pocket."

"When did you start telling other people that your name is Amelia?"

"My senior year, right before graduation. I told my mother then. She told me to leave, not to come back. I stayed at my guidance counselor's house. She helped me legally change my name, helped me buy new clothes. After I graduated, I got a job two towns over, restocking shelves at a medical supply warehouse. Everyone there knew me as Amelia."

"And when did you start medically transitioning?"

"Very soon after I started my job, I met with a doctor, and shortly after that I started taking hormones."

"Amelia, what's the next step in your transition?"

"Surgery. All my doctors think it's essential for me. For my mental health."

"And why is that?"

"I, uh." She took a deep breath, and the quick rhythm of their question-and-answer exchange stalled. "I have anxiety. And depression. It's hard to function some days. But in prison, you don't get to, you know, lay in bed all day, even if you're too paralyzed to move."

"And these bouts of depression and anxiety, how else do they affect you?"

Amelia looked her right in the eye and said as dispassionately as she could, "I've tried to kill myself twice since I've been in prison." Her voice wavered on *twice*, but she squared her shoulders and almost dared anyone in the courtroom to challenge her.

"Amelia, if you were to have surgery, what effect would it have on your overall health?"

"I… It's like I'm in a foreign country. And no one speaks my language. And the food tastes strange, and I don't understand how to use the crosswalks, because the cars are on the wrong side of the road. If I had this surgery, it would be like coming home again. Suddenly, things would make sense. I would make sense."

"Thank you, Amelia. No more questions, Your Honor."

Genevieve sat down, and a member of the opposing legal team, Tai Bolton, stood to cross-examine. Genevieve braced herself, and

Amelia bit her nail before stopping herself and slowly, intentionally returning her hands to her lap.

"Amelia, how long is left on your sentence?" Bolton asked.

What kind of question was that? Genevieve had expected cross-examination to target Amelia's character—to suggest that she had broken the law and therefore didn't deserve expensive, elective surgery.

"Eighteen months," Amelia said.

"Eighteen months. And, how old are you now?" Bolton paced a little, a sneer on her face.

"Twenty-nine."

"You are twenty-nine years old. You've lived for twenty-nine years in that body. Don't you think it's a bit much to ask the taxpayers of Michigan to pay for an expensive surgery for you, when you could wait a measly eighteen months and have the surgery once you've been released?"

Genevieve sucked in a breath. This wasn't a line of questioning she'd expected or spent much time preparing Amelia for. "Objection!" She jumped up again. "Argumentative."

"I'll rephrase," Bolton said. "Why does the state have to pay for this surgery, when a year and a half isn't a very long time for you to wait for it?"

There were two objections she could give, but Amelia started talking before she had a chance.

"I think what you're really asking is whether this is an elective surgery," Amelia said, and Genevieve wanted to applaud right then and there. *Way to get underneath her question and bring it back to the real issues.*

"That's not what I asked," Bolton said. "A year and a half is a relatively short amount of time for someone who's nearly thirty years old to wait for something."

"Objection." Genevieve might as well stand up during Bolton's entire cross-examination at this rate. "I'm sorry, Your Honor, but is there a question in here somewhere?"

"Ms. Bolton, please ask the witness a question."

Bolton was about to try again when Amelia answered anyway. "Eighteen months is an eternity for anyone living in prison. It's an eternity for anyone who feels like a foreigner in their own body. It's forever for a person who struggles to get out of bed every day. Put all of this together. Eighteen months is longer than I'll survive."

Bolton tried a few more times to get Amelia to say she could wait to have surgery until after her release—including suggesting that maybe Amelia might be eligible for release in nine months and asking how quickly it was even possible to schedule such a surgery.

It was an unexpected strategy. Bolton wasn't questioning whether Amelia needed the surgery—just when she needed it. She wasn't putting forward any arguments that could be construed as transphobic; she never implied that Amelia was really a man or that trans people were less deserving of state services or even that the surgery wasn't something the state should cover for incarcerated people. She just suggested that it might not be something it needed to cover for *this* incarcerated person who might be released before the surgery could even be scheduled.

Bolton concluded her cross-examination, and Genevieve rose to wrap up. "Amelia, has anyone, other than Ms. Bolton, right now, suggested to you that you might be released in nine months?"

Amelia shook her head with dignified certainty. "No. This is the first I'm hearing of it."

"And why do you think that is?"

"Well, maybe Ms. Bolton knows something I don't know. Maybe the prison wants to release me early so it doesn't have to pay."

"Objection," Bolton said. "Speculation."

"Sustained."

Genevieve nodded and continued. "And Amelia, have you ever discussed with a doctor what the process of scheduling such a surgery would be?"

"Yes. Surgeons schedule this procedure three months in advance. That's all."

"No more questions, Your Honor."

Amelia returned to her seat next to Genevieve, and after court was adjourned and everyone stood to leave, Genevieve hugged her. The prison guard escorting her took a step toward them, but she gave him a dirty look from over Amelia's shoulder. Still, she kept the hug brief.

"So. We wait now?" Amelia asked, crossing her arms and shifting her weight from foot to foot.

"Yep. I expect we'll hear in four to six weeks."

Amelia shrugged as if it didn't matter to her one bit, but she fidgeted with her fingers, then crossed her arms again. "Waiting sucks."

"I know. I want an answer yesterday too. I'm sorry that we had to go to trial and that things have taken this long. But I think we did well today."

"Yeah? You think we'll win?"

Genevieve hesitated. It was the worst question a client ever asked but also the most understandable. "I think we have a better case. We had better witnesses. Our legal theory—that there's an Eighth Amendment issue here—is solid. So I'm optimistic."

It wasn't a yes. But it was as close as she'd ever give a client.

Amelia nodded, and her escort stepped forward. "Thanks, Genevieve. For everything."

"Stay strong, Amelia."

The guard put a hand on her back and guided her toward the door. When he opened it for her, she glanced over her shoulder at Genevieve and waved.

It was strange, saying good-bye. The judge's decision would come down electronically; prison officials would download it from the Internet and give a copy to Amelia. Unless the decision was appealed, it was distinctly possible Genevieve wouldn't see her client again—barring a trip Genevieve made to the prison just to visit.

She'd done some work on depositions and securing the expert witness, and she'd done the direct examination of Amelia, but her legal team from HER had taken the bulk of the case, including handling the settlement conference entirely without her. She might think of herself as a litigation expert, but her best contribution to this case had been staffing it well.

Genevieve's 9:00 p.m. flight out of Michigan had her practically sleepwalking through the door of her townhouse at eleven thirty. She barely made it to her bedroom before collapsing and falling into a dreamless sleep.

On Friday, she woke up refreshed for the first time in months. There was nothing more she could do for Amelia's case, and she was proud of the way she'd argued it. She had some decisions to make now, including whether she wanted to continue litigating or move more into administration—it was increasingly draining to try to do both. Maybe she'd go for a run and do some soul-searching.

She stretched and grabbed her phone from her nightstand. There were a few e-mails from her staff, one from Jamie about their progress on the non-discrimination act and one from Penelope. She hesitated, then tapped it.

> Hi Genevieve,
>
> I know you had arguments in the sex reassignment case yesterday—how'd they go? Listen, if we're going to be friends, let's actually be friends. Want to grab a drink tonight and catch up?
>
> P

Well, that was unexpected. And very healthy. That was the thing about Penelope—she was so well-adjusted. Genevieve contemplated her reply, then wrote back:

> Hi Penelope,
>
> A drink sounds great. There's a wine bar in my neighborhood, unless you had somewhere else in mind. Let me know.

She stared at the e-mail for a minute, trying to figure out how to sign off. She settled for *see you soon. -Genevieve.*

Once she got caught up on e-mail, including a quick back and forth with Penelope confirming drinks at the wine bar at seven, she texted Frank that she'd be working from home that day. His reply was quick.

> Thank God. You must be exhausted. "Work" from home the way everyone else in the world does and watch Netflix. Or read. You're one of those people who reads, aren't you?

Spending the day in yoga pants, reading a novel, and snacking on pretzels sounded perfect, so that's exactly what she did. She went for a late afternoon run and was about to get in the shower when her phone buzzed with a text from Tori.

> *I know we're supposed to see each other tomorrow, and I know this is last minute, but I was wondering if you would meet me someplace tonight. There's something I want you to see. Can you be here at 7:00 p.m.?*

And there was an address for a place in Georgetown.

Tori being spontaneous? When was the last time that happened?

She rubbed her forehead and put her phone on the bathroom countertop. Drinks with Penelope or a mysterious date with Tori? A quick glance at her phone confirmed that it was too late to try to reschedule drinks for earlier and do both—it was already five forty-five, and she desperately needed to wash off the sweat from her run. The shower was already running, so she postponed her decision.

Cleaned and refreshed, she stepped out of the shower. Seriously, who was she kidding?

First, she texted Penelope.

> *I'm so sorry about this, but can I take a rain check on drinks? Something's come up.*

She then texted Tori.

> *I'm game. See you in a bit.*

Her phone buzzed almost immediately with a reply from Penelope:

> *Tell Victoria I say hi. See you later.*

She wasn't sure how to interpret that text, but before she could worry about it, her phone buzzed again, this time with a text from Tori.

Great! Looking forward to seeing you.

Not really knowing what she was getting into for the evening, Genevieve chose linen pants and a low-cut blouse. Almost as an afterthought, she also put on the pendant necklace Tori had given her. She wasn't really sure what to expect from their dynamic tonight, but she wanted to signal immediately that, as sentimental as it might sound, Tori was still close to her heart.

Traffic was worse than she anticipated, and at six minutes past seven, she pulled into the driveway of a house with a red door. She parked next to Tori's car and headed inside, wondering who lived here. The path to the front door was red brick, and the front lawn was well-landscaped. Whoever Tori wanted her to meet, they had good taste.

The door was slightly ajar, and she pushed it open and called out, "Hello?"

"In the kitchen." Tori answered.

The entryway was expansive and stretched upward two stories. A staircase to the second floor wound in an arc from her right to her left, and a contemporary chandelier of small chains and little glass balls filed with light hung above her head. The floor was black-and-white tile, with the railing and molding providing red accents. It was somehow both classic and mod, and she liked the aesthetic instantly.

She headed to her right, through a sitting room, and into the kitchen, where Tori and a man in a suit were talking about, of all things, plumbing.

286

Tori turned to her, and as soon as their eyes met, her chest and neck turned red, the way they did whenever Genevieve kissed her. "Genevieve, hi," she said a little breathlessly. She approached Genevieve, then stopped in front of her and hesitated.

They hadn't been this close to each other since Tori had kissed her on the cheek in the wine bar after Genevieve had broken up with her.

They stared awkwardly at each other for a long minute. *Don't overthink this.*

She grabbed Tori's hands, leaned forward, and kissed her on the cheek, lingering for the briefest of moments. While her lips pressed gently against Tori's skin, she inhaled, enjoying the smell of Tori's perfume.

Tori sighed softly, sending pleasant vibrations all through Genevieve. They pulled apart, but Tori's eyes remained closed for a beat, and Genevieve grinned.

When the man in the suit cleared his throat, Tori opened her eyes and smiled sheepishly. "Sorry. Raul, this is Genevieve."

They shook hands and Genevieve said, "How do you two know each other?"

Raul looked confused for a moment before Tori cut in. "We don't, really. Raul's showing me the house."

"Raul's showing you the...oh! Wait, you're looking to buy this place?"

Tori cleared her throat, then looked at Raul. "Would you mind if we looked around on our own for a bit?"

"Not at all," he said. "I'll be in the backyard if you have any questions."

Tori placed a hand on Genevieve's lower back, a proprietary and intimate gesture Genevieve was surprised Tori would do in front of a real estate agent, and led her into the dining room. "What do you think—do you like it?"

"I...What on earth is happening? Am I in some alternate dimension?" Genevieve walked around the dining room table. "Are you selling your house? You love your house."

Behind her, Tori trailed her hand across the backs of the chairs around the table. "I do. But you don't. Not really." She inhaled audibly. "And, Genevieve, I love you. I know you said that we don't work as a couple, but I still think we can. So I thought maybe if we found a place that was new to both of us—that wasn't mine and wasn't yours—well, maybe..."

She looked away.

Genevieve was in a strange house, with some strange version of Tori, standing in a strange room, with a real estate agent outside. The whole situation had her mind reeling. "I'm sorry." She rubbed her eyes. "What are you saying?"

"Look, if you don't like this place...we can keep looking together; or, if you're not ready to... It's just an idea. I just wanted to...be impetuous."

"Wait, are you... You're saying you want to buy a house with me?"

Tori looked at her, all vulnerability and hope, and Genevieve's heartbeat doubled.

"Yes. I want to live with you, and I think that's only going to make us both happy if neither of us moves in with the other. We should pick out a place together."

Her gaze searched Genevieve's even as Genevieve continued to gape at her.

"I've gone about this all wrong, haven't I? I'm not trying to force you into *this* house. We can look up listings together. Search together. I wasn't trying to pick out a house for you without your input. I get it—this is probably me just being controlling again, right? I'm sorry. We should just go. Let's talk about this some other time. I—"

Genevieve placed a finger on her lips. "Sh. Stop talking. You sound like a loon. Everything about this is entirely out of your comfort zone. It's super romantic. And it means a lot to me that you'd be willing to give up your sanctuary for me. For us. I can't believe you even would, after what an ass I was."

"We've both made mistakes. We need a new start. Maybe this place—or some place like it—could be it."

Genevieve raised her eyebrows. "You do know we're in Georgetown, right? Notorious for its impossible parking?"

Tori shrugged. "This place has a two-car garage. And we can walk to restaurants—no need to drive."

Genevieve walked to the windows and studied them, then turned to take in the flooring and the outlet locations. The ceiling looked solid. She pulled out her phone—cell service was good. "How many bedrooms?" she asked, turning back to Tori.

Tori's face lit up at the question. "Three. So we can each have a home office, or we can set one up as a guest room, or... How many bedrooms do you want?"

"And you're really ready to give up your house?"

Tori walked to her, stopping when their bodies were close. Genevieve could feel heat coming off her.

"Genevieve, it's just a house. I want more than that. I want you."

"I want you too—" Genevieve started, but Tori's lips were on hers, and Tori's hands were on her hips, and she forgot what else she was going to say. She slid her hands into Tori's hair, and when Tori pulled their bodies together, she moaned.

Tori's lips left hers, and she almost whimpered. With their foreheads resting together and their chests heaving in unison, Tori put her hand on Genevieve's cheek. "Take me back, Genevieve. Please."

Genevieve nodded, trying to catch her breath. "And here I thought I'd be the one begging for another chance."

"I don't need you to beg. I need to know what you want. There's all this white noise around us, this interference. It's just you and me right now. Tell me, do you want someone else? Something else?"

Genevieve laughed—evidently Tori did know how to do simple after all. "I want to buy a house with you and live happily ever after."

Tori's chuckle tickled Genevieve's mouth. "Oh, I doubt it will be that easy. We've proven more than once that we're capable of messing up pretty straightforward situations."

"I'm sorry I gave you reason to doubt me."

"I'm sorry you felt suffocated by me."

Tori's lips brushed against hers, a sweet kiss that held more innocence in it than should be possible between two people who had hurt each other this much. She stepped away from Genevieve, breaking all contact between them.

"You stay over there for a minute." She held up her hand as a kind of barrier. "You make my head spin when you're that close. And I need to know. Can we try again?"

Genevieve laughed and shook her head. "God, how can you be so charming?" She paused, her nerve endings craving Tori's touch, and called forth her self-control. "Yes, we're doing this. Getting back together. Now, can I touch you again?"

Tori melted into her, nuzzling her neck, then kissing it gently.

"Mm," Genevieve mumbled. "For the record, you make my head spin too."

"Good. We'd have real problems if I didn't."

Genevieve held her close for another minute, then held her hand and said, "Well, let's explore this house."

They went room to room slowly, discussing which of their furniture they'd keep and where it would fit. The house suited both of them—the clean, modern interior design for Tori and splashes of bright colors for Genevieve.

As they stood in the master bedroom, hand in hand, Genevieve said, "I think the only problem with this house is that we don't live in it already."

Tori rested her head on Genevieve's shoulder. "Well, let's get on that, then."

CHAPTER 30

Three days later, Genevieve and Victoria were again in the same room, only this time Tori was wearing her judicial robe, Heather and Crystal were holding hands in chairs next to Penelope, and Genevieve was in the balcony with the rest of the observers.

As the clerk read down the decision, and the justices who had signed onto it, Genevieve honest-to-God pinched herself. Had she heard right? Was it really a 7-2 decision? She looked at Tori, who met her eyes and beamed. Genevieve was still in shock, and Tori visibly stifled a laugh. She surreptitiously wiped her finger across her brow, as if smoothing the furrows on Genevieve's forehead.

A beat of silence passed after the clerk's announcement, and then the courtroom erupted into applause. Matthew Smith looked like he'd eaten a rotten egg. Kellen O'Neill was impassive.

The business of the Court continued, but Genevieve just stared at Tori. Had she always looked so smart, seated on the bench of the highest court in the land? She glanced around the courtroom, noting how many people were gazing adoringly at her. As the youngest justice, a brilliant woman who blazed trails, Tori was, well, impressive. Genevieve had spent so much time frustrated by Tori's career that, perhaps until this moment, she'd never truly appreciated how amazing it was.

When the Court adjourned, Genevieve stood to the side on the Supreme Court steps while Penelope, Heather, and Crystal spoke with reporters. It didn't hurt as much as she thought it would, watching it all happen instead of making it all happen.

She was musing about where to take them to celebrate when she heard Penelope say, "Why do I think we won so big? It has everything to do with the amazing trial record created by Genevieve Fornier, who filed the initial complaint. Genevieve!" she called out, beckoning.

The cameras turned to her, and their clicking grew louder as she walked over to Penelope and her friends. Heather and Crystal hugged her tight, Crystal giving her a kiss on the cheek.

"Genevieve, how does it feel to have won a case you didn't even argue?" a reporter called out.

With effort, she refrained from rolling her eyes. "It's not often you turn over the reins on a case to someone with the expertise, grace, and compassion of Penelope Sweet. It's an honor to work with her. And I'm overjoyed for my friends and for gay parents all over this country, who will no longer have to live in fear that their children will be ripped away from them. Today, the Supreme Court made this country more equal, more just, and closer to a more perfect union."

"Ms. Fornier, what's the status of your relationship to Victoria Willoughby?" shouted a reporter.

Despite herself, she opened her mouth to respond, but Penelope put a hand on her arm.

"Thank you, everyone, for your questions. We're going to go celebrate with our clients."

She ushered them down the rest of the Supreme Court steps and toward a black Suburban idling in wait. When they were all settled inside, Penelope told the driver, "Blue Duck Tavern," but before they could pull away, there was a tap on one of the tinted windows. Penelope rolled hers down to reveal Victoria.

"I just wanted to congratulate all of you," she said.

"Well, don't stop there. Join us—we're going to get a bite to eat and celebrate," Penelope said.

Victoria hesitated for only a fraction of a second. "I'd love to." She looked past Penelope to address Genevieve. "I have my car, so just text me directions?" She paused. "Genevieve? If you don't close your mouth, you're going to catch flies."

Shaking her head did little to dispel the shock. "Uh. You're coming?"

"If that's all right." Tori beamed, clearly enjoying the effect she was having.

"Uh-huh. I'll text you, then."

"Thanks, babe. See you soon, everyone!"

Penelope rolled up her window while Crystal and Heather nudged each other, and Crystal stage-whispered, "We're going to hang out with a Supreme Court justice."

Penelope whispered into Genevieve's ear. "She's not that bad. I suppose I see the appeal."

For the rest of the ride, Genevieve just held on and wondered if she was in the twilight zone.

Chapter 31

"Are you really sure this is the right decision?" Victoria asked Alistair.

Seated in one of the leather chairs in his chambers, Alistair nodded solemnly. "I've given this a lot of thought. Marcia may be in remission, but she could get sick again. And even if she doesn't, I've completed my tenure on the bench. I don't want to die in office—I want an actual retirement. I'd like to spend more time with my grandkids and garden and have my days to myself."

"The idea of days on end all to yourself doesn't scare you?"

"Only someone in their prime work years would ask that. It sounds like a little bit of heaven."

"Well, you've certainly earned it," Victoria said, patting him on the knee. "You'll be very missed around here, you know."

"Oh, I know. And I want to make something very clear to you, Victoria: I don't want us to drift apart just because we don't work together anymore. I expect you to keep in touch."

"Who else am I going to turn to when Kellen's bigotry makes me want to scream?"

Alistair shifted in his chair, and his voice deepened. "Victoria, I know you're mad at him about his vote on the gay parentage case."

"Out of three gay rights cases since I've been on the Court, he's voted twice to deny LGBTQ people basic civil rights," Victoria said. "*Twice*. In case you—or he—has forgotten: I am an LGBTQ person. How can he deny basic human dignity to a colleague and then make small talk with me during conference like it doesn't matter?"

"Victoria," he repeated as deep, grave lines carved into his expression. "I want to share something with you, something about our chief justice, and I honestly can't tell if you're going to like hearing it. When your predecessor stepped down from the bench and Obama had a vacancy to fill, Kellen came into my chambers and sat me down. He knew Obama would nominate a liberal judge— one with whom he would have stark ideological differences—and that the president was probably going to reach out to the senior justice on his side of the aisle for recommendations. Suggestions given aren't taken lightly, considering no one knows the demands of the job as well as sitting justices, and also, we know the members of the judicial community so well.

"I told Kellen I had no intention of wading into those waters, even if Obama asked, and to my surprise, he encouraged me to reconsider. 'Who would I even suggest?' I asked, and do you know who he recommended?"

Victoria rolled her eyes. "This is going to hurt my soul to hear, isn't it?"

"He said, 'I want someone smart. I want Victoria Willoughby.'"

Victoria's mouth opened and closed as she sat there in stunned silence, struggling to process this news. She'd met Kellen once or twice before her nomination, but they'd barely talked. Why would he want her? "But Kellen hates gay people. It doesn't make any sense that he'd want one as a colleague."

Alistair shook his head. "He doesn't hate gay people. It's... complicated, the divide between his religious beliefs and his intellect. I can't say I always understand it myself, and I'm sure it's the source of a lot of my disagreements with him. But he loves this institution, and he loves brilliant minds."

Replaying in her mind a handful of their recent interactions, Victoria looked for any indication that Kellen had singled her out for a spot on the bench or that he was disappointed in how his choice panned out. Most of his frustration, it seemed to her, was directed more at the press and small-minded people who would rather score political points than strive for true understanding.

"I… This… I don't know what to say."

"You don't have to say anything. In fact, I'm sure Kellen would prefer that you didn't."

"Why did you tell me this?"

"Because the Court's going to change next year. It's had the same members since you joined, so you've never gone through one of these personnel shifts. All of the dynamics change. You and I have been close, and I don't want you to feel unmoored after I leave. Of course, you still have Jason and Michelle, who will likely agree with you on most cases. But I want you to know that Kellen's an ally as much as an adversary."

Alistair brushed his knuckles against the collar of his jacket and smirked. "He can never replace my good looks and charm, naturally. But he can be a friend to you."

"But he hates gay people!" Maybe if she said it louder this time, Alistair would listen.

"Victoria," he said with an edge in his voice that he usually reserved for oral arguments, "he doesn't hate gay people. I understand that you two aren't going to be…braiding each other's hair." He winked at her.

Which was almost as shocking as finding out Kellen had drafted her onto the Court. "You saw that post?" she said weakly.

"I did, Justice Jax. And Kellen likes you a lot more than you think. Have an open mind about him. After all, that's what you want from him in return, isn't it?"

"I suppose," Victoria said.

"Good. Now, about my retirement party. Carrot cake is my favorite, and it's not a party without sliders."

Victoria held up her hands. "That's Kellen's territory, and he's quite possessive of it. He's in charge of the party, and that's that. So take it up with him."

"Sheesh. He'll probably make me submit my request in writing."

"Have one of your clerks hand-deliver it to his chambers."

"You know, that's not a bad idea."

"You two deserve each other, you know that?"

"I know a great many things, Victoria Willoughby. Maybe one day you'll know half of what I know."

She knocked her knee against his. "Smart-ass."

"Always." His hip popped as he stood. "I'm going to go over my press release and resignation letter one more time before, well, that's all she wrote." He walked her to the door.

"Don't go getting all nostalgic on me already, old man." She leaned over to kiss him on the cheek.

Back in her office, knowing Alistair wouldn't do it himself, she scribbled on a note, "Alistair likes carrot cake and sliders" and had one of her clerks deliver it to Kellen.

In the middle of July, Alistair Douglas officially announced his retirement. Standing on the Supreme Court steps with Kellen, Victoria, and the other justices on one side and President Obama on the other, he stood behind a microphone stand and cleared his throat.

"I am honored to have served as an associate justice on the United States Supreme Court for thirty-six years. During those decades, I have seen this country go through remarkable change. We've weathered recessions and boom years. Our partisan divides have ebbed and flowed. We've changed our understanding of security and broadened our definition of marriage. Through all this, one thing has remained a constant in my life: I have loved coming to work. My colleagues are men and women of integrity and passion, of profound intellect and careful attention to detail. I will miss them, and I will miss devoting my days to the law. Thank you for this opportunity to serve."

O'Neil stepped forward, and the two men shook hands. The bank of cameras recording this moment erupted as photographers scrambled to capture the two legal powerhouses together in one frame.

After Obama spoke about his responsibility to nominate a successor, the justices descended the steps, skirted around the cameras, and walked to the black limousine that Kellen had reserved for the occasion.

Once they were settled in the car, Kellen popped open a bottle of champagne, and they toasted to Alistair. The limo took them to Kellen's, where family and friends were milling around the backyard, waiting for them, and a sign reading *Congratulations and Thank You, Alistair* stretched between two trees.

Caterers had set up small circular tables with chairs all over the yard, and servers walked around with champagne and trays of food. Victoria wondered how much all of this was costing Kellen, but the chief justice had absolutely insisted he host Alistair's retirement soiree, and no one else was going to win that argument.

Marcia, small still, but with more color in her face than the last time Victoria had seen her, held out her hands to her husband as the justices entered the backyard, and he hurried to her. Near the end of the impromptu receiving line, Victoria barely overheard her say to someone at the front, "How was it? I wanted so badly to be present when he made his speech, but my doctors said no. Did he cry? Did Kellen?"

Too bad Genevieve was in Austin for a big fundraiser. But Michelle Lin was sipping wine and looking supremely bored, so Victoria wandered over, grabbing a glass of champagne from a waiter on her way.

"Obama gave a nice speech," Michelle said.

"So did Alistair." They drank in silence for a long moment.

"It's the changing of the guard, I guess," said Michelle. "I suspect as soon as we have a Republican president, Kellen will retire too. He joined the Court the year after Alistair, and I think he's tired. They've been my colleagues for sixteen years. I don't know what the Court even looks like without them."

"Do you think they felt that way once, when some of their mentors retired?"

"Probably. That's the Court, right?"

"I think that's life anywhere." Victoria watched, as Eliot McKenzie sat at a table with Alistair and Marcia. Jason Blankenstein was talking to Ryan Jamison, partisanship be damned. "Look at our colleagues. Such ideological differences. But sometimes, none of that matters."

"How are things between you and Kellen these days?"

"I think as long as we ignore some of our differences, we're great."

"Sounds fatalistic," Michelle said.

"Or pragmatic. I'm hungry—shall we see what our food options are?"

They milled around the yard, sampling the fig tarts, mini ahi tacos, and grilled asparagus.

"How's tennis these days?" Victoria asked.

"I need a new doubles partner. The woman I've been playing with for the past few years has tennis elbow and can barely squeeze a racquet. You don't play, do you?"

"No, I really don't. I play some badminton here and there, but that's the extent of my experience with racquet sports."

"You swim, right?"

"Yes, and I promised Genevieve I'd try yoga. Well, actually, I promised not to say a single derogatory thing about yoga or pass judgment until I've gone to five classes."

Michelle whistled. "Let me know how that goes. But Victoria, if you start coming to our conferences with kombucha instead of tea, Jason and I are going to stage an intervention."

"It's a deal."

Michelle headed off for more champagne, and Victoria wandered into the house in search of a restroom. She'd never spent much time on the main floor of Kellen's house—he typically hosted his gatherings in his drinking room downstairs. The layout was labyrinthine, and she had passed through a formal dining room, the kitchen, and a sitting room before she turned a corner and ran into her host.

"Oh, sorry, Kellen. I was looking for the restroom."

His good-natured smile bespoke happiness brought on by champagne. "I told my wife we should put up signs. It's that way." He pointed at a door over his shoulder, and she moved to pass him.

"Victoria," he said and leaned against the wall. "I know we don't see eye to eye on many things, and I know for you, some of those things are personal."

She waited for him to go on, not sure where this was headed.

He sighed, probably frustrated, but she wasn't going to make this easy on him.

"It may surprise you to know that Alistair has been, in many regards, my closest friend," he continued. "In addition to being friends, he was my best adversary. His opposition, and the way he framed it, made me a stronger and sharper writer. And while it may strain credulity, he did sometimes change my mind. If you asked him, I'm sure he'd say that the reverse is also true—that I sometimes changed his. I meant what I said in front of the cameras today—I will miss him. The Court and all it stands for will also miss him."

With his hands in his pockets, he scrutinized her for a moment. "I wondered if you would take his place, and be my new best adversary."

It felt very much like being asked to prom by a boy she'd never looked twice at.

"Kellen. I understand what you're saying about your relationship with Alistair. Political and ideological disagreements don't have to equal personal dislike. But what you don't understand is that your fundamental belief that I'm going to hell *is* personal. That's pretty hard to look past."

"There's a difference between religious views and person-to-person interactions," Kellen said, looking exasperated already.

"Only to someone who wants to intellectualize the issue. This isn't a court case or a constitutional issue, Kellen. This is my life."

"Protestants never understand that when the Catholic Church says 'hate the sin, love the sinner,' they mean it."

"I think Protestants believe that we are our actions. There's no separation between deed and person."

"But there is, in God's eyes," Kellen insisted.

"In the eyes of *your* god, maybe."

"But that's part of my point, Victoria. Whether you want to accept or reject wholesale my belief system, you have to understand the way it works internally. I might not approve of your relationship with Genevieve Fornier, but that doesn't make you any less of a person in my eyes. I don't approve of Alistair's preference for the New York Yankees over the Boston Red Sox, but I still love and admire him."

"You're comparing my love life to sports fandom?"

"Only literally," he said, but she didn't feel like joking. "Okay, yes, I did just do that. I was just trying to make a point."

Victoria ran her fingers through her hair. "Let me see if I'm understanding what you're saying. I might not buy into the logic that you can love the sinner but hate the sin, but as long as you're telling me that that's how you approach the situation, I should trust you?"

His head cocked to one side thoughtfully. "Yes, I think that's what I mean."

"Okay, and if I told you that I believe our actions determine who we are, and that your voting against gay marriage and same-sex parental rights tells me you're a person who doesn't think I'm worthy of full civil rights, would you find my world view internally consistent and, in turn, trust me?"

He laughed uncomfortably. "You're basically saying we're at a standstill."

"I don't like it any more than you do, but it's not enough for me that you think I'm smart and write good legal opinions when you find some fundamental part of me abhorrent."

"I never said abhorrent!"

"The Catholic Church does. Anyway, try this one on for size: Genevieve and I decide we're going to have a date, and we'd like to invite another couple to join us. We think you and your wife would be lovely dinner companions, so we ask you on a double date. Would you come?"

"Of course we'd come! This gets at the very point I'm trying to make. We'd love to have dinner with you."

"That dinner doesn't constitute a sin? It's indicative of our romantic relationship."

"You love each other. That's fine. Just don't, uh…"

"Don't invite you to join us in the bedroom?"

"Right."

"Jesus Christ, Kellen. Finally something we can agree on."

"I want us to be friends."

Something in his voice and posture reminded her of her grandfather. She hadn't thought of him in years, and she wondered briefly if he would disapprove of her life with Genevieve too.

It doesn't matter, she thought. "I want us to be friends, too," she said.

They nodded at each other with absolutely nothing specific resolved at all.

"When are we having that dinner date, then?" he asked with a grin.

She took a deep breath. "Kellen, I will agree to a dinner date with you, but you have to understand that I don't view it as purely social. I will spend the entire time trying to convince you that the Church's stand on homosexuality is wrong and that you need to understand that my love for Genevieve is no different than your love for your wife."

His jaw worked back and forth for a moment. "I accept your terms. I doubt you'll succeed, but you're welcome to try."

"Well, if Alistair could change your mind about things, understand this: I'm twice as persuasive as he is."

Kellen laughed. "I'll have my people call your people, and we'll make it happen. But first, the restroom's that way."

She stood alone in the bathroom and studied her face in the mirror. Maybe it was the dim lighting, but she looked more relaxed, more self-assured than she'd ever seen herself. She'd been afraid of this very confrontation with Kellen, but she'd survived it. And she felt fired up to argue with him—and convince him to rethink his position toward her, and the entire LGBTQ community.

She washed her hands and headed outside to help herself to a chocolate-covered strawberry from one of the caterer's trays. The groups had shifted, and Jason and Michelle now surrounded Alistair and his wife. She was heading in that direction, when a light touch on her arm stopped her.

"Missed you," Genevieve whispered in her ear.

Spinning around, she drew her arms around Genevieve and squeezed. "Missed you back." They kissed, and when they separated, Kellen appeared at their side with glasses of champagne for each of them.

"Genevieve Fornier—lovely to actually meet you," he said, and they shook hands. "I don't know if Victoria's told you yet, but you two are going on a double date with me and my wife."

Genevieve choked on a mouthful of champagne, and her eyes watered. "Oh? She hadn't mentioned that." She blinked, then shrugged and grinned at Kellen. "Sounds great. Where are we going?"

He rested a hand on Genevieve's shoulder, and Genevieve rolled her eyes. Genevieve contended with patronizing physical gestures from old men pretty much every time she was part of a roundtable media interview.

"Well now, I don't know," Kellen said. "Victoria?"

They both turned to look at her, and she laughed. "Um, Genevieve? Ideas?"

"Sure, let's do Blue Duck Tavern."

"Done," Kellen said. "Looking forward to it. Genevieve, thanks for coming—you two enjoy the party."

He drifted away, and Genevieve rounded on Victoria with an inscrutable look on her face.

"What have you gotten us into?"

"He said he wants to be, um, besties or something. Best adversaries. I don't know. I'm just rolling with it."

"I will too, then," Genevieve said, and she ushered Tori to an unoccupied table.

"How'd the fundraiser go?"

"Good. Exhausting, actually. Listen, there's something I want to tell you. I've been doing a lot of thinking—"

"That explains the migraines," Victoria joked, but Genevieve looked at her seriously.

"Actually, it might. I spoke with some of my doctors about my migraines, and it's distinctly possible that they're stress related. That I might be…overly optimistic about my superwoman skills when I think I can be an active litigator and the president of a civil rights organization. Neither Jamie nor Penelope actually do both with any regularity. I thought I could be different—better, maybe. But it's not a competition. It's my life, and I want to be happy."

Genevieve's hand was resting on the tabletop, and Victoria covered it with her own. "That's great, babe. I honestly have no idea what you're saying, but that's great."

After a short exhale, Genevieve said firmly, "I'm done arguing cases. Which fixes many issues, not the least of which is any professional conflicts between us."

The implications of this ran through Victoria's mind like movie credits. "Are you sure? I don't want you to give up something you love for me. For us."

"Because you're not giving up your house for us? I mean, we close on the new place next week, so if you're having doubts…"

"That's different," Victoria said.

"Is it? Regardless, this isn't entirely for us, but… I do have to give things up for us. That's what a relationship is—prioritizing things as a partner, not a single person. You've done that in a big way. It's my turn."

"Genevieve, I'm not keeping score," Victoria said.

"Look, if it makes you sleep better at night, we can say this is entirely for my health. Let's just try this for a while, and see if the migraines stop."

"And if you miss it?"

"The migraines? I think I'll live."

Victoria swatted at her shoulder. "Smart-ass. Arguing in court."

"I'm sure I will. I miss Chicago. Hell, I sometimes miss law school. Doesn't mean I want to go backward. It's just nostalgia."

Victoria took her hand, and they gazed around Kellen's backyard. "We've come a long way, Genevieve Fornier. Everything around us is changing—the Court will be completely different next year. Your work will be different. We'll live in a new house. And with all that change, I still feel stable. You make me feel stable."

She turned to look at Genevieve's face, to bask in her glow for a minute, but was surprised at the mischievous expression she found there.

"Yeah? You feel stable? Because I had a radical idea that might rock your world."

A prickle of fear rose up Victoria's throat, but Genevieve touched her cheek and whispered, "Wanna get married?"

Victoria managed to knock her elbow into her champagne glass in a moment of epic grace, and Genevieve laughed loudly. "Just the reaction I was hoping for."

Victoria scrambled to blot the spread of champagne across the white tablecloth with napkins, then froze and sat back down. She cocked her head at Genevieve. "Are you serious?"

"Sure. Why not?"

"Wow, talk about romance," Victoria said.

"Well, we can make this a big deal and throw a huge party, or we can just ask Alistair to do it in his backyard. I'm going to spend the rest of my life with you either way."

"Hard to argue with that logic."

"So you'll think about it? What kind of party you want, I mean? The marrying me part—that one you should just say yes to. Because we fought really hard for the right to do this. And we should use that right."

"Then, yes, you nut."

Genevieve kissed her, a sweet kiss full of promise, and Victoria briefly imagined what it would be like to kiss like that while wearing white dresses in front of all their friends and family. And reporters. And cameras. It would make Genevieve very happy, and honestly, it might make her happy too.

Their kiss was interrupted by Alistair clinking his champagne flute with his fork. He gave a speech thanking everyone for the party and the years of support and friendship—at least, that's what Victoria vaguely heard. All she could do was look at Genevieve's face and map the expression of love and happiness she found there directed at her. It was a lot like the way she looked in that picture of them that went viral. And a lot like the look Genevieve gave her when, two decades ago, Victoria had confessed she was in love with her.

She vowed to do everything in her power to keep Genevieve smiling like that for years to come.

Listening to Genevieve packing up the books from her study—or, rather, her colorful language as she wrestled with packing tape, turned out to be one of the more hilarious perks of helping her move.

"Need a hand in there?" she called from the living room.

"This...fucking...box," Genevieve grunted.

"Sounds like you've got everything under control. I'm ordering pizza."

Genevieve's head poked around the corner. "You are? Really? Why?"

Victoria knit her brows. "Because we're packing up your house... Isn't it a law that you have to eat pizza while packing?"

"Yes, that's a law I've defended in court many times."

Victoria rifled through one of the drawers in Genevieve's kitchen until she found a carryout menu for a pizza joint. There were grease stains on it, indicating the menu had been well used. She started to dial, then realized she had no idea what Genevieve liked.

The study was a mess—knickknacks, books, and office supplies were strewn everywhere. Genevieve sat on the floor trying to cram a book into a box that was already overflowing.

"I think maybe you're at capacity, babe."

"One...more...book...oof!" She pushed the hardcover so hard it cut through the side of the box.

"Right, well, good luck with that. What do you like on your pizza?"

Genevieve looked up and grinned, a trickle of sweat dripping down her temple. "There's something I never thought I'd hear you ask."

"Yeah, yeah, I get it. But if you don't answer, I'm getting Hawaiian."

"That's disgusting. Who puts pineapple on a pizza?"

"You don't see me judging how you pack boxes."

Genevieve raised an eyebrow at her.

"Okay, fine, I'm judging you."

"At least you're honest. I—"

Genevieve's cell phone rang. She started frantically sweeping books this way and that. "Shit! I have no idea where it is!"

Victoria rolled her eyes but started searching and finally located it underneath a pile of unassembled boxes. She noticed *Michigan Department of Corrections* on the screen as she handed it to Genevieve, who tapped it, held it to her ear, and waited.

Victoria started to leave, but Genevieve put a hand on her arm.

"You can stay if you want." Much louder, she said into the phone, "Yes, I accept the call. Amelia! Hi! I'm glad you got my message to call. How are you?"

Victoria organized some of the books on the floor while she listened.

"Good, I'm glad it's working. If anything changes—if they stop giving you your hormones—let me know right away. Listen, I wanted to let you know that the decision came down in your case. Amelia, you won."

Victoria half expected to hear screams of delight through the phone, but instead she heard only silence.

"Amelia?" Genevieve asked, "Are you still there?"

After a beat, her tone changed. "Hey, it's okay. I know. I know... No, of course it's okay to cry about this. It's been such a long journey for you."

Genevieve kept comforting Amelia, and her own eyes filled with tears as the call progressed. "Someone from our legal team will fly there next week to meet with you and help you schedule everything. I'm so sorry it won't be me, Amelia. But I'll come see you when I can—just for a visit. I'm so happy for you."

As soon as Genevieve hung up the phone, she started crying. With tears streaming down her face, she collapsed against Victoria.

"I wanted to fly there and tell her in person," she choked out between sobs. "But I also wanted to tell her as soon as possible, and I couldn't get on a plane today, and... I know I'm making the right decision, giving all this up. I feel better already—fewer headaches, and they're less intense. And Amelia doesn't need me anymore, if she ever did, and I—"

"Shh, it's okay, darling," Victoria said, stroking her back. "This isn't an irreversible decision—you can always go back to litigation."

She held Genevieve for a while, kissing her hair and murmuring words of comfort until Genevieve could speak again. "I know I can go back," she said, her voice cracking. "But I won't, and that's okay. It's good—it's really good. It's just hard."

"It is hard. But you've got me, and I'll help you."

"I know," Genevieve said, pulling back far enough to look at Victoria. "You already have."

"I have?" Victoria said.

"Yeah," Genevieve wiped her own tears off Victoria's cheeks and neck. "I just used your sweater as a Kleenex."

"Glad I could be here for you. Now and always, right?"

"Right. But I'm not eating pizza with pineapples on it."

"I'd never put you through such an ordeal. What else would you like, then?"

"Vegetarian, please. And, Tor, can we maybe put a pin in packing for the night?"

Victoria looked at the mess surrounding them. The moving truck would be there in two days, and they'd barely put a dent in packing up Genevieve's townhouse.

"Of course," she said with no regrets. "Let's just watch crappy TV and have pizza and beer tonight."

"Who are you, and what have you done with Victoria Willoughby?" Genevieve put her arm around Victoria and led her into the kitchen and away from the mess.

Well, out of sight, out of mind, at least for the evening.

Victoria kissed her and settled in for a thoroughly domestic night at Genevieve's place.

EPILOGUE

When the car stopped, Tori removed the blindfold and Genevieve blinked. A neon sign reading *Do Re Me* glowed in the window of the building next to them, right near a handwritten poster taped to the door with the words *Closed for a private event* scrawled on it.

"I thought we'd celebrate your birthday with song and dance," Tori said.

Genevieve turned to study her and smiled at the pride written all over her face. "Karaoke?"

"We have the whole bar to ourselves. Two bartenders, a blank stage, and over eleven hundred songs to choose from."

Genevieve trailed her finger around Tori's jaw. "You're adorable." Tori softened under her touch, and her expression took on that hazy quality Genevieve associated with their bedroom.

"Oh, no, you don't. We've got hours of partying before that happens."

Tori bit her finger, and Genevieve briefly pondered the wisdom of what she was saying. They could, of course, skip the party and just go home—their new home with the boxes in every room—where they would surely arrive at some kind of birthday present Genevieve found satisfying.

"Now who's thinking about sex?" Tori leaned closer to her until their lips were nearly touching. "I can always tell, you know. Your breath changes."

"How so?"

"You taste like freshly cut grass—sharp and sweet at all once."

Considering Tori had once used those words to describe how other parts of her tasted, Genevieve lost all sense of restraint, crushing her mouth against Tori's and slipping her tongue inside. Tori laughed and pushed her away.

"Darling. Don't get ahead of yourself. I promise that your birthday will be unforgettable, in many ways. Let's go inside, and you can have something to look forward to all evening."

Genevieve nodded dumbly and allowed Tori to grab her hand and drag her out of the car and toward the bar. By the time they reached the door, Genevieve's legs almost worked.

The bouncer opened the door for them and held out a bucket. "Cell phones, please."

Genevieve paused. "Are you joking?"

"No ma'am. Whoever organized this party instructed me to collect everyone's cell phone as they entered."

A quick glance at Tori confirmed it. "Why on earth?" Genevieve asked.

"I could say it's because I want people to be present in the moment and not distracted by their devices, but mostly I don't want videos finding their way online. I'm changing, but I'm not an entirely new person, you know?"

"Who all did you invite? Because Bethany knows you'd turn her to stone if she posted something as benign as your name online."

"Can you just surrender your phone and go inside, please?" Tori dropped hers into the bucket, which already contained at least twenty cells.

Genevieve shrugged and complied. In the darkened building, the ceiling was designed to look like a starry evening sky, with tiny dots of light barely illuminating the bar to her right and small round tables to the left. She stubbed her toe on a barstool and tumbled into Tori's back. "Damn!"

In a flash, the room was illuminated, and a bunch of people shouted, "Happy birthday, Genevieve!"

Once she blinked away the stars from her eyes, Genevieve spotted most of the staff from HER, Jamie and some of his HRC staff, Penelope, Bethany, Tara and Sonya, and Tori's brother and sister-in-law. Craning to look past them, Genevieve spied four of her closest friends from Chicago, whom she hadn't seen since she'd moved to DC, and, behind them, Heather and Crystal.

Tori placed a gentle hand on the small of her back and whispered in her ear, "I love you, babe."

While Jamie dazzled the room with a stirring rendition of Michael Jackson's "Black or White," Genevieve made the rounds, greeting people and thanking them for coming. Bethany placed a martini in her hand as she was mingling with her staff. By the time she'd reached her friends from Chicago, her first glass was empty, Tara had replaced it with another one, and Penelope was doing her best to sing "Jessie's Girl."

It had taken almost a year, but Genevieve had finally found something Penelope didn't effortlessly excel at. What she lacked in singing prowess, she made up for in queering a straight song, much to the entire room's delight. Bethany chose "Every Breath You Take," and managed to make it creepier than the original.

After a while, Genevieve started ignoring the performances happening on stage and immersed herself in the community of some of her favorite people. Will and Diane regaled her with stories of Tommy and Rebecca's latest antics, which included a fiasco at the park involving a mud puddle, litter, and a stray dog.

"Nothing says a successful morning with kids like a complete change of clothes before noon," Diane said.

"And how's work, Diane?" Genevieve asked.

"Pretty great, actually. Last week I got to do some translating for the secretary general of the UN—there were some activists here from Cambodia, and the secretary general doesn't speak Khmer."

"What's she like, the secretary general?"

"God, so smart. A little terse, but I think she tries to listen more than she speaks, which is a refreshing change from the way American politicians operate. And Will just landed a great new project." She put her hand on his back. "Tell Genevieve all about it, honey."

He rubbed the back of his neck, embarrassed. "Uh, well, the DC City Council is starting work on a new revitalization project, transforming some abandoned lots in Bellevue into public parks. The city is going to program evening events, but they want the space to function as a playground during the day. It was a bit of a challenge to arrive at a design that accommodated the space constraints, play structures, and performance requirements for the evenings, but my firm won the bid."

"He's so modest. It's entirely his design." Diane said, pride practically oozing out of her brilliant smile.

As Genevieve listened to them brag about one another, and watched them touch each other in small, insignificant ways, she was struck by the contrast between their relationship and the one she and Tori were working on. Maybe someday, once they'd been together for fifteen years like Will and Diane, Tori would be comfortable bragging about her and holding her hand in front of their respective staffs.

But they were definitely making progress, and the proof of it was all around her, drinking and dancing and having fun because Tori had gathered them together.

Diane slipped her arm through Genevieve's. "And you? How's work going for you?"

The gesture felt not just friendly but familial. Living an ocean away from her father, she hadn't felt that kind of connection in a long time. In some ways, Tori's family had taken to her more easily than Tori herself.

Speaking of, where was Tori?

Genevieve glanced around but couldn't see her anywhere in the dimly lit bar. She refocused her attention on Diane and Will. "Good. It's going well. My big priority has been a case about a trans woman in federal prison seeking access to the medical procedures related to her transition."

Genevieve glanced around again, thinking they'd probably had enough work-related talk and maybe she could go find Tori, but Diane tugged on her arm.

"What's the status of the case?" she asked.

"The district-level decision came down last week, and we won. Now we wait and see if the decision will be appealed."

"If you've won already, will you have to wait for the appeal before your client can start her procedures?" Will asked.

"Opposing counsel never filed for a stay of the decision, so we're proceeding as if they won't appeal. Amelia's surgery is scheduled for next month, and we haven't heard from them, which is a good sign. But it is possible that they'll appeal, and she'll have to wait for the new results."

"The law is so fascinating," Will said. "I mean, your client won her case, but she's sitting in a cell right now not entirely sure if that victory stands or if she has to win again."

"Yeah, there are ways in which the system feels unduly burdensome. Procedure often seems to matter more than substance.

But I honestly can't envision a way to improve things—there are just too many practicalities, and the same procedural rules that harm one client can benefit the next one." She was about to say something about how Civil Procedure was her favorite course in law school, when the dim lights suddenly cut out entirely, and the room fell silent. She turned around and squinted toward the stage—the karaoke jockey was somewhere over there. Maybe he knew where the fuse box was.

A single light at the back of the stage, pointed directly into the audience, nearly blinded her, but her vision adjusted and she could see a figure at the microphone in silhouette. Music started, and she immediately recognized the introduction to BØRNS's "Electric Love."

"I *love* this song," she said loudly, and everyone in the room laughed.

Side lighting suddenly illuminated three other people onstage, and as they started singing backup and executing choreographed dance moves, haze billowed up from the floor around the lead singer. The lights changed again, and Genevieve almost dropped her drink.

Victoria Willoughby gripped the microphone in one hand, her lips almost touching it as she sang. Leather pants so tight that Genevieve wondered if she needed oil to get them on clung to every curve of Tori's legs and hips. Her black top was cut in a deep V-neck that plunged past where a bra would be. The hand on the microphone had a black, fingerless glove, and her eye makeup was smoky and very glam rock. Her hair was teased to the point that it rivaled Bethany's in volume. She was the perfect mix of Joan Jett and Sandy from *Grease.* It was simultaneously hilarious and beyond attractive.

Genevieve spared a quick glance at Bethany, Tara, and Sonya, who were doing an admirable job as supporting performers, but her eyes quickly returned to Tori. As she sang, Tori threw her head back, snaked her body down the microphone stand and back, and pointed and beckoned to Genevieve. It was so over the top that the entire room was cracking up, but humor wasn't the most salient part of Tori's performance as far as Genevieve was concerned.

Clearly, Bethany had remembered that one time Genevieve had mentioned that the androgynous voice of the singer was sexy and that she wouldn't mind having sex to this song.

When Tori sang the word *taste*, Genevieve hoped to hell that no one in the room was looking her way, because whatever kind of poker face she might have in a courtroom, she surely couldn't mask how turned on she was. Her legs turned to rubber, and she wasn't sure standing was such a good idea anymore.

Tori slid the microphone out of its stand. As she continued to sing, she did a sinuous shimmy off the stage and walked slowly, purposefully toward Genevieve. Fumbling behind her, Genevieve's hands collided with a chair, and she tumbled backward into it.

Tori circled around her, slowly, as she sang the final verse. When she got to the last line, she slid a leg over Genevieve's, straddling her. She threw her head back to sing the final word, then held the microphone up in the air, to uproarious applause.

In the middle of the cheers, whistles, and laughter, Tori leaned down and gave Genevieve a long, sexy kiss. The world around Genevieve narrowed until everything was Tori and the way she smelled and the taste of her breath.

"Get a room you two!" William hollered at them, and Tori broke away laughing. She wiped her lipstick off of Genevieve's lips and headed back to the stage, microphone still in hand.

"How about a round of applause for my backup singers, everyone?" Tori asked, working the crowd in a way Genevieve would have never in a million years imagined she could.

The room went crazy, as the women onstage shared hugs and kisses with each other.

"While we have everyone's attention," Tori continued, "now seems like an excellent time for cake." She gestured to the bartender, who must have anticipated this moment; he leaned behind the counter and brought up a huge cake lined with candles.

"As you can see, fifty candles poses quite the fire hazard," Tori said, eliciting a chorus of laugher. "I've got extinguishers on standby."

"Oh, har-har," Genevieve called out, inciting more laughter as the bartender put the cake on the table next to her.

"Can we get everyone but Genevieve onstage, please?"

One of the bar's staff members brought out additional microphones, and someone else turned on all the lights so that as everyone sang "Happy Birthday," they had an excellent view of the birthday girl.

It was the most on-key rendition of "Happy Birthday" she'd ever heard, and someone even threw in some harmony.

When the song ended, Genevieve closed her eyes and wished that Michigan wouldn't appeal Amelia's case. It took three attempts before she was able to extinguish all fifty candles. By the time she'd finished, Tori was at her side with a grin reserved for her.

While Bethany served cake and guests mingled, Genevieve sat at a two-person table with Tori. "That was quite a performance."

Pride wasn't something Tori wore often, but she knew how to wear it well. "We practiced a lot. Bethany did the choreo—theirs and mine."

Genevieve toyed with Tori's fingers poking out through the glove that, upon closer inspection, was bedazzled. "Love the costume. You look ravishing."

"That was the intention."

"Now I understand why you had the bar confiscate all the cell phones."

"Well, it wouldn't do to have the media—or Kellen O'Neil—know how great I look in leather."

"Tonight was…unexpected. And perfect."

Tori caressed her cheek and smiled. "Who knew I wouldn't fall into a black hole if I kissed you in front of other people?"

Genevieve's heart swelled, and she took Tori's hands in hers. "I think that's what makes tonight so special to me. You made everything about what I wanted, and you took risks because you knew it would make me happy."

"Everything about being with you feels risky, Genevieve. But everything about you also feels satisfying."

"Essentially, you're saying I'm worth it, right?"

"You say potato…"

"Genevieve!" Bethany bellowed from across the room. Genevieve turned to find her standing on the stage twirling the microphone by its cord. "It's way past your turn. Get your sorry ass up here and sing to us."

Tori gently pushed her shoulder. "Go on, birthday girl. Give us a performance we'll remember."

Genevieve flipped through the binder until she found the song she'd been looking for. Bethany gave her a kiss on the cheek and pinched her ass as she handed off the microphone.

"I'm going to need a little help with this one," Genevieve announced. She curled her index finger at Tori, who laughed and headed toward the stage.

As "Take Me For What I Am" from *Rent* came through the speakers, there was no doubt in anyone's mind who would sing Maureen's part and who would sing Joanne's.

When the song was over and they left the stage, Heather and Crystal took their place to sing a duet of their own. Genevieve got pulled into most people's performances and spent most of the night laughing and dancing with everyone but Tori, who was making the rounds chatting with guests. But everywhere she went, she felt Tori's eyes on her, felt the brilliance of Tori's smile directed at her. Tori, who wasn't making any effort to hide her love—Tori, who was the same, but also so, so different.

Kind of like their relationship.

When the night was over, Genevieve and Tori stood side by side, hugging and kissing their friends good-bye. The last to leave, they walked down the sidewalk together, Tori's hand warm and soft in Genevieve's. Underneath a streetlight, Tori stopped and pulled her into a deep kiss that sent tingles all through her.

Maybe someone was photographing them. Maybe they'd need to talk about their renewed relationship in an interview. Maybe no one would care.

One thing was for sure: the only thing Genevieve cared about in that moment was in her arms.

About Blythe Rippon

Blythe Rippon is the author of *Barring Complications* (GCLS finalist for best dramatic fiction), *Stowe Away* and the short story "S. Claus" in the holiday anthology *Do You Feel What I Feel*. She holds a PhD in the humanities and teaches academic writing to undergraduates. When not grading papers or imagining plots for future novels, she is usually holding forth about the political injustice of the day, hiking, or experimenting in the kitchen. She has lived all over the United States and at present can be found in the San Francisco Bay Area, where she lives with her wife and children.

CONNECT WITH BLYTHE:

Website: www.blytherippon.com
Facebook: www.facebook.com/blythe.rippon
E-Mail: blythe.rippon@gmail.com

Other Books from Ylva Publishing

www.ylva-publishing.com

Barring Complications

(The Love and Law Series – Book 1)

Blythe Rippon

ISBN: 978-3-95533-191-7

Length: 374 pages (77,000 words)

When a gay marriage case arrives at the US Supreme Court, two women find themselves at the center of the fight for marriage equality. Closeted Justice Victoria Willoughby must sway a conservative colleague, and attorney Genevieve Fornier must craft compelling arguments to win five votes. Complicating matters, despite their shared history, the law forbids the two from talking to each other.

The Lavender List

Meg Harrington

ISBN: 978-3-95533-623-3

Length: 249 pages (62,000 words)

Aspiring actress Amelia Maldonado finds herself embroiled in the affairs of mobsters and spies in post-war New York, and the only ally she has is the mystifying girl she's got a crush on.

Cast Me Gently

Caren J Werlinger

ISBN: 978-3-95533-391-1

Length: 353 pages (100,000 words)

Teresa and Ellie couldn't be more different. Teresa still lives at home with her Italian family, while Ellie has been on her own for years. When they meet and fall in love, their worlds clash. Ellie would love to be part of Teresa's family, but they both know that will never happen. Sooner or later, Teresa will have to choose between the two halves of her heart—Ellie or her family.

Four Steps

Wendy Hudson

ISBN: 978-3-95533-690-5

Length: 343 pages (92,000 words)

Seclusion suits Alex Ryan. Haunted by a crime from her past, she struggles to find peace and calm.

Lori Hunter dreams of escaping the monotony of her life. When the suffocation sets in, she runs for the hills.

A chance encounter in the Scottish Highlands leads Alex and Lori into a whirlwind of heartache and a fight for survival, as they build a formidable bond that will be tested to its limits.

Coming from Ylva Publishing

www.ylva-publishing.com

UNDER PARR

(Norfolk Coast Investigation Story – Book 2)

Andrea Bramhall

December 5th, 2013 left its mark on the North Norfolk Coast in more ways than one. A tidal surge and storm swept millennia-old cliff faces into the sea and flooded homes and businesses up and down the coast. It also buried a secret in the WWII bunker hiding under the golf course at Brancaster. A secret kept for years, until it falls squarely into the lap of Detective Sergeant Kate Brannon and her fellow officers.

A skeleton, deep inside the bunker.

How did it get there? Who was he…or she? How did the stranger die—in a tragic accident or something more sinister? Well, that's Kate's job to find out.

PIECES

G Benson

Carmen is sixteen, homeless, and desperate to keep her and her kid brother out of foster care. Ollie, also sixteen, has a life that's all about parents, school pressure, and friends. One kiss changes everything. Ollie is captivated, but Carmen vanishes. When they cross paths later, everything is different. A young-adult, queer romance about what we're prepared to sacrifice for those we care about.

Benched
© 2017 by Blythe Rippon

ISBN: 978-3-95533-833-6

Also available as e-book.

Published by Ylva Publishing, legal entity of Ylva Verlag, e.Kfr.

Ylva Verlag, e.Kfr.
Owner: Astrid Ohletz
Am Kirschgarten 2
65830 Kriftel
Germany

www.ylva-publishing.com

First edition: 2017

Credits
Edited by Michelle Aguilar & Robin J Samuels
Proofread by CK King
Cover Design by Adam Llyod

49017963R00211

Made in the USA
San Bernardino, CA
10 May 2017